THE DAWN OF ECSTASY

Gabby lay still as Philippe's eyes became pools of gray velvet, his hands surprisingly gentle on her flesh. With every ounce of her strength she fought against the sensations that threatened to engulf her, knowing that once she submitted willingly she could no longer despise him for forcing himself on her. When Philippe enfolded her in his arms it was as if a bolt of lightning had pierced the very core of her. Yet he was gentle. Never had she known such tenderness from him. His passionate kiss was long and deep, and when he released her mouth she wanted him to claim it again. Her body trembled, tiny seeds of sensation bursting softly into bloom as waves of desire coursed through her. She no longer had a will of her own. Something was driving her on, insisting she find out the meaning of the powerful force pulsing within her.

"Don't fight it, *ma chere*," Philippe whispered. "There is no greater pleasure than that of the flesh."

Gabby experienced a terrible, rising ecstasy to which some secret place within herself was vibrating, his questing lips pushing her ever upward . . .

Also by Connie Mason:

**CARESS AND CONQUER
FOR HONOR'S SAKE**

Tender Fury

Connie Mason

A LEISURE BOOK®

Published by
Dorchester Publishing Co., Inc.
276 Fifth Avenue
New York, NY 10001

Copyright© MCMLXXXV by Connie Mason

Printed in the United States of America.

Part One

France and New Orleans

1814-1815

Chapter One

NOTHING IN Gabrielle La Farge's young, sheltered life had prepared her for this moment. There were many, she knew, who would consider the man standing beside her handsome. But his brooding good looks and cold gray eyes truly frightened her. Most girls her age would jump at the chance to marry a wealthy young man such as Philippe St. Cyr, or so her parents had informed her. Gabby only knew that she had no desire to become mistress of a plantation or wife of a planter in far off Martinique. But the choice had not been hers to make. She squeezed her eyes shut, her thoughts drowning out the priest's toneless chanting as she relived in her mind the events leading to this dreadful moment, events as crushing as Napoleon's defeat in October as his third army was driven across the Rhine by their allied invaders . . .

It had been barely a week ago that Gabby had been summoned into Mother Superior's small chamber. At first she thought that she had once again displeased that pious woman by some willful misbehavior, but try as she might could bring no such incident of late to her mind. In fact, since she had resigned herself to a religious life, she had been more content than at any other time during the ten years since she had come to live with the good sisters of St. Cecilia.

Ten years, Gabby fumed silently as she considered her bleak existence at the convent. And in all those years she had neither seen nor heard from her parents. In the early years she had fought bitterly against confinement and even yet there were times she longed desperately to break out of the somber gray walls of the convent—to run and laugh, to let her hair blow free in the wind. The hours she had spent on her knees in the chapel as penance for her youthful spirit and willful behavior were too numerous to count.

As the years passed with no word from Gilbert and Lily La Farge, Gabby began to despair. She would never leave the convent. She was destined to remain behind the walls until she died a withered old woman. She realized she could never face life on the outside on her own, for despite her nearly eighteen years she was as innocent as a child in the ways of the world. Finally, she had forced her mind to accept the inevitable. She was now prepared to join the order and become the bride of Christ. In less than a week, St. Cecilia's would become her home for the rest of her life.

The door to Mother Superior's chamber stood open and Gabby entered hesitantly, for some unexplained reason her heart beating furiously in her breast.

At first, nothing registered but shock and disbelief as Gabby slowly recognized the couple standing to greet her. Ten years had not changed Gilbert and Lily La Farge a great deal. Gilbert had put on weight but was still handsome with his large-boned frame and florid good looks. His hair was touched with silver now but the effect distinguished rather than aged him.

Lily, at thirty-six, could still be considered beautiful, although she could not hope to compete with her fresh-faced daughter whose dewy complexion still held the first bloom of youth. Lily pursed red pouty lips as her bright blue eyes took in the perfection of Gabby's willow-slim figure, fully a woman's beneath the coarse gray habit, thinking how the years had transformed her daughter from a gangling girl all arms and legs whose hint of beauty was barely visible into an astonishing lovely young woman who now stared at her through compelling violet eyes surrounded by thick feathery lashes. Though her hair was completely hidden by her wimple, her features, from arched eyebrows to full lips, were finely drawn and provocative.

"Well, daughter," blustered Gilbert, annoyed by Gabby's silence, "must you stand there mouth agape? Is this how you greet your parents?"

"I'm . . . I'm surprised to see you," stammered Gabby, shaken by their unexpected appearance at a time when she thought herself totally abandoned by them.

Gabby shifted uncomfortably under the couple's close scutiny. "You've changed, Gabby," Lily said, eyeing her daughter critically. "You've become a beautiful woman. Hasn't she, Gilbert?"

Turning to her husband, Lily was shocked and not a little jealous by what was clearly visible in his eyes. That he, too, thought the young woman before him lovely was all too evident by his leering look that was anything but fatherly.

"More beautiful than I would have imagined," agreed Gilbert placing his hand lightly on Gabby's upper arm in a motion that soon turned into a caress. It was difficult for Gibert to believe that this budding beauty standing before him was his daughter. He cleared his throat nervously. "Are you not curious why we are here?" he asked, his hand still resting on Gabby's arm.

"After ten years I suppose I should be," answered Gabby caustically, forgetting in a burst of resentment all she had been taught in ten years about obedience and respect.

Gilbert's hand tightened hurtfully and Gabby winced at the sudden pain. "Don't be disrespectful," Gilbert warned. "It was for your own protection that we left you with the sisters. After the Bastille fell we became enemies of the people. You were far safer in a convent than in hiding with us. I knew not what the future held at that time. You should be grateful you had a good home."

"But it's been *ten years*, Papa," she accused, unable to hide the hurt she felt from their neglect.

"And I trust your education has been completed in those

9

years," Gilbert retorted. "Your mother and I have made plans for your future."

"My future!" gasped Gabby. "My future has already been decided. I shall soon be eighteen and my novitiate completed. I intend to take the sacred vows and join the convent."

"I'm sorry, Gabby, but that is not possible," remonstrated Lily. "Tell her, Gilbert," she urged, turning to her husband.

"In good time, *cherie*, in good time," replied Gilbert as he took a large, white envelope from his pocket and wiped the beads of perspiration from his brow. "Have you heard the latest news from Paris, Gabby?" he asked in a placating tone. After Gabby's negative answer, he continued. "Paris has fallen; Napoleon has abdicated and has been banished to Elba. But his most stalwart supporters, myself included, have not given up. I have pledged all my resources and energies to see Napoleon restored once more as the illustrious Emperor of France."

"What has all this to do with me, Papa?" puzzled Gabby impatiently.

"Patience, daughter, haven't you learned anything in ten years? I would have thought you had been cured by now of the willful streak you displayed as a child." Gabby flushed at her father's rebuke but waited as patiently as her nature would allow for him to continue. "Soon your mother and I will depart for Italy along with a large group of Napoleon's staunchest supporters. Once there we will plan together for his return to power and triumphant march to Paris. But before we can leave France there is the matter of settling my debts."

"But I still don't . . . ?"

"Be still!" ordered Gilbert. "If you but give me a chance I will explain. During the citizens' uprising I lost a considerable fortune. Later I invested heavily in Napoleon's campaign. I now find myself in financial straits and unable to meet my obligations and fulfill my pledge to Napoleon.''

"Not to mention your debts of honor," interjected Lily. Gilbert's withering glance warned her to silence.

"I must also see to your future before I leave Paris," Gilbert continued smoothly, displaying an uncommon amount of parental concern.

"But my future is secure," Gabby insisted. "I already told you that I intend to pledge my life to *le bon Dieu* just as you have pledged yours to Napoleon."

Gilbert's scathing glance scalded Gabby. "I have arranged for your marriage." Gabby clutched at her throat and gasped with dismay. She felt as if the whole world was closing in on her.

The irony of fate! Just when she had reconciled herself to living a devout and prayerful life her parents had appeared and shattered her fragile peace. "I have no desire to wed, Papa," Gabby cried in desperation. "Please do not force me into a marriage I do not want."

As if on cue, the door opened, admitting a tall, sun-browned man whose cold gray eyes immediately sought and found Gabby. "Who am I to marry?" she whispered in a strangled voice, unable to tear her gaze from the man whose handsome dark features instilled terror in her wildly beating heart.

Smiling broadly, Gilbert La Farge motioned forward the tall, broodingly handsome man whose sun-darkened skin proclaimed him to be anything but a native of Paris. Turning to Gabby, he said, "Gabrielle, this is Philippe St. Cyr from the island of Martinique. If you meet with his approval, you will become his wife regardless of the fact that you have no dowry."

Gabby gritted her teeth, desperately wanting to lash out angrily at her father and the arrogant stranger whose approval meant nothing to her. She had no way of knowing that Philippe St. Cyr demanded only two things of his future wife,

11

—she must be virtuous, and she must be obedient to his will.

When St. Cyr had first met Gilbert La Farge at the card table in a certain club in Paris, he had taken an immediate dislike to the braggart who lost large sums of money and indiscriminately handed out his IOU. He personally held a small stack of these worthless notes. When in the course of conversation, Gilbert had learned that Philippe had come to France in search of a wife, preferably a convent-educated one, his eyes had become overbright as they thoughtfully contemplated the man who he also learned was a wealthy planter from Martinique as well as the owner of a fleet of ships. Philippe, for the most part, had ignored the man's fawning presence until Gilbert had drawn him aside and quietly spoken to him about his daughter. After much persuassion he had finally agreed to a meeting with the girl.

Now, as Philippe bowed before the petite Gabrielle, he was not at all certain she would do. Though no doubt she was virtuous, having been cloistered for the past ten years, she displayed a spark of defiance that set him on edge And her beauty startled him. He had thought himself finished with beauty and spirit. What he desired was an obedient, well-bred wife who would bear his children and become mistress of Bellefontaine, his plantation on Martinique. Once her duty was fulfilled he would demand nothing more from her. He had the delectable Amalie to satisfy his passion and intended to seek his wife's bed only to beget his heirs. To keep his beloved Bellefontaine he must have sons.

How was it then that he found himself lost in deep, shimmering pools of violet? Where was his willpower? Hadn't he told himself over and over he was finished with seductive beauty and spirit? When he spoke, his voice sent chills along Gabby's spine. "Mademoiselle La Farge," he acknowledged as he bowed over her slim hand, lightly brushing it with his lips.

A shudder passed through Gabby at his touch. "Monsieur

St. Cyr," she replied softly, remembering her manners.

"Your father has told me much about you and I can clearly see he did not exaggerate."

"I'm surprised he could remember anything about me," she murmured in a moment of pique.

Gilbert bristled at her remark but focused his attention on Philippe. "I told you she was well worth the trip out here," he boasted smugly. "Well, St. Cyr, what do you say? Do we have a deal or don't we?"

"I would like to hear what Mademoiselle Gabrielle has to say about your plans to sell her to me," Philippe said, oblivious of Gabby's feelings.

"Papa!" cried Gabby, drawing back in disbelief. "Surely Monsieur St. Cyr jests. You would not sell your only child!"

"Now, now daughter," soothed Gilbert, glancing reproachfully at Philippe. "Those are not the words I would choose. Monsieur St. Cyr has generously offered to cancel all my debts and to finance my venture in Italy in gratitude for supplying him with a suitable bride. And you, *ma chere*, are immensely suitable."

The knuckles of Gabby's clenched fists whitened as her whole body stiffened in defiance, negating in an instant ten years of discipline. "I am sorry, Papa, but I refuse to marry Monsieur St. Cyr! I choose to remain in the convent," she declared hotly.

Gilbert lashed out cruelly and the blow to Gabby's face resounded loudly in the small room. Philippe stepped menacingly toward Gilbert but at the last minute prudence intervened, and, shrugging, he fell back, deeming Gilbert's punishment justifiable in view of his daughter's rebellious nature.

"Gilbert, really!" Lily gasped. "Must you use violence? The chit will do as she's told whether she likes it or not."

"Of course, you are right, *cherie*," replied Gilbert guiltily. "I'm sorry, daughter, but I will not tolerate disobedience. I

13

have given my word to St. Cyr that you have been well taught by the nuns. Do not make a liar of me.'' Though his voice was soft, his words left little doubt that he would brook no interference with his well-laid plans. Gabby knew that no amount of pleading would dissuade her father from his course. She would become the bride of Philippe St. Cyr, if he would have her, and leave her beloved France. Still smarting from her father's blow, she lowered her head to hide tears of frustration and pain gathering in her eyes.

"Well, St. Cyr?'' Gilbert repeated impatiently. ''Does my daughter please you? Will you have her?''

Studying the girl through slitted eyes, Philippe saw that she now appeared submissive to her father's wishes. Perhaps she would do after all, he mused, his eyes drawn to the steady rise and fall of firm, upturned breasts beneath her drab garment. Even though he had not expected her to be so lovely, she would be a pleasant diversion on the long voyage ahead. Her young femininity was appealing and hard to resist, even to one who had forsworn such inducements. With the right clothes . . . His eyes drifted over the shapeless robe and ugly wimple concealing her hair. A sudden urge struck him and he was powerless to stay his words.

"Remove your headdress, Gabrielle,'' he ordered brusquely. Violet, mist-filled eyes stared at him uncomprehendingly as he raised her head. When she made no move to comply, he stepped forward and drew his breath in sharply as a cascade of silvery strands, pale as moonlight, tumbled down her back in a multitude of springy curls from beneath the cloth he had just plucked from her head. The sight strangely unsettled Philippe as he drew in his breath sharply. He found it difficult to still his wildly beating heart.

Gilbert smiled to himself. He was as good as on his way to Italy, he thought smugly. Although St. Cyr had expressed a desire for a virtuous, obedient wife, making no mention of beauty, he was a man, and what man would not want a young

14

and beautiful virgin such as Gabby gracing his bed?

When Philippe finally found his voice, Gabby knew that her prayers had been in vain. Her future had been decided without a thought to her own feelings or needs. "We have a deal, La Farge," Philippe said, reluctantly tearing his eyes from the vision before him. "The amount agreed upon will be deposited in your bank as soon as I return to Paris."

Lily flashed a pleased smile at no one in particular and Gilbert rubbed his hands together gleefully. "When do you wish the wedding to take place, St. Cyr?" he asked.

Involuntarily Philippe's right hand moved to his jacket, smoothing the imperceptible bulge made by the slim document he had sewn in the lining only this morning. Now that his mission was half completed he knew he must waste no more time. Ignoring Gabby, he said, "One of my ships now lies at anchor at Brest awaiting word from me. I see no reason to delay the wedding as I am anxious to reach New . . . uh . . . Martinique." He paused to ascertain whether anyone had noticed his slip of the tongue, and satisfied that no one had, continued, "The wedding shall take place in three days." Not once did his eyes slide to the small, wilting figure in the gray habit.

"The ceremony will take place in three days, at noon," announced Gilbert. "My daughter will be ready."

"*Bon!*" answered Philippe. "I will send a messenger ahead informing the captain on the *Windward* to be ready to depart Brest the moment I arrive aboard with my bride." Then suddenly remembering Gabby he turned his granite gaze in her direction. "Until then, Mademoiselle Gabrielle, *adieu,*" he said before turning on his heel and striding from the room, leaving Gabby breathless and shaken.

"How could you, Papa?" she exploded the moment Philippe was gone. "And you, Mama? How could you let Papa sell me to that insufferable man?"

"We did no more than other parents would do for their

15

children," replied Lily who had grown quite bored with her daughter's tantrums. "In these trying times we have done our best to provide for you. We can no longer remain in France to see to your welfare. You aren't the only girl whose marriage has been arranged, and quite admirably, I might add."

"Come now," cajoled her father, "there are worse things that could happen to a young girl than becoming the wife of a rich, important planter. One of them is hiding your beauty behind the walls of this convent." His glittering eyes roamed freely over his daughter's ripening figure. "I had no idea you had turned into such an enchanting creature. *Mon Dieu*, but St. Cyr is a lucky fellow!"

Lily bristled with jealous indignation. She thought Gilbert much too preoccupied with his daughter's looks. St. Cyr's money had earned him the right to deflower the girl himself no matter what Gilbert's intention.

16

Chapter Two

GABBY SHIFTED restlessly in her stiff satin wedding gown while the priest's toneless words bound her for life to the stranger who stood beside her. Her own voice wavered nervously as she repeated the sacred vows that could never be broken. Philippe scowled darkly at the shudder that passed through her body at the moment they were pronounced man and wife. Surely this was a bad dream and she would wake up safe and sound in her narrow cot in the convent. How she hated Philippe's arrogance, his possessiveness, his brooding good looks!

Suddenly the silence around them pierced her brain. Without warning her husband's hands were on her shoulders, pivoting her to face him. She turned ashen at his touch when she realized that Philippe was claiming the kiss that was now his by right of ownership. He had caught her unprepared with her mouth slightly open in surprise as he brushed his lips against hers. But when he felt the soft, warm breath escaping in frightened gasps from between her lips his cold reserve vanished for a moment as his kiss deepened and his darting tongue thrust fleetingly into her open mouth. Quickly gaining his composure once more, he abruptly released her, but not before scowling at her with a puzzled frown.

Gabby was shocked by the kiss. Though she had not participated in it herself, she did not find it too unpleasant once she had gotten over the initial shock. Surely Philippe could not kiss her like that if he did not feel something for her, she thought naively. Raising her head, Gabby met his eyes and was shaken to her very depths by the look of pure animosity directed at her, as if he held her accountable for his unexpected show of emotion.

Afterward Philippe led her into the small circle of servants and family friends hastily gathered for the occasion, but she was too numb to respond to their congratulations. Things had moved too fast for her. After all, this was only the second time she had ever seen the man she must now call husband. Her mind turned inward to that time three days ago when she had first seen him standing beside her parents in Mother Superior's chambers. She had thought him cold and arrogant then, his calculating gaze raking her insolently, and he had done nothing since to change that opinion.

Philippe's voice jolted her back to reality. "You seem far away. What are you thinking, *ma petite?*" His endearment seemed only to mock her and did nothing to dispel her dark thoughts.

"I'm thinking, Monsieur, that I wish myself back at St. Cecilia's," she blurted, finding in impossible to lie to him.

"My name is Philippe," he admonished softly, yet sternly. "I am your husband and you must not call me Monsieur."

"*Oui*, Philippe," she corrected dutifully, yet seething inwardly at his rebuke.

"Would you like something to eat or drink?" he asked, leading her toward the small buffet table set up in the chamber.

"*Non*, Monsieur, I have no appetite."

His hand closed hurtfully on her arm but at her small cry of pain immediately released his hold, his mouth drawn into a thin, white line as he frowned. She rubbed the bruise his grip had caused and vowed to remember henceforth to use his name. *Mon Dieu*, what manner of man was he? she thought, her mind stumbling over the unfamiliar oath.

"If you will excuse me then, I must speak privately with your father before we depart. I suggest you go to your room and change from that hideous wedding dress into something more appropriate for traveling."

"I'm sorry if my dress does not please you," Gabby shot back caustically, "but I could not do much better with only three days' notice to prepare for this wedding. You forget, I am newly arrived from a convent where such fripperies were unnecessary. If you desired me to be fashionably dressed, you should have allowed more time for a dressmaker to be hired and a proper trousseau made!"

"*Touché!*" Philippe smiled with a slight bow as he turned to join her father in the study.

Gabby breathed a sigh of relief as she watched Philippe's broad shoulders disappear from sight. She supposed, given different circumstances, she might find him attractive. From the back, she noticed how the fine cloth of his jacket clung to his wide shoulders and the way his well-cut trousers molded the muscular length of his thighs and legs. Even the midnight tendrils of hair curling at the nape of his neck would probably appear charming to another woman. But his cold, unrelenting eyes and the unmoving line of his mouth left her little doubt that he was a man who would demand complete submission to his will. Given time he would overpower her own indomitable spirit, manipulating her to his own purposes. She was not too naive to realize that she would eventually become the docile, obedient drudge he wanted, producing his heirs until she became worn and old beyond her years. On that unhappy note, she left the room to change her attire in preparation for the long journey ahead.

As Gabby passed her parents' bedroom on the way to her own room, she recalled the intimate conversation she had overheard the night before. She had been unable to sleep and was on her way downstairs to get a book from the library. The door to her parents' room was ajar and the only reason she had stopped to listen was because she heard her name spoken.

"Are you sure you are doing the right thing by allowing Gabby to marry that fierce St. Cyr fellow?" she heard her mother saying in a sudden burst of latent maternal misgivings.

"*Cherie*," her father answered in a placating voice, "St. Cyr is a rich man and she could do much worse. Besides, think of all the beautiful new Italian gowns you can buy to drape around that enticing body of yours." There was a significant pause before Gabby heard her mother's gasp.

"Ah, Gilbert, do not stop, please!" Lily's voice was low and throaty, the consistency of warm honey.

"You see the wisdom of my words, do you not, *cherie?*"

This time Lily's voice held a quality Gabby had never heard before. "*Oui*, Gilbert, *mon amour, oui!*" she moaned as her rising passion took over. "You are right, as always. I agree to whatever you say, only don't stop what you are doing."

"Never, *cherie*. But for your passion, I would have tired of you long ago."

Once again Lily's cries of pleasure filled Gabby's ears as she pressed her hands over them to blot out intimate sounds that caused her heart to beat wildly in her breast. She had been embarrassed to be privy to her mother's submission to the dictates of her body. Silently Gabby vowed never to allow any man to bend her to his will by controlling her senses.

Gabby tried hard to shake off the disturbing thoughts that the scene of the night before had aroused in her as she changed from the despised wedding dress whose prim lines could not hide the supple body beneath to another equally unbecoming traveling dress of brown velvet. She had just finished fastening the long row of buttons down the front of the dress when her mother appeared, arriving somewhat breathless and more than a little flustered.

"You are a lucky girl, Gabby," Lily gushed as she smoothed her honey-colored locks into place. "Your husband can be such a charming rogue when he wants to be." Her bright blue eyes grew hazy as she regarded her daughter with envy. "And extremely handsome in a devilish way. He could prove to be a resourceful and vigorous lover. I just encountered him coming out of your father's study and he asked me to speak to you."

"Speak to me, Maman?"

"About your wifely duties."

"Just what are those duties?" Gabby asked, wrinkling her nose.

"Did the nuns teach you nothing?" Lily exclaimed in exasperation.

"I know little of what occurs between men and women," Gabby admitted shyly.

"How can an innocent like you hope to please a virile man like Philippe St. Cyr? I wouldn't be surprised if half the women on Martinique were clamoring for his attention," Lily said, her eyes taking on a dreamy quality. "It's fortunate he wants you only for the purpose of producing his heirs, for I doubt he will derive much pleasure from your childish body."

Gabby eyed her mother with distaste. The number of Philippe's conquests were of no consequence to her. But what if she proved barren? Would he then cast her aside? she wondered. She would put no foul act past him.

"Maman," Gabby said, slowly thinking out her next words, "I suppose I am somewhat of an innocent, but I have a right to know just what Monsieur St. Cry expects of me in the marriage bed. The nuns were completely silent on the subject and there is no one else to ask but you."

Lily stared thoughtfully into her daughter's lovely face. Privately she thought herself a more fitting match for her virile son-in-law than her pale, inexperienced daughter who was likely to swoon at his first intimate touch. She shook her head to rid herself of the image of Philippe's powerful, nude body in full arousal. "Your duty is clear, Gabby," Lily finally said. "Your husband undoubtedly possesses vast experience as well as vast appetites, and will expect nothing but complete submission from you. He knows you are a virgin so will no doubt expect you only to accommodate him. If he wants more than that, he will teach you."

"Accommodate!" The word tasted like gall in Gabby's mouth, and told her little. "How must I accommodate him, Maman?" she asked, desperation making her bold.

Lily regarded her daughter as she would a backward child, then shrugged her dainty shoulders in disgust. "Philippe will do exactly as he pleases and you will do exactly what he tells you," Lily announced obliquely. "But for your own good, do not fight him, let him have his way with you. He is not a man to be put off."

"You mean I . . ."

"Enough! Enough! My head aches from your endless questions," Lily snapped, wanting nothing more than to escape from her daughter's vexing ignorance. "Come—if you are ready I will accompany you downstairs. Your husband bade me hurry you along." Reluctantly, Gabby followed her mother from the room and moved slowly down the staircase to join her husband.

Philippe watched Gabby's graceful descent and unwittingly his heart skipped a beat. She was so young, so innocent, as beautiful as a fragile flower, as fresh and dewy as a summer morn, yet so unaware of her own loveliness. Only the full, sensuous lips gave a hint of what might lie hidden beneath the vulnerable exterior. He felt a familiar tightening in his groin and a quickening in his blood that made him wish they were already aboard the *Windward*. There was no denying that he wanted the virtuous little chit. But he must be on his guard, he told himself. Never again would a woman enslave him with her beauty and spirit. Cecily had taught him well.

"Are you really to leave, *ma petite?*" he asked when she had reached his side. At her nod he propelled her through the door followed closely by her parents.

"Where will you spend the night, *mon ami?*" Gilbert asked, leering first at Gabby and then Philippe, leaving them little doubt as to his meaning.

"Except to eat and change horses and drivers, we will travel straight through to Brest. I have wasted enough time in France and am anxious to return to my plantation," answered Philippe blandly.

"Harumph!" snorted Gilbert derisively. "I certainly would not wait so long to bed my prize."

A small muscle twitched in Philippe's cheek as he fought to hold his temper in check. He felt nothing but contempt for a man who would sell his own daughter to finance a venture that was doomed to failure. Disdaining to answer, Philippe handed Gabby into the carriage and signaled the coachman to proceed.

Philippe watched with cool amusement while Gabby fit herself into the farthest corner of the seat. "I will not bite you," he said as he reached out and pulled her into his arms. Then, as if to prove his words, his lips closed on hers, seeking the tender shape of her mouth, molding it to his. Her eyes opened wide as his tongue forced her lips apart, slowly exploring with maddening thoroughness, and his hand cupped a soft undercurve of a breast.

When he released her she was breathless, a becoming flush staining her cheekbones. She was shocked at this invasion of her senses, more probing than she had ever known. Did he mean to consummate their marriage in the carriage? she wondered. Whatever was in his mind was beyond her limited knowledge of men. "Please do not shame me before your coachman," she pleaded, her violet eyes wide with fear.

"How could I shame you now that we are wed, *ma chere?*" he answered dryly. But he released her just the same and

23

settled himself comfortably into the cushions, promptly ignoring her as if she had never existed.

They spent three days and nights in the carriage, stopping only for meals, to change horses and to relieve themselves. Gabby had never been more miserable in her entire life. No amount of brushing could dislodge the layer of grime that covered their clothing. She had no idea why Philippe insisted on racing the horses at breakneck speed along the winding road to Brest. Fall rains had turned the dirt road into a muddy quagmire, but still he pressed on relentlessly, cursing when a wheel became hopelessly stuck in the gluey mud.

Once, when Gabby's head lolled wearily, Philippe drew her into the crook of his arm where she slept comfortably for hours. When she awoke to find herself still in her husband's arms, she drew away to huddle once again in the far corner of the coach, much to Philippe's amusement.

Gabby could not help but wonder at Philippe's preoccupation during their journey. Often his hand would stray to a place on his jacket just over his heart. She thought at first he was experiencing some sort of pain but it became increasingly evident that the pain was nonexistent for sometimes he took the reins of the carriage himself, propelling the horses forward at a pace that left her breathless as well as bruised from the constant jolting. Protecting herself from being thrown from the seat became a fulltime job.

Their fourth day on the road proved to be a day neither Gabby nor Philippe would soon forget. It was nearly dusk and Philippe had been dozing, muttering strange names in his sleep. Gabby knew from remarks he had made earlier that they were near to a village where they would eat and change horses and was gazing absently about the window thinking only of her aching bones and a hot meal. They had just entered a place where heavily wooded hills rose on either side of the road and she vaguely wondered what would happen if they met another carriage on that particularly narrow strip. Suddenly her thoughts turned to frozen horror as a huge boulder at the top of the hill on their right hurtled through space directly toward their carriage.

At her scream of warning, Philippe uncoiled from sleep like an alert animal, immediately assessing their chance for survival. Instantly he realized that the narrow, hemmed-in road afforded little or no room for maneuver, and even if the horses were to halt now, their momentum would still carry them into a collision course with the plummeting boulder. Acting swiftly, he pushed open the door to his side of the carriage, grasped Gabby about the waist and jumped to the ground, rolling to avoid the rear wheels of the coach, trying to cushion her body against the full impact of the fall. Gabby remembered the wheels yanking at the loosened strands of her hair as they passed dangerously close to her head . . . and nothing more.

When Gabby regained consciousness, the sun was in her eyes and she moved her head slightly to avoid its direct glare. She groaned as white hot pain seared the top of her head in a blaze of agony. Philippe was beside her instantly, concern flashing briefly on his dark face before assuming its normal cool reserve.

"Where am I?" she asked, gingerly touching her head. "What happened?"

"The coachman and I carried you here to the inn," Philippe answered. "You received a nasty bump on the head but otherwise you appear unhurt."

"Have . . . have I been unconscious long?"

"*Oui, ma petite,* all night."

"Who undressed me and put me to bed?" Gabby asked shyly. She was surprised upon awakening to find herself clad in her own high-necked nightgown.

"I did, of course. But do not fear," he hastened to add

when he saw her reddened cheeks. "I do not take advantage of helpless women." She hated the note of amusement in his voice.

"I remember nothing after you pulled me from the coach," Gabby put in quickly, thinking it best to change the subject. "The boulder, did it hit our coach?"

"Yes. If we had been inside we would now be dead."

She suppressed an involuntary shudder. "And the coachman?"

"He, too, had the presence of mind to jump in time. Even the horses escaped injury. But the coach was demolished."

"What an incredible accident!"

"Yes," Philippe agreed dourly. "It is truly an 'incredible' accident, just as you say." Somehow his words held little conviction.

"What do we do now?" Gabby asked, hoping she would be allowed to rest at the inn at least through the day before continuing their journey.

Philippe searched her face. "Do you feel well enough to travel right away? It is imperative that we reach the *Windward*."

"Why such haste, Philippe?" Gabby questioned irritably. "I hurt all over and I am exhausted. What does it matter if we reach Brest a day or two later?"

"Don't question me, Gabby," warned Philippe ominously. "Just tell me if you are able to travel. We have less than a day's journey ahead and I have spent most of the night searching for another coach. I'm tired myself and have more important things on my mind than coddling a complaining wife."

A red haze of rage pulsated behind Gabby's eyes. "Complaining wife!" she seethed angrily. "I would be safe behind convent walls if you hadn't come along. Does being an obedient wife mean following my husband even if he nearly gets me killed?"

Philippe held himself in check by the most stringent effort of will. What Gabby said was the truth. If what he suspected was right, then he was plunging her pell-mell into a dangerous situation that was none of her making. He should have followed his conscience and not complicated his life at this time by taking another wife. But once he had accepted this assignment, he had needed a cover for his activities, and what could be more natural than being in France to look for a bride? All the gentry of Martinique returned to France for wives, just as most of the island's young women married French aristocrats. His voyage to France must invite no suspicion, and if he must marry again, as he knew he must if he wanted an heir, who better than a convent-bred girl trained in obedience? Why, in the name of *le bon Dieu* had he chosen this little hellcat in nun's clothing who had so much to learn about docility and submission?

"If you are well enough to carry on like a shrew, then you are well enough to travel," Philippe informed her coldly. "I will give you one-half hour to ready yourself." Gabby's flashing eyes and the tantalizing treasures that he knew lay hidden beneath her prim nightgown almost tempted him to forget his urgency to reach the *Windward* and tarry long enough to consummate his marriage. He had been distressed and concerned for her the night before, but not too distracted to notice that his bride had a delectable body and was immensely desirable. Clenching his teeth against the sudden ache in his groin, Philippe strode from the room before he lost all control and joined her in the bed.

It had grown dark when they reached Brest that night and Gabby could see nothing of the city from the carriage window. They proceeded directly to the docks where the twinkling lights of ships anchored in the harbor appeared to her like mating fireflies. Philippe helped her from the coach and led her directly to the wharf where the *Windward* rode at anchor, then up the gangplank onto the ship. Gabby was astounded when the seamen around them immediately pulled in the gangplank and began preparations to hoist anchor and raise the sails. She watched forlornly as the ship loosed its moorings under the cover of approaching darkness and slipped stealthily from its berth, leaving behind the land she loved and the only life she had ever known.

Chapter Three

WHILE THE *Windward* was maneuvering past the line of ships achored in the harbor, Philippe and Gabby were joined by a man whose dress and air of authority proclaimed him to be the captain. "We expected you last evening, *mon ami*," the man said, directing wary, black eyes in all directions before speaking. "When you did not arrive, I began to fear something unforeseen had occurred to delay you."

"Something unforeseen did occur, Henri," Philippe conceded. "We were nearly killed when a wayward boulder destroyed our carriage on the road to Brest. We escaped just in the nick of time."

"*Sacre bleu!*" cursed the captain. "What caused the accident?"

"I returned to the scene later but saw nothing to indicate anything other than sheer chance. Evidently the recent rains had caused the boulder to pull loose, and the timing couldn't have been better—or worse, depending on how you look at it," Philippe added meaningfully. Suddenly remembering the girl at his side, he said, "Gabby, this is Henri Giscard, captain of the *Windward* and a good friend as well." And to the captain. "Henri, this is my wife, Gabrielle La Farge St. Cyr."

"Philippe, *mon Dieu*, you did not warn me your wife was so beautiful," chided Captain Giscard after bowing over Gabby's small hand. "But she is just a child, *mon ami*. How lucky you are to have captured beauty and youth in one small bundle."

"There was more involved than just mere luck, Henri,"

Philippe stated as he directed a raised eyebrow at Gabby who flinched, fearing he would reveal the circumstance surrounding their marriage.

Gabby breathed a sigh of relief when Captain Giscard cut in. "No matter, she will be a lovely addition to our little island. And you, Philippe, will be the envy of every man."

Gabby barely had time to acknowledge Captain Giscard's gallantry before Philippe took her by the elbow and steered her to a cabin in the stern that was to be their home during the coming weeks. He told her that there were other cabins below deck on either side of a long companionway but that they remained unoccupied on this trip. Their cabin was the largest, and always ready should he decide to sail with the *Windward* on one of her many voyages. With pride in his voice he informed her that he owned the *Windward* as well as three other ships just like her.

The cabin, though not luxurious, appeared comfortable enough at first glance, but try as she might, Gabby could not keep her eyes from straying toward the big bed that seemed much too large for the cabin. She noticed that her trunk had been carried aboard and placed next to a leather sea chest she supposed belonged to Philippe. A desk piled high with charts, a table and chairs bolted to the deck, and a washstand with the necessary accoutrements were the only other pieces of furniture in the room. The masculine odors of leather and tobacco assualted her senses as well as a fresh, clean smell of sea spray and witch hazel. There was none of the cloying, sweet aroma of pomade and perfume she noticed about her father's clothing and person.

Gabby started violently at he sound of Philippe's voice. "I realize these are rather cramped quarters, *ma petite*, but nevertheless, we must make do." For the first time he became aware of her weariness and state of near collapse, and he drew the cloak from her shoulders, speaking more gently than he had at any other time since their marriage, but still not conveying the warmth of a newly wed man. "I have urgent business with the captain, so I must leave you. I will arrange for a supper tray and you can retire whenever you wish. The journey to Brest hasn't been an easy one for you and I don't relish having a sick wife on my hands."

Gabby stared at Philippe through wary eyes, unwilling to believe that he had no compulsion to consummate their marriage now that they were aboard his ship. But when she saw that he was indeed preparing to leave the cabin, she murmured tiredly, albeit gratefully, "Thank you, Monsieur, your thoughtfulness is much appreciated." Too late she realized her slip of the tongue.

Philippe stopped dead at her words, swept his steely gaze over her slight figure and was beside her in two strides, grasping her small shoulders in his large hands until her fear caused her to cry out. "My name, Gabby—say it, damn you!" he growled. "Why do you continue to provoke me?"

"Philippe!" she cried through chattering teeth, terrified by his sudden change of mood.

"That's right. I am Philippe, your husband. Don't ever forget it," he warned, releasing her so abruptly that she staggered backward a few steps. Then he stormed fiercely from the cabin.

Alone at last, Gabby's relief was immense as she sagged onto the bed, emotionally drained and scarcely aware of the pain caused by Philippe's cruel fingers. For the first time in two weeks she gave vent to the traumatic upheaval she had experienced and began to weep uncontrollably, overcome with a despair so overwhelming that were she on deck she would have thrown herself into the sea. Soon she drifted into the healing arms of sleep.

Philippe's inexplicable flash of anger cooled somewhat as he made his way along the dark passageway to Captain Giscard's cabin. In fact, he had almost forgotten Gabby as his hand moved to the slight bulge in his jacket, as if assuring himself for the thousandth time that he still carried the document for which he was risking his life.

Philippe paused before Captain Giscard's door and was shaken to his foundation by voices coming from within. "*Mon dieu!*" he cursed aloud when he recognized the voice speaking to the captain. "It cannot be!" He burst into the cabin with a look of such pure rage on his face that both men inside the room felt they were facing a maddened bull.

"What is it, Philippe?" Captain Giscard cried in alarm when he saw Philippe's face.

"How in the hell did Duvall get aboard the *Windward*?" he demanded, pointing a finger at the tall, slim man regarding him through startling green eyes. "By whose authority is he on my ship? I gave strict orders that no passengers would be allowed on board this trip. You know the reason as well as I, Henri."

"I'm . . . I'm sorry, Philippe, truly I am," apologized Henri, astounded by the animosity displayed by Philippe toward a man who was considered by all to be his good friend. "When Monsieur Duvall came aboard late last night he assured me you would not object to his presence. It is well known that you and Duvall are neighbors as well as friends."

"At one time perhaps," muttered Philippe darkly. Then he turned to the elegantly dressed man toward whom his anger was directed. "What have you to say for yourself, Marcel? Why have you come aboard the *Windward* under false pretenses? You know as well as I that our friendship ended with Cecily's death."

"*Mon ami,*" Marcel Duvall began smoothly, all the while toying with the thin mustache gracing his upper lip, "you were the one who denounced our friendship. And at he time you were still grieving over the untimely death of your wife. I am prepared to overlook your rash actions and continue our relations as if nothing had happened."

"The devil take you, Duvall!" spat Philippe. "I meant every word I said. Cecily might still be alive today if it weren't for you. I want nothing more to do with you! You may have convinced Henri that we are friends but I know what lies between us and I warn you, keep out of the way." Suddenly his flinty eyes narrowed suspiciously. "Just what are you doing in France, anyway? When did you leave Martinique?"

Captain Giscard looked from one to the other, completely baffled by the turn of their conversation. He had no idea Marcel Duvall was in any way involved with the death of Cecily St. Cyr. If there was any connection at all, then he had done Philippe a grave injustice by allowing the man aboard the *Windward*.

"I left Martinique aboard the *Tristan* while you were on one of your trips to America," Marcel answered easily. "My business in France is simple; I hoped to arrange a suitable marriage for my sister, Linette."

"And have you?" demanded Philippe.

"Certainly, *mon ami,* and quite admirably," boasted Marcel. "Next year Linette will become the bride of Pierre Bonnard, the only son and heir of the founder of the great banking firm of the same name. Quite a match, I might add. A feather in my cap."

"*Oui.*" Philippe admitted grudgingly. "Ever one to further your own interests by uniting your family name to one of the great names in Europe, eh, Duvall? You must have offered a handsome dowry. Your fortune must be greater than I imagined. But tell me, how did you know the *Windward* was at Brest?"

"I did not know. It was just my incredible good fortune to find the *Windward* in port when I arrived looking for passage to Martinique. It seems I have been blessed with much good luck this trip," he said blandly.

"So it would seem," agreed Philippe without conviction.

33

"Now that you are aboard there is nothing I can do about it." With a wave of his hand he dismissed Marcel. "I have some private business to conduct with Henri, so . . ."

"Of course, of course. I do not wish to intrude, so I will bid you both good night. By the way," he added archly, "I understand congratulations are in order, that you have been successful in your quest."

"What!" exploded Philippe and Henri together.

"Why, what is wrong, gentlemen?" asked Marcel innocently. "I refer to your bride, of course. If I am to believe Captain Giscard, Madame St. Cyr is a raving beauty." After dropping that bombshell, he quickly left the cabin, humming a little tune as he strutted down the passageway.

"For a moment I feared he knew the real reason behind our journey to France," breathed Henri with obvious relief. "You don't think he could have found out, do you, Philippe?"

"No, Henri," Philippe replied with more conviction than he felt at that moment. "It's probably just a coincidence that the *Windward* was preparing for departure at the same time Duvall wished to return to Martinique." Then he looked sharply at the older man. "You mentioned nothing of our destination?"

"No! No!" Henri quickly assured him. "I thought you could tell him when the time is right."

Momentarily dismissing from his mind the man he had every reason to hate, Philippe turned to more pressing matters. He removed his jacket, and using a letter opener he found on the desk, carefully ripped open the seam, extracting a slim packet wrapped in oilskin. Only the hiss of air escaping from Henri Giscard's lungs invaded the silence in the room.

"You encountered no trouble, then?" Henri asked, casting a furtive glance around the small cabin.

"None at all. The document was delivered to me by a messenger at my hotel in the guise of an innocuous-looking missive from a nonexistent aunt. As far as I know, you and I are the only ones aware of its importance, besides the agent working for the American government.''

"And if others were to find out?"

"They would not hesitate to do whatever is necessary to prevent it from reaching its destination.''

"*Mon dieu,*" cursed Henri, breaking out into a sweat born of fear.

"I have memorized the contents and I want you to do the same. In case something should happen to these papers, one of us will be able to deliver the message orally.'' Philippe's voice grew ominous. "And if something unforeseen should befall one of us, the other is duty bound to see the mission to its conclusion. I suggest you memorize the contents immediately, then put the packet in the safe.''

What Henri didn't know was that Philippe intended to retrieve the document from the safe before morning and return it to his own cabin. If there should happen to be a spy aboard the *Windward,* the first place he would look would be the safe. And Philippe fully intended for the document to reach the Americans safely.

As Philippe walked back to his cabin, his mind kept returning to Marcel Duvall and his unwelcome appearance at Brest just hours before he and Gabby entered the city themselves. It seemed too well timed to be a coincidence.

Gabby was sleeping soundly, wrapped in the brown cocoon of her travelel-worn dress when Philippe let himself quietly into the cabin. An untouched tray of food lay on the table. He lit a lamp and studied the tear stained face of his young bride. She was like a child, a beautiful, innocent child, yet nevertheless a very desirable woman. Somewhere deep in his heart he felt a tug but failed to recognize it for what it was. He only knew that he desired her as a man desires a woman. He had no thoughts of Cecily, or even of Amalie as his eyes swept over her sleeping form. He shook his head as it to clear his mind of arousing thoughts, staring a few moments more at her peaceful face before dousing the lamp and creeping softly from the room to spend the remainder of the night under the stars while his wife slept in her virginal bed—a state of affairs he intended to remedy soon.

Gabby awakened the next morning confused and disoriented. Slowly she became aware of a gentle rocking motion. At the same time, she heard the creakings of the ship and rattling of the helm wheel chains and remembered that she was on a ship bound for Martinique accompanied by her husband. Her husband! Hesitantly, she reached a hand out beside her and was relieved to find herself alone in the bed and fully clothed. Philippe had chosen to sleep elsewhere! Dared she hope he would continue to do so?

She raised her stiff body to a sitting position and stretched, working out the cramps caused in part by the arduous journey and in part from being laced into a tight corset for days on end. She eyed the rumpled, sweat-stained dress she still wore with distaste, longing for a hot bath.

A noise drew her attention to the door and she was surprised to see Philippe lounging in the doorway. "Good morning, *ma chere*," he greeted gaily as he appraised her disheveled appearance with raised eyebrows. "I hope you slept well. Does the ship's motion upset you?"

"No, Monsieur . . . I mean Philippe," she corrected hastily as she rubbed the place where his fingers had bruised her flesh the night before. "I find the motion most soothing."

Philippe moved aside and two men entered carrying a large tin tub into the cabin followed by two others bearing buckets of hot water. Gabby was speechless. Though Philippe had gone out of his way to remain cool and aloof toward her, he still thought of her comfort. She watched with trepidation as he approached her once they were alone, his eyes clouded with a strange, smoky haze.

"You cannot take a bath with all your clothes on, *ma*

petite," he admonished gently. "Hold still and I'll unfasten your dress."

"I can manage quite well by myself," she insisted, taking a step backward.

"Nonsense! If your father wasn't so tightfisted he would have provided you with a maid. But then," he murmured huskily, "I would have been denied the pleasure of undressing you myself. I wouldn't, *ma chere,*" he warned sternly when she attempted to pull away from his questing hands.

Soon he had the row of tiny buttons down the front of her dress undone and the heavy material pushed from her shoulders, over her breasts and down past her hips where it spread out in a dark pool around her feet. He uttered an oath at the ridiculous number of petticoats she wore as one by one he loosed the strings at her waist until they, too, billowed around her ankles.

"Please, Philippe," Gabby pleaded as streaks of crimson stained her cheeks, "allow me to bathe in private."

"There is no need for privacy between us, Gabby. We are wed," Philippe informed her boldly. "*Mon dieu,* do you always wear so many layers of clothing?" She still wore corset, corset cover, chemise, and pantalettes. "You will soon learn that on Martinique it is much too hot for such encumbrances. This you have no need for at all," he said, wrinkling his nose with distaste as he pulled off her whalebone corset. Then to Gabby's dismay he walked to the porthole and tossed the offending garment into the sea. Dismissing her gasp of shocked outrage, Philippe turned once again to the pleasurable task of disrobing her. With deliberate calmness, belying the inferno raging within him, he added her pantalettes to the pile of discarded clothing. Only the thin chemise now covered Gabby's flawless skin. Philippe nearly lost control when he saw the pink tips of her breasts peeping through. Though Gabby protested violently, she could not prevent him from removing her remaining garment, leaving her exposed to his hot gaze. He reacted instantaneously. The full impact of pink-tipped, softly rounded globes tilting deliciously upward from tiny waist rising above gently swelling hips caused a painful tightening in his groin. His eyes fell to the juction of her thighs and the softly curled, pale hair, then slid down the sleek line of calf and ankle. He clenched his fits, swallowing hard to control his urge to fall upon her immediately. A constricted moan rose from his throat as he absorbed every inch of her beauty.

After bending to remove her shoes and stockings, Philippe lifted Gabby into the tub, ignoring her protests. Taking a piece of soap from the washstand, he rubbed her body until a thick cloud of lather rose up around her breasts. Gabby blushed profusely as his hands traveled intimately over her.

"Stand up!" Philippe ordered brusquely.

Somewhat subdued by his forceful manner, Gabby had no choice but to comply. The crimson tinge of her skin deepened. His intimate touches sent her senses reeling and turned her legs to jelly, but she stood as if carved from stone, eyes tightly closed, unwilling to betray her humiliation.

"Sit!" he ordered, speaking as if to a recalcitrant child. Automatically Gabby obeyed, only too glad to sink beneath the murky, concealing water. Then, to her further chagrin, he began to lather her hair, scrubbing until she cried for mercy. "Rinse!" he said as he turned away from her. Obediently, she immersed her head beneath the water to remove the soap. After several such dunkings that left her hair gleaming like a bright halo, she looked around for a towel and was startled to see that Philippe had removed his clothing.

"What . . . what are you doing?" she asked in alarm, lowering her eyes in embarrassment.

"Something I've wanted to do from the first moment I laid eyes on you but was obliged to postpone." He moved closer and handed her a towel.

"I'm not ready to get out yet," she insisted vehemently, sliding back into the cooling water, trying hard to avoid staring at his rigid manhood.

"Yes, you are, *ma petite*," he replied with aplomb as he lifted her bodily from the tub and rubbed her briskly with the towel until her skin glowed.

"Now what are you going to do?" Gabby asked, eyeing him warily.

Philippe drew back, a perplexed frown creasing his forehead. "Surely your mother spoke to you about what to expect? She assured me she would."

"She said only that I must submit to you, and little else." The defiant tilt to her chin told Philippe that she had no intention of following her mother's advice.

"*Mon dieu*, am I to be teacher as well as lover?" cursed Philippe disgustedly. "Well, my innocent, I see that I must explain to you that which your mother withheld." Without preliminary, and in blunt language, Philippe told Gabby exactly what he planned to do. It was time she learned the role she was to play in his life, he reasoned, a smile of indulgent amusement crossing his face as shock, disbelief, and finally outrage registered on her expressive features in that order.

Gabby's mouth formed a perfect "O" and her delicate, golden brows lifted several inches. "But that is not possible," she protested in a small voice. "You are much too . . . I mean . . . surely, I am too . . ." Embarrassment caused her to falter. His expression told her that he spoke the truth and that somehow she must endure this final degradation.

"Not only is it possible, *ma chere*, but altogether enjoyable," he promised mysteriously. Gabby opened her mouth to protest but found her lips captured in an agonizingly slow kiss, his tongue probing, demanding. She began to struggle, striking out at him with ineffectual blows to his powerful back and shoulders, her pleas and entreaties lost in the sigh of the wind.

He was like a man possessed. Her budlike nipples seemed made for his mouth as he coaxed them into erectness with his tongue. His lips and hands were everywhere as he attempted to arouse a spark of desire from her shrinking flesh. His passion grew as his kisses covered her breasts, her belly, but Gabby was like one dead inside, frightened out of her wits by the man ravishing her. Finally, unable to control the fire raging within him, he forced a knee between her thighs and grasped her buttocks to still her wild thrashings.

"Heed your mother's advice, *ma chere*," he urged, "for it will be harder for you if you continue to struggle. It will hurt at first, but I promise you it will be better the next time." Gabby chose to ignore his words as she steeled herself for his entry, gritting her teeth and tensing her body, silently vowing that she would never willingly submit to his depraved ruttings.

Although Philippe endeavored to be gentle, Gabby's struggles made it next to impossible. His lust was like a pulsating monster and his need so great that he was unable to stop his manhood from driving into her resisting flesh with brutal force. The pain was so intense she screamed aloud at the cruel violation. He knew he was hurting her but he could not stop as he moved with rapid, breathless strokes, pounding her slim form into the firmness of the mattress. His thrusts carried her into gasping darkness and just when she thought she could bear no more, he grew rigid, cried out, then spasmed, caught up in his own private ecstasy. Gabby was startled by the intensity of the shudders racking his body, amazed that the very act that caused her such terrible agony could bring him such obvious bliss.

"I'm sorry, *ma chere*," Philippe said raggedly, pulling away from her, "but you would not let me to be gentle with you. You fought me as if I were some kind of animal, so I acted like one. Dry your eyes," he admonished with a touch of tenderness. "Next time it will be better."

"You mean you intend to rape me *again?*" Gabby cried reproachfully.

"Rape?" Philippe repeated stonily, raising one eyebrow, giving his face a sardonic look. "Surely it is not rape for a man to make love to his lawful wife?"

Gabby's violet eyes grew big and round, brimming with unshed tears. He had been cruel and hateful, forcing her to his will by sheer strength. No longer was her body sacrosanct. He had taken her with brutal violence and as far as she was concerned, that was tantamount to rape. "So long as you continue to force yourself on me, rape is an adequate description of that disgusting act," she said dispassionately. "You took me by force, I'll never forgive you for that." By now the tears were flowing copiously down her cheeks. "I hate you, Philippe," she cried out, surprising even herself by her boldness, "I hate you!"

With an exasperated sigh Philippe drew back long enough to see the wild expression in her frightened eyes. She looked so young, so vulnerable that he was immediately sorry for the forceful way he had taken her. But in his mind to do otherwise would have been a mistake. He had to prove, if only to himself, that he could not be moved by her innocent beauty. She must learn from the beginning to be submissive to him in all things. So far she had exhibited none of the qualities he required in a wife, but in time she would learn that he could be a stern teacher.

Neither pleas nor struggles could forestall Philippe as desire stirred in his loins. Although he realized that losing her virginity in such a manner was a vicious assault upon her tender sensibilities, he was certain that she was not one of those cold women who tolerated the sex act merely because it was her duty. Once she became accustomed to the intimacies

41

of marriage, he had no doubt that he could arouse a passionate response in her. It was a delicious challenge, one he would enjoy. What better pastime than to teach the intricacies of love to his new bride during the long nights ahead? Then passion engulfed him like a raging tide as he moved to possess her once more, surprising even himself by his unquenchable thirst for the terrified young girl lying in his arms.

Chapter Four

MUCH LATER Gabby paced the deck finding it difficult to concentrate on anything but the soreness between her legs and the stiffness of her abused body. After Philippe's violation earlier that morning (she wondered why they called that painful act lovemaking for she still considered it rape), he had added insult to injury by sitting back and coolly watching her all the while she washed and dressed. Her cheeks flamed when she thought of the stained sheets and traces of blood clinging to her thighs. She had felt positively naked without her corset and had donned petticoat after petticoat while Philippe's laughter mocked her modesty.

She was only too glad to be alone for a while and vaguely wondered at the need for Philippe to confer with Captain Giscard so often. Gabby's eyes grew misty when she considered how differently things might be if she had taken the vows of a nun or had been allowed to marry someone who cared for her instead of Philippe, a cruel, hard man who proved to be totally unyielding in his mysterious attitude toward her. Somehow, she knew she would not be the frigid wife he thought her given the right circumstances, for even Philippe's hands on her body had sent unfamiliar sensations coursing through her veins.

As Gabby paced the deck she suddenly became aware that she was not alone. Abruptly, she turned to face a tall, lean man carrying a gold-headed cane who was rapidly approaching her. Absently she watched the play of sunlight on the head of the cane as he came nearer.

"I'm sorry if I startled you, Madame St. Cyr, but if we are

to be fellow passengers, then we may as well become acquainted," the elegantly dressed stranger said with a disarming smile that immediately put her at ease. "I am Marcel Duvall, and you can be none other than Philippe's lovely wife. He is a lucky dog, but then he always had exceptional taste in women," he added cryptically.

"You are a friend of my husband?" Gabby asked, completely captivated by his charming manner.

"*Mais oui!*" Marcel replied blandly. "We are neighbors, our plantations bordering on the slopes of Mt. Pelee. Did he not tell you I was aboard?"

"Philippe told me there were to be no other passengers this trip."

"That was before he knew I was aboard," replied Marcel, smiling in secret amusement. "Captain Giscard was right, you are a rare beauty. But such a child. Not at all what St. Cyr . . ." His voice fell off and his face reddened as if suddenly aware that he was talking too freely.

Gabby had never encountered such a man as Marcel. His charm and pleasant manner was the complete opposite of Philippe's dark, violent moods. She warmed immediately to him even though she knew she was being over bold by speaking with a strange man. "Monsieur?" she questioned, waiting for him to finish the sentence he had ended so abruptly. When he did not, she asked, "Did you also have business in France, Monsieur Duvall?"

"You must call me Marcel; after all, I will be your nearest neighbor on Martinique. And, *oui,*" he answered, "I have just concluded marriage arrangements between my sister and a son of the house of Bonnard." He looked expectantly at Gabby, as if waiting for her to acclaim the fortuitous alliance. But his words only turned her thoughts inward to her own arranged marriage and the hate and fear she felt toward her husband. Her violet eyes became dark, troubled pools and a small frown creased her forehead as she gazed out over the endless expanse of blue water.

"You are troubled, *cherie!*" Marcel exclaimed, noting her black expression. "What is it? How may I help? A new bride on her honeymoon should be too much in love to display even the smallest amount of unhappiness."

"Love?" spat Gabby bitterly. "Please, Monsieur Duvall, do not speak of love to me. You do not understand." Marcel was struck speechless by the animosity in Gabby's voice. Evidently the bride cared little for the groom, he thought with a kind of perverse satisfaction. He would give half his fortune to possess a woman such as the petite Gabby. Her soft, velvet eyes had the ability to melt the coldest heart, even one as cold as Philippe's, Marcel thought as he viewed her through startling green eyes. Although he estimated her age at seventeen or eighteen, there was nothing childlike about the lithe, supple figure that was deliciously rounded in all the right places. Time and again his eyes kept returning to the full, sensuous lips that promised a passion he wished was his to unleash.

All the while Marcel feasted his eyes upon Gabby, she studied him through lowered lashes. What she saw did not displease her. He was tall, yet did not have the ruggedness or look of strength about him that one noticed in Philippe, and appeared to be somewhere in his early thirties; but his vibrant green eyes made him appear much younger. A pencil-thin mustache and long, aristocratic face only served to enhance his distinguished features. Unruly brown hair and soft sensual lips saved him from appearing almost two handsome.

Suddenly aware of the growing silence between them, Marcel was the first to shatter the poignant moment. "Madame St. Cyr," he said with grave concern, "I do not know what troubles you, but I wish to be your friend. Someday you might have need of a friend and when you do, I shall be there."

Gabby was about to thank him when from the corner of her eye she caught a glimpse of an approaching figure, bearing down at them with alarming speed. She shrank back in fear when she recognized her husband's massive frame, the look of cold fury in his gun-metal eyes and a ferocious scowl on his darkening features.

"Is it your custom to speak to strange men, Madame?" he asked tersely, barely able to control his rising anger.

"You are unjust, St. Cyr," Marcel broke in. "The fault lies solely with me. I introduced myself to your lovely wife. Surely you would not have her ignore me under those circumstances?"

"Somewhat presumptuous of you, Duvall, knowing how I feel about you," Philippe retorted harshly. "Keep away from my wife. She is very young and inexperienced. I would not have her tainted by men of your calibre."

"I envy your good fortune, *mon ami*," smiled Marcel affably, choosing to ignore the insult. "Had I such a wife, I, too, would be jealous." Then he turned to Gabby. "Madame St. Cyr, it has been a pleasure talking with you." Fuming inwardly, Philippe watched him saunter off with maddening nonchalance.

Marcel's parting words had strangely unsettled Philippe. Jealous? Could it be jealousy he felt? It was not possible. He wished only to protect Gabby. Unbidden, his mind returned to the fun-loving Cecily and the child who had joined her in death. Bitter experience had taught him that Marcel was no friend. He would do whatever was necessary to keep Marcel from corrupting his innocent wife.

Gabby found herself being propelled along the deck and into their cabin, wincing in pain as Philippe's fingers dug cruelly into the soft flesh of her upper arm. "Well, *ma chere*," he said in a voice heavy with sarcasm. "Did you learn nothing from the nuns? Henceforth, you will not invite the

46

advances of strange men. Duvall is not a man to be trifled with."

"Nor are you, Philippe," Gabby shot back, hurt by his false accusations. "Surely there can be no harm in conversing with a man who is counted among your friends. We are the only passengers aboard the *Windward* and no doubt will see each other often."

"Duvall is no friend of mine, nor of yours!" he exploded.

"Am I to be allowed no friends? Am I to remain secluded, to be taken out and displayed at your whim?"

"I shall choose your friends!" Philippe shot back.

Red spots of rage gathered behind Gabby's eyes and her small, pointed chin tilted defiantly upward. "I choose my own friends," she retorted bravely.

Philippe took one step forward but quickly fell back, suddenly remembering Marcel's words. Was he jealous? Was there more to his rage at seeing her with Marcel than his need to protect her? His eyes narrowed thoughtfully. The sight of her, breast heaving with indignation, eyes blazing hotly, sent the blood coursing wildly through his body. His heart was beating so loudly he could hear it echoing in his own ears. Even though he deplored her show of spirit, he admired her for her courage. She was magnificent when angered, and she excited him beyond restraint. Unable to control his actions, he pulled her roughly into his arms, caressing her body with strong, demanding hands that were surprisingly gentle on her flesh.

Gabby recognized the naked desire in his eyes and immediately sensed his intentions. "Please, Philippe, not again," she begged, her eyes wide with disbelief. "It has only been a few hours since you . . . since we . . ."

"A few hours can be a lifetime with a bewitching creature like you arousing my senses," he drawled in a voice made husky with desire. What manner of woman was she? Philippe wondered as his body responded eagerly to her nearness. She

47

was innocent of worldly knowledge, yet extremely provocative. She was trained to be submissive, yet her very nature rebelled against authority. She taunted and baited him, yet he desired her with an all-consuming fire. When he spoke, his words sent chills of apprehension down her spine. "I will always want you, *ma petite*, if only to prove to you that you belong to me, that I am the only one with the right to take you, wherever and whenever it pleases me, no matter how many small flirtations you might conduct."

"But, Philippe," Gabby protested, "I did not . . ." The words died in her throat as Philippe claimed her lips.

Despite Gabby's feeble struggles, and given Philippe's superior strength, it took no time at all for him to disrobe them both and carry her to the bed. His ardent kisses and caresses failed to quiet her, but to her dismay she found that his hands began to force a strange reaction from her body. When he paused, she felt hauntingly hollow, as if craving something more. It took every ounce of strength she possessed to fight against the maddening sensations he was arousing in her. Turning her head from side to side she stifled the moan rising in her throat. Finally, Philippe flung himself atop her, plunging deep within her resisting flesh.

When the pain of his forceful entry diminished, Gabby's eyes opened wide at the pleasurable feelings coursing through her body, careful to give no hint to Philippe that she felt anything but repugnance, or that he was eliciting any kind of response in her. She nearly strangled suppressing the small gasps of pleasure beginning low in her throat, all the while despising the way Philippe's driving body roused her to wanton desire. Never would she allow herself to enjoy the things Philippe was doing to her! Suddenly his body grew rigid as he exploded in a thunderous climax, and Gabby breathed a sigh of relief.

During the entire ordeal Gabby had raged against the banked fires that threatened to engulf her as the overpowering need of her body began to overcome the dictates of her mind. Now, as he withdrew, she experienced a sharp pain of regret, as if she was on the brink of a great discovery and was denied the final knowledge. She sighed, partly from remorse, but mostly from relief. Relief that the act was over and she no longer had to fight against her own body as well as Philippe's.

"Why the sigh, *ma petite?*" asked Philippe, who had been watching closely the play of emotion upon her face. "Tell me truthfully, was not the pain absent this time as I promised?"

"*Oui,*" she admitted grudgingly, "but you will never make me want you or enjoy your so-called lovemaking."

As the ensuing days passed, Philippe continued to make love to Gabby almost nightly, striving mightily to elicit some response from her, until, in desperation, he took her roughly, disgusted with her lack of response. Even though his caresses turned her insides to the consistency of molten lava, Gabby fought hard to remain passive beneath Philippe. In her heart she knew that were she to give in to Philippe's passion, no longer would she be in control. It was obvious that his self-esteem was in jeopardy, for he was a man who prided himself on his sexual prowess. Somehow she sensed that her response to his lovemaking would please him and she had no desire to please him. Gabby was amazed at the direction of her thoughts. The shy inexperienced girl had come a long way in the few short weeks since her marriage.

It was days later before Gabby was to encounter Marcel Duvall. Since their first meeting he had been careful to avoid her so as not to provoke Philippe into violence. Even though they took meals together, they ate in silence, the scowl on Philippe's face deepening each time Marcel so much as glanced Gabby's way. Gabby had no idea whatever of the nature of Philippe's hatred for Marcel. She only knew that she felt a kindred spirit in the man who had offered a friendship she was afraid to accept.

49

Marcel's green eyes lit up in appreciation at the sight of Gabby standing by the railing, a brisk breeze whipping her skirts about her shapely legs and her silvery locks blowing about her face. He could not resist the urge to join her, and when he pointed out a school of porpoises her look of pure delight moved him more deeply than he would have imagined.

"How fortunate to find you alone," he murmured intimately, his voice barely audible above the wind. "Your husband guards you jealously, *ma chere.*" Gabby flushed becomingly, thinking how wrong he was about Philippe, but said nothing, turning instead to watch the cavorting fish arch high in the air. Soon Marcel's hearty laughter joined her merry peals, her gaity as infectious as her beauty.

Gabby was well aware of the dire consequences should Philippe find her alone with Marcel, but she was starved for companionship, and Philippe's moody company left much to be desired.

"Amazing, aren't they, Monsieur Duvall?" Gabby asked excitedly as she pointed to the frolicking porpoises.

"Quite amazing," he agreed, his eyes devouring her face, thinking how little it took to make her happy. "But you agreed to call me Marcel, remember?"

"Then you must call me Gabby."

Unconsciously, Marcel drew nearer until silky strands of wind-whipped hair brushed his face like fragile butterfly wings. It seemed only natural for Marcel to encircle her tiny waist with his strong arm as their heads bent toward one another to better catch their words made nearly inaudible by the wind. So engrossed were they that neither saw Philippe watching from a distance, his hands clenched into massive fists, eyes smoking with gun-metal hardness. Try as he might, he could not quite shake the feeling that it had all happened before.

The couple at the railing made no move to draw apart.

Philippe did not miss Marcel's bold gesture nor Gabby's willingness to accept Marcel's embrace. Abruptly, he turned from the scene, walking swiftly in the direction of his cabin.

It was some minutes before Gabby realized with a start that Marcel had become far too intimate. She pulled away sharply, aghast at his boldness as well as her own willingness to allow him such liberties. "I must go, Marcel," she said, her voice quivering nervously. "I tremble to think what Philippe might do if he found us like this."

"You are shivering, *cherie*," Marcel said, watching her closely. "Are you so terrified of your husband? Does he mistreat you? Tell me if he has hurt you in any way and I shall call him out and . . ."

Gabby blanched. There was enough animosity between them without her contributing further to it. "Oh, no, Marcel," she interrupted, "it's just that . . . I mean . . . our marriage was arranged and I am not accustomed to his ways yet. But having you for a friend means a great deal to me."

"Gabby, *cherie*, I will always be your friend. I would be more if you would allow it," he said meaningfully. "If ever you need my help, you have but to ask." Then he lifted one small hand, turned it upward and placed a warm, moist kiss on the palm.

His meaning did not escape her. With a sharp intake of breath, Gabby withdrew her burning hand and fled to her cabin, her mind a turmoil of emotions. She chided herself for acting like a young girl being courted for the first time by a handsome man.

Gabby entered the dimness of the cabin, her heart beating wildly, cheeks crimson, eyes sparkling. She rested a moment with her back against the door, trying to gain some measure of composure. She failed to notice Philippe seated at the small table, a glass of brandy in his hand and the half-filled bottle before him. The day that had begun in brilliant sunshine suddenly turned dark and forbidding as a squall swiftly gathered on the horizon; a storm no less fierce than the one raging within Philippe.

From across the room Gabby met his cold, gray eyes as he raised his glass in mock salute, a mirthless grin slashing his grim features. He jerked unsteadily to his feet and with sinking heart Gabby realized he was drunk. "I wonder, Madame," he drawled, slurring over his words, "if you would find Marcel Duvall's lovemaking more to your liking? It is obvious you hold mine in contempt. Perhaps you find me repulsive, or are more receptive to men who take that which belongs to another?"

Gabby turned to flee, but before she could Philippe propelled himself foward, putting one large hand against the door and pulling her roughly away from it with the other. When he released her, the abruptness of his action sent her flying to the opposite end of the room where she hit the bulkhead with a resounding thud, them crumpled to the deck like a rag doll. Barely conscious, she watched through frightened eyes while Philippe locked the door and dropped the key into his pocket before he turned toward her, a perplexed frown creasing his face when he saw her lying at his feet.

Swaying slightly he reached her side and bent to help her to her feet. Gabby shrank from his touch and Philippe raised his hand as if to strike her, but quickly lowered it when he realized his insane anger was causing him to do something he would regret later.

"Why are you doing this to me, Philippe?" she whimpered.

"You have the nerve to ask me why," he shot back, eyes blazing, "when night after night you lie beneath me cold and passionless, yet invite the embrace of a man you hardly know!"

Gabby's heart sank when she realized Philippe had seen her and Marcel together earlier. "You forget," she reminded him boldly, "that you are a stranger as well, and have shown me nothing but indifference and brutality in the short time we have been together. At least Marcel is kind and thoughtful."

"You do not know Marcel if you think he has nothing on his mind but friendship," Philippe raged.

Pushing aside Philippe's helping hand, Gabby rose unsteadily to her feet. "Don't touch me," she spat.

"You allow Duvall to touch you," he stormed. "I will kill him before I allow him to corrupt you!"

"Why do you hate him so?"

Her question caught him unaware but his brittle gaze did not waver as he answered with one word, "Cecily!"

"Who is Cecily?" The name meant nothing to Gabby.

Though befuddled and confused from too much brandy, Philippe knew he was not ready to tell Gabby about Cecily. Instead he said, "Don't trap me with your questions, Gabby, Cecily has nothing to do with you."

Then his glazed eyes fell on the neckline of her dress, which had become unfastened in the foray and hung open revealing a creamy breast. The flash of desire was swift as he ordered harshly, "Take off your clothes!" Gabby ignored his command with stony silence. "Did you hear me, *ma petite?*" he repeated. "Take off your clothes! Or I will tear them from your lovely, frigid body." Grimly Gabby raised her trembling hands to unfasten her dress. "Do not look so glum," Philippe laughed sardonically, "just pretend I am Marcel."

Gabby's neck corded, and anger was bitter on her tongue. His cruel words and filthy accusations stunned her. She longed to strike out at him but fear held her in check. "Hurry," he said as he poured himself another brandy and flipped it expertly down his throat, hot eyes devouring her as piece by piece her clothing dropped to the floor. "Tonight, *ma chere*, you will find paradise," he promised, his voice softening into a hoarse whisper. "I shall not allow you to suppress your natural passion with a pretense of frigidity. When I am through with you your thoughts will never again stray to another man."

Effortlessly, Philippe plucked her from the mound of discarded clothing at her feet and carried her to the bed, flinging his own clothes off before falling at her side. Gabby shivered, suddenly aware that the wind had risen and the ship was no longer the sedate lady she once had been. Though it had grown dark, streaks of lightning lit up the cabin while thunder rumbled across the heavens.

Gabby lay still as Philippe's eyes became twin pools of gray velvet, his hands surprisingly gentle upon her flesh. With every ounce of her strength she fought against the sensations that threatened to engulf her, knowing that once she submitted willingly she could no longer despise him for forcing himself on her. When Philippe enfolded her in his arms it was as if a bolt of lightning had pierced the very core of her, his body hot and demanding. Yet, he was gentle. Never had she known such tenderness from him. His passionate kiss was long and deep, and when he released her mouth she wanted him to claim it again. His lips etched a path along the smooth curve of her neck to the tip of her breast where he felt her nipple rise as his tongue flicked hotly against the pulsating bud before moving across the pale goblet of her belly, kissing and caressing all the small hollows and indentations along the way. Her body trembled, tiny seeds of sensation bursting softly into bloom as waves of desire coursed through her. By the time his lips reached the smooth, tender skin of her inner thighs, she no longer had a will of her own. Something was driving her on, insisting she find out the meaning of the powerful force pulsing within her.

"Don't fight it, *ma chere*," Philippe whispered, his mouth twisted in a crooked grin, all vestige of drunkenness gone. "There is no greater pleasure than that of the flesh." Then his lips were where no lips should ever be, teasing, nipping, tasting, as she experienced a terrible, rising ecstasy to which some secret place within herself was vibrating, his questing lips pushing her ever upward.

"Philippe," she begged in a haze of delirium, "have mercy!"

But Philippe showed her no mercy. Every muscle of her body was as taut as a finely drawn wire as she strove toward a truth she had long denied, even feared. Then all sense of time and reason receded as a million stars burst inside her head, hurtling her skyward to join the maelstrom of the storm raging outside the cabin, powerless before that long withheld surge of emotion until her body had nothing more to give.

When she was quiet Philippe raised himself and whispered in her ear, "That was for you, *ma chere;* now for me." She gasped as he plunged deep within her, moving with swift, sure strokes until Gabby felt once again the flood of warmth coursing through her veins. Her eyes opened wide in shock, confusion reigned. Could he be bringing her again to that pinnacle of towering passion in a repeat of the ecstasy she had known only moments before? Then all thought fled as she joined Philippe in his race to the summit.

Grabby drifted in an eddy of quiet contentment aware only of Philippe's cries of completion ringing in her ears. Before sleep claimed her she felt amazingly at peace. The briefest smile of triumph flitted across Philippe's face before he, too, sank into oblivion, both unaware of the raging storm and tumultuous sea around them.

The storm blew unceasingly for three days. It was not a full-fledged hurricane, but a fearsome squall nevertheless. During that time Gabby did not leave the cabin, and Philippe only once or twice, and then just long enough to check on the condition of his ship. But the passage of time was like nothing to the lovers as they rode out the storm as well as their pleasure locked in each other's arms, and time drifted sweetly on, the rocking of the ship a cradle of passion.

Sometimes Philippe made gentle, tender love to her, her rapture more intense than any she had ever known. At other times his fierce ardor swept her along on a tide of passion so consuming that she was left drained and exhausted. Then there were times when just lying side by side, bodies touching, was enough.

The innocent, convent-raised, untutored virgin no longer existed. In her place dwelt a woman who had learned volumes about loving, and recorded a thousand ways to please and be pleased. But not once had Philippe's words implied she meant anything more to him than a vessel for his lust. He still remained a mystery to her. Why did Philippe treat her so shabbily? No matter how intimate they became she could not penetrate his cold reserve. There was always a part of him held back, even in his greatest moments of ecstasy. Sometimes Gabby hated him, as well as her own traitorous body. No word of love passed his lips. And always that same triumphant smile tugging at the corners of his mouth each time she cried out for pleasure.

Chapter Five

GABBY AWOKE just as the day was dawning with a blush of crimson in the eastern sky and realized that the storm had finally blown itself out. Busy sounds drifted in and she knew that the ship was once more responding to the directions of men instead of its capricious mistress, the sea. She ventured a glance at Philippe and saw that he still slept, looking much like a little boy, all the lines in his face smooth and his black curly hair lying unruly upon his forehead. She stifled an urge to brush her fingertips across his brow and arose from the bed careful not to disturb him. She shivered in the cool morning air, hugging her arms across her naked breast.

She was unaware that Philippe had awakened and watched her through slumberous eyes while she washed and dressed. Her fragile beauty never ceased to amaze him. When a knock shattered the silence he was instantly up and donning his trousers. Their early morning visitor was the cabin boy with a request to join Captain Giscard for a hot breakfast, their first in three days.

If Gabby thought Philippe's attitude toward her had altered during those three days when he had become a tender lover, she was mistaken. His manner remained cool and aloof, as if their shared intimacies meant nothing to him. She choked back the resurgence of hate that rose like gorge in her throat, seething bitterly as she recalled the carnal pleasures he had taught her to enjoy in just three short days.

Philippe's voice startled her from her reverie and she was surprised to see him dressed and shaved while her mind wandered. "Gabrielle, I expect that Duvall will be at the captain's table," he said sternly, as if lecturing a willful child. "You will do well to remember all that I have told you about him and act discreetly."

Gabby bristled with indignation and her eyes flashed violet flames. She opened her mouth to utter a scathing retort but Philippe forestalled her.

"You cannot begin to know what Duvall is like. You must trust my judgment in these matters. Your experience in the ways of the world is sadly lacking."

"But I am learning fast, am I not?" she mouthed contemptuously.

Philippe frowned menacingly as her chin shot defiantly upward. "I am beginning to think I made a dreadful error in marrying you," he said. "Your father was mistaken if he thought the convent had gentled you."

"I was innocent when I left, Philippe! And you have managed to take my innocence forever. But no one, not even you, can destroy my spirit."

"Your innocence was not too difficult to take, *ma petite*," he laughed cynically. "It seems you were ripe for the plucking and I got more than I bargained for. I knew you could not remain an ice maiden forever. But I warn you," he said, his features darkening, "your treasures are mine alone, bought and paid for. There will be no question of whose child you carry when that day arrives." He thought of Cecily and the child who might have been his.

"How dare you, Philippe," cried Gabby, shocked by his words. "I am legally your wife and although I never wanted this marriage I have no intention of breaking those sacred vows. I did, after all, learn something in the convent."

"More than Cecily, I should hope," he muttered cryptically.

"Cecily!" Gabby repeated. "Who is Cecily and what has she to do with me?"

"Cecily, *ma petite*, was my wife," he replied in a sudden burst of confidence.

"Your . . . your . . . wife?" Gabby stammered.

"*Was* my wife," Philippe emphasized.

"I had no idea you had been married before. What happened to her?"

"She is dead! As well as the child she carried."

Gabby's natural curiosity ran rampant. There was no way she could have stopped the next question even if she had guessed at the shocking answer and the effect it would have upon her life. "How did she die?"

Philippe debated the answer in his own mind, fighting to control the turmoil of his emotions. Only when his anguish subsided and he gained a semblance of control did he speak, his voice flat, devoid of feeling. "I will speak of this only one time and then never again. Do you understand?" When Gabby nodded, he continued. "I killed Cecily."

Gabby sucked in her breath, her gasp of horror shattering the silence. Fear raged within her and unanswered questions, ones she dare not ask, died in her throat. Did he intent to kill her also when he tired of her? What had the hapless Cecily done to warrant her untimely death? Why hadn't the authorities arrested him for murder? *Mon dieu*, what manner of monster had she married?

Gabby shrank from his touch when he came forward to usher her from the cabin, her eyes wary and distrustful. Suddenly it came to Gabby that she would not hesitate fleeing from the man she had married.

Breakfast was an ordeal Gabby could have done without. Time and again Marcel tried to draw Gabby into conversation. "I see you have weathered the storm in good condition, Madame St. Cyr," he said, addressing her directly.

"*Oui*," she answered, dropping her eyes discreetly to her plate of food.

"You were not seasick?" he asked, hoping to elicit more of a response from her.

"My wife was not seasick," cut in Philippe rudely. "In fact, our seclusion was well spent in pleasurable pursuits." No one could mistake his meaning.

Gabby flinched, a hot flush spreading across her cheeks when the full impact of his words struck her. Even Captain Griscard cleared his throat in embarrassment. Smiling a secret smile Philippe went on to thoroughly enjoy his breakfast, blissfully unaware of Gabby's discomfort or of Marcel's covetous glances.

The following weeks brought little change to the status quo. Philippe continued his assault upon her night after night. And she was powerless to resist. As long as she responded he became a tender, consummate lover, striving to satisfy her as well as himself. He carried her to heights she never knew existed or had even imagined so long ago when she lay alone in her hard convent cot. How could there be so much contradiction in one man? she wondered dismally. By night her rapture knew no bounds, his gentleness deceiving, for during the day his brooding silence clothed her in a cloak of fear. She did not mention Cecily again nor did he.

When they entered southern waters, Philippe's dark moods lightened somewhat and he grew almost loquacious when she asked him to tell her about the island that would soon be her home. For the first time since their marriage, except when he was making love to her, the harshness of his face gave was to a soft, wistful look.

"First you must know that Martinique is one of the Windward Islands in the Lesser Antilles," Philippe informed her in a voice that showed excitement for the first time since she had known him. "The Antilles chain stretches across the Caribbean Sea from the eastern reach of the chain between the islands of Dominica and St. Lucie. It is approximately 431 square miles in size and very mountainous."

"Is it dry like a desert?"

"Just the opposite," laughed Philippe, showing her dimples she never knew existed. "It is mostly a jungle. Mount Pelee, an active volcano, rises four thousand five hundred fifty-four feet on the northern shores. In the south, low hills rise one thousand to two thousand feet. There are numerous streams and several large rivers."

"An active volcano!" Gabby repeated with awe. "Is there much danger?"

"None whatsoever, else a city such as St. Pierre would not thrive. The city is located at the foot of Mount Pelee. Although it periodically belches smoke and ash, there has not been a major eruption for years. Of greater danger are the hurricanes that occasionally batter the island, and, of course, the fer-de-lance."

Gabby shuddered, "Hurricanes? Fer-de-lance?" It was clear she knew practically nothing about either.

"Hurricanes are winds that sometimes reach one hundred miles per hour, accompanied by drenching rains that strike during the months of July through November. In fact, I'm surprised we haven't encountered one since entering southern waters. The havoc they wreak is indescribable. Huge waves can destroy entire cities with great loss of life."

Gabby prayed that she would never experience a hurricane. "And the fer-de-lance?" she asked.

"A deadly snake whose bite is sure death," Philippe answered grimly. "They are everywhere, in the jungle, in the cane fields, in trees, in grass, in bushes. They can be any color or hue. There are eight varieties on Martinique alone, and it has the unpleasant habit of hiding in the roots of trees or in a stalk of bananas. Now is as good a time as any, Gabby, to warn you of the danger. Never, never, put your hand on a tree or your foot anywhere you aren't sure is safe. Once a fer-de-lance strikes, you are as good as dead."

Gabby listened with quiet horror while Philippe explained

about the deadly snake. When he finished, she shuddered in revulsion and promised never to venture anywhere on her own. She vaguely wondered if he weren't exaggerating in hopes of frightening her so she would be afraid to leave the plantation. Did he mean to terrorize her into submission?

As the days drifted endlessly into one another, Gabby learned more about Martinique and Bellefontaine, Philippe's plantation on the slopes of Mt. Pelee above St. Pierre. He told her he kept a townhouse in St. Pierre as did most of the other planters on the island because of the active social life in that city, especially at Carnival, and a much more popular business and cultural center flourished there than at Fort-de-France, the seat of government.

Gabby found herself eagerly looking forward to reaching Martinique, for she felt stifled by Philippe's constant attendance. The days were bad enough with his changing moods, but the nights were agony and ecstasy at the same time. To her horror she found that her body was responding to his skills, even while her mind rejected him utterly. And always, his words came back to haunt her. "I killed my wife."

One particularly warm afternoon, Gabby decided to abandon the sun-washed deck in favor of the dim coolness of her cabin. She removed her dress and stretched lazily on the bunk, drifting almost immediately into a light sleep. She awoke with a start to the sound of angry voices coming through the open porthole. She was sure she had heard her name spoken and recognized the voices as belonging to Philippe and Marcel. She arose stealthily, edging toward the porthole, straining to catch their words.

"You seem quite enamored by your *petite* Gabrielle, *mon ami,*" Gabby heard Marcel saying.

"And you, Duvall, seem overly concerned with my wife and my marriage."

"Does your bride know about Cecily?" Marcel asked slyly.

"She knows I was married before," replied Philippe between clenched teeth.

"I'm sure you have not told her the truth," Marcel implied.

"Keep away from Gabby, Duvall," Philippe warned ominously. "If you interfere this time I will kill you. I should have done so long ago."

"I was not the cause of Cecily's death," Marcel emphasized. "You were the one who forced her to conceive a child she did not want. You were the one who sent her fleeing through the jungle in the dead of night. You . . ."

"Enough, Duvall! It is over and done with. It is Gabby I am concerned with now. She is not cut from the same cloth as Cecily. She is a true innocent and knows little of men like you. Stay away from her!"

"Ha!" laughed Marcel derisively. "What about men like yourself, *mon ami*? Who will protect her from your jealous rages, or your insatiable lust? What about that, St. Cyr? Let us speak of your lust. Have you told your little innocent about Amalie, the beauteous, passionate, Amalie? Amalie will not take kindly to your new wife."

"I can't see where it's any of your concern, Duvall," Philippe said coolly, "but if it makes you feel any better, Amalie expects me to return from France with a bride."

"I can well imagine how that wildcat took the news when you told her you were ready to take another wife," smiled Marcel with secret amusement.

"As I said before, it is none of your concern. Amalie will do and act as I say," insisted Philippe.

"Since when did Amalie follow orders?" Marcel laughed derisively. "No, *mon ami*, Bellefontaine is not big enough for both wife and mistress." He smoothed his mustache and licked his lips, thoroughly enjoying Philippe's discomfort. "I will be happy to take the little baggage off your hands."

Philippe turned on him with such a black scowl that Marcel was momentarily at a loss for words. "Amalie will remain at Bellefontaine," he growled. "It is her home. Whether or not she remains my mistress is none of your business."

"I have no doubt whatsoever that she will continue to warm your bed, especially when little Gabrielle's belly begins to swell with the heir you seem to want so much."

"Why is it, Duvall, that my women interest you more than any others?" asked Philippe venomously.

"But, *mon ami,* you have such superb taste in women. Take your innocent wife, for instance. I do believe she surpasses even Cecily in beauty. When you succeed in driving her away, I shall be there to pick up the pieces."

Gabby did not hear Philippe's angry retort because Captain Griscard chose that moment to join the two men and his booming voice soon put an end to the alarming conversation that cast a pall upon her immediate future. She should have known that Philippe had no intention of keeping his marriage vows!

That night, if Philippe noticed any reluctance on Gabby's part to participate fully in the farce he called lovemaking, he made no mention of it. His tenderness in bed not only puzzled her but infuriated her as well. She longed to confront him with what she had learned that afternoon and decided to do just that when he finally lay quiet beside her, his mood mellowed by sexual fulfillment.

"Philippe," she said hesitantly, running her hand along the muscular planes of his chest.

"What is it, *ma chere?* Have I not satisfied you enough for one night?"

"Please, Philippe, be serious for a moment."

"I am serious," he said, moving his hand lightly over her body.

Gabby realized that if she did not say something to stop him his insatiable lust would soon forestall any conversation. "Who is Amalie?" she asked boldly, unprepared for the violence of his reaction as Philippe reared up as if bitten by a snake.

"You have been talking to Duvall behind my back!" he accused angrily. "What did he tell you about Amalie?" His fingers dug hurtfully into her shoulders.

"I have not spoken to Marcel," Gabby protested. "Please stop, Philippe, you are hurting me!"

"Where did you hear about Amalie?" he persisted, gripping her even harder.

"I overheard you and Marcel talking earlier today. I could not help it. I was resting inside the cabin when you stopped near the porthole. You both spoke so loudly I could not help but overhear."

"*Mon dieu*," he cursed, releasing his hold upon her. "I had hoped you would not learn of her so soon, but since you have, I will not lie. She was my mistress."

"Was or is?" asked Gabby contemptuously.

"That remains to be seen," he answered archly. "As long as you continue to satisfy me I have no need of a mistress."

The answer did not satisfy Gabby. She had been humiliated enough already without having to live in the same house with Philippe's mistress. "I care not what you do, Philippe," she said carelessly, "but as long as I am your wife, I refuse to have your mistress sharing my home. You will have to set her up elsewhere."

Philippe laughed uproariously, but his laughter held no mirth. "You are truly amazing, Gabby," he said, pulling her roughly into his arms. "Come, demonstrate to me how you intend to distract me from my mistress."

Later, sleep eluded Gabby as she lay listening to Philippe's even breathing. She thought of the hollow victory she had just won be remaining passive in Philippe's arms. With a disgusted grunt he had rolled away from her when it was over, immediately falling asleep.

When Philippe's light snoring told her he would not awaken easily, Gabby stealthily slid out of bed, donned a shift, threw a shawl around her shoulders and let herself quietly out the door. Once on deck she drew in great lungfuls of warm, salt-laden air. The deck was deserted except for the watch and the helmsman at the wheel. She leaned against the railing, a mystical figure whose wind-whipped, silvery locks appeared as illusive as angel wings beneath the shimmering moonbeams. Her mind drifted back to her life in the convent and how safe and secure she had felt. She sighed. Oh to be that innocent and protected again.

"Do you mind if I join you?" Gabby nearly jumped out of her skin as the voice materialized from out of nowhere. "I did not mean to startle you, *cherie*," said Marcel.

"Oh, Marcel, you gave me quite a start," breathed Gabby with a ragged sigh. "I couldn't sleep and the night is so lovely."

"It is indeed a beautiful night," agreed Marcel. "Look at the moon, *cherie*. It is a lover's moon."

The moon hung in the sky like a huge, golden ball, its beams dancing amid the gentle swells like cavorting sea nymphs. A smile of delight curved Gabby's lips.

"You should always smile, *cherie*," Marcel whispered, his breath warm upon her face. "You outshine even the brightest star in the heavens."

Gabby flushed becomingly. His presence, though welcome, made her uncomfortable, especially in view of the growing intimacy he displayed toward her.

"Do you ever visit Bellefontaine?" she asked, hoping to break the spell the moon and the night had cast upon them.

"Long ago, I did, but I am not welcome there anymore," he answered lightly.

"Did you know Cecily?" She watched him closely for his reaction.

Her question all but floored Marcel who was startled by the directness of her query. "What do you know of Cecily?" he asked, his eyes narrowing suspiciously.

"Only what Philippe has told me," she admitted. "I know that she was his wife and that she is dead."

"Did he tell you how she died?"

Gabby's eyes great large and luminous in the moonlight, her answer barely audible. "He said . . . he said . . . that he killed her." Fear nearly strangled the words in her throat.

"Mon dieu!" Marcel exclaimed uneasily. "If that is what he told you then it must be the truth. The exact cause of her death has never been made public, but according to rumor she had been strangled."

Gabby started violently, clutching at her throat, causing Marcel to wish he had bitten his tongue rather than add to her distress. Hoping to still her fears, he drew her into his arms, and when she did not protest, ran his hand boldly down the silken curtain of her hair, coming to rest on the curve of her waist. He could feel her trembling beneath his touch and instinctively pulled her closer, feeling her body soft and pliant against his. Suddenly a great surge of tenderness welled up in him for the vulnerable, young girl in his arms. He wanted nothing more than to protect her forever.

"Marcel," Gabby began timidly, "Philippe intimated that you had something to do with Cecily's death." She knew in her heart that if Marcel was in any way connected with the death of Philippe's wife she could never accept his friendship.

"Sacre bleu!" cursed Marcel. "I was not even present at the time of her death. I only befriended her, *cherie*, just as I would you. When Philippe's raging jealousy became intolerable, she came to me and I welcomed her in my home. Philippe soon came after her, forcing her to return to Bellefontaine."

"What happened then?"

Marcel paused dramatically, gazing upward as if scanning the heavens for an answer. "He forbid her to leave Bellefontaine for any reason, forcing himself on her again and again until she conceived. He mistakenly thought a child would tame her, bind her more closely to him."

"What happened after she became pregnant? Why did he kill her?"

"To my regret I know nothing of the circumstances surrounding her death. Because Cecily came to me when she needed protection your husband somehow held me directly responsible for the events leading to her death. Believe me, *cherie*," he said, his face a mask of innocence, "I am guilty of nothing more than succoring the poor girl in her hour of need. Philippe St. Cyr must face *le bon dieu* on judgment day, not I."

"*Merci,* Marcel," Gabby said, "for telling me this. How can I live with such a monster? Your words have given me courage. When the time comes I'll know what to do."

"Come to me when you need me," offered Marcel blandly. "I will help you, whatever you wish to do."

"My wish is to leave my husband," avowed Gabby fervently. "I am well educated and I can earn my own way. I shall leave Martinique and take a post as governess someplace where Philippe won't find me. If you could help me find such a position I would be eternally grateful."

Marcel's expressive face grew thoughtful. "My sister, Celeste, lives in New Orleans with her husband and children. They have a large home on Rue Dumaine and her three little ones are just about the age to require a governess. I will write to her and when you are ready to leave I will find a way to get you on a ship without Philippe's knowledge. I could even arrange to go to New Orleans with you, *cherie,* so you would not be alone."

Gabby wasn't at all sure about Marcel going with her, but she was too appreciative of his efforts on her behalf to protest. "I must go, Marcel, before Philippe awakens and finds me gone," she insisted, suddenly realizing how long she had been out of their cabin. She shuddered violently at the thought of having to climb back in bed with a murderer.

"*Oui*, perhaps it is best, *cherie*. We do not want to arouse your husband's suspicions if we are to safeguard our little secret." Then, before she could protest, Marcel lowered his head and softly brushed her lips with his, his touch so gentle that after he released her she was uncertain whether his hands had lingered on her breasts or if she had just imagined it. Then he was lost in the swirling mist that arose from the sea.

Gabby held her breath as she reentered the cabin, slowly letting it out when she saw Philippe still sleeping peacefully. She crept into bed and moved as far away from him as possible. But he somehow sensed her movement and reached out to draw her tight against him. "You are so cold, *ma petite*," he murmured, still half asleep. "Don't pull away. How can I keep you warm if you draw away from me?" Finally Gabby gave up and snuggled into the curve of his body until his warmth lulled her to sleep.

Loud knocking and urgent voices outside the door startled them from sleep. Gabby sat up and clutched the blanket to her breasts while Philippe moved swiftly to pull on his pants before lurching to the door. An agitated and distraught cabin boy stood before Philippe wringing his hands and jabbering incoherently.

"The captain, Monsieur St. Cyr," he babbled, "it's terrible. Please come quickly. The captain . . ."

Then Gabby heard no more because Philippe had closed the door. Moments later he stepped back into the room, his face taut and unreadable, his emotions held tightly at check. Only after he had dressed did he speak to her.

"Lock the door after I leave and let no one in," he ordered brusquely.

"What is wrong, Philippe?" Gabby asked with growing alarm. "Has something happened to Captain Giscard?"

"Later," he answered curtly. "Just do as I say." Then he was gone. Gabby locked the door just as Philippe ordered and padded back to bed, speculating on the meaning of the cabin boy's frightened words. There was nothing for her to do but wait for Philippe to return.

Philippe reached the deck just steps behind the cabin boy and surged ahead of him to the bridge where the large circle of men milled around a still figure lying on the deck in a pool of blood. Roughly Philippe pushed his way through until he stood beside the motionless form. But even before he examined him Philippe knew Captain Giscard was dead. The first mate, an experienced seaman named Mercier, was kneeling beside the body shaking his head sadly.

"What happened, Mercier?" Philippe asked brokenly. He had loved Henri Giscard like a brother but there was time later to give in to his grief.

"An accident, Monsier St. Cyr," the shaken first mate replied. "A terrible accident. Evidently the captain arose early this morning and reached the bridge before I did. Perhaps if I had been there a few moments earlier the captain would still be alive."

"Go on, Mercier," Philippe urged gently. He knelt beside the captain's body, first examining the fearful wound in his neck and then the jagged weapon that had caused it.

"No one saw it happen," lamented Mercier. "There was no outcry, no warning. The broken spar you see there came hurtling down from the rigging just as the captain stepped on the bridge. The poor man probably never knew what hit him. He died instantly. As you can see, the jagged end of the spar struck him in the neck, severing the jugular vein. He bled to death before anyone was aware of what had happened."

Philippe tore his eyes from the captain's body to gaze upward at the place where the spar had been broken. Then he examined the piece still embedded in the captain's neck. Gritting his teeth, he deftly removed the instrument of death and studied it from every possible angle.

Frowning darkly, he asked, "How could something like this happen on my ship?" His steely gaze moved from man to man until finally alighting on Marcel Duvall who had just joined the circle of onlookers.

"I can only guess," Mercier said with a puzzled shrug, "that the spar splintered when we were pounded by the storm we encountered a few weeks out of Brest and has been dangling, ready to drop off at any time. It must have become dislodged when the wind freshened this morning and Captain Giscard had the misfortune to step on the bridge at that exact moment. *Mon dieu,*" he cursed, eyeing the men gathered around him, "I will have someone's head for such negligence!"

Philippe said nothing as he continued to study the deadly missile. After much thought he said, "Looks like it came from the gaff. Send one of the men up to see if they can find where."

Immediately a seaman detached himself from the group and started up the rigging. Then Philippe and Mercier carried the captain's body to his cabin to be prepared for burial. All the while Philippe's mind worked furiously. He had not only lost an excellent captain but an old and trusted friend as well. He couldn't help but think the accident too contrived, the timing too incredible. Besides, the jagged end of the spar that had killed Henri appeared much too sharp, as if a point had been whittled by hand. He was almost positive that Henri's death was not an accident, that it had something to do with the secret document they both had memorized and promised to deliver in New Orleans. With Henri gone, Philippe knew that the life and death of an entire city, maybe an entire nation, depended upon him. The responsibility was awesome.

When Philippe had first entered Henri Giscard's cabin he had immediately sensed that something was wrong but could not put his finger on it. Suddenly it came to him; the cabin was too neat, as if everything had been put in order. It was not in Henri's nature to be so orderly. Even maps and papers that usually lay scattered carelessly about were piled neatly in stacks. That was not at all like Henri who could reach for whatever document he wanted amid the disarray. He had often chided Henri about his sloppy habits but the good-natured captain had only laughed and said housekeeping was a woman's job. There was no doubt in Philippe's mind that Henri's cabin had been thoroughly searched and each article put back into place more neatly than it had been before. Of one thing Philippe was certain; whoever had searched the cabin had not found what he was seeking. Once Henri had read the secret document and put it in the safe, Philippe had returned to the cabin, and, unbeknownst to Henri, had retrieved the papers. Being owner of the ship he naturally had the combination of the safe. The document now lay hidden at the bottom of Gabby's trunk. Upon further thought Philippe had every reason to believe that his own life was in danger.

Later, when Philippe returned to his own cabin, Gabby's heart immediately went out to him when she noticed the fine lines etched around his mouth and across his forehead. It was as if he had aged ten years in just a couple of hours. "Philippe, tell me what has happened!" she cried when he walked tiredly into the room. "I can hear voices and everyone seems to be in a state of shock."

"Captain Giscard is dead," Philippe intoned dully, his own face mirroring her shock.

"Dead! How! Why!"

"An accident, on the bridge early this morning."

Suddenly all his defenses were down and the agony in his eyes was a terrible thing to see. Philippe silently mourned. If he hadn't elicited Henri's help on this mission the poor man might still be alive. Was there no end to the path of death that followed him and took everyone he held dear? he wondered. How could he endure the guilt of yet another life being snuffed out because of him?

"Who will guide the *Windward* to Martinique?" Gabby asked, shattering the painful silence.

"First Mate Mercier is quite capable but I intend to take over the helm myself. I often captain my own ships."

Another long silence ensued while Philippe fought hard to come to a decision. A decision that included Gabby; yet one that could lead her into danger. Did he want to involve his innocent bride in the intrigue he had willingly flung himself into? He had no choice. For a long time he studied her intently, until Gabby began to squirm uncomfortably under his scrutiny.

"What is it, Philippe? Why are you looking at me so strangely? How can I help you?" Unwittingly, she had made the decision for him.

"What do you know about the war began in 1812 between England and America?" he asked, puzzling her by his abrupt change of subject.

"Not much," Gabby admitted. "What are they fighting over?"

"It's mainly due to Napoleon that they are at war; to him and to the acts of piracy on the high seas perpetrated on the American ships by the British. Not to mention the illegal impressing of American men into the British Navy."

"What has Napoleon to do with it?"

"The Americans were more or less forced to take sides with the French when the British imposed blockades on their ports so they could not carry crucial cargo to French or Spanish ports. And because the British could not patrol all the major

American ports they took to stopping all ships carrying the American flag on the high seas and seizing their cargoes as contraband. Even food and nonwar supplies were considered contraband to the British.''

"But, Philippe, what has all this to do with Captain Giscard's death?"

"I was just coming to that, *ma petite*," he said grimly. "Captain Giscard and I were entrusted with an important document that had been smuggled out of England. It is to be delivered to General Andrew Jackson who is in New Orleans at this time to prepare that city for an attack by the British. The document in my hands confirms that the British intend to attack New Orleans by sea. It not only pinpoints the exact date of the siege but the number of ships and men they can expect. So you can see how imperative it is that the document reaches General Jackson without delay."

"And you believe that Captain Giscard's death is related to thse secret papers?''

"I must assume so. I don't like the looks of that 'accident.' ''

"Then you never intended on sailing directly to Martinique?" Gabby asked, tryng to sort out in her mind all that Philippe had just divulged. As she thought about New Orleans a little seed began to take root and grow in her brain. New Orleans was a big city. Perhaps she would find a way to slip away from Philippe once they docked. It shouldn't be hard to find Marcel's sister and begin a new life for herself.

Unaware of the direction of her thoughts, Philippe said, "Captain Giscard and myself were the only ones who knew our destination was to be New Orleans. We feared spies might be planted aboard or that the document would be stolen should our destination be made known. That's why I was so upset when I learned Duvall was aboard. I instructed Captain Giscard to book no other passengers for this voyage but because Duvall was my neighbor and a loyal French man, he was allowed to purchase passage. Giscard wrongly assumed our friendship was still valid."

"Surely you don't suspect Monsieur Duvall of being a spy!" Gabby protested.

Philippe scowled darkly. "I would put nothing past him. But Henri is dead and I must assume full responsibility for the safe delivery of the document."

"Why are you telling me all this, Philippe?" Gabby asked quietly.

"If something unforeseen should happen to me before we reach New Orleans I want you to deliver the papers to General Jackson."

For a moment Gabby's heart stopped. Something happen to Philippe? *Mon dieu!* Aloud, she said, "Are you saying that if someone aboard the ship killed Captain Giscard because of those secret papers, they would not hesitate to kill you also?"

"Exactly."

"And you trust me enough to tell me all this?" Gabby asked with amazement.

"There is no one else," he replied carefully. "The papers are hidden in your trunk beneath your clothing. In case of my death, take them directly to Jackson's headquarters in New Orleans. For your own safety let no one know that you have any knowledge of this. Mercier has orders to pilot the ship to New Orleans if I cannot." Suddenly he grasped her shoulders in a bruising hold. "Promise me you will trust no one, Gabby! No one! Do you understand? No one!"

"I promise, Philippe, I promise," gasped Gabby. Only when he had extracted her promise did he release his grip on her tender flesh.

"Tomorrow we enter the Florida Straits and then the Gulf of Mexico," he went on after he had regained his composure. If Duvall is a spy, Philippe thought to himself, he has little time remaining to do his worst.

"New Orleans is French, is it not?" Gabby asked.

"There are some old Spanish families in New Orleans but most are French or Creole. Of course, since 1803 when Napoleon sold the territory it has become part of the United States."

Gabby tried hard to assimilate all Philippe had told her but found she was mostly confused by all the talk of wars, spies, and secret documents. But she had given her promise and she intended to keep it, even if the thought of Philippe's death left her feeling strangely bereft.

The next day Gabby spied the first land she had seen since they had left Brest. Philippe explained that they were only small islands or keys but land nevertheless. From a distance they appeared like jewels in the azure sea. The sight of pure white beaches and vegetation held her in thrall. She was so engrossed with the tiny isles floating by that she had hardly noticed Philippe's grim look as he nervously eyed a bank of seemingly innocuous, fluffy white clouds. He didn't appear one bit surprised when Mercier approached with the information that the barometer was falling at an alarming rate. Only then did Gabby turn her attention to the lowering sky. What had earlier seemed like brisk breezes had suddenly turned into threatening winds as the ship skipped across the water with frightening speed. Already she could see men working furiously at the sails while others scurried about lashing cargo to the deck. From the amount of activity around her Gabby realized that this would not be the same kind of storm that had blown them harmlessly about the Atlantic for three days while Philippe tutored her in the art of love. They were in tropical waters now and this could be one of those hurricanes Philippe had spoken of.

"How long do you think we have before we feel the full brunt of the storm?" Gabby asked as Philipe guided her back to their cabin.

"It's hard to tell," he replied, "but it's the right time of year for hurricanes and judging from the barometer we are in for quite a blow, probably before the day is out." He left her rather abruptly at their cabin door, his mind already occupied with the safety of his ship and men.

Gale-force winds lashed the ship the rest of that day and far into the night, reminding Gabby that the sea was a naughty mistress ever ready to tease, caress, or to devour if she became angry—and it became increasingly clear that she had never been more angry than she was now. No sooner had one gigantic wave hit broadside than another would rise up and take its place. Gabby's stomach was in a constant turmoil and she swallowed to keep the nausea from rising in her throat as she clung tightly to the sides of the bunk to keep from rolling off.

Philippe had returned to the cabin several times, his face a white mask of exhaustion, his clothing dripping despite the oilskin he wore. On his last trip, he saw immediately that Gabby was ill and quickly hurried to her side. With a great show of tenderness he brushed the tendrils of pale hair from her damp face then kissed her forehead.

"Soon, *ma chere*," he murmured. "Soon it will be over. Do not fret, I shall take care of you." He did not turn away in revulsion when she began vomiting into the slop jar, but held her close when she trembled from weakness. Never had she known such kindness from Philippe; but it had come too late. After consoling Gabby until the sick spell left her, Philippe, reminded of his duty by the howling wind, reluctantly released her and turned to leave.

Afterward, what transpired next was never quite clear in Gabby's mind. Where she found the strength to do what she did or why she even did it remains locked away in some remote compartment of her heart. At the same time Philippe opened the door to leave the cabin an enormous wave slammed into the ship causing it to tilt to such a degree that it nearly capsized. Before Gabby's horrified eyes the door was wrest from Philippe's grasp and he was thrown to the wind-whipped deck. She watched in frozen terror as a barrel of nails that had been lashed to the deck broke loose and careened menacingly toward him. He saw it coming and attempted to rise to his feet but the sea-washed deck and roll of the ship made him awkward and slow. He had risen no farther than to his knees when the barrel struck, smashing him into the railing. The next roll of the ship sent the barrel in the opposite direction leaving Philippe unconscious and in a precarious position against the rail where the next swell could easily sweep him overboard.

Gabby staggered unsteadily to her feet and slowly made her way to the door calling Philippe's name over and over as if unaware that she could not be heard over the din of the storm. Looking anxiously up and down the deck, she saw that no one was aware of Philippe's predicament, darkness and rain making visibility impossible. No matter how much Gabby hated Philippe she could not allow him to be swept overboard! With strength born of terror she moved cautiously from the shelter of the cabin onto the deck, pushing herself beyond her limited endurance to where Philippe lay. Twice she was knocked off her feet by a blast of wind and had to crawl, and once she clung to a broken mast for support as a tremendous swell washed over the deck. But somehow she reached Philippe exhausted and panting for breath, but intact. She blanched at the sight of the deep gash on his forehead and still white face as she tired to staunch the flow of blood with a corner of her shift. Realizing that they could not remain where they were lest they both end up in the sea, she called for help, but none could hear or see them in the murky darkness over the roar of the storm. It was up to Gabby to save them both.

Grasping Philippe beneath the arms, she began dragging him inch by painful inch toward the nearest mast, stopping often to catch her breath and gulp down the nausea that wracked her slight form. Philippe's dead weight put a great strain upon her faltering strength but she would not allow the sea to claim them. By the time she reached the mast with Philippe's unconscious body she ached in every muscle and was as near to collapse as she had ever been in her young life.

Gasping for breath, Gabby propped him against the mast and reached for a line broken loose from the rigging and dangling free. Working instinctively, for she knew she could not make it back to the cabin with Philippe in tow, she took the only course that lay open to her at that moment. With great effort of will she proceded to lash him to the sturdy upright, making certain that the knots were secure. Only then did she allow herself the luxury of respite, collapsing beside Philippe, chest heaving, pain seering her exhausted body. Finally, when she had regained a measure of strength, Gabby reached up for another line with which to tie her own body to the mst. And she very nearly succeeded. Struggling upward she was unware of the enormous swell rising up behind her, nor did she hear Philippe's voice when he suddenly surfaced into consciousness to witness the bizarre scene unfolding as if in a terrible nightmare. His warning cry was lost to the wind.

Philippe watched in abject horror as the killer wave rose from the depths of the angry sea and struck with a vengeance even as Gabby clung doggedly to the line. He lowered his head against the force of wind and water, and when he raised it, she was gone; gone as if she had never existed. Then, he, too, was drowning in a sea of black oblivion.

Chapter Six

THE PAIN was excruciating. Just opening his eyes caused Philippe untold agony. The top of his head was afire and his body ached in places he hadn't known existed. The first face he recognized was that of Mercier, the first mate, who was looking at him with such pity that Philippe became immediately alarmed. Slowly the rest of the faces came into focus, and among them was Marcel Duvall's. But the face he searched for was missing.

"Ah, Monsieur St. Cyr," Mercier said in obvious relief. "I am happy to see you are finally back with us. You gave us quite a scare."

Philippe tried to sit up but was gently but firmly pushed back into the pillows. "No, no," Mercier admonished. "I am no doctor but it is obvious that your head wound could have caused a severe concussion. It is best you do not exert yourself for a while."

"The ship . . . the storm?" stammered Philippe, still too dazed to think clearly.

"All is well," assured Mercier. "We sustained some damage but nothing that cannot be repaired once we reach New Orleans."

"How long have I been unconscious?"

"Nearly twenty-four hours!"

"*Mon dieu*," Philippe cursed weakly. "What happened?"

"We were hoping you could tell us," Mercier said, sliding his eyes from Philippe's as if he had something more to say but was reluctant to say it.

"I remember nothing from the time I left my cabin after

checking on my wife until this moment," said Philippe, gingerly touching his head where a thick bandage covered an angry lump. "What hit me?"

"As far as we can surmise, a keg of nails broke loose from its lashings and hurled you into the railing. We can only guess at what happened after that. As soon as the sky lightened we found you securely tied to the mast, unconscious and bleeding from the head wound. Whoever had the presence of mind to lash you to the mast probably saved your life."

Marcel stepped forward, his eyes bleak. "Can you remember nothing, Philippe? Think man, think!" he implored. "Do you remember nothing of your wife's sacrifice?" He seemed quite beside himself with grief and Philippe frowned in concentration as he tried to focus his fuzzy mind on the events that were causing Marcel such anguish.

"Leave us!" ordered Mercier, glancing around to include several seamen crowded inside the cabin. Finally no one remained but Marcel, Mercier, and Philippe. "Now, Monsieur St. Cyr," Mercier began, "it would help if you could recall something of what took place on deck during the storm, for it is my sad duty to inform you that your wife is missing and we have every reason to believe she was swept overboard. We can only assume that she was the one who lashed you to the mast. The great tragedy was that she was unable to save herself as well."

Mercier paused to give his words time to penetrate Philippe's muddled brain and was unprepared for what followed. Memory swept back with frightening clarity as Philippe surged from the bed in a show of strength that was sadly short-lived. When his feet hit the floor his head exploded into a million jagged fragments and he clung to consciousness through sheer strength of will.

Philippe allowed himself to be eased back into bed. The

pain of full recollection washed over him like the huge wave that hurled Gabby overboard. He buried his head in his hands, overwhelmed with grief. His voice sounded like it came from a great distance.

"Gabby must have witnessed my accident through the open cabin door, for the next thing I remember was finding myself secured to the mast, regaining my senses in time to see her swept into the sea." A gray cloud had drifted into his eyes obscuring his vision. "*Mon dieu*, it is all too much; she saved my life but lost her own. Am I cursed? Must I be the cause of the death of every woman I hold dear?"

"You said it, St. Cyr, not I," came Marcel's emotional reply. Turning on his heel he left the cabin to grieve in private for the flaxen-haired, violet-eyed woman who had come to mean more to him than he could ever imagine. Fate had intervened and taken an innocent life instead of the one he had intended. No woman had ever made such an impression on him in such a short time as Gabrielle St. Cyr!

Philippe would not allow Mercier to set a course directly for New Orleans even though it was determined that they were within one day of that city. Instead, he ordered the ship about to begin a criss-cross pattern to cover the area where Gabby might have gone overboard. It was a gamble, albeit one that did not pay off. For three days the *Windward* covered a large portion of the Gulf of Mexico just below the mouth of the Mississippi while the entire crew focused eyes upon socres of tiny uninhabited islands and cays where Gabby might have been washed ashore. It was a hopeless task. No one knew for certain their position at the time she had disappeared. There were no witnesses at all to her heroic deed. Philippe, still weak from his head wound, stood from sunset till sundown at the ship's rail, endlessly scanning the sea and jewel-like islands dotting the horizon.

Finally, all hope gone of finding Gabby alive, they abandoned the search and entered the Mississippi River for the 107 mile journey to New Orleans. Philippe still had a mission to complete, but nothing could purge from his mind the memory of that silver filly, with hair like moonbeams come to life, he had tried to tame . . . and failed.

Shortly after Captain Giscard's death Marcel had been apprised of their destination by Philippe. He had displayed great surprise and anger at being diverted from his passage to Martinique but Philippe had not been taken in by his performance. He could not help but suspect that the man he hated was somehow involved in the accidents that had plagued him since starting on this mission.

Now, as they entered the Mississippi, Marcel brooded silently, casting furtive glances at Philippe who seemed unaware of anything save his own abject misery. It would be easy to lose himself in the crowd once the *Windward* docked, he surmised. He hadn't succeeded in doing what he set out to do but there was still a remote possibility he might still be able to complete the task and turn failure into success. Much depended on his leaving the ship quickly after it docked and working out the necessary arrangements before Philippe set out to report to General Jackson.

Marcel hurried down the gangplank and disappeared into the streets crowded with longshoremen and military men as soon as the *Windward* had been secured to the pier jutting out into the river. Philippe paid him no heed as he, too, prepared for his own departure ashore.

Only after giving Mercier instructions concerning the repair of the *Windward* did Philippe retrieve the packet lying at the bottom of Gabby's trunk. At the sight of her clothing Philippe nearly lost control of his emotions and had to force himself to leave the cabin where reminders of her were everywhere. Slipping the packet into an inner pocket of his jacket he walked woodenly from the ship onto the levee. Everywhere he looked he saw evidence of a city under or about to be under siege. Large stockpiles of arms and food supplies dotted the wharves and streets around the levee. Even the people themselves appeared in a turmoil. Philippe walked the short distance to the Place d'Arms, later to be renamed Jackson Square, where he knew General Jackson established headquarters while in the city. If the large number of American soldiers in the city were any indication, then he would assume General Jackson was preparing to defend New Orleans against full-scale British attack. Crossing the street to enter the Place d'Arms, Philippe was suddenly aware of danger, sniffing it out like a hound dog. A loud clatter called his attention to a carriage racing toward him at breakneck speed. Even from a distance he could see that there was no driver, giving it the appearance of being a runaway.

Philippe realized that he could neither retrace his steps nor gain the other side of the street before the carriage would be upon him. He had but one alternative; to attempt to dodge the horses' hooves and carriage wheels. Accordingly, he dropped to the ground, rolling himself into a tight ball, and when the horses passed over him, successfully maneuvered his body between their driving legs, sustaining a fair number of bruises for his efforts. But the worst was yet to come. The carriage was upon him before he was able to roll completely clear and the right wheel grazed his head, reopening the wound suffered during the storm. In minutes it was all over. People on the streets were crowding around him and several soldiers hurried across the street from the Cabildo to help him to his feet.

"Are you hurt, sir?" asked one of them, brushing the dirt from his coat. "Looks like a nasty gash on your forehead. Best you see a doctor right away." "*Merci*, thank you," Philippe repeated in English, moving his hand automatically to his pocket. "I am not seriously injured, just shaken. Did you see where that carriage came from?"

"No, sir," replied the soldier. "One minute the street was empty and the next that carriage was headed straight for you.

We managed to stop it but no one was inside nor did anyone show up yet to claim it. A mystery, it seems," he said shaking his head.

"*Oui*, a mystery," agreed Philippe cryptically as he dabbed his handkerchief at the bloodied gash on his head, which by now had begun throbbing painfully.

After he asked directions to General Jackson's headquarters, Philippe's mind was fertile with speculation. For the third time since undertaking this mission he had nearly lost his life. Already two people were dead—he winced when he thought of Gabby—one more death would mean nothing to the person or persons who would kill to prevent the document he carried from reaching General Jackson.

Philippe paced Jackson's outer office for several minutes before the door burst open and a guant, white-haired man with tired eyes hurried forward to greet him. "St. Cyr, we have been anxiously awaiting your arrival." Then he spied the blood on Philippe's head and noticed the condition of his clothing. "My God, St. Cyr, what happened to you? Come into my office. Sit down, sit down, man. I will call our doctor to see to your injury."

"It is nothing, General," protested Philippe who nevertheless took the chair Jackson offered. "An accident outside; a runaway carriage nearly succeeded in ending my life."

Jackson stared at him fixedly and raised one shaggy eyebrow while Philippe described the accident. "The entire voyage was plagued by senseless accidents. Even the weather was against us. Captain Giscard was killed and . . . and . . . my wife was lost overboard during the hurricane that struck several days ago." The bleakness of Philippe's voice distressed Jackson greatly but he said nothing, waiting for Philippe to continue. "I'm convinced that the accidents that led to those deaths and the attempts on my own life were the work of a spy bent on keeping the document I have in my possession from reaching you." Then he reached into his inner pocket and extracted the packet that he had protected at great personal sacrifice.

Deep furrows etched their way across General Jackson's already lined face as he sought the words to express his gratitude, knowing that nothing he could do or say would bring back Philippe's wife or Captain Giscard.

"What can I say, St. Cyr," said the general in genuine sympathy, "except that you have the undying gratitude of the American people and the French government. With the information in this document we will know for a certainty if the British plan on attacking the city of New Orleans or have some other target in mind."

Then he tore open the packet and quickly scanned the several pages, his taut face lightening considerably. "By sea," he announced, eyes glowing. "And soon. It also says that the British plan to enlist the aid of Jean Lafitte. The Baratarian gulf is an important approach to New Orleans and they need the cooperation of Lafitte to gain access."

"I am aware of the contents," said Philippe. "Both Captain Giscard and myself read the document as a precaution. But isn't Lafitte a pirate?"

"He goes under many names and pirate is one of them. But if he agrees to help the British we are as good as defeated."

"Do you think he will?"

"I wouldn't blame him if he did," grunted Jackson. "Governor Clairborne recently ordered American Navy ships to Barataria, Lafitte's stronghold, where they shelled the island, sank several of Lafitte's ships and captured some of his men. What is amazing is that Lafitte did not fire back. He later sent a message to the governor saying that he considered himself an American and would not fire upon his own country's ships. Then he offered to help fight the British when the time came."

"And did the governor accept Lafitte's offer?"

"The stupid man still does not trust Lafitte, but I intend to deal with him myself to judge if he is sincere in his wish to aid us. One of his lieutenants has agreed to guide two of my men to Barataria to learn where Lafitte's loyalties lie."

"Is the city prepared to fight?" asked Philippe. "What of the citizenry?"

"Most do not believe the British are a threat. I'm sure they would rather be under British rule than American. But now that I have proof of the imminent attack I will redouble my efforts to alert the people and prepare them to defend their city."

"On my way here I saw stockpiles of weapons and supplies along the levee. Seems like you have a good start."

"Were that only true," sighed Jackson wearily. "We are woefully short of certain arms and of musket flints and are now in the process of scouring the countryside for our needs. According to this," he said, indicating the secret papers in his hand, "I have little enough time in which to fortify and arm the city and prepare its citizens to fight." He sighed again and ran his long, bony fingers through his thatch of white hair. Philippe sensed his preoccupation with war and its portents and rose to leave. Jackson noticed Philippe's movement from the chair and seemed startled to see him still in his office, as if thought of war had banished all else from his mind. Graciously, he offered his hand once more to Philippe.

"St. Cyr, again, I thank you on behalf of the American people. I only wish I had the power to bring your wife back. If there is anything I can do, please feel free to ask."

Philippe grasped the gnarled hand, moved by the sincerity of the great man and said, "There is one thing, General."

"Anything within my power, St. Cyr, anything," replied Jackson sincerely.

"There is a remote chance that my wife may have washed ashore on one of the many islands and cays dotting the mouth of the river and might still be alive. If you could alert your men to be on the lookout for her I would be more than grateful. I am prepared to offer a five thousand dollar reward for information leading to her discovery, if alive, and her body, if dead.''

General Jackson's deepset eyes were full of pity as they regarded Philippe. He knew the man's wife had not one chance in a million of surviving. Even if she had washed ashore alive she would immediately become alligator bait. But he had not the heart to say those words. Instead, he said, ''Very generous of you, St. Cyr. I will be glad to circulate a description of your wife among my men. You can rest assured that if she makes her way into the city I will know it.'' Though his voice remained optimistic his eyes betrayed him. In his heart he knew St. Cyr's efforts to locate his wife were useless.

Nevertheless, Philippe wrote out a description of Gabby and handed it to Jackson who read it in silence. ''There will be no mistaking your wife for another if she is found,'' he said. ''There surely can be no other woman in New Orleans matching your wife's attributes. I take it you plan to remain for a while in the city?''

''*Oui*, I will sleep aboard the *Windward* while she is being repaired and refitted. Once she becomes seaworthy again I shall make a decision on whether to take lodgings in the city or return to Martinique. Much depends, of course, on whether or not I find my wife . . . or her body.''

''Keep in touch, St. Cyr,'' urged Jackson who had already begun sifting through a stack of papers on his desk. ''If I have any news at all I'll know where to find you.''

The interview had ended. Philippe walked from the office into the broiling sun, suddenly overcome by a bone-deep weariness and a feeling that his meeting with General Jackson was anticlimatic and everything that had happened during the voyage a bad dream. Only it wasn't a dream. And now that the document was in safe hands there was nothing left to occupy his mind except thoughts of Gabby. He could clearly picture the defiant tilt of her chin the first time he had taken her; the look of shocked outrage when he described what he intended to do to her and the response of her warm body when he had finally broken through her icy reserve and unleashed a towering passion he was not likely to forget. Even now he could feel the lush thickness of her curls, the soft curves of her slender form, the silky softness of her flesh next to his, and his body ached for her. When he had married her he had expected a sweet, pliant girl who would bear his children and make no demands upon him. What he had gotten was a bewitching, untamed, hellcat who had surprised and angered him by her unquenchable spirit and fierce ardor.

From the first moment Philippe laid eyes on Gabby he realized she would present a problem to his scheme of things. But, *mon dieu*, he had wanted her! Neither harsh treatment nor debasement could tame her into submission. He only succeeded in pushing her further into rebellion, even into Duvall's arms. If Gabby could have only known his actions were spurred by thoughts of Cecily and what had been. He could still see her, eyes spitting violet flames then turning to molten lava as his kisses and caresses tormented her body into the only submission she had ever granted him. Even that would be enough to satisfy him if *le bon dieu* would give her back to him!

Chapter Seven

GABBY SAW the wave only moments before it struck because of the solid curtain of driven rain. She had time for nothing except a brief prayer. Then she felt herself being lifted on the crest and all the bright hurts she suffered during the struggle to save Philippe's life dimmed in the strangely restful ebb and flow. She was sinking beneath it. Deeper, deeper . . .

She was dead. There was no other explanation for it. She was reclining on a white cloud and there was even an angel staring solicitously down on her. An angel, with incredible, black, thickly fringed eyes and ebony hair.

"Mademoiselle is awake." It was a statement more than a question and the angel's voice was as arresting as her appearance. The soft, lilting words conveyed her concern and she spoke pure French.

Gabby stirred and was immediately aware of hundreds of aches and pains throughout her body. That was the moment she realized she was not dead. Dead people don't suffer hurts and she had hurts aplenty. She started to rise but the beautiful woman hovering over her gently pushed her back against the soft cloud of the bed.

"Where . . . where am I?"

"You are among friends, Mademoiselle. No harm will come to you here."

"The ship . . . Philippe . . ." Gabby stammered, cradling her head in her hands, rendered speechless by pain. When she lifted it she saw that a man had entered the room. He was tall and slim and graceful when he moved. His entire attitude suggested great strength. His hair was long, sleek, and jet black, as were his sparkling eyes, mustache, and sideburns. Gabby thought it strange that he wore a long, dangling gold earring in one ear. The high jackboots that molded his muscular legs clunked noisily against the floor as he neared the bed.

His voice was surprisingly gentle. "It is good to see the color of your eyes, Mademoiselle. For a while we feared you would never open them and that would have been a pity for never have I seen any more beguiling. One does not often see violet eyes in New Orleans." He laughed, showing an extraordinary expanse of strong, white teeth.

Gabby smiled in spite of herself. "Monsieur, could you please tell me where I am and how I came to be here?"

"Certainly, Mademoiselle. You are on Barataria. I am Jean Lafitte and this is my island stronghold. As to how you came to be here, well, I can only partially answer. Evidently you were washed overboard during the hurricane and *le bon dieu* must have not wanted you for you were tossed upon Barataria where my men found you. The rest, *ma petite*, you shall have to supply."

"I was on a ship bound for New Orleans when the storm overwhelmed us," Gabby said. "Do you know if the ship sank or did it make it to New Orleans?" Somehow it was important that she know if Philippe lived.

"The ship's name?" asked Lafitte.

"The *Windward*."

"We saw no sign of wreckage so we can assume the ship reached New Orleans safely. I will send one of my men to check on it. Now, Mademoiselle, if I may know your name . . ."

Gabby hesitated, then shrugged her shoulders. "I am Madame Gabrielle St. Cyr."

"Ah, you have a husband. Then we must inform him immediately of your safety. He will be frantic by now, thinking you dead."

91

"No, no!" Gabby cried out in great agitation. "Please, I don't wish to return to him. Do not send me back. I beg you."

"Madame St. Cyr, calm yourself. We will not talk of it now. Later, when you are stronger we will discuss this further. You are welcome to remain on Barataria as long as you wish. Though some call me pirate, smuggler, and assassin, you shall not be harmed while under Jean Lafitte's protection."

"And are you any of those?" Gabby asked, suddenly frightened.

He laughed uproariously. "All of them, Madame, all of them. But above all, I am a gracious host and you are my guest for as long as you wish. I leave you in the tender hands of my own Marie." He flashed a brilliant smile at the tiny, exquisite woman beside him.

When he left, Gabby looked questioningly at Marie. "Is he really a pirate?"

"*Oui*, you could call him that," she answered, although the love shining from her eyes suggested that he was anything but that in her heart. "But he only attacks the galleons of the accursed dons, the Spanish. All of New Orleans seeks Jean out to buy the treasures he has taken from the dons. Never has he attacked an American ship," she vowed, "yet they spurn his help."

Gabby was confused by Marie's words and the girl must have realized it for she quickly changed the subject. "But never mind, Madame St. Cyr, it is important that you rest and heal your body. We shall talk later."

"Please call me Gabby," she insisted.

"*Merci*. Gabby it will be."

"How long have I been here, Marie?" Gabby asked while Marie fussed over her, making sure she was comfortable.

"One week."

"One week!" exclaimed Gabby in disbelief.

"*Oui*, and we were not certain you would awake at all. But

you have and now you must concentrate on getting your strength back," Maria insisted. "I will leave and see that something nourishing is prepared for you. Meanwhile, try to rest."

When she was alone, Gabby could not help but think of Philippe. Her eyes grew bleak as she wondered if he had survived and if her apparent death had saddened him. No, she decided, her passing could not have caused him too much grief. And if she had her way, he would never learn that she was alive. Eventually she would make her way to New Orleans and find Marcel's sister. But she would stay on Barataria with Jean and Marie until she was certain Philippe was safely back on Martinique.

It was the better part of two weeks before Gabby felt strong enough to venture outside. Most of those two weeks were spent in the delightful company of Marie in the room Gabby had come to view as her own. Jean Lafitte visited as often as his duties allowed and he was always polite and concerned. No mention was made again of informing Philippe of her whereabouts even though Jean's men had learned that the *Windward* was docked in New Orleans.

One day Marie appeared with an armful of beautiful dresses and underclothes. There was an array of silks, satins, cambrics, and brocades in every color of the rainbow. "These are for you," she said, laughing at Gabby's dismay.

"All of them?" Gabby gasped. She had never seen anything more lovely than the dresses spread out upon her bed. Surely the trunk full of clothes she had brought from France contained nothing half so beautiful.

"They are a gift from Jean. He wishes you to join us for dinner tonight. We have guests coming and we are to act as hostesses. That is if you feel up to it," Marie amended.

"Of course I feel up to it. You and Captain Lafitte have been so kind to me that I will be glad to do something in return."

"Eh bien," said Marie. "Now come, let us choose our dresses carefully. We do not want it said that the mistress and guest of Captain Lafitte were anything but resplendent."

Gabby stared openmouthed at the beautiful, vivacious girl. For some reason she thought Marie to be Lafitte's wife. Each displayed so much love for one another that it was impossible to think them anything but husband and wife.

Marie saw the expression on Gabby's face and hastened to reassure her. "Does that shock you?" she asked. "That I am Jean's mistress, I mean."

Gabby blinked but tried not to show her dismay. "No," she quickly assured Marie. "But you and Jean are so much in love that it is hard to understand why he does not marry you. Surely you are not content to remain his mistress?"

"But, Gabby, is it possible that you don't know?" asked Marie with amazement.

"Know what?"

"That Jean cannot marry me no matter how much he might wish it!"

"But why? I do not understand!"

"I am an octoroon. *Une fille de couleur.* Jean can never marry me."

Gabby gaped at Marie in shock. The girl's skin was nearly as white as hers and whiter than Lafitte's. How could anyone consider Maria to be anything but white?

"Do you hold it against me, Gabby?" Marie asked timidly when she could no longer stand the silence.

Gabby immediately took the girl in her arms. "I hold nothing against you, Marie, only against the society that would label you inferior. Surely you are more beautiful, gentler, and kinder than any French girl in New Orleans."

"*Merci*, Gabby. If only everyone thought as you do. Then my Jean and I could be happy forever."

They were silent for a while as they sorted through the stack

94

of dresses. Then Marie spoke again. "You have not told me about your husband, or why you wish to remain dead to him. Is he so old and ugly that you cannot stand him?"

Gabby grew thoughtful as she pictured Philippe's handsome face and strong, virile body. "I'm sure most women would find Philippe extremely handsome. Certainly he does not have the classic features of most Frenchmen, but rather a strong, rugged face. One senses an animal magnetism about him."

"And you are hiding from him?" asked Marie in disbelief. "I certainly would not run from such a man."

"But you do not know him, Marie. He is cruel and domineering. He married me only to bury me on his plantation and bear his children. I'm sure Bellefontaine means more to him than I do. He even admitted that he had a mistress."

"Surely you hold yourself in too little regard. A woman with your beauty and obvious charms should have no problem holding on to a man such as your Philippe. If he does not love you now, I'm sure he would grow to love you within a short time."

"You do not know Philippe. There is no room in his heart for love."

"But was he not a good lover?"

"Lover and love hold two difference meanings," Gabby scoffed. "For some reason unknown to me, Philippe wished a wife raised in a convent. My father sold me to him promising that I was submissive and docile. Little did he know that I was unwilling to become the placid brood mare he sought."

"Your father sold you to him?" Marie was aghast with shock. Things like that did not happen to the white gentry.

"No matter how you look at it I was sold. From the first Philippe made it known that he paid off my father's debts in return for my hand in marriage. Then he became angry when

I refused to become the tame plaything he thought me. He even discouraged me from becoming friendly with a . . . with a passenger aboard the *Windward*."

"*Mon dieu,* he must have wanted you badly."

"*Oui,*" Gabby admitted, "he wanted me. And he wasn't satisfied until he taught my body to respond to his. He used me as he would a finely tuned instrument and I had no control over my own emotions. I hated him for teaching me the many ways to love and I hated myself even worse for becoming such an avid pupil!"

"Ha! Then he was a good lover!"

"I have nothing to base his performance on but if making a woman feel as if . . . as if . . .! Oh, Marie, I cannot begin to describe the ecstasy I found in his arms!" Gabby's face heated as she thought of past intimacies.

"I would find it difficult to leave such a man," Marie said dreamily.

"What if he had committed murder? Would you still refuse to leave him then? Has your Jean killed a woman or child in cold blood? Philippe admitted to me that he had killed his wife and the child she carried."

"What are you saying, Gabby? Is this the truth?" Marie's fathomless black eyes regarded Gabby with some skepticism.

"All of it, I swear, Marie. He told me himself. Philippe was married to a beautiful woman named Cecily. He killed her and when she died so did their unborn child. After his shocking disclosure I vowed I would not remain with him. Somehow, somewhere, I would find the opportunity to leave him. I could never live with such a wicked man."

"*Mon dieu,*" cursed Marie, hastily crossing herself. "I understand perfectly and would do just as you are doing."

"If I stayed with him I would live in fear that sooner or later he might become angry enough to kill me. And perhaps, I, too, would carry an innocent babe to its death."

"You are safe enough here with Jean. No one would dare come here for you. I will explain to him why you do not wish to return to your husband and he will understand just as I have."

"You are the first true friend I have ever had, Marie, and I thank you both for your kindness," said Gabby. "But I cannot remain on Barataria forever. I must make my own way. I know of a woman in New Orleans who might have need of a governess and soon I must leave here and find her."

"We will speak of that later," Marie said, pushing the subject of departure aside. "But for now, let us concentrate on which dress will most dazzle our guests."

While she dressed, Gabby glanced out the window and was surprised to see several English ships achored in the sheltered bay next to Lafitte's own ships. She wondered why the British should approach the smuggler's base. Was Lafitte about to betray the Americans? Evidently the British were to be their dinner guests that evening. A chill of apprehension prickled the nape of her neck as she remembered the important document Philippe had in his possession; a document that Captain Giscard had died for. She wondered if it had been delivered safely to General Jackson and if Philippe was even now heading back toward Martinique. She watched as an oarsman cast off a small boat from the flagship to make its way ashore. Aboard the corsair ships, all gunports were open and agile seamen swarmed into the riggings. On shore, the Baratarians gathered in apprehensive clusters, some standing ready at the breastwork cannon guarding the island.

Jean Lafitte greeted Gabby and Marie when they walked into the main room later that day. Gabby was fashionable garbed in violet watered silk that made the color of her eyes more startling than usual and Marie's dress was a sea blue that highlighted her creamy golden complexion. The room was ablaze with soft candlelight and the rich brass candle sticks glowed dully in the diffused lighting. "How beautiful you ladies are," Lafitte said with a small salute. "*Les Anglais* will be envious of my two ladies."

Gabby admired Jean as he walked around the room inspecting the china and table arrangements. He wore a crisp, white shirt and a captain's coat with brass buttons; his shiny hair was combed back and his mustache waxed. Only his rapier hung at his side; his pistols had been put aside this night.

"Ah, a signal from the beach," he said, cupping his ear to the sound. "Our guests are coming." Then he turned to the ladies. "I ask only that you look lovely and be gracious to His Majesty's emisssaries." His black eyes twinkled mischievously.

Gabby heard the tramp of boots upon the veranda steps then saw a group of three rather staid navy officers, resplendent in blue uniforms enter behind one of Jean's lieutenants. Marie stood poised by Lafitte's side as if she were gentry instead of mistress to a notorious pirate.

The first Englishman to enter the room immediately introduced himself. Bowing stifly, he said, "Mister Lafitte, I am Captain Richard Tremaine, His Britannic Majesty's navy. My aide," motioning to a young man behind him, "Lieutenant John Lockly; and Captain William Johns of the army. Also in our party is a royal envoy, Mr. . . . ah . . . Smythe. But he was struck by a fever and unable to accompany us ashore. I have come to present you with a missive from our commander, and Mr. Smythe has entrusted us with a document direct from the British government."

Then Captain Tremaine held out two separate oilskin-wrapped packets. Lafitte accepted both but tossed them carelessly upon the table without bothering to break the seals. "On Barataria hospitality always comes before business. And Jean Lafitte never puts business before pleasure. Please be seated, gentlemen; but first allow me to introduce to you my two lovely ladies. My hostess and my guest.'' Then he in turn introduced Marie and Gabby.

Gabby could sense the Englishmen's curiosity about her. Did they assume that both she and Marie were Jean's mistresses? Both girls exchanged mischievous smiles for they knew they were confusing the British by their presence. One beautiful mistress was understandable . . . but two?

Not until the last dish was cleared from the table did Jean pick up the packets that had lain there through the meal, break open the seal, and read each with deliberate thoroughness. His face was expressionless and completely unreadable. Gabby was beside herself with suspense. Would Jean banish her and Marie from the room before he broached the business at hand? It was clear they expected him to do just that.

But Jean surprised everyone by immediately addressing the English without first dismissing the ladies. "It seems, Captain Tremaine, that both your commander and your government suddenly hold me in high regard. So highly that I am offered a captaincy in the Royal Navy for my cooperation.'' He spread out his hands beseechingly. "But why, Captain? What need have you of a smuggler and pirate?''

Captain Tremaine cleared his throat nervously. "As you know, control of the Baratarian Straits is crucial if we are to capture New Orleans. They offer an important approach to that city. Your cooperation will insure our success.''

Then Jean shocked the captain into silence when he handed the documents to Marie. "What do you think, *cherie?*'' he asked carelessly. "Should we allow the British ships into Barataria?''

Marie quickly scanned both documents. "Thirty thousand dollars is a lot of money, Jean,'' she acknowledged, "but a mere pittance compared to the profits from your lucrative business in New Orleans with the Americans. The treasures you relieve the dons of now decorate the finest homes in New Orleans.''

"But remember the captaincy, Mr. Lafitte. You will be a respected member of the Royal Navy. No longer will you be a feared pirate."

Jean tilted his head back and roared uproariously. "If you do not believe I am respected, ask any citizen of New Orleans about me. They will tell you that I am not only respected but revered."

"Then you do not accept our offer?" asked Captain Tremaine stiffly.

"I did not say that," Lafitte answered smoothly.

Gabby's heart sank. Surely Lafitte would not join the English? But it sounded as if he was considering the offer. Her face was so serious that Marie nudged her under the table and whispered that she should not worry, Jean knew what he was doing.

"I will consider your country's offer, Captain Tremaine," Jean said expansively. "Where might I contact you when I decide?"

"You cannot contact me directly but the envoy I spoke of earlier will be in New Orleans. He has a house at number thirty Rue Dumaine and you can send word of your decision there."

Shortly after that the Englishmen rowed back to their ship. Nothing more was said about them, or the documents that still lay on the table.

"*Merci*, Gabby," Jean said, using her first name, "for gracing our table with your beauty and charm." Then he turned serious. "Marie explained to me why you do not wish to return to your husband and I am in total agreement. You may remain as our guest for as long as you like. Now that you are fully recovered from your ordeal at sea you may feel free to explore our little island. Go wherever you like. No one here will harm you."

"*Merci*, Captain Lafitte," Gabby said gratefully. "I will

stay only until I am certain my husband is no longer in New Orleans. Then I shall make arrangements for my future.''

The next morning the English ships were gone, only Lafitte's fleet rode at anchor in the bay. After breakfast Marie took Gabby on a tour of her lover's great house. It sprawled, but not without design, for Lafitte had planned it for comfort and entertaining. It was magnificent, surrounded by a long veranda that shaded against the summer sun and protected against winter winds. Heavy wooden shutters could be swung to protect its screened windows.

Opulence was the key; its richness a bit overdone with silver, tapestries, ornate furniture, gold statues, and priceless carpets. The kitchen contained every food imaginable and the cool wine cellar dug beneath the house contained brandy and wine from dozens of countries.

Sometimes alone but mostly accompanied by Marie, Gabby explored Barataria. The island itself was well fortified, although some of the battlements had been destroyed earlier by American Navy ships. She learned that there was a strict code of honor governing the people who lived there. Women had as much right as men. Although they were every hue from white to the darkest ebony, they were free to bed or wed whomever they chose. The white sand beach surrounding low hills were scattered haphazardly with shacks, overturned ships' gigs, and long racks for drying meats and fish.

Most of the smugglers were rough men who looked and acted like the pirates they were. Although many of them eyed her covetously, none dared approach her, especially while in Marie's company. Some of the women envied her position and she could feel their animosity directed toward her as she strode about the island.

Gabby learned from Marie that Lafitte was putting off the English while sending urgent letters to Governor Claiborne and General Jackson. Of late he was so preoccupied that he barely noticed her presence and more and more of his men began ogling her openly. She knew her time on Barataria must end soon.

One day, nearly a month after the English had come, Marie told her they would again have important guests for dinner that night. "Americans, this time," Marie said. "Representatives of General Jackson himself. Maybe now they will believe Jean and accept his help."

"Has he refused the British offer?" Gabby asked.

"Mon dieu!" Marie exclaimed. "He never even considered it. Besides the thirty thousand dollars and the captaincy they offered, the British wanted Jean's pledge that he would not attack any Spanish ships. The second document from the Royal Navy carried a direct threat; help fight the Americans or Barataria would be destroyed by English ships. Jean was so angry it was all he could do to keep from throwing them off of Barataria."

"Do you think they will attack if Jean sides with the Americans?" Gabby asked.

"It is a worry, for even now the English wait out there somewhere," she said pointing beyond the bay. "But a bigger problem right now is that Jean's men are still imprisoned in New Orleans and the Governor doesn't even answer Jean's letters. He is under a terrible strain. That is why he went directly to General Jackson. He was getting nowhere with Governor Claiborne and time is growing short."

"Then General Jackson must consider his offer to help a serious one or he would not send his men to deal with Jean."

"That's what Jean hopes," sighed Marie thoughtfully. "Jean may be a Frenchman, but above all he is a Louisianian and an American."

Both women had taken great care with their appearance that evening. Gabby's long, silvery locks and violet eyes were set off perfectly by a dress of tawny silk. Her creamy shoulders and tops of her breasts rose majestically above the deep decolletage. Marie's dark beauty was enhanced by the green satin that molded her firm, young body like a second skin. Jean's black eyes shrone appreciatively as he introduced them to the two young men who had already arrived and were in deep discussion with him. They spoke in English, as had the British officers, a language Gabby had learned to speak fluently in the convent. Jean used only her first name when she was introduced because she had asked him not to divulge her last name in the event that these men might be acquainted with Philippe.

The older of the two men, Captain Robert Stone, seemed unable to tear his eyes from Gabby from the moment they were introduced. The younger man, Lieutenant Peter Gray, eyed her speculatively but was friendly enough with his greeting. Upon hearing her name, a glance passed between both men, causing a chill of apprehension to run down her spine.

As the meal progressed, Gabby became more and more uncomfortable as Captain Stone's vivid blue eyes continued to devour her. Even Marie noticed his preoccupation with Gabby and arched her delicate eyebrows when she caught Gabby's glance. Gabby studied the captain through lowered lids while Jean had momentarily captured his full attention. His face seemed so boyish and open compared to Philippe's brooding countenance. He was nearly as tall and rugged with a magnificent physique but there the comparison ended. His unruly blond hair had a way of falling into his guileless eyes whenever he moved his head in a certain way. His wide, boyish grin was completely disarming and Gabby blushed profusely whenever it was directed at her, which was quite often. In no way was he threatening, his eyes gentle. Try as she might, she could not picture him as a soldier for he hadn't the looks of a killer.

Lieutenant Gray, though younger, appeared older. His gray eyes reminded her of Philippe's and their flinty barrier she could never penetrate. He appeared wise beyond his years and instinctively she knew he would encounter no difficulty killing. Gabby shivered whenever his gaze fell on her. He looked on her not as a desirable woman but as a marketable commodity. He made her extremely nervous and she was glad when the meal ended and Jean took the men into his study to discuss business over brandy and cigars. A courtesy he did not extend to the English. Gabby did not linger to talk with Marie, but went directly to her own room.

Once alone, Gabby brooded for what seemed like hours over the look the Americans exchanged when she had been introduced to them and the speculative gleam in Lieutenant Gray's eyes. What did it mean? Questions ran haphazardly through her mind. Was Philippe still in New Orleans after all this time and did he believe her still alive despite finding no trace of her? During her endless pacing she could not help but glance out the windows to the bay; the sparkling water, the shimmering moonlight, the softly scented breeze mysteriously beckoning her. Pulling a robe over her nightclothes she quietly let herself out of the house and descended the veranda steps. All was still and Gabby knew Jean and the Americans must have long since concluded their business and gone to bed. The oystershell path crunched under her slippered feet as she headed toward the white sand beaches. She passed a sentry but he did not stop her. She recognized him as one of the men who had a wife and family on Barataria.

Finally she stood just beyond a line of palm trees along the perimeter of the beach. The moon was high and each ship anchored in the bay was clearly outlined. It was an impressive sight, one Gabby would long remember. Almost at the same time she heard the crunch of a footfall behind her and a voice saying, "A beautiful sight, Mademoiselle Gabrielle." Gabby started violently but the softly drawled words fell pleasantly on her ears setting her immediately at ease. She much preferred these Americans' English to the harsh, clipped tones of the British. And for some reason she did not fear Captain Stone's presence.

"*Oui,*" Gabby answered dreamily as she gazed out to sea, "lovely."

"I'm not talking about the scenery," he whispered softly. She could feel his warm breath on the nape of her neck and was disturbed. But he made no move to touch her.

"Please, Captain," she demurred, wishing he would not continue with such talk.

"I'm sorry, Mademoiselle, but I could not help but make that observation. You are the loveliest creature I have ever seen."

Gabby was glad the darkness concealed the crimson staining her cheeks. His voice was so sincere, so intense that she knew he really meant it and was not accustomed to throwing compliments around impulsively. She smiled in spite of herself and was happy it was Captain Stone and not Lieutenant Gray who had found her alone on the beach.

"I see you, too, could not sleep," she said to cover her embarrassment.

"The balmy night drove me from my room," the captain admitted. "Now I'm grateful to fate for aiming my steps in this direction."

"Is your ship out there?" Gabby asked, nodding at the sheltered bay.

"No, we came down from New Orleans by pirogue. Dominique You guided us here."

"How long will you stay?"

"That hasn't been decided yet, but probably no longer than a fortnight. Lieutenant Gray and I have been commissioned by General Jackson to inspect the island and its battlements as well as the effectiveness of Lafitte's fleet should we decide to accept his help. After I am satisfied with his sincerity to aid us I will make my report to the general."

Gabby began walking along the beach and Captain Stone

paced his steps to her, taking it for granted that his company was welcomed. They walked side by side, enjoying the silence, the night, and their companionship. Before long Gabby turned and they returned their steps back to the house where they parted after a softly murmured, "Goodnight."

During the following days, no matter how many hours Captain Stone was closeted with Lafitte and Lieutenant Gray, he still managed to find time for Gabby. Usually it was during the late hours of the night when they strolled the beach together. Neither Jean nor Marie failed to notice the growing friendship between them, but did not question her actions. She was their guest and they would not think of limiting her freedom. On Barataria, each was free to choose for themselves and she was no different.

One night Gabby was occupying her usual place beneath the palm trees waiting for Captain Stone when she heard a familiar crunch on the oystershell path. With a welcoming smile she turned and was shocked to see Lieutenant Gray coming down the path instead of the captain. "What are you doing here?" she blurted out.

"Were you expecting someone else?" he asked pointedly. "A lovely evening for a tryst, Madame St. Cyr. I wondered what Captain Stone found so intriguing on the beach at this time of night and now I know."

Gabby blanched, the use of her full name stunning her. To cover her confusion, she said with as much contempt as she could muster, "You are rude, Lieutenant Gray!" Then she turned on her heel.

"Not so fast, Madame St. Cyr," he said silkily as he grasped her arm. "You're not fooling anyone. Both Captain Stone and myself know who you are. Your husband had your description circulated all over New Orleans. What would he do if he found his wife living with a group of dirty smugglers and pirates and carrying on with another man?"

"My life is none of your concern," she retorted hotly. She

was deeply hurt that Captain Stone had not told her that he was aware of her identity.

"I'm making it my concern," Lieutenant Gray countered as he ran a hand insinuatingly down her arm. Gabby shivered. "Your husband must place great value upon you. He has offered a five thousand dollar reward to anyone who brings him information concerning your whereabouts or proof of your death. What I'd like to know," he asked thoughtfully, "is why you choose to let him believe you are dead? Surely a loving wife would fly swiftly back to her husband. It is obvious you are not being held against your will." His eyes narrowed cunningly and his grip tightened on her arm.

Gabby cried out, alarm creasing her lovely features. What was he saying? Philippe wanted her back enough to offer a reward? She had been so certain he would be gone from New Orleans by now, but if what Lieutenant Gray said was true, then he had no intention of leaving before learning what had happened to her or gave her up for dead.

"I intend to collect that five thousand dollars, Madame St. Cyr, and I have no desire to share it with Captain Stone."

"Did I hear my name?" Captain Stone had come quietly up behind them and sized up the situation in one glance. Immediately, Lieutenant Gray released Gabby and stepped back.

"I just informed Mademoiselle Gabrielle that we are aware of her identity and would see that she is safely returned to her husband," Lieutenant Gray proffered.

"Did you have to manhandle her?" demanded Captain Stone when he saw Gabby rubbing her bruised arm.

"I'm sorry," apologized the lieutenant with mock contriteness. "I guess I became excited thinking how happy St. Cyr would be to learn his wife is alive and well."

"Leave us," Captain Stone ordered. "I will speak with Mademoiselle . . . with Madame St. Cyr." All the while they spoke Gabby remained silent. How far could she trust Captain Stone? she wondered. Why hadn't he confronted her before now? Did he, too, want the reward offered by Philippe?

"Are you hurt?" Captain Stone asked anxiously after the lieutenant's retreating figure disappeared through the trees.

"I . . . I . . . he did not hurt me," she answered hesitantly.

"Gabrielle . . . Gabby," he said softly as he drew her into her arms. Gabby stiffened but did not resist.

"Why, Captain Stone? Why didn't you tell me you knew who I was before this? Did you plan on dragging me back to my husband after you had gained my confidence?"

"At first I thought to wait and see if you would confide in me."

"Captain Stone . . ."

"My name is Rob."

"Rob, then," she agreed. "Just tell me if you intend to collect the reward offered by my husband. It is a great deal of money. More than a captain in the army would make I am sure."

"From the first I had no intention of informing your husband that you are on Barataria. I know you must have a very good reason for not returning to him. And as I came to know you I realized that I didn't care if you never returned to him. I find you to be a beautiful, warm-hearted woman who would not run from her husband without good reason." His show of concern was so different from Philippe's arrogant disregard; and yet, Rob seemed such a boy compared to Philippe.

"I love you, Gabby," confessed Rob, his sincerity warming Gabby's heart.

"Captain Stone . . . Rob . . . you don't know what you are saying! You do not really know me," Gabby protested as she gently disengaged herself from his embrace.

"I know all I need to know about you."

"I am a married woman."

"Yes, but one who obviously does not love her husband." Rob said with conviction. He pulled her into the circle of his arms once more. "Gabby, darling, come back to New Orleans with me."

"Rob, I can't!" Gabby protested. "Philippe will find me."

"He will find you here, also. You can be certain that Lieutenant Gray will go directly to him the minute we are back in the city. But if I leave Barataria before the lieutenant perhaps I can arrange for you to leave with me without his knowledge. By the time he informs your husband we will be long gone. Trust me, Gabby. I will take care of you."

He was so good, so gentle that Gabby almost believed he could protect her from Philippe. But in the end she knew Rob would only be hurt. "No matter where you hide me, Philippe will find me. You don't know him," she despaired.

"Then I shall send you to my parents in South Carolina. I will tell them that you are my wife and no one will ever doubt it."

"But I can never be your wife!"

"To me you would be my wife and when the battle for New Orleans is over we will live in South Carolina as husband and wife. St. Cyr would never think to look for you there." In his own mind it was all settled.

"*Cheri,*" Gabby whispered, touched by his feelings for her, "I cannot do that to you. You deserve a wife who could be legally yours. Our children would not even be legitimate."

"To me they would be," he insisted stubbornly.

Gabby raised her head to caress his strong, boyish face and to push back the hank of hair that had fallen across his forehead. That simple act seemed to unleash a furor in him as he molded her slender form against his own hardening body, capturing her lips in a fierce kiss while his hand cupped the soft underside of a breast. When he released her lips she was breathless and her heart pounded wildly against her ribcage. He, too, appeared thoroughly shaken by the experience as he lowered his head to nuzzle the hollow between the base of her neck and tops of her breasts.

"No, Rob," Gabby cried, feeling her resistance ebbing. "I am still married and I have always held that marriage vows were sacred. I am not ready to break them and go against everything I have been taught."

"And I will not force you to, Gabby," Rob answered, reluctantly releasing her. "But think about what I said. I don't know why you refuse to return to your husband but when he comes for you Jean Lafitte can do nothing to prevent him from taking you. You are his legal wife."

Gabby did think about Rob's words. All that week, in fact. She didn't see Jean alone during that time but she did confide to Marie that her identity was known to the Americans and that Lieutenant Gray intended to collect the reward offered by Philippe. Marie promised to speak to Jean about her problem.

To Gabby's chagrin, Jean told Marie that if Philippe came to Barataria, he would have no choice but to release her into her husband's custody. Evidently Philippe had General Jackson on his side and Jean would do nothing to hinder the fragile negotiations taking place between him and the Americans. Marie pitied her friend but Jean's word was law. Getting his men released from jail and the defense of New Orleans were more important than problems between husband and wife. In the end Gabby had no choice but to allow Rob to help her.

Rob was ecstatic when she told him she would accompany him to New Orleans even though she insisted she would make her own way in the city once Philippe returned to Martinique. It seemed that while she was making up her mind on whether or not to accompany him, he had worked out a feasible plan for their departure.

In two days he would return to New Orleans leaving Lieutenant Gray behind for yet another week on a final inspection of ships anchored in the bay. Gabby would accompany him disguised as a boy. They would leave at night using the darkness as a cover. If Lieutenant Gray became suspicious of her absence the next day Marie was to tell him she was ill. Later, Rob would find different lodgings so Philippe could not easily trace them.

Marie proved a willing accomplice to Rob's plan, thinking it all very romantic. She provided Gabby with boy's clothing and even secured Jean's promise to delay Lieutenant Gray on Barataria as long as possible.

"If you do not love your husband you could do worse than Captain Stone," Marie giggled. "He is quite handsome. Not so handsome as my Jean, but nonetheless virile and rugged. I have watched how he worships you with his eyes."

"I am still married," Gabby answered somewhat primly.

"*Mon dieu*, but you are an innocent," shrugged Marie. "You must follow your heart, *cherie*," she advised in a rare moment of insight.

The night of their departure arrived and Rob informed Lieutenant Gray, who seethed angrily at having to stay behind, that Lafitte wanted it that way. Even though Rob assured the lieutenant that he would not claim the $5000 reward from Philippe St. Cyr, he did not trust his superior. He wanted to be the first to reach New Orleans. He was so agitated that he was absent when Rob departed aboard the pirogue with the important letters from Lafitte tucked snugly beneath his belt. If he had been present he might have seen a slim, boyish figure wearing a cap pulled low and carrying a bundle slip noiselessly into the pirogue just minutes before it slid silently into the dark waters.

"These small boats tip easily so be very still and hang onto the sides," advised Rob when they were well out into the narrow stream. "But they can go where large ones cannot, through hummocks and across mud bars, even."

Gabby watched fearfully as one of Lafitte's men poled the narrow, shallow boat. Rob held a lantern high to guide their way. "Do not panic if an alligator rises nearby, for they hunt at night." The water was lapping at her hands as she clung to the sides and the tiny boat rocked alarmingly but soon settled down to an easy glide.

In places the water was shallow and dotted with many marsh islands, sometimes turning and twisting into many false channels. Gabby knew now why they needed a guide. Only Lafitte's people could find their way, others would become hopelessly lost in the myriad swamps.

Damp, chill air penetrated Gabby's thin clothing and she flinched when an owl shrieked close by. She was sure she could hear the swish of heavy tails in the water and huddled close to Rob as their guide deftly poled the small craft first into one channel between hummocks, then into another. Gabby nearly screamed when a ghostly flutter of moss caressed her face. Rob put his arm around her and held her close until she stopped shivering.

They seemed to have been in the boat for hours when a small light winked in the distance. As they drew closer, Gabby saw that it was a campfire. She breathed a sigh of relief when the pirogue slid silently to a stop against solid ground. Rob helped her out and she stood trembling in the darkness as their guide spoke rapidly to five men gathered around the campfire. One of them disappeared into the darkness and returned leading a beautiful black horse with a distinctive star on its forehead.

Rob approached the horse and spoke to it gently before coming back for Gabby. Then he placed her on the horse's back, handed her her bundle of clothing and lifted himself up behind her. With a salute to the men around the campfire they rode into the blackness. It seemed to Gabby that they followed a winding trail forever before finally coming onto a road. Only then did Rob speak to her.

"Are you cold, darling?" he asked solicitously, pulling her body snugly against him.

"A little," Gabby admitted, welcoming the warmth his arms offered.

"Thunder will get us to New Orleans soon," he said, affectionately patting the animal's sleek flanks. "By the way," he added, eyes twinkling mischievously, "you make a fetching boy." Gabby blushed furiously but was grateful for his lighthearted mood.

"Is Thunder your horse?" she asked.

"Yes, Lafitte's men cared for him while I was on Barataria."

They rode in silence for a while longer before Gabby asked, "How much farther to New Orleans?"

"Not too far now. My rooms are in the *vieux carre* on Rue Royal. We'll spend the rest of the night there. I'll sneak you up the back stairs, then tomorrow look for different lodgings after I deliver Lafitte's letters to General Jackson."

"Will Lafitte join the Americans?"

"I am convinced of Lafitte's sincerity in his desire to aid us. He asks only that his men be released from jail as well as a full pardon tendered for him and his men."

"Will General Jackson go along with that?"

"I'm sure of it after he gets my full report and reads Lafitte's letters."

Lights of the city soon guided their way as they rode through the silent streets. They entered a gate into an inner

113

courtyard and Rob walked Thunder to a stable where he dismounted, lifting Gabby to the ground. Putting a finger to his lips, he took her hand and guided her from the stable to an iron stairway that took them to a second floor of a two storied building where Rob stopped before a door and produced a key, pulling Gabby inside the moment it was unlocked.

Rob lit a lamp and Gabby gazed around with interest. The room was immaculate, but sparsely furnished. She looked with longing at the bed, it had been a long night, but quickly turned her eyes from it when she caught Rob staring at her with a strange look on his face.

"Gabby, you must be exhausted," Rob said, taking the bundle from her arms. "Come, you must rest."

Giving her no time to protest, he swooped her into his arms and laid her gently onto the soft surface of the bed. He removed her concealing cap and watched entranced as long, silvery locks cascaded over her shoulders. He took the silken strands in both his hands and lifted them to his face, breathing deeply of the clean, lemony smell. "Gabby, I . . ." he began hoarsely.

"No, Rob," Gabby breathed, aware of the emotions surging through him, "Do not say it. I beg you. We are good friends; we can be nothing more." Hurt immediately clouded his clear blue eyes but he did not dispute her words.

"I'm sorry, Gabby. Truly I am. I love you and want you desperately, but I will not force you. When the time is right I'll make you mine and marriage vows be damned. But for now, sleep." Then he pulled a quilt from the bed and prepared to make a pallet on the floor. Gabby was stunned by his easy acceptance of her wishes. If only Philippe had displayed a little of Rob's patience and love.

Gabby blinked awake to a roomful of sunlight. It took only a moment to remember where she was and another moment to realize that Rob was not in the room with her. The quilt he slept on had been neatly folded and placed at the foot of the bed. On top of the quilt lay a piece of paper. Reading Rob's note Gabby learned that he had gone to see General Jackson. She was to wait for his return and not venture out alone.

Spying a pitcher of water on the washstand, thanks no doubt to Rob's thoughtfulness, Gabby washed and dressed in a simple gown she had brought along with her. Marie had made sure that she had enough clothing to get her by until she found employment. Then she sat by the window studying the scene below with rapt attention.

The city that had been so silent the night before had come to life. Vendors, hawking their wares, raised their voices above the din of mule-drawn drays. Gabby could even hear the sing-song voices of Negro longshoremen coming from the direction of the levee.

Concentrating on her immediate surroundings, Gabby marveled at the beauty of the little courtyard they had entered the night before. It was beautifully landscaped with stables in the rear. Hibiscus rioted beside oleanders and palms. A bougainvillaea sent a shower of blood-red blossoms up beside and over the lattice work iron balcony that ran the length of the second floor overlooking the narrow cobblestone street.

When the small enclosed carriage entered the courtyard Gabby paid it little heed until she recognized Rob as the driver. Her obvious joy on seeing him as he entered the room made his face light up with pleasure. He cared little that she was another man's wife, he was determined to persuade her to go to his plantation in South Carolina and wait for him, especially since he had just learned he must soon leave the city on yet another mission for Andy Jackson.

"I brought you some croissants," Rob said, setting a small sack on the table. "Eat up while I pack my belongings. I rented us a room with kitchen at Patalba Apartments on Rue Chartres."

While Gabby munched contentedly on croissants, Rob

packed his gear and carried them, along with Gabby's meager belongings, to the carriage. He had already seen the landlady and paid her, deliberately leaving no forwarding address. After Gabby had eaten, he hurried her down the back stairs and into the carriage. Soon they were traveling through one narrow street after another until Rob finally drove through a gate and into a courtyard much like the one they had just left. As he had done the night before, Rob led her quickly up a flight of stairs and into a large, airy room that served as bedroom and sitting room. A smaller room served as kitchen. It was not an unpleasant apartment. French doors opened onto a small lacy balcony overlooking the busy street. On the opposite end of the room another pair of French doors led to another, larger balcony and the stairs they had just ascended.

"When did you have time to do all this?" Gabby asked, motioning around the room.

"I didn't sleep well last night," Rob said with an impish grin, "and was up very early this morning. Luckily General Jackson also is an early riser, and when our meeting concluded I went apartment hunting. Do you like it?" His boyish enthusiasm was infectious.

His desire to please made Gabby feel guilty. There was no way to repay him for his kindness. "It's perfect," she said. His delighted smile was like sunshine spreading across his face.

For a while they busied themselves putting away their clothing. Then Gabby said, "Tell me about your meeting with General Jackson. What has he decided to do about Jean Lafitte?"

For a brief moment a frown flitted across Rob's forehead and Gabby mistakenly thought it boded no good for Lafitte and his men. But Rob quickly put her mind at ease. "General Jackson is desperate for aid to defend the city since the citizens themselves seem unwilling to defend themselves. After reading Lafitte's letters and listening to my firsthand recommendations, he has decided to accept, and gladly, Lafitte's help to fight the English.''

"What about Governor Claiborne?''

"The governor will do as Jackson says. He has no choice in the matter.'' He looked searchingly at Gabby. "The document your husband brought over from France was enough to persuade Jackson of the real threat to New Orleans and made him realize how unprepared the city was to defend itself. Did you know your husband carried those secret documents, Gabby?''

"*Oui*, I knew, Rob. He told me about them after Captain Giscard was killed. He suspected someone aboard the *Windward* was a spy. He also believed his own life was in danger and asked me to deliver the papers to the general should something happen to him.''

"Yet it was you who nearly lost your life while St. Cyr made it safely to New Orleans,'' mused Rob thoughtfully. "I've never asked you this, but how did you come to be on deck the night of the hurricane instead of safely in your cabin?''

Gabby's face clouded as she relived those moments when she half-dragged, half-carried Philippe across the slippery deck and tied him to the mast. She shuddered, visibly shaken by thoughts of the ordeal. She could almost feel the force of that huge wave that carried her overboard. Rob was immediately contrite as he pulled her trembling body into his arms. "I'm sorry, darling,'' he soothed, caressing the bright curtain of her hair. "I did not mean to dredge up painful memories. You don't have to tell me if you don't want to.''

"Maybe sometime, Rob, but not now. It's too fresh in my mind.''

Before he could stop himself Rob captured her mouth with

his, the gentle pressure of his lips easily parting hers. His tongue, soft as velvet, made her head spin giddily and her heart beat with quick force. Suddenly her emotions were at war with her strongly nurtured conscience and her strict moral values. But it had been so long since Philippe had loved her that her body ached with a need she found hard to deny. Only when Rob's nimble fingers had unbuttoned her dress and slipped it from her shoulder to bare a firm, white breast did Gabby come to her senses.

"No, Rob," she pleaded, flashing him a look of entreaty. "We must not."

"But you want me, Gabby, I can sense it from your response. I love you and I think you love me."

Love? Did she love Rob? She was grateful to him and knew of no one else she liked as well as him. But love? Perhaps she did love him, she reasoned, still at odds with her raging emotions. But that still did not permit her to break her marriage vows.

"I don't know what I feel, Rob," she finally said. "I have known no other man save my husband, and him hardly at all, before I was forced into marriage. I did meet another man aboard the *Windward* but Philippe's jealousy made it impossible for us to become friends. So you can see my experience with men has been necessarily limited."

"This other man," asked Rob, experiencing a pang of jealousy, "did you fall in love with him?"

"No!" denied Gabby. "We were only friends."

"And I offer you my undying love." Then Rob kissed her again, deeply, thoroughly and Gabby thought she would faint from giddiness. Nothing in her life had prepared her to handle such a situation.

Although she was one man's wife she found herself physically wanting another man. Somewhere in the back of her mind she remembered her mother's desire-filled voice begging her father to take her and her own vows that she would never allow pleasures of the flesh to dominate her life. Only then was she able to resist Rob's passionate onslaught.

"I am not free to accept your love, Rob," Gabby said, gently disengaging herself from his arms.

Rob's face was flushed and his body shook with repressed desire but he was determined to wait until she came to him. With trembling hands he helped her pull the bodice of her dress into place to cover the tantalizing flesh he had bared just moments before. "Forgive me, Gabby, I will not pressure you although it is torture for me to remain near you and not have you," he said, disappointment bitter in his voice. "If I cannot know your love at least once leaving you will be all the harder."

"Leaving!" gasped Gabby with dismay. "So soon? Where are you going?"

"General Jackson has ordered me on another mission. The army is in such short supply of flints and ammunition that he is sending foraging parties all over the countryside in seach of them. At the end of the week I will lead a small group of men up to Natchez where a scout has heard about a cache of arms and flints hidden someplace in Natchez-under-the-Hill. I must locate t hem, buy them and transport them down river to New Orleans."

"Is it dangerous?" Gabby asked, suddenly fearful that she would never seen him again.

"Don't worry, darling. It's not a particularly dangerous mission."

"How long will you be gone?"

"Not any longer than I have to. Certainly no more than a month," he assured her. "I have just enough time to arrange for you to go to South Carolina to my parents' plantation. They will take care of you. Please, darling," he pleaded when she began shaking her head in protest, "how can I leave knowing you will be alone?"

"I will be safe enough here while you are gone," she

insisted stubbornly.

Rob frowned, deep lines creasing his usually sunny countenance. He knew he could not force her to leave. "Will you promise not to run off on your own in a strange city?"

"I promise," she answered solemnly.

"Gabby, I have never questioned you before, buy why are you reluctant to return to your husband? I don't know him but General Jackson thinks highly of him."

"Then your general does not know him!" spat Gabby vehemently. "He is a killer, a man who murdered his own wife!"

"My God, Gabby! Do you know what you are saying?"

"He told me himself and I have no reason to doubt him. He is cold, arrogant, and hateful; he treats me as a possession, not as a wife. I never want to see him again!"

"And you never shall, darling. When this battle is over nothing will prevent me from taking you to South Carolina. Not even your own protests."

The following days passed swiftly. Gabby did not attempt to leave the small apartment but sat often on the balcony. Rob was gone much of the time, caught up with duties and his expedition to Natchez. He did manage to find time to stock the kitchen with supplies, and to take her out into the French marketplace disguised as a boy to acquaint her with the place in the unlikely event he should be gone longer than anticipated.

Each night, after a look of intense longing at the bed, Rob made his pallet on the floor without comment. On their last day together he took her out of the *vieux carre* in a closed carriage for a picnic along the banks of Lake Ponchartrain. The days were turning cooler but the sun was still warm when they reached the secluded spot Rob had chosen for their outing. She felt like a child on her first picnic, which in truth it was. She sipped cool wine and ate crusty bread and cheese as if it were the most extravagant feast in the world. Later they

120

walked hand in hand along the beach and explored the surrounding woods. Rob was attentive where Philippe had been uncaring of her feelings; Rob was warm and gentle where Philippe was cruel and arrogant. Why then did she not love Rob? They lingered long enough to view the perfect sunset to end a perfect day.

Rob was full of last minute instructions when they returned to the Patalba Apartments. "Don't go out without your disguise, for St. Cyr is still in the city," he warned. "Lieutenant Gray has returned to New Orleans from Barataria and your husband must know by now that you are alive. There is enough money in the bureau drawer to last until I return. When I return things will have to be settled between us, darling, because I cannot continue like this. Your nearness has driven me mad these past days." Then he drew her into his arms. "Promise me you will not leave in my absence. That you will be waiting for me when I return."

"I shall be here when you return," promised Gabby, touched by his caring.

That night, as usual, Rob made his pallet on the floor and after a goodnight kiss which Rob seemed unwilling to break off, both retired to their own bed. Gabby could hear him tossing and turning on the hard floor, but hardened her heart against his need. Finally she fell asleep, troubled by her dreams as she squirmed restlessly on the bed suddenly grown too big for one person. She dreamed she was aboard the *Windward*, in the cabin she knew so well, with Philippe. She could almost feel his hands upon her body, arousing her in the many ways she had come to know, to desire. Suddenly she was wide awake. The hands exploring with gentle firmness were as real as the warm presence next to her. Shocked, she started to rise.

"No, Gabby, stay with me," Rob begged. "Let me love you this once before I leave, my darling. My God," he sobbed, "I want you so badly. Please let me love you!"

His kisses felt soft and gentle on her lips but did not stop there. With trembling hands he drew her nightdress over her head, tossing it to the floor, then proceeded to discover all the sweet, secret places of her body for himself. Her feeble protests went unnoticed as she vainly tried to push him aside.

"God, Gabby," he groaned hoarsely, "don't stop me now. I've waited so long for you. You're so incredibly desirable and I love you so much."

Even if she wanted to, Gabby could not have stopped him. Suddenly her need for this gentle, sweet man overwhelmed her; she desperately wanted to be consumed by his passion; needed to have Philippe cleansed from her mind and soul forever.

"Stay, Rob," she urged, desire flooding her loins. "Love me! I'd be lying if I said I didn't want you and I was never any good at lying."

Then there was time for no more words between them as Gabby rose eagerly to accept his weight. His passion sparked hers and transported her into a world she had known only with Philippe as he kissed her breasts, her belly, then moved back to her lips in an unhurried and sensuous exploration. The taste of him filled her mouth. He was a tireless, consummate lover whose imminent departure the next morning made him all the more passionate. He was also a gentle, thoughtful lover, exhibiting none of the wild fire that raged within Philippe when he took her. And although her pleasure was nearly as complete as Rob's, it ws not as dramatic or violent as she had known before. But the sweetness of fulfillment with Rob was like balm to her soul, unlike anything she had ever experienced. When dawn streaked the sky, she fell asleep with Rob's golden head resting on her breast. Darkness made it impossible to see the tears that sprang to her eyes and spiked her eyelashes with tiny dew drops but nevertheless Rob sensed the turmoil within her heart.

Rob arose the next morning before Gabby was awake. He

dressed in silence, then stood beside the bed gazing down at her with loving eyes, as if trying to memorize her features. The golden lashes were like butterfly wings against her cheek and his heart contracted violently at the sight of her curled childlike and innocent amidst the rumpled bedding. But there was nothing childlike or innocent about her response to him last night, he thought, his body hard with remembered passion. Somehow, when he returned he must find a way to persuade her to return to South Carolina with him. He perched at the edge of the bed and gently nuzzled a bare shoulder.

"Gabby, darling, I'm leaving," he said softly so as not to startle her.

Gabby stretched like a playful kitten before coming full awake. "There is something you should know before I leave. I didn't tell you everything yesterday for fear of spoiling our last day together."

"What is it?" Gabby asked, little fingers of fear playing along her spine.

"I did not tell you that Lieutenant Gray has already collected the reward offered by your husband. I saw him in General Jackson's office yesterday."

"Does he know I am with you?"

"No, thank God," sighed Rob. "He still believes you on Barataria and that's what he told St. Cyr."

"Then Jean and Marie must have convinced him that I was ill," breathed Gabby with relief.

"Nevertheless," warned Rob ominously, "when St. Cyr finds you gone from Barataria he will scour the city until he finds you. Unless you wish to return to him," he paused dramatically, searching her face, "you must remain inside our apartment until I return."

"I have no desire to return to Philippe," Gabby denied fiercely as she threw her arms around Rob's neck. "Oh, Rob, I would be a fool to refuse your love."

"Gabby, sweetheart, does that mean . . . dare I hope . . . I mean, could you love me?" His eyes were alight with happiness.

"We'll discuss it further when you return," she promised. "For now just know that your love has made me very happy. Never have I known such sweetness."

He kissed her deeply, gratefully, then drew away reluctantly. "I must go. Remember your promise to me. And, darling, in my heart you will always be my true wife, legal or not." His eyes held all the promise of tomorrow. Then he was gone and already Gabby could feel the empty days and nights stretching endlessly before her.

Gabby remained true to her promise and did not venture from the apartment on Rue Chartres for nearly two weeks after Rob left. Sometimes she sat on the little balcony, other times she wandered around the tiny courtyard. She read the few books lying around but in the end boredom became her greatest enemy. One day, after discovering her larder nearly depleted, Gabby donned her boy's garb, wound her long, pale locks beneath a cap and set out for the French market, the promise of adventure coloring her cheeks. Stuffed in her belt was the pouch of coins Rob had left her.

She felt gay and lighthearted as she jauntily drank in the sights and sounds of the *vieux carre*. Women of various hues, dressed in gaudy outfits and wearing madras turbans chatted gaily as they headed for the market with baskets slung over their arms or balanced on their heads. Many were very beautiful and looked haughtily down on their lesser sisters. Before long the acrid odor of the waterfront assailed her nostrils and she wrinkled her nose at the combined smell of fish, decaying fruits and vegetables, and human waste.

Gabby passed back and forth in front of the many stalls before deciding upon her first purchase, a plump hen. She pulled the pouch from her belt to pay for her purchase unaware of the pair of sharp eyes watching her movements. She was so caught up with her choice of vegetables to accompany the hen that she failed to see the small, ragged urchin dash from the throng of people crowding around the vendors until it was too late to prevent what happened next. The frail body, exhibiting surprising strength, lurched into Gabby, knocking her off her feet. In a trice the urchin's agile hands snatched at the money pouch. Before anyone in the milling crowd of onlookers knew what was happening the ragged child had disappeared, the pouch clutched tightly in a grubby fist.

"Help!" Gabby cried when she finally found her voice. "Stop that child! He stole my purse!"

Immediately two soldiers were beside her helping her to her feet. "Are you hurt, sonny?" asked one of them kindly. "What happened?"

"I am not hurt," Gabby explained, "but a ragged street urchin knocked me down and stole my money."

"It happens all the time," sighed the other soldier, shrugging his shoulders. "They are too swift for us to catch. But surely you were aware that these things happen along the waterfront and should have been more careful with your money."

He looked sharply at her, taking in the dainty, almost girlishly slim figure and pretty features. Gabby raised her hand to her cap to assure herself it was still in place.

"What's going on here, Sergeant?" The authoritative voice came from behind Gabby but she recognized it immediately. She lowered her head under the penetrating gaze of Lieutenant Gray.

"Aw, nothing much, Lieutenant," shrugged the sergeant. "Seems like this here lad was robbed by one of them street urchins. But he wasn't hurt none, were you, sonny?"

"No," whispered Gabby.

Lieutenant Gabby studied the slight figure standing before him with shrewd eyes, then asked, "What is your name, boy, and where do you live?"

"I am Gilbert La Farge," replied Gabby, lowering her voice an octave. Her father's name was the only one she could think of on the spur of the moment. "I live . . . I live . . . on Rue St. Charles."

Lieutenant Gray's deepset eyes did not waver from her face and Gabby became increasingly uncomfortable under his close scrutiny. Only when he reached out a hand to remove her cap did she realize that he had seen through her disguise. Instinctively she ducked, and quick as a flash her slim body slipped between the two soldiers on either side of her.

"Stop that boy!" shouted the lieutenant as Gabby moved swiftly into the surrounding crowd.

"What's he done, Lieutenant?" asked the sergeant scratching his head in bewilderment.

"Don't question me, just do as I say," Lieutenant Gray shouted as he took off after the fleet figure. "Catch him and find out where he lives."

Gabby found it difficult to lose her pursuers in the narrow maze of streets. No matter where she turned either the lieutenant or one of the soldiers were close behind. She dare not return to Rob's lodgings and she had no money with which to pay for another room for herself, thanks to that ragged child who had robbed her. With growing alarm she realized that eventually she would be forced to return to Philippe. The streets were no place for a woman alone with neither friends nor money.

Gabby had just turned a corner and stopped to catch her breath when she happened to glance up at the street sign she was leaning against. It read: Rue Dumaine. Then she remembered. Marcel's sister lived on Rue Dumaine. But which house? The street appeared to be several blocks long and she only recalled that his sister's last name was Gaspar. She glanced furtively around and breathed a sigh of relief when she found the street nearly deserted. Perhaps she had lost her pursuers, she hoped, silently praying for that miracle. But it was not to be for at that moment Lieutenant Gray rounded the far corner.

"Mon dieu!" Gabby cried aloud, casting frightened eyes to the other side of the street where she spied an open gate leading into a courtyard surrounded by a high wall. Without a second thought, Gabby dashed into the street hoping to gain the safety of those walls before Lieutenant Gray saw her.

But fate intervened. Gabby was nearly to the open gateway when a carriage suddenly appeared beneath the portals and she found herself lying in the street dazed and bruised but alive. The cap concealing her bright hair lay some distance away and those glorious locks spread about her still form like a cascade of silvery moonbeams.

The carriage ground to a halt and the driver crouched down beside Gabby making clucking noises in his throat.

"What is it, Pitot?" asked a voice from within the carriage.

"A boy, Monsieur, no, it is a girl," Pitot corrected. "He . . . she . . . is injured."

The passenger stuck his head from the window in exasperation. "Move him . . . or her aside and let's be off," he ordered impatiently.

Just then the glitter of silver caught his eye and he turned shocked eyes to the still figure on the ground. A shimmering curtain of pale hair surrounded a white face he knew so well. *"Dieu!"* he exclaimed, his voice quivering with disbelief. "It is not possible!"

A shiver went through him as he felt the full impact of violet eyes gazing up at him. "Gabrielle? Is it really you, Gabby, *ma chere?*"

"Marcel!" Gabby cried with joyful recognition. "Help

127

me, please!'' She didn't know where Marcel had come from but his appearance at this moment was providential.

"Quickly, Pitot, get her into the carriage," Marcel ordered briskly. A crowd had begun to gather in the streets and from it an American officer started forward.

"Wait, sir!" called Lieutenant Gray as he pushed his way through the people milling around the carriage.

"Please hurry, Marcel," Gabby pleaded, violet eyes glazed with fright, "he intends to take me back to Philippe!"

"Forward, Pitot," Marcel called to the driver. "Make haste!" Pitot flicked the whip over the horses and the carriage lurged forward, soon leaving the crowd and the American officer behind. Only after Marcel was certain they were not followed did he turn his attention to Gabby.

"Are you hurt, *cherie?*" he asked with concern.

"Only shaken and bruised, Marcel," she assured him. "I am just thankful that you came along when you did."

"I can't believe you are alive! It's like a miracle. Everyone though you had drowned. Where have you been all this time and why didn't you let Philippe know you were alive?"

"Please, Marcel, not now," pleaded Gabby. "I am still too shaken."

"Forgive me, *ma petite*, for being thoughtless," Marcel murmured solicitously. "You are safe with me. I will take you to my sister's house where no one will find you. You can tell me everything in your own good time."

It seemed to Gabby that they spent an inordinate amount of the time winding in and out of alleys and narrow streets before they finally entered a courtyard. Just before they had turned in she saw the number 30 emblazoned on the door to the imposing brick house. Almost at the same time she recognized the street as the same one she had been on earlier. In fact, the courtyard they had just entered was the very one she had thought to hide in. They were at number 30 Rue Dumaine. Gabby wrinkled her brow in concentration but her head hurt too badly for her to associate this fact with something she had heard weeks before.

The carriage halted and Pitot jumped down from his perch to close the gate while Marcel helped Gabby, ushering her immediately inside the house where he turned her over to a tall, dour black woman.

"Lizette is my cook and housekeeper. She will take good care of you, *cherie*," insisted Marcel when he noticed Gabby's reluctance to accompany the woman. "After you have rested we will speak further." He chastely kissed her cheek and Gabby had no choice but to follow Lizette up a long flight of stairs.

Much later, bathed and dressed in clothing belonging to Marcel's sister, Gabby joined Marcel in the salle. She wondered where Marcel's sister and her family were but Lizette proved highly uncommunicative when questioned, answering in a guttural jumble of French and Creole Gabby found hard to understand.

Ah, *cherie*," greeted Marcel warmly, running an appreciative eye over her slim form, "now you look more like yourself. You do justice to my sister's gowns."

"Where is your sister, Marcel? I am anxious to meet her and thank her for the loan of her clothes."

"That is not possible at this time. The entire family are north for an extended vacation." Gabby's distress was so obvious that Marcel immediately took her arm and led her to a chair. "What is it, *cherie*? What have I said? Are you still shaken from your harrowing experience?"

"Nothing like that, Marcel. It is just that I had so counted on seeking employment as a governess to your sister's children," Gabby said dejectedly. "Now I must find another position."

"No!" Marcel objected. "The position is yours as soon as Celeste and her family return, which should be soon after the battle for New Orleans is resolved one way or another. Meanwhile, you are my guest.''

"When do you plan on returning to your home on Martinique?''

"Not many ships are leaving the city right now," he explained. "Somewhere out there is the English fleet."

"Oh, *oui*," said Gabby, "I have met their commander."

"You what?" asked Marcel startled by her words.

"*Oui*, on Barataria, several weeks ago."

"You were on Barataria with Jean Lafitte's smugglers? But how . . . ?"

"I'll have to start from the beginning, Marcel," Gabby sighed as she settled back and prepared to relate the events that led up to this moment.

She started with the storm, minimizing her part in saving Philippe's life and continued straight through to the moment she ran into his carriage on Rue Dumaine. When she had finished speaking, he regarded her with astonishment.

"These pirates, *cherie*, they did not . . . did not harm you in any way?"

"I was Lafitte's guest and none dared touch me."

"Not even Lafitte, himself? I hear he has an eye for beauty. He must have been quite taken with you," Marcel said, green eyes boring into her.

"I told you," insisted Gabby, "I was his guest. Besides, he has a beautiful octoroon mistress who does not take kindly to his philandering," Gabby laughed, recalling Marie's flashing black eyes whenever Jean so much as looked at another woman. "Then, too," she added thoughtfully, "his mind was taken with more serious matters."

"What do you know of his plans?" Marcel asked with intense interest.

"Little, except that he does not take the English seriously."

"Then he intends to help the Americans?" Marcel persisted. A certain note in his voice alarmed Gabby and she wished he would leave off with his line of questioning, but he persevered. "This army captain who brought you to New Orleans, you say he carried letters to General Jackson?"

"*Oui*, I believe he did, but I know nothing of their contents."

"This Captain Stone, he had been your . . . uh . . . protector since you left Barataria?"

"He . . . he offered me a place to stay until Philippe left New Orleans."

"He is your lover?" Marcel implied, impaling her with his emerald gaze. When no answer was forthcoming, and seeing her confusion, he quickly added, "Never mind, *ma chere*, your silence speaks more eloquently than your words ever could. It's a pity you never learned to disguise what is in your heart." Her downcast eyes caused him to laugh. "Come, come, do not be so glum. Who could blame you? Certainly, not I."

"Please, Marcel, let us speak of other things," said Gabby, acute embarrassment flooding her cheeks with color.

"After you explain why you left Captain Stone," Marcel replied.

"General Jackson sent him on a mission to buy ammunition and flints for the army."

Marcel stiffened. "Where did he go?" he asked tersely.

"To Natchez, I think," answered Gabby. "An agent reported a cache of shells and flints in a warehouse somewhere in Natchez-under-the-Hill."

"Did he go alone?"

"He led a party of men. I'm unsure of the exact number." Gabby was baffled by Marcel's absorption with Rob's mission.

"When did he leave?" When Gabby did not answer immediately, Marcel seized her wrist in a bruising grip.

131

"When did he leave?" he asked again, this time more forcefully.

"Two weeks ago!" gasped Gabby. "What is it, Marcel? Why are you so interested in Rob? You are hurting me!"

Abruptly he released her wrist and at once became contrite and tender. "I am sorry, *ma chere*, but I allowed my emotions to rule my head. It angered me to think of you in a strange city all alone after your captain had left. But now you are under my protection and I shall be everything to you that Captain Shore has been," he said meaningfully.

"Marcel, I am grateful to you for coming to my aid, but that is all. We can never be more than friends. I fully intend to earn my own way and once your sister returns I no longer will need anyone's protection."

"And your lover? What of him? Are you in love with this Captain Shore?"

"I . . . I don't know," shrugged Gabby. "But my feelings for him, whatever they may be, can change nothing. He deserves someone who can be a wife to him and bear him legitimate children." Silence prevailed while she relived their last moments together. "I must admit that I have never met and probably never will meet a kinder, more tender, loving man."

"I will try to remedy that," murmured Marcel, "if you but give me a chance."

Gabby was glad that Pitot chose that moment to announce dinner, for it extricated her from an embarrassing situation. What had happened between her and Rob was something special but she didn't intend the same thing to happen between her and any other man.

At the conclusion of the excellent meal, Marcel informed Gabby that he must leave for a short time but would return before she retired for the night. He left her in the salle surrounded by several good books he hoped would entertain her in his absence.

But no matter how hard Gabby tried to concentrate on the words, a multitude of thoughts flashed through her mind. Why was Marcel so interested in Rob's mission to Natchez? Would Philippe search for her in the *vieux carre?* She knew she couldn't go back to the Patalba Apartments for fear of being discovered. She would stay with Marcel for the time being and contact Rob when he returned. He would be upset to find her gone, she knew, but somehow she would get word to him. Finally, exhaustion and the late hour took its toll and she dropped off to sleep sitting on an overstuffed chair.

It was nearly midnight when Marcel returned to the house on Rue Dumaine. He was deeply apologetic when he awoke Gabby. "I'm sorry, *cherie,* but my business took longer than I had anticipated. You must be chilled sitting here like this," he cried when he saw her shiver. "Come, I will see you to your room."

With an arm around her shoulders he led her up the stairs. When they reached her room, he opened the door and followed her inside before she could protest. He gazed at her longingly but did not try to touch her.

"Something unexpected has arisen and I must leave in the morning," he said glibly. At Gabby's gasp of dismay he continued quickly, "I don't expect to be gone long, a fortnight at most. But you need not worry. Pitot and Lizette will take good care of you and see that you lack for nothing until my return."

"I shall be fine," Gabby replied. Actually she was relieved that he would not be around for well she knew his feelings toward her and hated to hurt him after he had been so good to her. "But I hate to impose on you. Perhaps I should return to Captain Stone's lodgings," she insisted.

"No! No!" protested Marcel. "By now Philippe has heard

133

that you are somewhere in the *vieux carre* and will leave no stone unturned until he finds you. After all, you are still his wife. Just think about Cecily and you will realize that you must remain here.''

"Of course, you are right, Marcel,'' Gabby agreed readily when she thought about the alternative.

"Then I will bid you goodnight, *cherie*. And *adieu*, until I return. Remember, trust no one but Pitot and Lizette.''

Then he surprised her by pulling her into his arms and kissing her with a longing that left her breathless. "Just to speed me on my way,'' he explained with a wolfish grin. Then he was gone.

Chapter Eight

WHEN PHILIPPE received the message summoning him to General Jackson's headquarters, he intuitively knew it had something to do with Gabby. Two months had elapsed since she had been swept overboard during the fateful storm and despite the $5,000 reward he had heard nothing. He had always heard the sea refused to give up her dead and now he believed it. He could not even give her a decent burial. Of one thing he was certain, he would never marry again. First Cecily and now Gabby. Surely there was a curse on him and the women he loved. He refused to inflict a sure death sentence on another woman by marrying her. Poor, innocent Gabby. She had died while saving his life. He could still picture in his mind the defiant tilt to her stubborn little chin and the violet flames flashing from her eyes. He had admired her strength and will, passionate spirit, unbending pride. When she angered him he wanted to break her. A crooked grin twisted his mouth. Though he knew in his heart she could never be tamed he longed for her sweet, supple body in his arms.

In the months since her death he had come to the realization that he loved her. Why couldn't he have told her before it was too late? Why had he remained a stubborn, unfeeling fool? Marcel had been right. He had acted like a jealous husband aboard the *Windward*, trying to protect what was his. But who could blame him? If Marcel hadn't fed Cecily's discontent she would still be alive today. How could he have stood by and allowed Marcel to destroy Gabby's life, for

Gabby was far more innocent and vulnerable than Cecily had ever been.

Philippe was in General Jackson's outer office only a few minutes before the general appeared. "Good to see you again, St. Cyr," he said, extending a hand in greeting. He seemed to have grown even more gaunt and hollow-eyed since Philippe had last seen him. "I will get right to the point because I know you will appreciate not having to wait for the news I have for you."

"My wife . . ." began Philippe, the words catching in his throat.

"Is alive," finished Jackson.

Philippe's whole body seemed to collapse as he grasped the edge of the desk to support himself. "Where is she?" he asked when he finally found his voice.

"I'll let Lieutenant Gray tell you for he is the one who found her." Only then did Philippe see a young officer step from the shadows and approach him. He looked expectantly at the lieutenant, waiting for him to speak.

"I have seen and spoken with your wife, Mr. St. Cyr," Lieutenant Gray announced importantly.

"*Mon dieu*, man, tell me, where is she?" shouted Philippe, unable to contain his growing excitement. "Is she well?"

"I have recently returned from a mission to Barataria where I found Madame St. Cyr."

All the breath went out of Philippe. "The pirate stronghold?" he asked with dismay. "Are you telling me she is a hostage of Jean Lafitte? I received no ransom note."

"She is no hostage, sir," countered the lieutenant smugly. "She was introduced to myself and Captain Stone as Lafitte's guest and we had no reason to believe otherwise. She obviously had the run of the island."

"How did she come to be on Barataria?"

"She didn't say, sir."

"Did you have private words with her?"

"Once," replied Lieutenant Gray slyly. "She was walking late one night along the beach when I encountered her. I let her know I was aware of her identity and asked her to accompany me back to New Orleans."

"What did she say to that?" asked Philippe, becoming more and more uneasy as the facts unfolded.

"She told me to mind my own business, that she didn't intend to return to you."

"*Mon dieu,*" cursed Philippe. "You mean to tell me she would rather remain with a lot of freebooters than return to me, her husband?" When Lieutenant Gray nodded his assent, Philippe was stunned into silence.

"Captain Stone returned from Barataria a week before you did," broke in General Jackson, addressing his question to the lieutenant. "Why do you suppose he failed to inform us about Madame St. Cyr? Has he no need of five thousand dollars?"

"Who is this Captain Stone?" asked Philippe.

"He was the officer in charge of delivering letters to Jean Lafitte and sounding out his loyalty to America," answered Jackson. "A good man. I have just dispatched him on another mission to Natchez in search of ammunition and flints."

"Captain Stone and your wife became very . . . uh . . . friendly," offered Lieutenant Gray.

"Be careful what you are implying, Lieutenant," warned Jackson.

"I'm sorry, sir," replied the lieutenant, not sounding sorry at all, "but I believe Mr. St. Cyr should know the facts."

"Go on, Lieutenant," said Philippe in a tight voice.

"I watched them meet every night and walk along the beach together. They appeared quite . . . intimate . . . if you know what I mean, sir."

Philippe tried hard to ignore the implication of his words.

"You said that Captain Stone left Barataria a week prior to your own departure," said Philippe. "What did my wife do then?"

"I did not see her after that. Mr. Lafitte and his mistress both told me she had taken ill and needed bed rest. I left a week later without encountering her again."

"You must forgive me for my close questioning but I find all this very hard to assimilate," apologized Philippe. "Did she appear well when you first arrived on Barataria?"

"She appeared and acted very well, indeed. She is a beautiful woman. Nothing was ever mentioned about how she came to be with Lafitte or the condition she was in when she arrived. To my eyes, there was nothing wrong with her."

"There is but one explanation," put in Jackson. "She washed ashore on Barataria and was found by Lafitte or one of his men. Your wife must be very lucky to be alive at all. Surviving the sea is astonishing enough but finding her a guest of Jean Lafitte instead of a hostage is a miracle. But then," he added thoughtfully, "of late Lafitte has been on his best behavior. He wants a full pardon and his brother and followers released from jail in exchange for his help in repulsing the English."

"Is there anything else of important you have to tell me, Lieutenant?" asked Philippe hopefully.

"No, sir."

"Do you believe my wife to be on Barataria still?"

"Yes, sir, I do."

"Thank you, Lieutenant, you have been most helpful. If you come aboard the *Windward* this evening I will see that you receive your reward."

Lieutenant Gray's dark eyes gleamed at the mention of the coveted prize. "I will be there," he answered, barely able to contain his glee. When he saw the interview had ended, he saluted General Jackson and departed.

"What will you do now, St. Cyr?" Jackson asked when they were alone.

"I am going to Barataria after my wife," Philippe answered unhesitatingly.

"You will never find the way," Jackson said. "No man has found it without a Baratarian to guide him."

"Then I shall find a guide," insisted Philippe, undaunted.

"I can be of some help," offered Jackson. "I don't know why your wife acted as she did, and I will not ask, but if you insist on traveling to Barataria, then I would ask you to act as emmissary for me. In return I will tell you where to obtain a guide to his stronghold."

"I am rather good at carrying documents," grinned Philippe. "I will be happy to be your messenger again."

"Good! You proved trustworthy before and I know you will not fail me this time, either."

"Tell me what I have to do, General."

"Do you know the Absinthe House?"

"I have heard of it."

"It is a meeting place of many of Lafitte's men. At exactly ten o'clock tomorrow morning go to the Absinthe House and ask for Dominique You. Tell him I sent you. He will know why you are there and see to it that you reach Barataria."

"Will there be an answer to your messages?" asked Philippe.

"None will be necessary. Governor Claiborne has agreed to release Jean's brother Pierre and the rest from jail in addition to granting a full pardon for all."

"Can you trust Lafitte?"

"I believe that he will do all in his power to prevent the British from seizing New Orleans," said Jackson with firm conviction.

By noon the next day Philippe was on his way to Barataria. He had found the Absinthe House easily enough and had only to wait one hour while someone went for Dominique You. After listening to Philippe, Dominique called to one of the disreputable looking men sitting around a table drinking and before he knew it he was on a horse heading out of the city. The freebooter guiding him might have been mute for he said not one word until they reached the edge of the swamp about eight miles from town where several fierce-looking pirates were milling around a makeshift camp.

Philippe dismounted and followed his guide, standing aside while two men dragged a pirogue out from under a clump of bushes and put it in the water. Only then was he spoken to. "Get in, Monsieur," were the guide's brief words.

During the next hours Philippe thanked *le bon dieu* almost constantly for the guide. Never in a million years could he have found his way amid the maze of bayous, channels, and swamps. In places the fog was so dense it covered the water in a thick, gray blanket. But the pirate guide poled unerringly to their destination. It seemed to Philippe that he had been in a pirogue for hours when the island suddenly loomed out of the mist and the boat bumped into shore.

Immediately a group of ragged men and women crowded around and Philippe was amazed at the number of persons engaged in various pursuits in the immediate area. He had no idea so many people, including women and children, lived on Barataria under Lafitte's protection. They were a motley and ill-assorted group at best. He heard English spoken, and French, Spanish, and other languages he didn't recognize. In the distance he could make out a low log fort and its cannons. As he was being led to Lafitte's house he studied the people he saw along the way. Some men were young and cocky, some old and gray bearing many battle scars. All were marked by the harsh wind and sea. Long, pointed swords clanged at their sides, pistols were shoved into their belts. There appeared to be so many races, so many tongues that he soon gave up trying to sort them out.

Jean Lafitte awaited Philippe in the main room of the rambling house. "I am Jean Lafitte," he said with a slight bow. "And you are . . . ?"

"Philippe St. Cyr," replied Philippe. If the name meant anything to Lafitte he didn't show it outwardly; his smooth face betrayed nothing.

"I believe you have something for me, Monsieur St. Cyr."

"I do," anwered Philippe, quickly reaching into his pocket and extracting the packet entrusted to him by General Jackson.

Almost immediately the packet was in Lafitte's hands and he scanned the pages, a pleased smile creasing his handsome features.

"*Eh bien!*" he exclaimed excitedly. "This General Jackson is a man of action and he won't be sorry he trusted Jean Lafitte! Together we will send the English back to England in defeat." Then he turned to Philippe. "*Merci*, Monsieur St. Cyr. No answer is necessary. My brother Pierre and my men will be released from jail and a full pardon for all is being drawn up. Just inform the good general that he will not be sorry. As for you, St. Cyr, you shall be my guest for the night and in the morning I will see that you are returned safely to New Orleans."

For all purposes Philippe was being dismissed. But that was not his intention. "I have come to Barataria on a mission of my own as well as the one I performed for General Jackson," he explained briefly, forestalling Lafitte's imminent withdrawal. "I understand that my wife is on your island."

Lafitte studied the handsome, intense husband whom Gabby had chosen to abandon in favor of another, and instinctively knew that this man could never be guilty of cold-blooded murder. Especially the murder of his own wife. Somehow, something was very wrong. Jean felt in his heart that St. Cyr was owed an explanation.

"Your wife is no longer on Barataria, Monsieur St. Cyr,"

Lafitte said, watching closely the other man's reaction. What he saw must have satisfied him for he continued. "We found her nearly drowned and covered with bruises on our shore. My own Marie nursed her back to health and they became close friend. I offered her haven on my island."

Philippe's face was carefully blank as he asked, "Why did she choose to remain on Barataria once she had recovered? Wasn't she aware that everyone assumed her dead?"

"I did not pry, Monsieur. She obviously had her own reasons for wishing to remain dead to you," shrugged Lafitte. "In truth, I was much too caught up in more pressing matters to investigate her motives. I know only what Marie has told me, and I swore I would not betray her confidence."

"May I speak with your woman?"

"That is not possible, I'm sorry. Marie is now in New Orleans visiting her sister."

"Please, Captain Lafitte, I must find my wife," Philippe pleaded. "Do you know where she went after she left Barataria? Once I find her I'm certain we can overcome our differences."

Somehow Jean believed Philippe. "I don't know where your wife is, and it may even be too late for you once you do find her," Jean confided, "but I can tell you that she left Barataria two weeks ago with Captain Stone, one of Jackson's officers."

"Captain Stone!" Philippe felt as if someone had just punched him in the stomach. "Are you telling me that they are lovers? That she has been with him since they left here together?"

"Easy, Monsieur St. Cyr," soothed Lafitte. "Everyone on Barataria is free to choose whomever he or she wishes, but in truth I do not believe that they had become lovers while on my island. What transpired after they left here I cannot say." Then he turned back to his letters from General Jackson. "I can tell you nothing more and I have pressing matters to

142

attend to," he said, dismissing Philippe with a shrug of his shoulders.

The next day Philippe was once again seated in General Jackson's small office. Lieutenant Gray was also present. After giving Jackson Lafitte's verbal message, and telling him that Gabby was no longer on Barataria but in New Orleans, he was surprised to see a smug smile flash across the lieutenant's face.

"If I may interrupt, sir," Lieutenant Gray broke in. "I saw your wife after I left here yesterday. She was in a marketplace disguised as a boy. When she realized that I recognized her she darted off into the crowd."

"I cannot believe she would go to such lengths to avoid me," said Philippe, shaking his head in bewilderment. "Did you follow her?"

"Yes, sir," said the lieutenant. "Two enlisted men and myself gave chase and almost had her cornered when she darted into the street and was knocked down by an oncoming carriage."

"Mon dieu," cried Philippe as he jumped from the chair in alarm. "Is she hurt? Where is she now?"

"I . . . she . . . I don't know," admitted the lieutenant, licking lips that had suddenly gone dry. "The carriage stopped and before I could push through the crowd the man and his driver had her inside and sped off."

Philippe's thoughts were in a jumble. Had Gabby been abducted, or had someone befriended her? Aloud he asked, "Did you recognize the man in the carriage?"

"I never saw him before, but he appeared to be a gentleman of means."

"I thought perhaps it might have been Captain Stone," Philippe said thoughtfully. "I may as well tell you, my wife and Captain Stone left Barataria together. Has the captain returned from Natchez yet?"

"I knew there was something going on between them,"

gloated Lieutenant Gray. He would have continued but Philippe's icy stare stopped him cold.

"Perhaps your wife is at Captain Stone's lodgings," offered General Jackson. "I know he lives not far from here on Rue Royale."

"*Merci*, General, I will go immediately," said Philippe, making straight for the door.

"One moment," cut in Jackson with such solemnity that Philippe stopped dead in his tracks. "I did not tell you this sooner because it seemed to have no bearing on your wife's disappearance but I can see now that it might be of great import to you."

Philippe's full attention was on Jackson. "Captain Stone is dead. He and his men were transporting the ammunition and flints he had purchased down river from Natchez on barges when they were attacked by Choctaws who came out from the riverbank in canoes."

Both Lieutenant Gray and Philippe sucked their breath in sharply. "How do you know this?" asked Philippe.

"Only one survivor lived to tell the tale. He was badly wounded and left for dead but was picked up by a trapper and brought back to the city," answered Jackson.

"I thought the Indians were friendly," said Philippe, still stunned by Jackson's disclosure.

"Mostly they are. But many of them have been recruited by English agents to aid their cause. I suspect that is the case here. Somehow, they learned of Stone's mission and wanted to stop the delivery of ammunition. The corporal who survived the attack said a white man, probably an English agent, directed the slaughter from the riverbank. Not only have I lost an excellent officer but ten men and the badly needed supplies," lamented Jackson. The pain and weariness in Jackson's care-lined face caused Philippe a moment of concern for the tall, gaunt soldier whose bent shoulders bore so much.

"I must find my wife," declared Philippe earnestly. "With Captain Stone gone she is alone in the city. She is very young and has no experience to cope with the dangers around her. If luck is with me I will find her at Captain Stone's lodgings on Rue Royale. If not . . ." His face, too, bore lines of anxiety and worry as he thought of the many unpleasant things that could happen to a woman alone in a city like New Orleans.

Luck had deserted Philippe. Captain Stone's former landlady at number 52, Rue Royal explained that he had given up his lodgings about two weeks earlier and left no forwarding address. She could not even tell Philippe if he had been alone or had a lady with him. The only thing left was to enlist the aid of his crewmen on the *Windward* and scour the *vieux carre* for Captain Stone's new lodgings.

Nearly a week was to pass before First Mate Mercier happened upon the Patalba Apartments and found that a Captain Stone and his wife occupied rooms on the second floor. But, according to the landlady, the captain had been gone for three weeks and his wife for two, although the rooms were paid for until the end of the month. Philippe hurried to the Rue Chartres address to question the landlady himself but learned nothing new. He did manage to persuade her to let him inside the rooms, and although he found a small amount of woman's clothing, there was nothing to suggest Gabby had ever been there. He thanked the woman with a general sum of money and returned to the *Windward*, his emotions in a turmoil.

Evidently Gabby had broken her wedding vows and lived openly as the wife of Captain Stone! It galled Philippe to think that she had willingly lain in another man's arms, responding to him with her own special kind of sweet ardor, freely giving what should have been his alone. That image, etched on his brain, was enough to drive him crazy. What if she carried her lover's child? He clenched his fists until his knuckles grew white. Once he found her did he love her enough to forgive her? he wondered, yet knowing in his heart the answer.

Long into the night Philippe paced his cabin trying to sort out his feelings. No matter what Gabby had done he still wanted her. Everything that had happened, even her refusal to return to him, was of his own making. He should have known from the start that she was not like Cecily. He realized now that he had dealt too harshly with her; he had been stern and arrogant, and yet, damnit, he had acted like a jealous fool instead of a loving husband with a lovely, young bride whose only fault was that she was too spirited for his liking. If he found her, could he become the kind of husband she deserved without allowing his jealous, overbearing nature to destroy her? How would he feel when he held her in his arms knowing another man had possessed her sweet body, known her wild passion? He smashed his fist into the bulkhead and cursed loudly as pain radiated clear up into his shoulder. Finally he went to bed with nothing settled in his mind except the knowledge that he would leave no stone unturned until he found his wife. He was certain that one day she would return to the rooms on Rue Chartres and he would be there waiting when she did.

Gabby had been at Gaspar house for nearly two weeks and in all that time she had not ventured outside the house or gardens within the neat little courtyard. Neither had she heard from Marcel. She had no complaints for she had been well looked after by Pitot and Lizette, but the boredom after the lively comings and goings on Barataria with Marie as a companion was nearly more than she could stand. She had exhausted the meager supply of books and both Pitot and Lizette proved decidedly taciturn. As time elapsed she began to fear that Rob would return from his mission and find her gone after she had promised she would be there waiting for him. Nearly a month had passed since he had left for Natchez

146

and she knew she must let him know she was safe. She thought about sending Pitot with a note but decided she didn't trust him enough for that. In the end she donned her carefully preserved boy's clothing and slipped out of the house unnoticed. If Rob was not at their rooms, she would leave a message and hurry back before she was missed. When Rob returned he would know where to find her.

The streets were crowded as usual and no one paid much attention to the slim lad who kept his eyes trained on the sidewalk as he passed. Gabby reached the Patalba Apartments without mishap and hurried up the iron stairs. When she fished the key from her pocket and opened the door she was disappointed to find the rooms deserted with no sign that Rob had returned. His clothing and gear were still missing and the apartment damp and dusty. Chills of foreboding prickled the nape of her neck as she sensed rather than felt something threatening in the empty rooms. She hurried to the desk to pen a note to Rob, all the while averting her eyes from the bed where once they had found happiness in each other. A faint noise alerted her and she looked up just as the door opened.

"Rob!" Gabby cried joyfully, expecting to see Rob's wide, boyish grin.

"Hello, Gabrielle," said Philippe softly. "I've been waiting for you."

"Philippe! You! How . . . how did you know where to find me?" Seeing him so unexpectedly had left her thoroughly shaken.

"I learned that Captain Stone and his 'wife' had taken these rooms," he replied, stumbling over the word wife.

Gabby flinched but held her ground. "I suppose you have already spoken to Lieutenant Gray?"

"*Oui*, and Jean Lafitte, when I went to Barataria."

"You went to Barataria?" gasped Gabby in amazement, wondering what Jean thought when Philippe St. Cyr came looking for his wayward wife.

"*Oui.* But I was too late. Lafitte told me you had already left with Captain Stone."

Gabby lifted her chin defiantly but said nothing to defend her actions.

"Do you love this captain so much that you would forsake your marriage vows?" asked Philippe bitterly.

"Rob is the kindest, gentlest man I have ever known," Gabby declared hotly. "What have you shown me except cruelty and unprincipled arrogance?"

"I asked you if you loved him, Gabby," persisted Philippe, gentling his voice.

"I don't know, Philippe," she answered honestly, averting his eyes. His granite gaze seemed to pierce her very soul. "But Rob loves me and wants me to be his wife."

"Impossible! You are my wife!"

"Divorce is not unheard of. Difficult, yes, but not impossible," she shot back.

"Gabby," began Philippe in a voice Gabby had never heard him use before, "say no more. There is something you should know."

"Nothing you have to say will change my mind about you, or about Rob."

"He is dead, Gabby. Your Rob is dead."

There was no way to soften the blow, Philippe reasoned as he watched all the color drain from Gabby's face. She had to learn the truth. With a cry of alarm Philippe leaped forward to catch her in his strong arms before she hit the floor. He laid her gently on the bed, noticing for the first time the snug fitting trousers she wore and the way her shirt pulled tightly across her swelling breasts.

Gabby slowly threaded her way through the maze of unconsciousness to surface into a world of sadness. Dear, sweet Rob was dead. She would never again see his merry, blue eyes smiling at her with their own brand of laughter. Tears sprang to her eyes as she recalled their last tender moments together.

"Captain Stone was your lover!" Philippe's voice was accusing, his flinty eyes chilling. "*Mon dieu*, Gabby, what has happened to you? Where is the girl who wanted to dedicate her life to *le bon dieu?*"

"You married her, Philippe, and she was never the same after that," replied Gabby flatly. "How did Rob die?"

After Philippe told her all he knew concerning Rob's death Gabby sobbed quietly, feeling more alone than she had ever been in her life.

Moved by her tears, Philippe sat on the bed next to her and smoothed the pale hair from her damp forehead. "I don't believe you really loved him, Gabby. But all that doesn't matter now. Can't you understand? He is dead and I am still your husband." Gabby grew very still. "Is it too late to start over? You must have felt something for me to have saved my life. I . . . I care for you, *ma chere*. And . . . and I still want you."

Astonishment followed disbelief across her face. What Philippe was asking was nearly impossible. She would always live in fear. She doubted that Philippe could forget so easily that Rob had been her lover. Even if he did forget, he could never forgive. Neither could she forget Cecily nor forgive him for murdering her.

"Would you strangle me as you did your first wife when the thought of another man possessing me begins to eat into your soul?" Gabby taunted, unable to keep her thoughts to herself.

"Gabby!" Philippe gasped, visibly paling. "Where did you ever get the idea that I strangled Cecily? How could you believe me capable of such a horrible deed?"

"You told me yourself that you killed your wife," Gabby

retorted. "Marcel said that she had been strangled. What else was I to think?"

"Marcel!" Philippe spat, the name bitter on his tongue. "Of course he would twist my words around to suit his own purpose. *Mon dieu,*" he cursed when he realized what she must have been thinking all this time. "And you thought you would be my next victim?" When she did not reply he knew he had hit upon the truth. The reason Gabby was unwilling to return to him was because she feared for her life. How could he have been so stupid?

"Listen to me, *ma chere,*" he said earnestly, "I did not kill Cecily with my own hands. I only felt responsible for her death, and still do."

"But . . . I don't understand."

"Please, just listen, then judge for yourself." Philippe pleaded, his eyes smoky with entreaty. "I met Cecily after I had returned to Martinique from France where I had attended school for ten years. I returned when I received news of my father's death. Bellefontaine was mine as was the responsibility of running a large sugar plantation. I worked hard for three years, and must have been quite a serious young man for I rarely ever entered into the gay, social life of St. Pierre as did my good friend and neighbor, Marcel Duvall. One day he introduced me to Cecily and my whole life changed overnight.

"On all of Martinique there was no one quite as beautiful as she and I fell in love with her beauty as well as her vitality and restless, fun-loving spirit. She flirted outrageously and seemed to come alive under the barrage of compliments showered upon her by the group of men who seemed always at her beck and call. I pursued her relentlessly and judging from her behavior during the few times we were alone together, I thought she returned my feelings. I proposed and she promptly rejected me, saying she was not ready to settle down, especially to a place as remote as Bellefontaine.

"But I was unwilling to accept that. She was like a sickness in my blood. Marcel warned me that she was not for me but of course he was jealous of my attentions toward her. Finally, in desperation, I approached her father with my offer of marriage. The poor man would have liked nothing better than for his rebellious daughter to marry me and settle down. I was immensely prosperous and considered a good catch for any girl on the island. He worried that Cecily would never find a husband to suit her. Between us we pressured her into marriage . . . but not before she extracted my promise to live in St. Pierre. I could deny her nothing." Philippe was on his feet now, nervously pacing back and forth. He paused to gaze out the window, his sightless eyes turned inward.

"Go on, Philippe," Gabby urged gently.

"We were deliriously happy, or at least I was, even though she turned down a honeymoon voyage aboard the *Windward*. She claimed that being penned up for so long would bore her to distraction. I was often away from the house, occupied with business having to do with my shipping lines. Cecily was free to do much as she pleased in my absence and I never questioned her. She spent money at such an alarming rate that finally I was forced to speak to her about it and that was our first serious quarrel.

"We had been in St. Pierre nearly a year when I received an urgent message from my overseer informing me that a fire had burnt the entire west section of cane including the distillery. I was needed immediately to bring some semblance of order to the chaos. When I told Cecily we were going to Bellefontaine for an indefinite stay she cried, fought, and railed againt it, but in the end was powerless to do anything except follow my wishes. That's when the real trouble started." He was looking directly at Gabby now, as if begging for her understanding of what transpired next.

"From the first day we arrived at Bellefontaine Cecily refused me her bed. And I, like a besotted fool, made excuses

151

for her behavior, telling myself that she would adjust and soon be in my bed again. One thing I can say about Cecily—she was an exceptionally passionate woman and I knew the dictates of her body would soon overrule her childish behavior.''

"And did they?'' asked Gabby. She could almost picture the willful, beautiful Cecily whom Philippe adored.

"Just the opposite," he admitted, his face bleak with remembrance. "She barely spoke to me. And then I did something that may inadvertently precipitated her death. I turned to Amalie for solace. I found in her arms that which my wife withheld.''

"Your mistress!''

"*Oui*, but she became my mistress only after Cecily refused to be a wife to me. I am a man, Gabby,'' he stated flatly, as if that explained everything. "When Amalie generously offered what Cecily denied, I accepted and found that when I was in her arms I could forget, if only for a time, what Cecily's constant refusals did to me.''

"Just who is Amalie?'' Gabby asked, curiosity getting the best of her.

"She is the daughter of Tante Louise, my housekeeper, and Gerard, my right hand man on the plantation. Both belong to me as well as Amalie and all three have always lived at Bellefontaine. Amalie is incredibly beautiful, as well as desirable,'' he added, sensing Gabby's next question.

"Is she black?'' asked Gabby, her eyes wide with disbelief. Surely Philippe would not bed a black slave!

"She is an octoroon and no darker than either of us.''

Gabby digested that statement, thinking of Marie, Jean's lovely mistress, before asking, "How did Cecily react to your taking a mistress?''

"One day she took the carriage and disappeared. I searched the plantation and when she did not return by nightfall I immediately set out for St. Pierre, thinking to find her at my townhouse. But she was not there, nor was she anywhere else in St. Pierre. After one week I returned to Bellefontaine, distraught, determined to give up Amalie when Cecily returned. After all, Cecily was my wife and would one day become the mother to my heirs. She was more important to me than anyone else. I still loved her desperately and was positive that the rift between us could be healed, even if I had to promise to return to St. Pierre to live as soon as the plantation was in order."

"And did she return?" Gabby was completely engrossed in the tale.

"No," said Philippe sadly. "I heard nothing from her or about her until two weeks later when Marcel Duvall's sisters came to Bellefontaine and informed me that Cecily had been staying at Le Chateau with Marcel. He had forbidden them to come to me but it seemed my willful wife had made a nuisance of herself. According to the Duvall girls, she began ordering the servants around and disrupting the entire household with her demands. So, risking their brother's anger, they decided to ask me to come and get my wayward wife. Needless to say, I went immediately.

"When I reached Le Chateau and confronted Cecily, she refused to return with me. It was obvious to me that she and Marcel had become lovers, but both vehemently denied it. Even the Duvall girls could neither prove nor disprove my claim. Marcel, who had been my friend, insisted he had only offered Cecily his hospitality. In the end I forced Cecily to return to Bellefontaine." Philippe ceased his incessant pacing and sat once more on the bed beside Gabby.

"I swore to Cecily that Amalie meant nothing to me, but she only laughed, saying I could take a dozen mistresses if I wished. She still refused to have anything to do with me and said she would leave me again if given the opportunity. I knew then that I must take drastic measures or risk losing her. I had her watched constantly during the day, and during the nights I stayed with her myself, forcing her to share my bed. A plan began to take shape somewhere in the dark recesses of my mind; I believed that once she became pregnant her whole attitude toward me and Bellefontaine would change; that she would once again become the loving, passionate woman I had married. By sheer brute force I overcame her weak protests in my efforts to impregnate her, forcing her submission until she conceived. I could sense her growing animosity, but she was a passionate woman and soon accepted my attentions once I broke through her feeble resistance.''

Gabby thought of her own surrender to Philippe and knew full well how relentless he could be once he set his mind on something.

''In a surprisingly short time Cecily told me she was pregnant. I believed her only when a doctor confirmed her condition. I was ecstatic to think that my plan had worked so well. Just as I had surmised, Cecily seemed to welcome motherhood and became surprisingly sweet and loving. It was like a miracle. I told Gerard to cease watching her movements and she was free once more to go wherever she desired. I even promised her we would divide our time between St. Pierre and Bellefontaine once the child was born.''

''If you were so happy why is she dead?'' asked Gabby with a puzzlied frown.

''It turned out I was the only one happy. One night, after we had just made love, she told me she would never again be a wife to me. She accused me of being selfish and thoughtless of her feelings. She said I was stifling her and that she intended to leave me and live in St. Pierre. I made the mistake of not taking her seriously, knowing pregnant women often have outbursts of that sort. I laughed and told her she was foolish, that the next day things would look brighter.

"Cecily jumped out of bed in a rage. I had never seen her angrier or more distraught." Philippe paused dramatically, his voice quivering. Gabby reached out and touched his arm. Her touch seemed to give him courage as he cleared his throat and continued. "She told me . . . that . . . that the last laugh was on me; that the child she carried was not mine. She said that Marcel had fathered her child."

"Oh, no," cried Gabby, feeling his pain in her own heart.

"I was stunned. I could not even move to stop her when she dashed from the bedroom. After all, where could she go at that time of night? I had misjudged her desperation to leave me and Bellefontaine. She fled the house and took a horse from the stable before I realized her intent. Only when I heard the pounding hoof beats did I rouse from my stupor and follow. I knew from the path she had taken through the banana groves that she was going to Le Chateau and Marcel. I was beside myself with fear. Just being in the groves was risky business and at night the danger was multiplied a thousand-fold. And she had at least a five minute head start while I had been immobilized by the bombshell she had just dropped.

"While in pursuit, I convinced myself that she had lied to me; that she said what she did to hurt me. True, she had been at Le Chateau two weeks but she and Marcel had both denied being lovers. As the minutes passed I became more and more certain that the child she carried was mine and I was determined to think of that innocent life in no other terms.

"Suddenly I heard a strange sound in the darkness ahead and spurred my own mount through the dense groves, ducking thick, ropy vines blocking my path. And then, *mon dieu*," Philippe gasped, reliving the horror of that night. "I saw her. She was hanging by the neck from a thick coil of vines; her horse stood nearby. I cut her loose, but it was too

155

late. She was already dead. Evidently she hadn't seen those vines in the darkness and rode straight into them. She was literally lifted from the horse's back and strangled, struggling, her feet just inches from the ground.''

Gabby put her face in her hands and quietly wept for the gay, misguided creature who could not stand the isolation of Bellefontaine and in the end had masterminded her own release. "I'm sorry, Philippe, truly sorry," she whispered. "But why did you tell me you had killed Cecily when in truth it was an accident?"

"Although the authorities were satisfied that it was an accident I judged myself as guilty of murder as if I had strangled her with my own hands."

"How can you say that?" protested Cecily.

"I tried every way I knew to keep her at Bellefontaine, even forcing a child on her she didn't want. I did my best to make her love me, but in the end succeeded only in destroying her and my child."

"You were certain then that the child was yours?"

"I suppose that is something I shall never know for sure. Even if Cecily and Marcel had been lovers, she herself could never have known for certain to whom the child belonged. She was my wife, so no matter what—I was the father. But from that day forward I could not think about Marcel without wanting to kill him. I will always blame him for feeding Cecily's discontent and encouraging her to leave me.''

"When did you decide to take another wife?"

"Not for a long, long time. I turned more and more to Amalie for solace, and to the sea," he replied. "More often than not I accompanied Captain Giscard aboard the *Windward* as supercargo, traveling up and down the American seaboard dodging English ships to reach port. By that time America and England were engaged in war and the *Windward* had become adept at running the blockade. We were in Boston when I was approached by a government agent who had heard of our prowess on the high seas. He asked if I would undertake a mission for the American government. I was to take the *Windward* to France and on a certain day contact an undercover agent in Paris. He was English but leaned toward the American side. He was supposed to have in his possession secret documents confirming that a major American port city would be attacked by the English, the probable dates, and the number of ships and men involved."

"New Orleans!" exclaimed Gabby.

"Exactly," replied Philippe. "I readily agreed to the mission. I had no reason to return to Martinique, and the mystery and danger of the mission appealed to me. The rest you know."

"No, Philippe, not all," insisted Gabby. "When did you decide to marry again, and why did you select me?"

"I had many lonely nights aboard the *Windward* and so many long hours to think. I had no heir and no one on Martinique I wanted to marry, although I could have had my pick of dozens of willing women. The more I thought about it the more I realized that I would never marry for love. My only reason for marrying was to produce heirs for Bellefontaine. As long as I was going to France I felt it was as good a time as any to choose another wife."

"But that's so cold and unfeeling," Gabby protested.

"That's how I wanted it," insisted Philippe. "I was determined to look to a convent for my next wife. I would choose someone far different from Cecily. My only prerequisite was good lineage for the future mother of my children. Beauty was not even an important consideration in the woman I would choose; innocence and submission were far more desirable to my thinking."

"But I possessed none of those qualities," Gabby remarked dryly. "Even the sisters said I was willful and too proud for my own good. Why, then, did you marry me?

Surely there were other women more tractable? Women you wouldn't have had to pay for as you did me. Or were you taken in by my father's gift of persuasion?"

"When first I met your father over the game table I thought him a braggart and wastrel. He lost heavily and handed out his IOUs until his creditors began demanding payment. I knew he was in trouble. Somehow he learned that I was in France looking for a wife and he approached me. He told me he had a daughter who would fill my needs perfectly. If you pleased me, a marriage could be arranged in return for the payment of his debts plus enough money to permit him and his wife to travel to Italy to take part in some half-witted scheme to put Napoleon back on the throne. But to answer your question, no, *ma chere,*" he said, riveting her with his smoky gaze, "I needed no persuasion to marry you. You were definitely not the kind of wife I hoped for, or even wanted, especially after Cecily, but once I looked into the depths of those violet eyes I was helplessly lost."

"You treated me with contempt from the very first," Gabby reminded him, the hint of accusation heavy in her voice.

"Don't you understand, *ma chere?*" Philippe said gently. "I had no choice. In order to maintain my authority over you I had to subdue the spirit you exhibited from the moment I met you. I vowed to tame you until you were meek and submissive before we reached Martinique. I could not allow myself to show my love again for fear I would destroy you just as I did Cecily. Finding Marcel aboard the *Windward* was a stroke of incredible bad luck and I had to be constantly vigilant when I detected your interest in each other. From the moment I saw you standing before me demurely attired with that awful headdress concealing your glorious hair I knew I had to have you. I . . . I think I loved you even then with your defiant little chin tilted in the air as you argued with your parents against marriage."

Gabby's heart lurched in her breast. If only he had told her of his love before now. If she had known she would never have turned to Rob.

"Don't look so astounded," Philippe said when he saw her dismay. "When I believed you dead I was devastated. That you should die thinking me cruel and heartless was unbearable. I vowed that if a miracle happened and you were restored to me I would make it up to you. Something held me in New Orleans. I refused to accept your death and even offered a reward, hoping, praying, to find you alive somewhere. It succeeded, because I have found you."

It seemed only natural for Philippe to take Gabby in his arms. "Is it too late for us, Gabby?" he asked aware of the tears trickling from beneath her lowered lids.

"What about Rob?" she asked hesitantly, fearfully.

"He's dead! Forget about him! Think only of us!"

"Can you live with the knowledge that he . . . that he and I . . . ?"

Philippe tensed. Only a twitch in a muscle that ran along his jaw revealed his inner turmoil. His continued silence sent Gabby's hopes plummeting.

"I don't think so, Philippe," Gabby said sadly, answering her own question. "I know your temper and your dark moods. You will never find it in your heart to forget . . . or forgive me for Rob."

"I drove you to it," Philippe stated emphatically. "It's not your fault you turned to Captain Stone in your loneliness. I . . . in a way I am grateful to him for bringing you back to me."

No matter how hard she tried Gabby could not make herself believe that Philippe was ready to take her back with open arms without recriminations. She wasn't even sure of her own feelings. Suddenly she thought of a way to test this newfound virtue of his.

"Philippe," she plunged on recklessly, "haven't you

wondered where I've been since Rob left?"

Her query startled him and he regarded her suspiciously for a moment, his eyes wary. It was true, he thought. In his excitement over finding her again he had not thought to ask where she had been during the past weeks, or how she had existed. He was not even sure he wanted to know. His brooding silence did not speak well for his earlier resolve to forget and forgive.

Lifting her chin and speaking slowly, Gabby said, "I have been with Marcel Duvall!"

"Marcel Duvall!" Philippe repeated, his face colorless beneath his tan. "Will that man never be out of my life? I thought him gone from New Orleans long ago. Where did he find you, Gabby? Or did you find him?"

"We sort of found each other. And purely by accident," Gabby explained. "His carriage ran into me when Lieutenant Gray was pursuing me. He took me to his sister's house. I hoped to become the governess of his sister Celeste's children when they returned to the city."

"Ah, *oui*," muttered Philippe thoughtfully, "Lieutenant Gray said he did not recognize the man who carried you off in his carriage." He looked at her sharply. "If Marcel's sister and her family were out of the city then you and he were alone in the house." His eyes became hooded but not before Gabby noted their icy glaze.

Gabby knew that the moment of truth had arrived. Would Philippe believe nothing had happened between her and Marcel? Aloud she said, "Marcel offered me a place to stay until Rob returned. I was grateful to him."

White ridges of barely suppressed anger formed around his mouth. "How grateful, Gabby? Did you offer him your body in gratitude as you did your captain?"

Her hand swung back in a wide arc and struck with resounding force. Suddenly all the anger rushed out of him and she felt almost sorry for him as his body appeared to deflate before her eyes.

"Marcel has never been my lover nor did I ever intend him to be! In fact, he left the day after I arrived at his sister's house and I have not seen him since."

She was startled by the look of pure joy in Philippe's eyes. Did he really believe her? she wondered. His accusations had pained her but if he believed her now there might still be hope for them. "You do believe me, don't you, Philippe?" she asked with bated breath.

His eyes gentled to a blue-gray haze and it took him only a moment to answer. "*Oui, ma chere*, I believe you. Those hateful words were out before I could stop them. It's just that I cannot bear to hear Marcel's name without becoming enraged. He had insinuated himself into my life too many times with disastrous results."

He kissed her then, slowly, longingly, as a spasm of erotic quivers splintered through her and a flood of remembrances drowned her in desire. Her thoughts were of eternal, love-filled nights spent in his arms; of a storm that had swept away her innocence forever and of the tender man she had caught fleeting glimpses of when she had pierced through his armor.

When Gabby neither protested nor pulled out of his arms, Philippe became bolder, moving his lips to the hollow at the base of her neck where a pulse throbbed wildly, then to her breast after he had released the top buttons of her shirt. She moaned low in her throat, spurring him on as his hands worked furiously to remove the rest of her clothing. His own clothes seemed to fall away of their own accord and Gabby felt the hot length of his muscular frame stretch out beside her.

"I want you, Gabby," he whispered hoarsely. "*Mon dieu*, how I've missed you!"

His lips left little ridges of fire along the length of her body and his hands found her ready for him as he probed her innermost places. She was excited and aroused as she never had been that one time with Rob. Rob's lovemaking had been gentle and achingly sweet, but Philippe's left her breathless with desire, consumed by an unquenchable blaze of passion.

Suddenly, through a haze of rapture, Gabby became aware that Philippe's hands had abruptly left her body and he was staring at her with smoky intensity. "Don't stop, Philippe," she pleaded, hardly aware of what she was saying.

But still he held himself in check. As much as he wanted her, Philippe realized that he could not ake her until he asked a question of her, even if it meant losing her. Never again would he suffer through the hell of Cecily's last words that fateful night of her death.

Drawing a deep, steadying breath, he asked, "Gabby, *ma chere*, you may hate me for asking this of you, but I cannot continue until I know. Never again will I be tortured by doubts and you have never lied to me yet." He paused dramatically while Gabby struggled to grasp his meaning.

"I must know, Gabby? Are you . . . I mean . . . you are not carrying Captain Stone's child, are you?" he blurted out. "Can you understand why I must ask this? Try to put yourself in my place."

"What if I am expecting a child, Philippe?" asked Gabby, anger building in her blood.

"I will accept it because it is yours, and, *oui*, damn it, even love it for the father was a brave man who loved you. But the child can never become my heir."

Slowly her anger diminished as Gabby digested Philippe's words. In her own mind they proved that he had truly changed, and that he did love her. She knew for a certainty that she did not carry Rob's seed as a result of their one night together and quickly put Philippe's mind at rest.

"Philippe, *cheri*, Rob and I had but one night together

and I know without a doubt that I am not pregnant from that encounter.''

''Ma chere! Mon amour! Let us hope this encounter will prove more fruitful,'' he cried joyfully as he sought to reignite the flames that nearly devoured them moments before. Gabby felt his hunger, was overpowered by it, and then she felt her own hunger being drawn out as he lost himself in her velvet softness. She began to move in abandon, in a longing so intense that her body began to hurt, then grow wings as she exploded in a million tiny fragments, just moments before Philippe's own searing climax.

Chapter Nine

AFTER THEIR climactic reunion, Gabby returned to the *Windward* with Philippe. Their plan was to sail for Martinique as soon as possible. The entire city of New Orleans was in turmoil. They had received word on December twelfth that the English fleet, under Admiral Cochrane, was anchored off Lake Borgne. General Jackson was under the impression that the English would not row sixty miles across the lake to attack so he had left the lake guarded only by a small flotilla of gunboats that were quickly captured on December fourteenth.

Jackson did not know that the English had started ferrying their 5,700-man army halfway across Lake Borgne in scrounged flatboats to Pea Island. Then, in a stroke of good luck for the English, a cooperative Spanish fisherman, for a sum of money, showed them the Bayou Bienvenue, the only waterway leading toward New Orleans that hadn't been blocked by Jackson. It led to the left bank of the Mississippi, less than eight miles from the city.

It was supposed to have been guarded by Major Villiers, whose family owned the land along the bayou. Villiers mistakenly believed there was little chance for attack there so he left only a token picket guard.

On December twenty-third, the English entered Bayou Bienvenue and seized the Villiers plantation along with Major Villiers himself, and rested there until the entire troop had been ferried across Lake Borgne. Somehow Major Villiers managed to escape and make his way into New Orleans to warn Jackson that the English were within eight miles of the city with hundreds of men.

When Philippe heard the news, he hurried to Jackson to put at his disposal his entire crew from the *Windward*. The general accepted with alacrity, then left immediately to set up his line of defense behind Rodriguez Canal. It was there he intended to wait for the English to attack. On December twenty-fourth, Christmas Eve, Philippe said goodbye to Gabby.

Although she had anticipated his departure, she could not still the pang of fear his leaving caused her. "Please, Philippe," she begged, "let me go with you. There must be something I can do, even if it is to look after the wounded."

"No, *ma chere*," he admonished in a voice that brooked no opposition. "You will remain here until I return. It is too dangerous out there amid the rifle shot and exploding shells. I won't risk losing you again."

"What about you?" she stormed, unwilling to be put off so easily. "There is danger for you also."

"But I can take care of myself, *ma petite*," he replied, ignoring her display of anger. "Come," he teased, "kiss me goodbye like a good soldier's wife." She flew into his arms and later tried mightily to remain dry-eyed while he loaded his men and weapons into a wagon and took off without a backward glance.

Christmas Day was a dreary affair and Gabby left the ship to go out into the streets hoping to glean news of the battle filtering into the city. She learned that one of Jean Lafitte's ships, *Carolina*, was pounding the English on the left while American troops were attacking the right, blunting the English spearhead. Gabby breathed a silent prayer for Philippe and her Baratarian friends and returned to the *Windward*.

She heard nothing more until December twenty-eight

165

when the city was agog with the news that another armed Baratarian ship, *Louisiana*, had begun raking the English, hopelessly pinning down Sir Parkenham's troops, who had begun an attack on the American lines. Needless to say, the attack had finally been called off.

On January 1, 1815, after three days spent bringing up ten eighteen-pound guns and four twenty-four pounders from their ships, floating them on canoes and dragging them through swamps, the English, under cover of darkness, scooped out four batteries only 800 yards from General Jackson's lines. They used sugar casks to build up the parapets and opened fire as soon as the early morning fog burned off. It was ten minutes before the American guns, manned mostly by Jean Lafitte and his men, opened fire, but when they did the effect was devastating. The reverberations were heard all the way to New Orleans. With amazing accuracy, sugar and splinters flew in all directions as Lafitte's big twenty-four pounders and thirty-two pounders pulverized the English batteries. In contrast, little damage was inflicted on the American line as most of the Englishmen's shots plowed harmlessly into the American earthwork. The defeat was mostly due to the expert marksmanship of Lafitte and his Baratarians, who had remained true to their commitment to fight for Louisiana.

When Philippe did not return to New Orleans, Gabby could not stand the waiting and not knowing if he were dead or alive. In a surge of restlessness she dressed in her boy's garb and, determined to find a way to reach the battleground, went again into the streets in an attempt to locate a conveyance. But to her chagrin it seemed that there wasn't a horse, carriage, or wagon in all New Orleans that wasn't already put to good use by Jackson and his men. She dejectedly began retracing her steps back to the *Windward* when she heard a voice calling her name.

"Gabby, *mon dieu,* is that you?"

Gabby whirled, her eyebrows raised in surprise, for she knew no one in New Orleans except for Marcel, and the voice greeting her was female. Her look of surprise quickly turned to that of pleasure when Gabby recognized Marie perched atop the driver's seat of a small wagon. "Marie! How good it is to see you again!" she cried, quickly reaching Marie's side.

"And I you, *cherie*," Marie answered. "But where are you going dressed like that? Is your Captain Stone at Rodriguez Canal fighting the English?"

"Rob is dead," said Gabby, fighting to keep the tremor from her voice. "I am back with my husband and he is fighting with Jackson."

"Ah, I was wondering if your husband ever found you. Jean told me he showed up on Barataria looking for you. All is well, then?" she asked, taking it at a glance Gabby's bright eyes and flushed cheeks.

"I . . . *oui*, I think all is well. But tell me, where are you headed and what are you doing in New Orleans?"

"I have been in the city several weeks to help my sister who recently had a baby. Now I go to join Jean on the battlefield."

It was as if Gabby's prayers had been answered. Here was a way to reach the battlefield, to help her friends from Barataria, and at the same time to search for Philippe. "Take me with you, Marie," she begged, breathless with excitement. "I can do anything you can do and I owe so much to you and Jean. Let me repay my debt by offering my help."

Marie looked doubtful. "What will your husband say? Evidently he left you behind where you would be safe."

"I haven't seen Philippe for over two weeks," lamented Gabby. "Perhaps he is already dead. But no matter what, I cannot sit idly back and do nothing. If you will not take me I will find my way by myself."

Marie knew Gabby well enough to realize that she would indeed find her way to the front and perhaps be in more danger than if she were among friends, "Get in," she finally said, "Jean will welcome your help."

In no time at all they were out of the city and on the road to Rodriguez Canal. The date was January 7, 1815. Gabby used the time it took to reach the Baratarian camp to tell Marie all that had happened to her since she had left the island. Marie listened in rapt silence, clicking her tongue several times throughout the telling.

"Perhaps it has all worked out for the best, *cherie*," consoled Marie when she heard the details of Rob's death. "It's obvious to me that you are happy with your husband."

Along the way they passed groups of laughing Creoles, young men shouting and cavorting as they made their way to join the war. Marie and Gabby traveled as far as they could along the road and then Marie drove part way into a field and stopped. "We've got to walk from here," she advised as both girls jumped nimbly from the wagon.

They continued on, passing men who were busily scooping dirt from a wide dry ditch and others who were unloading bales of cotton from wagons. Beyond the ditch lay a treeless field and farther off stretched the river. Soon they saw the big cannon and Marie ran the rest of the way to reach Lafitte who was resting under a sprawling live oak tree.

The lovers were in each other's arms, hugging and kissing when Gabby approached. "Did you bring help?" Jean asked skeptically as he ran an appraising eye over the slim youth accompanying his beautiful mistress.

Marie clapped her hands delightedly and laughed. "It is Gabby, *cheri*, she has come to help."

Jean looked dubiously at the slight figure but nevertheless gallantly welcomed her. Many hands would be needed to help load the big guns he had brought from his stronghold and he put her into the able hands of Dominique You who explained to her what must be done. Her job would be to dip the rammer into a bucket of water, then use it to cleanse and cool the bore and to tamp the cannonball. The instructions were simple enough and in no way did You minimize the danger to her while exposed to enemy fire. He gave her all the time in the world to change her mind but there was no pulling back now. She was determined to do her part and fight beside her friends.

Up and down the line word was out that the English would attack at dawn the next day, January 8, and Gabby spent an uncomfortable night huddled in a blanket, staring into the embers of a dying fire, wondering if Philippe was alive and if so if he was nearby.

It was nearly dawn when she jerked awake as someone handed her a tin cup of coffee and a hard roll. She ate it gratefully, peering into the wet mist shrouding the oaks until they appeared like grotesque ghosts reaching out moss-covered tentacles. Suddenly a high explosion echoed through the fog and she jumped to her feet.

"Hold fire!" shouted Dominique You to his anxious comrades. "When I see their guns I will give the order to fire." He trained a ship's glass across the field and gave a sigh of contentment when he saw a flash as one of the English cannon roared into action. He made a few adjustments with a gunscrew before he cried, "Now!" and lit the touchhole with a match.

After that Gabby was kept too busy to think about anything except darting through the cotton bales, swabbing the throat of the cannon, waiting until powder and shot had been fed it, then seating the ball firmly with her rammer. She caught glimpses of English soldiers but was much too occupied to worry about musket balls picking away at the barricade or the cannon balls roaring dangerously overhead. The noise was devastating. Her ears rang painfully with shouting men, rifle shot, and thundering cannon. The mingling of sounds became as a sword, driving into her perspiring, exhausted body.

The acrid taste of gunpowder was thick in her mouth and her face and arms were black with it. Even though her limbs ached from the unaccustomed exercise, she drove herself on until, blessedly, the guns felt silent. Someone was handing her a cup of water and she drank greedily. "It is over?" she asked Dominique hopefully.

"I do not think so," he answered, "but rest while you can. They probably are bringing up replacements."

The battlefield was cluttered with dead and dying brave men on both sides. Then the big guns jumped into action and once again Gabby took her place beside the long barrel.

Gabby had no conception of time, aware only of the cries of the wounded around her and of the weariness eating into her bones. The big guns continued unceasingly until the first hints of scarlet tinted the evening sky. The rifles stopped firing first, and then the cannon, too, fell silent before Gabby realized that an encompassing stillness had fallen over the battlefield. It took her several minutes to come to the conclusion that the attack had been destroyed and the Americans victorious. She collapsed on a mound of dirt, tired beyond belief but immensely proud of her part in the melee.

"It is over, *cherie*," said Dominique, hunkering down beside her. "Your help was invaluable. You are a good cannoneer." In her weariness she was unable to respond to his compliment. He patted her shoulder and left her to a well-earned rest.

Gabby leaned her head against a bale of cotton and closed her eyes. Somehow she slept, blocking out the gory sights and gruesome sounds. She heard nothing when Jean Lafitte approached with a tall man who was blackened with gunpowder and limped from a flesh wound in his thigh. Her cap had long since fallen off and dirty strands of pale hair was plastered across her grimy face, but to Philippe she was the loveliest sight he had ever seen!

170

After the battle had ended, Philippe was dispatched to the Baratarian camp with a message from General Jackson and had been astounded with the news that Gabby was here, on the battlefield. What's more, he learned from Lafitte that she had fought bravely alongside the best of his men.

Philippe was undecided whether to kiss her or beat her, but when he saw her, filthy and covered with bruises, he thanked *le bon dieu* for keeping her safe. She did not awaken even when he picked her up and placed her in the wagon Jean had put at his disposal. It was not until Philippe was stripping the grimy clothing from her after they reached the *Windward* that she opened her eyes. She was too tired to speak but her smile was enough.

Two days later the English fleet slipped anchor and sailed back to England in defeat. Jean Lafitte was given a full pardon and Gabby and Philippe attended the dinner given in his honor by Governor Claiborne. Lafitte and his men were recognized for singularly distinguishing themselves in defending the city of New Orleans against the British.

With the British gone, Philippe made plans for their departure to Martinique, and two days before they left, they learned that on February 11, 1815, the British sloop, *Favorite,* carrying a flag of truce, slipped into New York harbor bringing copies of the peace treaty signed in Ghent in December. It was ironic that although peace had actually been reached on December 24, the battle for New Orleans was fought after the treaty was signed. But the battle was a great moral victory for America. Jackson's victory was so emphatic that it gave birth to a legend of American invincibility that would live on and on. A new feeling of national pride invaded the country and the decisive victory gained it new respect abroad.

On March 1, 1815, the *Windward* slipped her moorings and glided into the mist on a long delayed voyage to Martinique. If Gabby looked forward to a life of bliss and happiness she was in for a shock. A whole new world awaited her on the sun-drenched island of Martinique.

Part Two

Martinique

1815-1817

Chapter Ten

IT WAS seven days before the *Windward* cut a path through the Yucatan Channel and sailed into the Caribbean Sea. It was another seven days before they approached a cloud-shrouded island that seemed to spark Philippe's excitement.

"That's Saba," he pointed. "It's the first of a chain of islands you'll see as we near Martinique."

"It looks majestic," ventured Gabby.

"It's a volcanic island. All these islands are. Some are desert and some are covered with dense jungle."

"And is Martinique one of the jungle-covered islands?"

"Yes, so thick you need a machete just to take a walk. The first French settlers literally drove the jungle back to clear the way for the cane fields."

"Then it truly is a wilderness," Gabby said with dismay.

"Hardly a wilderness," Philippe laughed. "St. Pierre is a favorite port for all the sailors in the world. If the wind holds out we should reach St. Pierre within two days."

At first sight, each mist-shrouded new island to come into view seemed but a dim silhouette. As they drew nearer the beauty of bending palms and villages built on the shore as well as in extinct volcano craters took Gabby's breath away.

Never had she seen such an incredible, luminous blue sea where water and horizon blended into the azure of the sky. Lush green islands surrounded by white rings of sand appeared to float atop the water. She lifted her face to the hot Caribbean sun that seemed to welcome her to paradise. Philippe's arm tightened around her waist and for a moment she was truly content. She closed her mind to what awaited her on Martinique. Nothing existed now except the man by her side and her new life at Bellefontaine. Only time would tell if she was a child living with childish dreams, for at the end of their journey awaited . . . Amalie.

Just as Philippe predicted, two days later Martinique appeared as a misty gray shadow on the morning's horizon. Entranced, Gabby watched as its mass grew and changed from blue and then to emerald in a turquoise sea. It wasn't long before she could see the mountains and long, green spurs of land reaching like fingers out to the sea, the aftermath of ancient lava flows now overgrown with tropic growth. Philippe explained that the sweeps of gold plain in the jungle were cane fields. But the dominating feature was Mt. Pelee rising majestically more than 4,000 feet above the ocean, the dangerous, brooding giant that gave birth to Martinique. Gabby eyed the massive monster somewhat skeptically until Philippe assured her it was now extinct, its cone asleep in a bed of fluffy, white clouds.

St. Pierre was on the lee side of the island, in the shadow of Mt. Pelee. The town appeared to hug the white crescent of beach all but obscured by lush growth and tall swaying trees. Terraced tiers of pale yellow houses with red tile roofs rambled along narrow crooked streets shaded by towering palms. A high ridge circled the town from behind, thick with trees, overhanding vines, and brilliant blooms. Philippe pointed out two rivers running through the town into the harbor. It was like something out of a picture book.

"Look!" pointed Gabby excitedly, "Canoes are coming out to meet us."

Philippe smiled when he saw a flotilla of canoes packed with naked brown boys come nearer. They appeared to be between ten to fourteen years old and were using pieces of flat board for paddles. Their precise movements were poetry in motion.

Gabby let out a small gasp when she realized the boys were

GET UP TO 4 FREE BOOKS!

You can have the best romance delivered to your door for less than what you'd pay in a bookstore or online. Sign up for one of our book clubs today, and we'll send you **FREE* BOOKS** just for trying it out...**with no obligation to buy, ever!**

HISTORICAL ROMANCE BOOK CLUB

Travel from the Scottish Highlands to the American West, the decadent ballrooms of Regency England to Viking ships. Your shipments will include authors such as CONNIE MASON, SANDRA HILL, CASSIE EDWARDS, JENNIFER ASHLEY, LEIGH GREENWOOD, and many, many more.

LOVE SPELL BOOK CLUB

Bring a little magic into your life with the romances of Love Spell—fun contemporaries, paranormals, time-travels, futuristics, and more. Your shipments will include authors such as LYNSAY SANDS, CJ BARRY, COLLEEN THOMPSON, NINA BANGS, MARJORIE LIU and more.

As a book club member you also receive the following special benefits:

- **30% OFF all orders through our website & telecenter!**
- **Exclusive access to special discounts!**
- **Convenient home delivery and 10 day examination period to return any books you don't want to keep.**

There is no minimum number of books to buy, and you may cancel membership at any time. See back to sign up!

*Please include $2.00 for shipping and handling.

YES! ☐

Sign me up for the **Historical Romance Book Club** and send my TWO FREE BOOKS! If I choose to stay in the club, I will pay only $8.50* each month, a savings of $5.48!

YES! ☐

Sign me up for the **Love Spell Book Club** and send my TWO FREE BOOKS! If I choose to stay in the club, I will pay only $8.50* each month, a savings of $5.48!

NAME: _____

ADDRESS: _____

_____

TELEPHONE: _____

E-MAIL: _____

☐ **I WANT TO PAY BY CREDIT CARD.**

☐ VISA   ☐ MasterCard   ☐ DISCOVER

ACCOUNT #: _____

EXPIRATION DATE: _____

SIGNATURE: _____

Send this card along with $2.00 shipping & handling for each club you wish to join, to:

Romance Book Clubs
20 Academy Street
Norwalk, CT 06850-4032

Or fax (must include credit card information!) to: 610.995.9274. You can also sign up online at www.dorchesterpub.com.

*Plus $2.00 for shipping. Offer open to residents of the U.S. and Canada only. Canadian residents please call 1.800.481.9191 for pricing information.
If under 18, a parent or guardian must sign. Terms, prices and conditions subject to change. Subscription subject to acceptance. Dorchester Publishing reserves the right to reject any order or cancel any subscription.

JOIN NOW!

nude but could not turn her eyes from the beautiful, lithe forms. Before she knew what he was doing, Philippe reached into his pocket and tossed a handful of coins overboard. The boys, who had moments before been calling out in Creole French, plunged into the water, diving after the coins until the sea around the ship was alive with small bodies thrashing and diving into the cool blue depths.

The ship continued to ease toward the pier and soon men began scurrying about preparing to dock. As soon as the gangplank was in place, Gabby gave one final backward glance to the place where she had been forced into womanhood before allowing Philippe to guide her down the gangplank.

Gabby's passage through St. Pierre was an adventure of sights and sounds, a kaleidoscope of colors and of happy, smiling people whose skin ranged from light yellow to ebony. Laughter was punctuated by calls of women vending vegetables and fruits and carrying around loaves of bread from flat, wooden trays balanced on their heads. They wore plain robes of vivid hues, girded close to their bodies to leave their dark, flashing legs bare and free. Each bright costume was topped by a headdress consisting of a magnificent madras kerchief wound like a turban around the head with one corner pulled through the top at the front.

Some of the light-skinned women wore rich finery more opulent than any worn in the courts of France. The loose embroidered blouses dipped low in front to reveal smooth skinned, golden bosoms, and skirts, called jupes, rising shorter in the front, hugged slim supple hips that swayed provocatively as they walked. Below the brilliant yellow or stripped turbans, huge dangling earrings glittered in the sun. Some wore as many as five strands of gold beads around willowy throats rivaling the flash of earrings. Philippe explained that the colorful madras turban was worn by all *filles de couleur*.

The shiny skins of the men glistered with health, their trim figures bereft of the slightest bulge except for rippling muscles that corded arms and thighs. They wore little more than modesty demanded, their entire costume consisting of a single pair of trousers cut off or torn at the knee and held with a rope belt.

Gabby's head was awhirl by the time they reached Philippe's townhouse, a pale yellow structure with thick, stuccoed walls and red tile roof. The house was in a quiet section of town built around a garden shaded with silk cotton trees and tamarinds. Gabby found it tastefully furnished and more comfortable than any home she had previously known.

A staff of three was in attendance; cook, maid, and butler, and they welcomed her with a show of childlike affection. Speaking in a corrupt form of French called *patois*, Matilde the cook insisted on preparing a true Creole meal for them while Jeanette, the pretty mulatto maid, fluttered about the bedroom clicking her tongue over what she called her new mistress's woeful lack of adequate wardrobe.

Gabby was hard put to follow the *patois* spoken by the house servants. Mainly she waited for Philippe to translate for her.

True to her word Matilde set out a tempting feast for the newlyweds. There was a gumbo soup, called *calalou*, fish broiled with pimento, peppers and onions, and a pudding of molasses and manioc flour called *matete*. When Gabby exclaimed over the simple but delicious meal Philippe told her that the meal was little more than country fare, that at Bellefontaine meals would be more elaborate, prepared mainly in European style. Still, Gabby ate with shameless gusto, each tasty morsel a delicacy after the monotonous fare aboard the *Windward*.

"Are there many servants at Bellefontaine?" Gabby asked after the meal was concluded and they were seated side by side on the settee in the *salle*.

Philippe swirled the amber liquid around in his glass a moment before answering. His thoughts seemed only on the excellent brandy he was about to consume. "Altogether there are five hundred slaves on Bellefontaine," he said slowly. "Twelve or so are house slaves and the rest work in the cane fields and banana groves."

"Philippe!" gasped Gabby. "You said slaves. Do you own these people? Have you bought and paid for them? Are they yours to do what you will with them for the rest of their lives?"

"Just as I have bought and paid for you, *ma petite*, to do with what I will for the rest of your life," jibed Philippe thoughtlessly.

Gabby's head shot up and she drew back as if slapped, the sharp intake of her breath audible in the stillness of the room. Once again he had stunned her by his cruelty. "I am your wife, Philippe," she lashed out defensively. "Surely I am more to you than your black slaves?" The knowledge that he had paid her father for her still rankled as did the idea that he owned other human beings as well.

Suddenly aware of the hurt in Gabby's eyes Philippe was immediately chastised. What made him say such a cruel thing? he wondered as he sought to soothe her bruised feelings. "Forgive me, *mon amour*. I don't know what made me speak to you like that," he apologized, taking her into his arms. "I do not enjoy owning another human but it is the way of things here. Without slaves it would not be possible to run our plantations or work our fields. We, on Martinique, are completely dependent on slave labor. Someday, though, I foresee a time when all slaves will be free, but at least on my plantation I know they are happy, well fed and well cared for. You shall see the truth of my words for yourself once we are at Bellefontaine."

Somewhat mollified, Gabby relaxed in the protective circle of Philippe's arms, ignoring the small tugging deep within her heart. It was difficult to believe Philippe could speak so harshly to her after what they had shared, after his declaration of love. Or was he still punishing her for Rob? Finally, his lips, insistent upon hers, dissolved her plaguing thoughts into nothing more than vague misgivings as he led her into a world of delight. Philippe made love to her with slow, dizzying passion, his hands and lips fanning the embers of her feelings into leaping flames until her mind could no longer function.

The days that followed were happy ones for Gabby. Whenever Philippe wasn't busy at his office on the docks he took her about in the carriage to show her St. Pierre. She was charmed by the city even though they were obliged at times to leave their carriage behind and walk through the narrow streets broken by steps that ascended the ridge of dark lava rock now overgrown with vegetation. The same clear water that bubbled along the gutter cooling the city fed the sparkling fountains.

Once again Gabby was struck by the beauty of the dark-skinned people. Particularly the quadroons, those having one-fourth Negro blood, whose dresses were the richest and most ornate. Philippe explained that even French girls of good breeding were able to walk the streets in safety as long as they were accompanied by a chaperone.

The marketplace was in the savanne, a paved square around a fountain where every manner of fish was sold as well as vegetables and exotic fruits, most of which Gabby had never seen before. Some were identified to her as guavas, mangoes, avocadoes, and nutmeg.

Oftimes they stopped at a sidewalk café for a cool drink before returning to the townhouse. At first Gabby disliked the taste of the concoction Philippe ordered, called *bavarois*, a mixture of mostly milk with a touch of rum and sugar and whipped to a foam, but before long she came to savor its refreshing taste. Always they returned to the townhouse by midafternoon, sleep and the cool interior of the stucco building the only reprieve from the afternoon heat. Gabby grew to enjoy the long naps to awaken refreshed as the sun hung low in the western sky.

Many days were spent at the dressmaker on Rue des Urselines, for Gabby owned nothing suitable for her role as wife of an important sugar planter. The dresses Philippe ordered from Madame Corday were cool, featherlight, and of the most expensive fabrics. They were feminine, adorned with rows of lace and shirring. A parasol to ward off the hot sun accompanied each costume. The lingerie was whisper soft, extravagant and quite immodest to Gabby's eyes. But she did not protest, taking girlish delight in the lavish profusion of light, airy costumes Philippe chose for her. The cost seemed a small fortune to her, which in fact it was. When she ventured to mention his extravagance he told her that if she must take her place in society she must dress accordingly. One day she would be obliged to be his hostess, to entertain other planters and their wives.

Little occurred to mar Gabby's happiness during those weeks spent in St. Pierre except a small, plaguing physical complaint that she tried hard to hide from Philippe. At first the mild bouts of nausea that struck shortly after he had arisen and left for the office weren't hard to conceal, but as time passed they occurred with frightening frequency, becoming more and more virulent. Still she would not tell Philippe of the strange malady. It was only by chance that he discovered her illness. He had already departed the house one morning when he realized he had left an important manifest at home. Retracing his steps back to the bedroom he found Gabby, weak and pale, retching into the slop bowl, her trembling body bathed in sweat as waves of nausea convulsed her slight form.

"*Mon dieu*, Gabby," he cried in alarm as he rushed to her side. "You are ill, *ma petite*. Why haven't you told me?" Tenderly he brushed strands of damp hair from her white face. "How long has this been going on?" he asked, gesturing to the slop bowl.

"Nearly a fortnight," Gabby grimaced, her hand to her roiling stomach.

"A fortnight!" Philippe repeated angrily. "And you have not told me? Don't you realize you may have contracted some dread tropical fever or disease? Get back in bed," he ordered, softening his voice when he saw her stricken face, "and I will summon the doctor immediately."

Dr. Renaud, a kindly mannered, white-haired man with a droopy mustache, regarded Gabby from merry blue eyes for some minutes before abruptly dismissing Philippe from the room. Then he addressed Gabby in a fatherly tone, putting her completely at ease before asking some rather pointed questions that left her pale cheeks becomingly tinged with crimson. His examination was through and he grunted in satisfaction when his probings seemed to confirm his initial diagnosis. Such was her innocence that Gabby gaped in wide-eyed wonder when the doctor disclosed the nature of her illness. A baby! She hugged the thought to herself, picturing in her mind's eye a miniature of Philippe; someone all her own to love who would love her in return with no reserve or recimination. Gabby and the doctor discussed at length such things as the date of birth and precautions she should take to assure a healthy child and safe delivery. Then he left her to her own happy thoughts.

Dr. Renaud found Philippe in the salle nervously pacing the floor, rum glass in hand, positive that Gabby suffered some fatal, rare disease. He started violently when the doctor announced his diagnosis.

"Are you certain, Doctor?" Philippe asked worriedly. "My wife is still a child herself. Will there be any danger to her?"

"Believe me, Monsieur St. Cyr, all will go well. 'Tis true she is young and not quite as robust as our island-bred girls tend to be but my advice is to take her to Bellefontaine where Tante Louise can pamper her and fill her with some of her famous tsannes. Her health is good, and given her youth, I foresee no problems. The nausea should disappear in a few weeks. When her labor starts summon me if Tante Louise cannot handle it or expects some difficulty."

"And when is the delivery to take place?" queried Philippe, still in a state of shock.

"In about six months I should think."

"A baby," Philippe repeated. "You must pardon me, Doctor, though I had hoped for an heir I had not expected one so soon." His chest seemed to expand with pride before the doctor's eyes.

"Bah! It is always the same with you new husbands," announced Dr. Renaud with an exasperated shrug of his shoulders. "You impale your brides nightly like a mighty stallion put to stud and then act surprised when the natural culmination of your ruttings comes to fruition. But if I am any judge, an heir will not displease you."

"An heir will be most welcome," Philippe averred heartily. "It is just that my wife is still so young."

"Eh? Did you think to spare her the ordeal of losing her maidenhead?" guffawed the doctor, his eyes twinkling mischievously.

Philippe's reddened face caused Dr. Renaud a moment of merriment before he went on. "I thought not. Well, do not worry, *mon ami,* your wife will survive motherhood several times over, no doubt; for a lusty fellow like yourself will likely sire many children."

Philippe had but one question to ask. "Will it harm her if I . . . that is . . . if we . . . ?"

"Do not worry, *mon ami,*" laughed the doctor, "you and your beautiful bride may indulge yourselves as you wish as

183

long as you keep your lovemaking within reasonable limits. But only until six weeks before the expected birth," he warned, suddenly turning serious, "for after that the danger to mother and child increases."

After Dr. Renaud's departure, Philippe hesitantly entered the bedroom, unsure of Gabby's reaction to a pregnancy coming so close upon the heels of her wedding. But his fears were groundless. The dreamy smile on her face told him volumes about her state of mind.

"Philippe!" she cried when she spied him balancing his large frame nervously in the doorway. Her arms stretched out invitingly, happiness clearly etched on her face. "Have you spoken with Dr. Renaud?" she asked shyly.

"*Oui, mon amour,* I have," Philippe replied tenderly as he approached the bed.

"And are you happy?"

He shot her a piercing glance before answering her question with one of his own. "Does it make you happy, Gabby? You are so young."

"If I am old enough to respond to you as a woman I certainly am old enough to bear your child," Gabby replied with surprising maturity. "As to your question, having a child makes me extremely happy."

"As it does me, *ma petite,* as it does me," whispered Philippe, strangely moved.

The next day preparations commenced for their departure. Although Gabby had grown to love St. Pierre and the townhouse, she nevertheless looked forward eagerly to seeing the much heralded Bellefontaine and the beloved Tante Louise and her husband Gerard about whom Philippe had spoken so glowingly.

"I thought Tante Louise was a slave," Gabby had asked Philippe, still confused about the relationship between slave and master.

"She is a slave, yet not a slave. How can I explain? She has been with our family since before I was born and suckled me along with her own children. She raised me as much as my own mother has. She rules the household with an iron hand and she orders me around shamelessly," Philippe explained with good humor. "I realize it must be hard for you to understand unless you were born here on the island as I was."

Gabby was eager for any information concerning her new home, listening intently to Philippe, thinking that she had never heard him mention either of his parents before. It seemed to her that he was unusually reticent about bringing up any aspect of his childhood. He had told her once that his grandfather built Bellefontaine for his grandmother before they were married. He also mentioned that he had no living relative. More than that he would not divulge.

In less than a week they were in a carriage on the road to Bellefontaine. All their baggage, including trunks full of beautiful new clothes, had been sent ahead two days earlier along with a message informing Tante Louise of their imminent arrival.

Their passage to Bellefontaine took most of the day on a narrow road winding over steep mountain crests. The road etched its way along the top of ravines so sheer Gabby hung on to Philippe for dear life. It seemed the peaks should have been snowcapped instead of dense, scrubby growths of vegetation and palms. Some of the hairpin turns doubled back upon themselves so many times that Gabby was sure they traveled twice the distance to Bellefontaine before they finally arrived. The scenery along the way was breathtakingly beautiful. The color and variety of growth were endless. The gorges and ravines were overrun with ferns, bamboo plumes, and wild bananas, and breadfruit trees hung with vines.

Then slowly, coconut palms, bananas, and bamboo gave way to cane fields, ringed with the omnipotent jungle whose tall trees were like sentinels standing guard. An eerie feeling came over Gabby, for now she understood just how isolated life would be on the plantation.

Bellefontaine sat high on a cliff above the sea, the surf beating on the grayish sand below visible from the long driveway leading to the house. As they turned into the gates, Gabby saw a long avenue bordered by palms and a low growing hedge abloom with bright colored flowers. She drew in her breath sharply at her first glimpse of the house, an Indian style mansion rising majestically two stories into the air. It was constructed of thick stone with rows of windows whose shutters were flung open to catch the faintest whisper of a breeze. A pillared veranda ran the length of the building, shielding the rooms within from the sun.

"It . . . it's magnificent," stammered Gabby, finally finding just the right word to describe the imposing structure.

"It may be imposing," laughed Philippe, "but it is also cool and comfortable."

When they halted before the house, Gabby exclaimed in delight over the expanse of grassy lawn and the formal garden displaying every plant imaginable in every color of the rainbow. Shrubs and bushes were laid out in a geometric design that must take at least five men to maintain adequately. A low stone wall held back the jungle. In the distance she could see stables and outbuildings.

Philippe had just handed her down from the carriage when suddenly a slim, golden-skinned figure dashed from the house and flung herself headlong into his arms, purposefully ignoring Gabby who fought against waves of vertigo that had assailed her the moment her feet touched the ground. As if from a long distance, she watched the warm welcome tendered by the girl, their voices receding farther and farther into the background; the girl's shapely, bare legs flashing alluringly in the dying rays of the sun as Philippe placed his

186

hands about her tiny waist and whirled her around, jupe skirts flying, full, ripe breasts bouncing, evidently delighted to see her.

The girl squealed in delight, tiny, pearl-like teeth bared, full, red lips parted. "But why have you stayed away from your Amalie so long, *mon amour?*" she asked breathlessly.

"If I had but known what an exuberant welcome awaited me I would have hurried back sooner," Philippe teased, giving her pert nose an affectionate tweak. Then, as if suddenly remembering he had a wife, he reluctantly released the lithe body pressed close to his muscular form and turned to Gabby who by now was clutching desperately to the side of the carriage, intuitively aware that her happiness and the welfare of her unborn child depended upon the capricious whims of a man who evidently expected her to share his affections with his mistress!

"*Ma petite,*" said Philippe, pushing the golden girl forward, "this is Amalie, the daughter of Tante Louise and Gerard."

Amalie's name was on her lips as everything around her dimmed and she pitched forward, her crumpling body caught up by Philippe only moments before she hit the ground.

Gabby slowly surfaced into consciousness aware of a humming in her ears. After a few moments she realized that the humming was nothing but low pitched voices speaking in quiet tones. She recognized Philippe's voice immediately but not that of the female speaking to him. Because her eyes remained closed the couple talked freely, thinking her still asleep.

"The long, hot trip was tiring for the *petite fille*, especially in view of her condition. But she will be fine, Monsieur Philippe, as soon as Tante Louise gets one of her tsannes into her stomach." It was difficult for Gabby to follow the *patois*.

"I hope you are right, Tante," said Philippe worriedly.

"Dr. Renaud assured me she was in good health and should encounter no problems with her pregnancy."

"She is so young," added Tante Louise thoughtfully.

Philippe shot her a sharp look. "I admit that Gabby is young and has much to learn," he said brusquely. "I did not think she would conceive so soon but we both welcome this child."

Tante Louise's knowing black eyes studied Philippe until he became restive under her scrutiny. She knew him better than he knew himself. "May I speak frankly, Monsieur Philippe?" she asked, intending to speak her mind no matter what.

"When have you hesitated to do otherwise?" Philippe answered tartly.

"Surely you must realize that Amalie will not take kindly to your wife. It would have been best for everyone if she were to remain in St. Pierre. Or else send Amalie away. She is my own daughter and I know her well," she muttered ominously.

"Amalie appeared to take my marriage well," replied Philippe with typical male conceit.

"You do not know my daughter if you think she accepted your wife," Tante Louise warned.

"You worry unnecessarily," Philippe chided, more upset by his housekeeper's words than he cared to admit.

"You must think of your petite wife and your child."

"What makes you think I do not?" Philippe scowled, annoyed by the turn the conversation was taking.

Tante Louise wagged her turbaned head from side to side in apparant disgust. "Do not be taken in by Amalie's wiles. She will never reconcile herself to the idea that you have a wife. What will Madame Gabby's reaction be to Amalie? How will it affect your child?"

"Madame Gabby is my concern, as is my child," Philippe asserted with a hint of underlying anger in his voice.

188

"Forgive my boldness, Monsieur Philippe, but it is your bride I think of now, not my daughter." The strong-featured black woman looked at her master with bold eyes, holding no hint of subservience. Her next words stunned Philippe. "What place will Amalie have in your household now that you have a wife? Will she continue to warm your bed?"

"You go too far!" Philippe exploded angrily, unaware that Gabby was listening intently to the exchange.

"Forgive me, Monsieur, but I think only of your wife; Amalie can take care of herself but your *petite fille* seems unprepared to face the harsh realities of life. Perhaps it would be better for all concerned to send Amalie away."

"This is Amalie's home! This is where she belongs!" retorted Philippe unreasonably. "I will not send her away, but you can rest assured that I have no plans to take her into my bed again. I no longer have need of a mistress, even one as tempting and bewitching as your Amalie." Tante Louise clearly remained skeptical despite Philippe's declaration.

Gabby's gasp of surprise at Philippe's announcement immediately alerted the speakers. Almost instantly Philippe was beside her, followed by a tall, handsome black woman whose commanding presence seemed to fill the room. She was large without being fat and her wrinkleless face was a well-oiled ebony. It was difficult for Gabby to believe that the petite, golden-skinned Amalie was this woman's daughter. She stood a majestic six feet tall with her multi-colored turban adding at least another six inches. Her ponderous breasts were like ripe melons and her hands were as large as Philippe's. She pushed Philippe aside with ease as she bent over Gabby, studying her from large, velvet eyes as black as Hades.

"Ah, *ma petite*, you are awake," she crooned in a gentle, sing-song voice using the *patois* Gabby was just beginning to understand. "You are home where you belong and Tante Louise will take good care of you and the babe."

189

Gabby made to get out of bed but one of the big woman's hands held her captive to the mattress. "No, no, you must rest," she insisted firmly. Then she turned to Philippe and ordered brusquely, "You, Monsieur Philippe, shall see that your *petite fille* remains in bed." Gabby watched in awe as the woman strode majestically from the room.

Gabby studied her surroundings and what she could see in the dim light pleased her, though the room seemed somewhat masculine with its massive pieces of furniture. A gentle breeze from opened windows lining the opposite ends of the room cooled her feverish skin. Her eyes finally alit on Philippe hovering over her.

"How do you feel, *cherie?*" he asked solicitiously. "You gave us all quite a fright."

"Well enough, Philippe," she responded weakly. "But Tante Louise is right, it would be best if I remained in bed for a day or two. I hadn't realized the trip to the plantation would be so arduous. I wouldn't want to do anything to harm the babe."

"Certainly you must rest, *ma petite*," Philippe readily agreed, relieved that she wasn't about to protest the enforced bedrest he was going to insist upon. Placing a chaste kiss on Gabby's forehead he tiptoed from the room anxious to confer with his overseer whom he had not yet spoken with. Sugar cane harvest was in full swing and the field hands were working around the clock. Soon they would begin distilling rum in the big cauldrons in a building adjacent to the cane fields, and he knew his days as well as many nights would be taken up with duties.

Lulled into sleep by one of Tante Louise's soothing tisanes Gabby was unaware that Philippe had come in much later and taken his place beside her in the big bed, cradling her in his arms through the long night. He was already gone when she awoke the next morning, the only visible sign that he had been in the bed with her the indentation his head made on the pillow. Because her weakness still persisted, Tante Louise ordained that she must remain in bed several days, and Philippe echoed her words.

In any event, Gabby found herself more or less isolated while the cane harvest continued at a frantic pace. Even the house servants were pressed into service and she saw little of anyone except Tante Louise. When she saw Philippe in the evening, he seemed brusque and preoccupied. He had not attempted to make love to her since their arrival at Belle-fontaine, falling in bed at night too tired even to talk. At times he remained away the entire night and Gabby had wild imaginings of him with the beauteous Amalie. Somehow his words to Tante Louise insisting he had no need for a mistress held little comfort. Soon she would be large with child and she wondered if Philippe would take up with his mistress when her grotesque body repelled him.

Once Gabby's health and vitality were restored she set out to explore all the rooms of the house, from the wine cellar to the huge ballroom on the upper floor. Tante Louise explained to her that all the rooms were in a single line with a veranda on either side to catch the slightest breeze. The rooms were light and airy with pastel colors on the walls. The furniture throughout most of the house was of French design fashioned mostly from native woods. Gabby was delighted with the house and surprised at the large staff of servants it took to run it.

When Gabby met Tante Louise's husband, Gerard, she was shocked. The man towered above his six foot wife with lofty majesty; a crop of grizzled, white hair hugged his large head as well as his chin. The muscles that rippled along his massive torso and thighs were awesome, but they were not the most amazing thing about the powerful slave. The most incredible, the most shocking, was his skin. He was white! As white, or nearly as white, as to be indistinguishable from Philippe or herself. Now she understood Amalie's golden complexion.

As Gabby learned her way around the house she realized that there would be little if anything to occupy her time. She was not about to usurp Tante Louise's position or insert her authority into such a well-run establishment. Nevertheless, she adapted easily to the indolent life of a planter's wife expecting her first child. She was cosseted and pampered and learned to live with the intense heat, even enjoying the long afternoon naps when Philippe usually joined her in the big bed.

Even after Gabby had recovered from her early illness, Philippe still seemed reluctant to approach her with his love-making, fearing it would precipitate another attack of weakness and endanger the child. One day Gabby took it upon herself to intiate the resumption of their former intimacy, hinting that their loving would neither hurt the child nor harm her. The first time they made love, Philippe held her like a fragile doll, afraid she would break. But soon her desire turned his own passion into a blazing inferno. He had lain beside her far too many nights, holding her close, feeling her body warmly curled next to his, yet hesitant to approach her. He tried to be gentle but they were soon eagerly devouring one another. When at last he pierced her softness, she gasped with pleasure as she rose to meet him. Swiftly he brought her to completion before crying out his own joy. After that they made love regularly, Philippe's fatigue vanishing the moment he drew Gabby into his arms.

Gabby's first visitors at Bellefontaine were Marcel Duvall's sisters, Honore and Linette. She was completely captivated by the two high-spirited girls who were ecstatic to find that Philippe's wife was near their own age. Honore, the youngest, was seventeen. Her pert face and saucy manner soon had Gabby smiling. Auburn curls fell in sausagelike rolls around her pixie face and she stared at the world through vivid, blue eyes. Linette, at nineteen, seemed much more mature but nonetheless beautiful. Her raven waves cascading down her back were held in place by a ribbon. Her green eyes were startling in their clarity and her petulant, sensuous mouth reminded Gabby of Marcel. Linette was to be married soon after the new year. Though she had never met her husband-to-be, she unquestioningly trusted her brother's judgment in arranging the match. After marriage Linette would live in France with her husband leaving Honore alone at Le Chateau until a suitable marriage could be arranged for the younger girl.

From the sisters Gabby learned that when on Martinique Marcel resided mainly in St. Pierre, preferring the townhouse and the active social life of the city to the dull country existence of the gentleman planter. Several times a year the girls would join their brother, spending days on end visiting friends, shopping, and attending the theater. Carnival season always found them in St. Pierre, for Marcel was an indulgent guardian of his young sisters. From them she also learned that Marcel had returned to Martinique shortly after she and Philippe.

The Duvall girls were frequent visitors to Bellefontaine and as long as Marcel remained in St. Pierre Gabby was free to return their visits. Le Chateau proved to be as well run and well kept as Bellefontaine despite the fact that Marcel left the running of it to his overseer and his sisters.

The cane had been harvested and not any too soon. The rains began with drenching regularity, commencing nearly every morning with torrential downpours but clearing up by midday when the sun appeared high in the sky. Gabby found she was able to bear the dampness and gloom only because of the breaks between rainy days lasting anywhere from thirty-six to forty-eight hours, enabling her to resume her visits with the Duvall sisters.

Gabby had neither seen nor heard from Amalie since that day she arrived at Bellefontaine. If she was still on the plantation there was no evidence of it. Perhaps Philippe had followed Tante Louise's advice and sent her away. Philippe was still absent much of the day, and since the harvest had been completed often traveled into St. Pierre, remaining at the townhouse several days at a time. His fleet of ships was constantly coming and going with cargo to all parts of the world and Gabby began to realize the immensity of his wealth and holdings. With all his prosperity any girl on the island would have jumped at the chance to become his wife, yet he had traveled all the way to France for his bride. It seemed incongruous that he should have paid for what would have been freely given by any woman in her right mind.

Though she was somewhat in awe of Tante Louise, the woman daily proved her devotion to Gabby and her unborn child. She watched over her *petite fille* as if she were her own daughter and daily concocted delicacies to tempt Gabby's sluggish appetite, the heat often dulling her taste for food. Through it all Gabby managed to thrive as did the babe within her.

The first time she had felt movement in her womb her startled cry awakened Philippe who had been sleeping soundly beside her. He stared at her in wonder as he rested his hand lightly on the soft mound of her stomach and felt for himself the flutterings of the tiny life they had created.

"It's a boy, Gabby," Philipe proudly proclaimed. "And after this one we shall have another, then another . . ."

"Philippe," Gabby chided gently, "I am not sure I wish to produce a child a year." Although her words were said jokingly, the thought was sobering. Would she become a brood mare only to be caste aside when she was worn out in favor of Amalie or another like her?

"Having children is a natural culmination of our passionate natures," Philippe said dryly. "Would you have me take a mistress so that you might be spared the rigors of childbearing? Of what use would you be to me, then?" he asked with overbearing arrogance.

Gabby was stunned into silence. Just when she thought herself free from his cruelty he taunted her with threats of a mistress, calling her useless if she failed to serve her purpose in life.

Seeing her face, Philippe was immediately contrite. What made him hurt her when she deserved much better? he wondered, hating his own thoughtless words. She had adapted admirably to the isolation of the plantation and welcomed the coming child despite her tender years. She had even learned to respond to his lovemaking with an ardor that matched his own. Why then this compelling need to punish her? In his original plans Gabby was meant to play a minor role in his life. But she had become much more. Could it be he was afraid to show his love? Did thoughts of Cecily still haunt him?

"I'm sorry, *cherie,*" Philippe murmured contritely. "I don't know what comes over me at times. I would not deliberately hurt you. Please believe me."

Gabby forgave but did not forget.

That night was the first time Gabby became aware of the drums. She had heard about Voodoo or Obeah, snake worship as it was practiced here on Martinique. She had assumed that the natives were Catholics, like the French, but Philippe had informed her they were very much involved in Obeah as well as Catholicism when it served their purpose. The priests, he explained, tried to flog Obeah out of the slaves but were unsuccessful. No one on the island scoffs at the Obeah curse, she had learned.

The drums unsettled Gabby, and she drew closer to Philippe. They seemed to bode evil for her. She hadn't realized that the Bellefontaine slaves practiced Obeah but should have guessed they would be no different from the others. Later, she dreamed of sleek, black bodies writhing and dancing around an altar upon which a nude, golden-skinned woman held a snake aloft, inviting it to become a part of her own body. She awoke drenched in sweat, clutching at Philippe who spent the remainder of the night soothing her fears with soft words and love.

The following morning Gabby awoke to a blaze of sunshine so intense that her fears from the night before were immediately put to rest. After days of rain and gloom the warming rays of the sun were a welcome sight. With an air of contentment she donned her gayest dress, one she had let out but which still fit reasonably well considering the rounded bulge beneath the waistline. Gabby hummed a happy tune while she planned a leisurely visit with Honore and Linette at Le Chateau. She hadn't seen them since the rains had begun and sorely missed their company and witty chatter. So impatient was she to be off that she begrudged the time it took for Francine, the pretty mulatto maid, to arrange her silvery locks becomingly atop her head. After breakfast she left word for Philippe that she would not be home for lunch, then set off for Le Chateau in a carriage driven by Gerard.

When Gabby reached Le Chateau no one ran out in joyful welcome as was the Duvall sisters' usual custom. Hesitantly she approached the door and was rendered speechless when it was flung open by Marcel who seemed inordinately pleased to see her, drawing her into the cool hallway.

"Gabby!" Marcel exclaimed in obvious delight. "How good it is to see you again." She could only stare as he drew her into the salle and seated her in an overstuffed chair. "I hadn't expected to see you at Le Chateau since my sisters are in St. Pierre."

"I . . . I didn't know they were gone," stammered Gabby, still flustered.

"It is their intention to buy out St. Pierre," laughed Marcel indulgently. "I shall join them in a day or two, as soon as I have cleared up my business here." His green eyes glittered like emeralds and Gabby blushed as his gaze swept over her burgeoning figure. "But enough of me," he said, turning serious. "What of you? Are you happy? I missed you when I returned to my sister's house in New Orleans. How did Philippe find you?"

At that moment a servant appeared with refreshments and Gabby sipped her *bavarois* with relish while she considered her answer. Finally, she said, "I am content, and happy. I think Philippe has changed. He . . . he . . . is so looking forward to the birth of our child." She hung her head shyly at the mention of the babe.

Marcel eyed her skeptically. "You mean to say that Philippe is the perfect husband? I hardly thought him capable." Gabby did not miss the note of sarcasm in his voice.

"If you are thinking of Philippe's past involvement with Amalie, Marcel, you need not worry. He no longer has need of a mistress," Gabby said meaningfully. "Philippe has time for no one but his wife and the child soon to be born."

"Would that child were mine," muttered Marcel, his eyes straying again to Gabby's waistline before returning to gaze into her violet eyes.

Gabby was startled by the depth of feeling in Marcel's voice, and dropped her eyes to cover her embarrassment. As if sensing her discomfort, he took her hands in his and began speaking of things that would give her no cause for embarrassment. Warming to his charm, Gabby relaxed and soon they were chatting easily, unmindful of the passing time.

Meanwhile, Philippe, hot and dusty from the distillery, returned to the house earlier than usual because of a breakdown of machinery, his thoughts on a leisurely bath and spending the hot afternoon in the coolness of his bedroom with Gabby beside him, either making slow, lazy love or just resting side by side if she weren't up to the former. He smiled in anticipation, for Gabby rarely rejected him, even as she grew large and bulky. He was more than a little annoyed to learn that Gabby was visiting Le Chateau and not expected to return until later in the day. His frown deepened as he absently ordered a hot tub to wash away his sweat and labors from the frustrating morning attempting to repair broken machinery. Philippe stripped and poured himself a generous measure of rum to ease his tensions and agitation. Finding the fiery liquid immensely soothing, he quickly downed another and another until he was well on his way to forgetting all about Gabby and her delicious little body.

Immersed in a steaming tub of water, Philippe's thoughts strayed once more to Gabby and his thwarted plans for the afternoon. He had looked forward with eagerness to holding her sweetly curving body close to his, allowing her to slowly arouse him, savoring the moment he finally took her. Scowling, he realized his line of thought had aroused him and cursed under his breath. Why wasn't his wife here when he needed her? Just then he heard a noise and, rising from the tub, looked expectantly at the door, a pleased smile curving his lips, certain that Gabby had returned early and his afternoon would not be wasted after all.

Philippe's smile turned to stone when he saw Amalie advancing on him, her seductively arrayed body voluptuous in a low-necked, white blouse displaying the sharp tips of her pointed breasts, stretching the material almost beyond reasonable limits. Her boldly striped jupe skirt hugged her lithe hips and rose nearly to her knees in front. With an amused smile she viewed Philippe's obvious state of arousal, and with hips swaying provocatively moved forward until they stood only inches apart. Philippe was too stunned to move when Amalie reached for a towel and began drying his body with excruciating thoroughness.

"What are you doing here, Amalie?" Philippe croaked, the words nearly strangling him as her hands worked furiously.

"I grew lonely for you, Monsieur Philippe," she purred silkily.

"I explained to you that I no longer needed a mistress," Philippe said, an underlying thread of anger in his voice. "You were ordered not to come to the big house and upset my wife." He strove mightly to impress her with his words but found it extremely difficult while her hands moved with such dexterity over his body.

"Poo!" Amalie scoffed. "How can your wife hope to please you now that her belly grows large. Soon she will no longer be able to accommodate you. Besides," she said huskily, her cat-soft touch affecting him more than he wanted to admit, "Madame Gabby is not here and I am, *mon amour*."

She reached her arms to encircle his neck and nibbled at an earlobe with small, sharp teeth, laughing delightedly as his manhood gave a leap at her boldness. "I knew your body had not forgotten the touch of mine so soon." Her voice was the consistency of poured honey.

Moving backward a few steps Amalie shrugged the blouse from her dainty shoulders uncovering the golden globes of her breasts. Her nipples were already erect ripe cherries. With a flick of her wrist her jupe skirt fell to the floor. She wore no underclothes and Philippe's eyes were riveted to the curling black triangle now damp with her desire. "You are eager for me, *mon amour*, just as I am eager for you," breathed Amalie, never more certain of her allure. "Come, let us taste one another again and seek the rapture we once knew together."

Philippe drew his breath in sharply as Amalie moved so close to him that her pointed nipples burned into his chest like a searing flame, melting his resistance. Using every ounce

199

of strength he possessed, he drew away from her. "Put your clothes on, Amalie," he said hoarsely. Even though he meant what he said, he was tortured with desire for his ex-mistress. "I have a wife who is expecting my child. I will do nothing to upset her and endanger the life of my babe."

Philippe's self-righteous words affected Amalie not at all. "You want me, *mon amour*, I can see it in your eyes. Even your body speaks of your desire for me. Let me stay, Philippe," she begged. "Allow me to please you as only I can."

Before Philippe could stop her she slipped to her knees before him, encircling him with her lips as the room reverberated with his agonized cries of surrender.

Roughly, he pulled her to her feet. "You wicked, tantalizing witch," he groaned, as if in pain. "How could I forget your golden, tempting body, or those lips so ready to consume? *Oui*, I want you, damn it! I want you with every fiber of my body!"

Lifting Amalie easily in his arms, Philippe carried her to his bed while the room trilled with her exultant laughter.

"Philippe, Philippe," she moaned as his hands began their intimate assault upon her breasts. "How I have longed for you these long months. How I've wanted to come to you knowing that your pale wife was not woman enough for you but afraid you would be angry with your Amalie. I see now how wrong I was. You have been waiting for me."

Barely able to contain his lust, Philippe ran his tongue along the outline of her lips, then plunged the tip into her mouth. Guilt, he knew, would come later. But for now it was enough just to concentrate on the passionate, writhing body beneath him, exciting him beyond physical endurance. His probing fingers found her ready for him and she clasped him to guide him into her body. But he needed no help as his manhood unerringly found its mark.

With a cry of delight Amalie raised her hips to meet his thrust and Philippe sank into the depths of her, filling her so completely she nearly swooned. Eyes glazed in passion he threw back his head in utter abandon, his face contorted with the cataclysmic explosion of his climax, his cries cutting into the afternoon heat.

At that fateful moment, Gabby quietly opened the bedroom door expecting to find Philippe sound asleep. She had not remained long at Le Chateau when she found the Duvall sisters gone and herself alone with Marcel. She remembered Philippe's rage the last time he had discovered her alone with him. She was in high, good spirits when she hurried to their room anticipating a warm, perhaps even a passionate welcome. The shocking sight that greeted her plunged her to the very depths of Hell. Eyes wide in shock, she stifled a gasp of horror and outrage with a tightly clenched fist pressed to her trembling mouth. Philippe's enraptured expression and blissful cries of completion assaulted her vision and hearing. Her eyes were riveted upon the naked, golden form that was the cause of her husband's ecstasy. Amalie's undulating body was beaded with a fine coating of sweat and she glowed with a pagan beauty. Gabby stood rooted to the spot, enthralled by the lovers caught up in the act of gratification. She felt like an intruder. Cringing inwardly, she watched as Amalie's lovely features grew tense, her need for surcease spellblinding. But before Amalie lost herself in the throes of her own climax, she turned her head in Gabby's direction, her cat's eyes glistening with triumph.

It was more than Gabby could bear. She had thought being sold by her father the final degradation of her life; but she was wrong . . . wrong . . . wrong. Her own husband had just succeeded in topping her father's disgusting deed. Gabby's hand flew to her stomach as the child convulsed in her womb. As if in a dream, she fled from the scene of her betrayal, stumbling clumsily down the stairs and through the house, encountering no one in her hasty flight. Escape was uppermost in her mind. Escape from the sights and sounds forever etched upon her brain. Unthinkingly she headed for the stables, hoisting her swollen body atop Philippe's horse already saddled from his return to the fields. Gabby was not a skilled horsewoman and her pregnancy made it increasingly difficult for her to keep her seat, but she resolutely took up the reins and spurred the horse into the banana groves, toward Le Chateau . . . and Marcel, a friend whom she needed badly at this moment.

Trembling violently, Gabby felt as if a knife had been plunged into her gut, a knife wielded by Philippe and twisted by Amalie. The horse beneath her skittered and shied, as if aware of the inexperienced rider clinging to his back. Suddenly, her mount halted, refusing to budge no matter how Gabby urged him on. In her recklessness, Gabby did not heed the animal's sixth sense and she dug her heels into his flanks, causing him to rear in protest, his forelegs pawing the air wildly. Unseen by Gabby, a fer-de-lance that lay concealed in a bunch of bananas slithered down the tree trunk and into the path of the terrified horse. In a moment of desperation, she clung to the horse's mane, too frightened to scream, to think. As if in slow motion she began to slide backward until her grip loosened and she tumbled to the ground, rolling to a sudden and painful halt against the trunk of a banana tree, unaware of the fer-de-lance that lay dead in the path, trampled by the horse's flying hooves. The one thing she was aware of was the stabbing, excruciating pains tearing her body apart.

Chapter Eleven

GERARD WAS in the stable when Gabby's riderless horse returned. He had not known Philippe's mount was even out of the stable and was surprised to see him coming from the direction of the groves lathered and badly frightened. Chills of apprehension prickled the back of his neck. He knew that Monsieur Philippe was in his bedroom napping and that Madame Gabby had gone immediately upstairs when he brought her home from Le Chateau. Shaking his head in bewilderment he went to confer with Tante Louise and together they decided to awaken Philippe to tell him of the strange occurrence.

When neither Gabby nor Philippe answered his knock, Gerard took matters into his own hands and bravely pushed open the unlocked door. Gerard's second shock of the day came when he recognized the golden body of his daughter beneath Philippe's muscular frame. He could only gape, forgetting for a moment his reason for entering the room. When he regained his senses he knew intuitively that Gabby must have come upon this scene and, shocked out of her wits, taken Philippe's horse and ridden into the banana groves toward Le Chateau. He blanched. To attempt such a feat in her condition was tantamount to suicide.

When Philippe saw Gerard inside his bedroom he was livid with rage. Not so much for entering unannounced, but for discovering him in bed, arms and legs entwined, with Amalie.

"What do you want?" Philippe bellowed, disentangling himself from Amalie's clinging limbs.

Gerard could only stare at his daughter stretched in obvious contentment, purring like a pleased kitten. Finally, dragging his eyes from her nude form, he looked at Philippe, his face purposely blank, hiding his disgust behind a frozen mask.

"Well?" Philippe demanded, hastily pulling on a robe. "This had better be good, Gerard, or I'll have your hide!"

"It's Madame Gabby! I think she . . . I think she . . . !"

"Out with it, man, what about Madame Gabby? Has she returned from Le Chateau so soon?" Beads of sweat broke out on his forehead as latent pangs of guilt assailed him. Had Gabby come upon the sight of him and Amalie making love? Was she ill? Fear prickled the nape of his neck.

"The Duvall sisters were in St. Pierre so we returned from Le Chateau earlier than expected," Gerard said, fighting to keep his voice level.

Casting a shamed look toward the bed where Amalie had half risen on one elbow, Philippe asked, "Where is Madame Gabby now?"

"That's what I'm trying to tell you, Monsieur Philippe," Gerard insisted. "Moments ago your horse returned to the stable sweating profusely and badly frightened. Since no one else had taken him out I could only assume that Madame Gabby rode him into the banana groves and has met with an accident. Tante Louise has searched the house for her and she can't be found."

"*Mon dieu!*" cursed Philippe, a hard knot of panic rising in his chest. Was Gabby to become another Cecily? Already he could picture her death. Leaping into his clothes, he started from the room.

"Monsieur Philippe, what of me?" Amalie pouted, stretching out a slim hand in his direction.

Philippe turned toward the bed as if shocked to find Amalie still alluringly arrayed upon it. He wrinkled his brow

204

in distaste, and said, coldly, deliberately, "Get out! Don't be here when I return." Then he was gone. As he followed close behind, Gerard's departing scowl eloquently displayed his displeasure with his daughter. Amalie's gloating smile was her only answer.

Soon Philippe and Gerard were carefully picking their way through the banana groves, Philippe's features distorted, his shoulders stiff as he searched the path for telltale signs of Gabby's passage.

Suddenly, Gerard's voice rang out. "Up ahead, Monsieur Philippe!"

Almost immediately Philippe spotted the small, still form lying at the foot of a banana tree in a crumpled heap. "Gabby!" he cried in a strangled voice, springing from his mount and vaulting the short distance to where the motionless figure lay.

An agonized wail thundered from his lips. Blood was everywhere. It stained the skirt that had risen above Gabby's knees and ran down her legs in rivulets. A short distance away lay the fer-de-lance neatly cut in two by pounding hooves. No explanation was necessary. Gerard had told him that Marcel was at Le Chateau and Philippe instinctively knew that Gabby, once she had seen him, decided to leave him again and go to Marcel, just as Cecily had done so long ago. In the far reaches of his mind was the nagging suspicion that Gabby had intruded upon the intimate scene with Amalie and fled, hell bent for suicide. But he immediately dismissed it from his mind, preferring instead to place the blame on Gabby's head, leaving him blameless, or nearly so, in his own eyes. Damn her fickle heart! he cursed unreasonably. In her haste to leave him she had committed murder! His child was dead, the tiny fetus lying in a pool of blood beneath her thighs.

Philippe sighed with relief when he saw the thin rise and fall of her breast. From the enormous amount of blood surrounding her, Philippe realized that he must act quickly if she were to be saved. He made to lift her onto his horse.

"No, stop, Monsieur Philippe!" cried Gerard before Philippe could carry through. "There is no time. The bleeding must be stopped now, immediately! To carry her back to the house would spell her death. We must first staunch the flow of blood. Quickly, your shirt," he ordered crisply, taking the decision out of Philippe's hands.

Hesitating only a moment, Philippe peeled the soft linen shirt from his back and handed it to Gerard who immediately tore it into long strips. Grunting in satisfaction at the pile of linen before him, Gerard grimly set to work to save Gabby's life. Gingerly he raised her skirts above her waist, ignoring Philippe's horrified gasp when he saw the tiny, bloody form that had once been a living thing. Try as he might, Philippe could not turn his eyes from his dead child.

"Monsieur Philippe," Gerard said gently, "I know what must be done. And when I am finished we must have a litter to carry her back to the house. Ride like the wind, Monsieur, and alert my wife. She will know what to do."

Reluctantly, Philippe left after one last agonizing look at Gabby's still, white face. He barely remembered his ride back to the plantation or his return with the litter.

Working swiftly after Philippe's departure, Gerard cut the umbilical cord and, pushing the fetus aside, began to stem the flow of blood still issuing forth with the linen strips, packing them tightly. When the bleeding had slowed to a slow ooze, he pulled off his own shirt, ripped it down the middle and used part of it to wrap the bloody fetus and the rest to wipe the excess blood from Gabby's legs. He pulled her skirts down to her ankles just as Philippe returned with four men bearing a litter.

Seeing the stricken look in Philippe's eyes, Gerard quickly assured him, "She lives, but we must hurry."

Philippe would allow no one but himself to place Gabby on the litter. In his anxiety over Gabby he failed to notice the tiny, swaddled bundle in Gerard's arms as they started down the path toward Bellefontaine.

Tante Louise met them at the edge of the groves, uttering a cry of dismay when she glimpsed Gabby's white face and still form. She delayed but a moment to speak with Gerard and peek at the tiny bundle he held before hurrying after Philippe and the litter bearing Gabby.

With Philippe hovering nearby, Tante Louise worked feverishly to save Gabby's life. Patiently she spooned infusions of herbs and medicines meant to clot blood down Gabby's throat. She used clean linen pads to staunch the bright flow that slowly drained her of life until nothing more than a trickle remained. All through the night Tante Louise sat beside the motionless form, and when morning came, so did the fever. Philppe was dismayed by the violence of the shudders that racked Gabby's tiny body. He helped bathe her burning flesh while Tante Louise fought to keep a steady flow of life-giving liquids down her throat.

It was four long, nerve-wracking days before Gabby's fever broke and they knew she would live. Only then did Philippe, a shadow of his former self, allow himself to dwell on the accident that had cost him dearly. But when he did, his anger at Gabby exploded into harsh reality. Once again Marcel Duvall had unwittingly intruded upon his life in a way that had left him devastated. Gabby's thoughtless, reckless ride to be with Marcel had cost him the life of his child and heir!

Gerard had informed Philippe that the child had been a boy, and he had grown bitter, completely ignoring his own treachery that precipitated Gabby's foolhardy action. He thought only of the many times he had warned her of the danger lurking in the jungle. In his sorrow over the loss of his child he convinced himself that Gabby had deliberately set out to murder his child. Forgotten was his passionate tryst with Amalie, his betrayal of his marriage vows, his lust for his former mistress. Not even the knowledge that Gabby would have other children eased his tortured thoughts. And eating away into his vitals was the terrible conviction that Gabby had risked her life and that of her child's to be with Marcel!

During Gabby's illness Philippe had moved to a spare bedroom so as not to disturb her rest. On the day her fever broke he made his way to his room so exhausted he could barely move one foot in front of the other. Bone weary from his long vigil at Gabby's besdide, he sank gratefully into bed, falling almost immediately asleep. Suddenly he was jolted awake by small, impatient hands tugging at his clothes.

"Amalie!" Philippe cried in dismay, catching both busy hands in one strong fist. "What the devil . . . ?" He tried to rise up but her lithe body pinned him to the mattress.

"You need me, Monsieur Philippe," Amalie purred. Philippe was mesmerized by the small tongue that darted between pearly teeth to moisten full, red lips, immediately struck by her resemblance to a small, predatory animal. "It is I who has remained faithful to you," Amalie continued, relentlessly pursuing her objective. "I do not flee to the arms of another man. If I had your child in my belly I would not kill it."

Philippe blanched, but in his tortured state recognized the truth of Amalie's words, or what he considered the truth. Gabby had deliberately killed his son! He sighed, and loosened his hold on her hands, allowing her to resume her tiny flutterings and caresses.

"Let me love you, Monsieur Philippe," Amalie murmured soothingly. "Let me heal your pain." Her body was silken upon his.

His passion flared, and suddenly Philippe was desperate for Amalie. His arms clung to her as if he were drowning. "Your love never changes, *ma amour,*" he said brokenly, his mind unconsciously thinking back to Gabby's infidelity with Rob. "You will never betray me." His lips found hers and his body came alive, her hands found him more than ready for her. Soon Philippe was lost in her golden flesh, her small cries of pleasure drowning out the voice of his conscience.

Gabby found it difficult to accept the loss of her child. She was left with a deep feeling of emptiness. She knew that during her fever Philippe was constantly with her, but since she had come to full awareness she had seen little of him. And when he did appear at her bedside, he seemed remote and distracted. Finally, unable to bear his brooding silence any longer, Gabby deliberately brought up the subject that they had both avoided.

"Was the child a girl or boy?" she asked, her voice low and sad.

"A son," replied Philippe stonily. "He was buried in the family plot should you be interested." His voice was implacable, without kindness. Gabby began to sob softly but Philippe remained unmoved. "Why, Gabby?" he asked bleakly. "Why did it happen?"

"You dare ask me that, Philippe?" she asked, dismayed by his audacity. "Surely you share the blame." He was totally unreasonable in his anger.

"It wasn't I who rode recklessly through the jungle while large with child!" Philippe exploded, his anger awesome. "I hold you fully responsible for the murder of my son!"

"You honestly hold yourself blameless, don't you, Philippe," retaliated Gabby, her violet eyes shadowed with hurt and shock. Murder her own child?

Seeing her stricken face Philippe wavered but accusation never left his icy eyes. Weakness caused Gabby to tremble. It seemed that Philippe harbored no guilt feelings for what happened that afternoon when she interrupted his passionate love scene with Amalie. For all she knew Philippe and Amalie had carried on behind her back since the day she arrived at

Bellefontaine. From what little she witnessed Philippe's lust for Amalie was enormous.

Resignation prompted her to speak. "It matters little who was to blame, Philippe," she said tiredly. "We both must live with our own guilt."

"You were going to Marcel," accused Philippe.

"I . . . I had nowhere else to go," she whispered sadly.

Philippe's face hardened and a small muscle on his chin twitched, but he said nothing, aware of the violence ready to burst to the surface. Knowing what he was capable of doing when angered beyond endurance, he realized that separation at this time seemed the best remedy for their fragile relationship. He needed space, time to think, time to recuperate from his anger and heartache. Retreat would give them both time to heal. There were things they both needed to forget . . . and forgive. Perhaps later they could take up their lives where they had left off. Time had a way of dimming old memories and hurts. And the sooner he told her of his decision the easier it would be for both of them, he reasoned.

Philippe cleared his throat. "I came to say goodbye."

Gabby paled, her eyes huge in her pinched face. "Goodbye?"

"The way I feel now I am doing neither to us any good by remaining here. Tante Louise and Gerard are quite capable of caring for you in my absence."

"Where . . . where will you go?"

"In two days the *Windward* begins a voyage to New Orleans and ports in North America. I intend to be on board when she sails."

Gabby wanted to ask if Amalie would accompany him but pride forbade it. Instead, she nodded mutely, too weary and sick at heart to reply.

"You should be restored to full health when I return and we will both be better prepared to discuss our differences. A short separation seems best at this time."

Gabby was dismayed by Philippe's cool manner, but realized she had neither the will nor strength to argue. "Goodbye, Philippe," was all she said in a voice devoid of all emotion. He was gone before he heard her heartrending sobs.

Chapter Twelve

THOUGH GABBY'S body healed her heart remained heavy. She feared to ask the question that burned on the tip of her tongue. Was Amalie aboard the *Windward* with Philippe? She had seen nothing of Amalie since that fateful day that lingered in her memory like a bad dream.

Not the least of her worries were the eerie drums reverberating throughout the long nights in her lonely bed. Not one night had gone by since Philippe's departure that the drums didn't add to her wakefulness. Gabby found them vaguely threatening even though Tante Louise assured her they were just a means for the slaves to work off their frustrations. But to Gabby they sounded sinister. She remembered how they had frightened her the night before she discovered Philippe's unfaithfulness and lost her child. Even visits from Honore and Linette failed to raise her spirits.

One day, nearly a month after Philippe's departure, Marcel was ushered into her room by a scowling Gerard. It was clear that the slave held little esteem for the man Philippe hated with a vengeance. Gerard left them alone only after a warning frown directed at Gabby. It was obvious that he intended to remain close by.

"I'm truly sorry, Gabby," Marcel said gently when he had seated himself next to the bed. "I know how much the child meant to you."

"And to Philippe," added Gabby, her voice tinged with regret.

"*Oui*, and to your husband," allowed Marcel grudgingly.

"Is it true you were riding to Le Chateau when the accident occurred?" he asked, taking her slim hand into his.

"*Oui*, Marcel," admitted Gabby, eyes lowered.

"Do you wish to tell me about it? I fail to understand why your husband chose to leave for an extended journey at a time when you most need him. I am your friend, *cherie*," Marcel emphasized, "you can tell me anything and I shall understand and help you if I am able."

Tears welled in Gabby's eyes and fell like rain drops down her pale cheeks. Whatever Marcel was to anyone else, he was a friend to her. Marcel whipped out his handkerchief and tenderly dabbed at Gabby's tears, then sat back until she was able to speak.

"I was on my way to Le Chateau, to you, Marcel, the only friend I have other than your sisters, when the horse I was riding reared and threw me."

Marcel was aghast. "But what happened after you left my plantation to cause you to mount a horse in your condition and ride headlong into the jungle?" Somehow he knew Philippe was behind her reckless deed.

"Amalie!" ground out Gabby, choking back a sob. Marcel's green eyes grew brittle with speculation but he said nothing. "Upon my return to Bellefontaine I found Philippe and Amalie in . . . in my bed, make . . . making love!" Bitterness was heavy upon her tongue. "I was blinded by all but the sight of her naked body clutching at Philippe's flesh and the sound of their cries and groans of bliss. I thought only to flee from the sight and sounds of Philippe's lust for his mistress. I . . . I had nowhere else to go but Le Chateau, and the quickest way to get there was on horseback. What Philippe said was true, I totally disregarded the danger to my unborn child. My rashness lost not only my child but my husband as well."

"Ah, *cherie*," consoled Marcel, "what a terrible shock to

one of your delicate sensibilities. You are much too hard on yourself."

"It's true that Philippe must share the blame for allowing his lust for Amalie to come between us, but I am the one who mounted that horse."

"What does Philippe think?" Marcel asked gently.

"He holds me responsible for the death of our child!" With tremendous effort she fought to control the hysteria rising in her breast. "To Philippe's thinking it was my reckless deed that killed our child, not his liaison with Amalie. Right now there is no room in his heart for forgiveness, but then, there is none in mine, either."

"*Cherie,*" Marcel consoled, "you have suffered greatly for Philippe's misdeeds. And now he has left you?" Did Gabby detect a note of hopefulness in his voice?

"Oh I am sure he intends to return when I am fully recovered and better able to withstand his anger and recriminations," said Gabby scornfully. "But for now I am certain he is enjoying his freedom, just as I am certain that Amalie is with him."

"You mean he has taken her aboard the *Windward?*" Marcel frowned. "That does not sound like him."

"Of course I can't be certain that Amalie is with him but I know my husband and long nights at sea alone in his bed hold little appeal for him. But of one thing you can be certain, he will return one day. As his wife I am the only woman who can give him an heir. Oh, *oui,* he will return, if only to plant his seed." Her voice trembled with suppressed anger.

"How may I help you, *cherie?*" Marcel asked with grave concern.

"You have already helped me just being here and listening to me," smiled Gabby through a veil of tears.

"I shall always be here for you, Gabby," replied Marcel.

Her trust in him moved him more than he cared to admit.

At that moment the imposing figure of Tante Louise darkened the doorway. "Madame Gabby must rest now," she asserted authoritatively. "You go!"

If Marcel thought to ignore the towering women's dictum, he had only to glance past her to see Gerard ready to evict him bodily if he failed to heed her words. He rose, raised Gabby's slim hand to his lips and said meaningfully, "I shall not be far away. If I am not at Le Chateau then you can find me in St. Pierre. Rest and get well for you must be sufficiently recovered to attend Linette's wedding. She is counting on seeing you there." With regret, Gabby watched him leave.

Time passed slowly for Gabby with no word forthcoming from Philippe. Nor did she expect any. Gabby had regained her full strength and was allowed to come and go at will, albeit under Gerard's watchful eyes. Thus far, she had no desire to leave the plantation and was undecided whether to attend Linette's wedding. She hated the thought of attending without Philippe beside her, yet she knew Honore and Linette would be disappointed by her absence. She knew she must make her mind up soon.

Almost nightly the drums persisted with their eerie serenades. Gabby could not help but recall Philippe's description of Obeah or snake wordhip as it was practiced on Martinique. No matter how hard she tried she could not rid herself of the feeling that something sinister was about to take place. Something involving her. Each morning she awoke with a sense of impending doom.

One night Gabby lay wide awake in bed, listening to the pagan beat wafting through the open windows. Suddenly she stiffened in fright, the wild, frenzied sound becoming painful to her ears. Though she wanted desperately to get up and shut the windows against the incessant tattoo of the drums, she found herself lethargic, nearly paralyzed. A whisper of sound caused the hair at the nape of her neck to rise. Dark shadows loomed before the open windows. Fear constricted her throat as the shadows materialized into menacing figures entering the room on stealthy feet. By the time Gabby collected her wits about her it was too late to scream or attempt to alter the course of events.

Gabby gagged and sputtered when a cloth was pushed rudely into her mouth. Two dark figures bent over her and she felt herself being lifted from the bed by strong arms; a musky odor assailed her nostrils and then she saw nothing more as a rough sack was pulled over her head. No amount of struggling helped as she was carried through the windows and into the flower scented night. They moved unerringly in the direction of the drums.

While she was borne toward some unknown evil all sorts of wild imaginatings crowded her brain. She had heard of slave uprisings where whites were slaughtered but she had thought Bellefontaine slaves to be content. Instinctively Gabby knew that whatever was about to happen was meant for her alone.

They had reached their destination. Against the echo of hundreds of chanting voices the drums were strangely silent. Gabby sensed rather than saw the multitude of sweaty bodies pressing in upon her. A pungent odor assaulted her senses. She stiffened when she felt herself being lowered, and then her back came in contact with a hard, cold surface. Full realization came upon her the moment the covering was removed from her head. She was meant to be sacrificed to Damballa! She lay on a stone altar on a raised dais, hundred of glazed eyes staring at her. The scene was so bizarre, so unreal, that Gabby expected to wake up at any moment for this frightening nightmare.

Gabby gaped in horror as Amalie's lithe form stepped to the front of the congregation, a deadly fer-de-lance coiled around her outstretched arms. Screaming silently, Gabby shrank within herself. She could look to no one for help. It was obvious to her that the throng of slaves were under some kind of spell fired by Amalie's lust for blood . . . hers. Mesmerized, Gabby eyes were riveted on the snake as the drums began to beat with renewed frenzy whipping the slaves into orgasmiclike movements, twising and gyrating around the sacrificial altar, their bodies glistening with perspiration, their faces saving with lust, chanting, "Damballa! Damballa!"

At a nod from Amalie two brawny men positioned themselves at Gabby's feet and head, each grasping an arm and leg, securing them with leather strips to rings in the stone slab, rendering her incapable of movement. Still gagged, Gabby watched with wide-eyed horror as Amalie drew near and with one slim hand curled at the neck of her nightgown, ripped it from her body. At the sight of Gabby's exposed, white flesh, a cry rose up from the frenzied crowd. Soon, couple after couple dropped to the ground joining with lust-crazed abandon wherever they fell, the drum beat keeping time to their undulating bodies.

Her heart beating wildly in her ribcage, Gabby closed her eyes, preferring not to witness what she could not understand, praying for this horrible nightmare to end. Suddenly, a great hush fell over the thong and Amalie's voice filled the silence. The slaves responded to her words with much yelling and waving of arms, their eyes glued to Gabby's nude form, glowing like pale alabaster in the moonlight. Their chant became like thunder in Gabby's ears. "Damballa! Damballa! Damballa!"

She was driven to the brink of insanity, violet eyes glazed over as Amalie, the fer-de-lance now draped about her neck, approached the altar and drew a razor sharp fingernail between Gabby's breasts, drawing a thin line of blood all the was to her navel. Gabby blinked at the sudden pain, but

Amalie was not yet finished with her. A collective sigh arose from the crowd as Amalie pulled the gag from Gabby's mouth and proceeded to paint her lips with the blood she had just drawn. Screaming, fighting against the leather thongs that bound her to the altar, Gabby knew death was at hand when Amalie placed the fer-de-lance on her stomach, then stood back, a sardonic smile distorting her beautiful face. An icy rivulet of fear ran along her spine and cold trickles spread through her body until her breath came fast and ragged, almost in a sob.

A prayer for her immortal soul on her lips, Gabby stared at the snake slithering across her quivering stomach. Amalie's cat's eyes gleamed malevolently as her body moved seductively to the tempo of the drumbeat, joyfully anticipating the death of the woman who stood between her and the man she loved. A huge muscular slave whose black skin glistened wetly in the firelight seized her around the waist and threw her to the ground, stradling her. With eager hands she grasped his engorged organ and drew him down, into her writhing body.

Immobilized by fear, Gabby felt the snake inch downward along her prone form. Then she screamed . . . and screamed . . . and screamed, on the verge of madness, the fer-de-lance now entangled amid the curling strands of the silky triangle at the juncture of her thighs. Through her madness appeared the vision of a huge form weaving around the tangle of copulating bodies and frenzied dancers, his booming voice casting a pall upon the pleasure-seeking group of slaves. The drums stopped, and all eyes turned toward Gerard, but he had eyes only for Gabby as his gigantic hand fearlessly grasped the snake by its neck and tossed it aside as if it were a toy. Enraged, he turned to Amalie, dragging the still pumping body from atop her and pulled her roughly to her feet. One by one the slaves began melting into the surrounding jungle. The last thing Gabby saw before she blacked out was Gerard's huge fist drawn back to strike his daughter.

Chapter Thirteen

GABBY STRUGGLED into consciousness aware of the bright sun warming her face and of two people gazing at her with grave concern. Tante Louise and Gerard breathed a collective sigh of relief when Gabby regarded them through eyes that held none of the madness of the night before.

"How do you feel, *ma petite?*" asked Tante Louise, a worried frown creasing her careworn face.

"Amalie! The fer-de-lance!" Gabby cried, reliving in her mind the horror of the Obeah ceremony. Tremors shook her slim body as she moaned softly.

"It's over. Nothing or no one will harm you again," soothed Tante Louise, brushing strands of silver hair away from Gabby's damp brow. "Amalie may be my daughter but this time she went too far. I don't know what Monsieur Philippe would do if anything happened to you." She rolled her black eyes to better emphasize her words.

Gabby looked skeptical. She was certain Philippe cared more for his mistress than he did her. But no matter, never again would she allow Amalie to harm her, she promised herself. She would put herself as far away as possible from Philippe's cold brutality and Amalie's hatred. She doubted if she could ever be the same after what had happened to her last night at the altar of Damballa. During that diabolical ceremony a different woman had been born; one who would live her own life; one who would not, could not live under the domination of Philippe St. Cyr! Accordingly she made her plans.

It took several days for Gabby to recuperate from her harrowing experience, but when she did she informed Tante Louise and Gerard that she planned to attend Linette's wedding at St. Pierre, and remain several weeks as houseguest of Honore. With hooded eyes and clacking tongue Tante Louise made known her disapproval. But neither she nor Gerard had the authority to stop their mistress from doing as she pleased in Philippe's absence. Philippe's explicit orders had been to protect and care for her, nothing more.

Two days later, a scowling Gerard handed Gabby into the carriage and they set out for St. Pierre. Gabby thought back to the last time she had traveled along the breathtakingly beautiful roads as Philippe's happily pregnant bride. She wondered how she could have been duped by Philippe's empty promises and false words of love. She sighed, bitterness a hard knot in her breast. She had allowed the dictates of her body to cloud her thinking and she had paid dearly for it. Never again would she be that naive girl who thought her love for her husband could conquer all.

The trip was long and exhausting and Gabby had plenty of time to think carefully about what she planned to do with her future. When St. Pierre loomed ahead of her, she still had not deviated one iota from her original decision. In her heart she knew she could no longer live with Philippe!

According to Gabby's instructions, Gerard drove directly to Marcel's townhouse, stiff disapproval mirrored in his dark eyes and in the firm line of his broad shoulders. As fate would have it, Marcel was arriving home from his office at the same moment Gabby alit from the carriage in front of his gate.

"Gabby, *cherie!*" he exclaimed as he rushed to help her. "Linette will be so pleased that you decided to attend her wedding." Marcel's warmth spread over Gabby like a cheerful fire on a damp night, and she felt as if she had come home.

"When should I return for you, Madame Gabby?" Gerard asked, flashing Marcel a scathing glance.

Marcel faced Gerard's grim face with composure. "I shall see Madame St. Cyr back to Bellefontaine myself when she is ready to return," he replied haughtily, forestalling Gabby's answer. "Leave her trunk at the gate and my man will carry it in." Then, as he offered Gabby his arm they entered the house while a disgruntled Gerard looked helplessly on. He knew Philippe would be far from pleased by the turn of events, but deep in his heart he could not fault Gabby for fleeing from a situation that had caused her so much grief and terror. He blamed his own beautiful daughter for attempting to harm his mistress and his master for leaving his young wife unprotected.

Inside the house, Gabby was so happy to be away from Bellefontaine and danger that she nearly collapsed with relief.

"What is it, *cherie?*" Marcel asked when he noticed her pallor and violent trembling. "What has happened? More than the wedding has brought you here. Do you wish to tell me about it?"

Unable to contain her emotions for a minute longer, Gabby burst into tears, whereupon Marcel gently drew her into his arms and led her to a sofa, letting her cry out her frustrations into his chest.

"Is it Philippe?" he asked, his jaw tightening. "Has he hurt you? I thought he was still aboard the *Windward.*"

Clinging to Marcel, Gabby gasped out, between sobs, the events that sent her from Bellefontaine in fear of her life. When she finished Marcel's mouth was agape with shock and his hard, emerald eyes wide with distress.

"I would not have thought Amalie would go to such lengths to rid herself of a rival," he muttered darkly. "To think that St. Cyr would leave you at the mercy of that witch is inconceivable. You poor child," he consoled, barely able to contain his anger at Amalie for putting Gabby through an ordeal that might have damaged her mind had she been a weak woman. "You need never return to Bellefontaine if that is your wish. My home is yours for as long as you care to remain. Amalie cannot harm you here and Honore will remain in St. Pierre after the wedding to forestall any gossip attached to your visit. It is well known that you and my sisters are great friends.''

"No matter what Philippe thinks about you, Marcel, you have been a true friend to me and I shall never forget it," Gabby said gratefully. "I have no desire to return to Bellefontaine and I'm afraid to stay at Philippe's townhouse where either he or Amalie can easily find me. As long as it is agreeable to you I will stay here until I decide where my future lies.''

"What do you have in mind, *cherie?*" Marcel asked, searching her violet eyes hopefully.

"I can no longer live with Philippe," Gabby declared firmly, her small chin thrust forward, eyes unwavering. "I intend to leave him. Will you help me?"

"Asky anything of me, Gabby," Marcel said fervently.

"Does your sister in New Orleans still need a governess for her children? If so, I would like to apply for the position.''

"The job is yours, *cherie,* and I will be happy to see you to New Orleans personally if you are still determined to leave your husband," he quickly replied.

"I have no choice. I am afraid of Philippe and fear Amalie even more.''

"After the wedding . . ." But Marcel got no further. Honore and Linette burst into the room throwing themselves upon Gabby.

"Gabby!" exclaimed the volatile Honore. "You've come!"

"We were afraid you would not come to the wedding," explained the less dramatic but nevertheless sincere Linette. Then, being a very perceptive young lady, she noticed Gabby's red-rimmed eyes and immediately voiced her concern. "Why have you been crying, *ma chere?* Is something amiss?''

Almost immediately she realized her blunder, remembering the recent loss of Gabby's child, and blushed furiously.

But it was Honore who surprisingly voiced Linette's feelings. "You dunce, Linette," she rounded, "Gabby has a right to be sad, but now that she is here we will keep her too occupied to have sad thoughts."

"Gabby has consented to stay with us for a while," interposed Marcel, "so you will have plenty of time for gossip. Right now she must be exhausted after the long, hot ride from Bellefontaine so why don't you two take her to her room so that she may bathe and nap before dinner. Don't tire her with your jabber," he warned with mock severity.

Gabby glanced around appreciatively at the handsomely appointed room to which the Duvall sisters had taken her. She noticed that her trunk had already been unpacked and a change of clothing laid out on the bed. A tub of steaming water sat upon the hearth. Gabby had so many reasons to be grateful to Marcel. Honore and Linette made to leave but Gabby urged them to stay and talk while she bathed.

"Tell me about your husband-to-be, Monsieur Bonnard. What is he like?" Gabby asked Linette while she undressed. She could not help but think of her own hastily arranged marriage and how she had railed against becoming the bride of the cold, aloof stranger her parents had chosen for her.

The radiant smile on Linette's face told Gabby volumes about the bride-to-be's feelings. "He is so handsome, Gabby," enthused Linette happily. "Although Marcel told me I would find Monsieur Bonnard pleasing I somehow pictured him anything but handsome."

"She nearly swooned when they met," giggled Honore.

After a sharp, albeit fond look at her sister, Linette continued shyly, "I . . . I think he found me attractive, also." Her cheeks flushed becomingly.

"Of course he did," Gabby smiled indulgently, feeling more like a mother to Linette than someone her own age.

"He would be a fool not to. But tell me more. Have you had an opportunity to be alone with him?"

"We . . . we . . . had a few moments in private," admitted Linette, flashing a grateful glance at her beaming sister.

"And?" prompted Gabby, rising from the tub and wrapping herself in a large bath towel.

"He said . . . he said he loved me already and hoped I would come to love him. He promised to treat me gently. I think . . . I think . . . I love him, too," whispered Linette awestruck by her temerity.

Remembering their brother's warning not to tire Gabby with their chatter, the girls soon left, and Gabby sank gratefully into bed, falling asleep almost immediately. The dreams that marred her rest began the moment she closed her eyes. She saw, as if from a great distance, her own nude body stretched upon a cold, stone slab, a fer-de-lance resting across her stomach. She writhed and twisted, dislodging the bath towel from around her body even though she did not awaken. Disembodied faces floated around her, laughing and leering evilly. And Amalie was there! A seductive smile curving red lips dripping with blood. She felt as if her soul had left her body as she watched the snake move lower on the body bound to the altar, seeking the secret opening. Suddenly, in her dreams, Philippe appeared and flung the snake aside, taking its place between her trembling thighs. His kisses and caresses nearly drove her mad. Then she awoke, sweating profusely yet strangely chilled.

Marcel was holding her quivering form in her arms, soothing her, speaking to her gently as she came to her senses. It took her some minutes to realize that Marcel was moving his hands intimately over her nude breasts and stomach. With a cry of dismay she pulled away and desperately sought to cover herself with the sweat-drenched towel she had cast aside during her nightmare. Though every nerve ending seemed to strain toward Marcel's arousing hands, Gabby realized that her relationship with Marcel must never go beyond friendship. She had no desire to further complicate her life by taking a lover.

No, *ma chere,*" Marcel whispered when he felt her stiffen and pull away. "Let me love you. Allow me to show you the meaning of gentleness and tenderness." His hand moved to explore the tender skin of her inner thigh, his lips teasing an already erect nipple.

"No, Marcel," gasped Gabby raggedly, pushing Marcel's hands and lips aside. "You take unfair advantage of me. I am too vulnerable, too fresh from hurt. Too much has happened to me and my mind is in a turmoil. I implore you to stop. I am too exhausted in mind and spirit to commit myself. I have no desire at this time to take a lover, but your friendship means more to me than anything in the world at this time. If . . . if that is not enough for you I shall be forced to leave."

"You want me, *cherie,* I can feel it in every fiber of your delightful body," Marcel insisted, refusing to give up.

"My body could not help but respond to your caresses, Marcel, but my mind and heart tell me otherwise. You would not take me against my will, would you, Marcel?"

The pleading in her wide, violet eyes was too much for Marcel. Never had he felt such tenderness toward a woman, never had he wanted to make love to a woman as he did Gabby. He found it difficult to admit, but the lovely, very hurt young woman he held in his arms meant as much to him as did his own sisters. Reluctantly he allowed Gabby to slide from his embrace and even surprised himself by helping her to refasten the towel about her slim body. "Will you be all right?" he asked as he made to leave.

"*Oui,* I'm fine . . . now," replied Gabby shyly.

"Nothing or no one will harm you while I am here to protect you," promised Marcel gravely. And he never meant anything more in his whole life. He would kill anyone, even

Philippe, who obviously cared little for his lovely wife and appreciated her even less.

Linette's wedding was a delightful affair, the affection displayed between bride and groom touching. Linette was enchanting, her bright beauty a perfect foil for Pierre Bonnard's dark handsomeness. Gabby's high regard for Marcel increased each time Pierre Bonnard leaned protectively toward his radiant bride throughout the long nuptial mass. Marcel could have chosen someone old and ugly or someone cold and possessive, like Philippe, for his shy, reserved sister. But instead he had picked a man who seemed to appreciate Linette's many qualities. If only Philippe had been half as devoted as Pierre Bonnard, Gabby thought bitterly. Nothing remained of the tender, caring man Philippe had become when he first learned she carried his child. Had it all been a charade?

Gabby appeared but briefly at the wedding reception. Linette and Pierre had already left to board a ship that would carry them to their new home in France and Gabby did not linger once she had wished the young couple a long, happy life.

During the following days, Honore thanked Gabby time and again for remaining with her and taking up the void left in her life by the departed Linette. Honore could not know that she too was like a balm to Gabby's deflated spirits. Honore's youth and exuberance helped greatly to dispel Gabby's recurring nightmares of sacrificial altars and snakes.

Finally the day came when Gabby could no longer delay her departure from Martinique. The passionate, beseeching looks aimed in her direction by Marcel left little doubt in her mind that he would not long be satisfied with their relationship based on friendship alone. She also began to fear that Philippe would appear and demand her return to Bellefontaine. That thought alone made her decision for her.

Accordingly, she voiced her wishes to Marcel. "You have been content here, haven't you, *ma chere?*" asked Marcel, unhappy with her decision.

Gabby stared thoughtfully at Mt. Pelee before answering. She sensed in it a sleeping giant, ready to erupt at any time, just like Philippe. Sighing hugely, she finally replied, "Too happy, Marcel. In fact, so content that I had nearly forgotten that Philippe could return at any time and force me to return to Bellefontaine, just as he did Cecily so long ago. I am convinced he will never send Amalie away and I could never be a wife to him under those conditions." Gabby's violet eyes turned dark as she fought back tears of remorse. "Don't you see, Marcel? It's imperative that I leave Martinique before Philippe returns. I'm afraid that the next time Amalie will succeed in her diabolical plan to do away with me. Will you help me, Marcel?" she beseeched.

"*Cherie, cherie,*" crooned Marcel, running his hand along the soft curtain of her hair. He saw how terrified Gabby was of Amalie and Philippe and decided to work it toward his own purposes. *Le bon dieu* knew how much he wanted her and once she was away from Philippe he was certain she would come to love him in turn. "Of course I will help you, even if it means parting with you for a short time. How soon do you wish to leave?"

"The sooner the better," came Gabby's determined answer.

"I will make inquiries on the docks this very day. Leave matters to me, *cherie*. I shall arrange everything to our mutual satisfaction. You will go to my sister in New Orleans. And Honore shall accompany you."

"*Merci!* I knew I could depend on you," cried Gabby throwing her arms impulsively around Marcel's neck.

The imprint of her soft body pressed so intimately against his was too much for Marcel. With a groan of surrender he drew her ever closer and captured her slighty parted lips in a fierce, demanding kiss that left her breathless and confused. Gabby resisted only for a moment, then responded more out of gratitude than love. Fired by her response, Marcel became more than ever determined to have her for his own. He would finish his business on Martinique and follow her to New Orleans. To his way of thinking nothing mattered except having Gabby all to himself, in every way. With the greatest effort of will he removed his hands from her soft body and broke off the kiss, his head awhirl with plans for a future that would place Gabby exactly where he wanted her . . . in his bed.

Two days later arrangements for Gabby's and Honore's passage to New Orleans were complete. When Honore found she and Gabby were to travel together to New Orleans for a visit with her sister, her dark eyes sparkled and she clapped her small hands happily. "You are so good to me, Marcel," she laughed. "It's been ever so long since I've visited Celeste that the children must have forgotten me already. And Gabby," she said, turning to Gabby with outstretched hands, "you are so kind to accompany me. It would be impossible for me to travel unchaperoned."

"Gabby realized that you could not make the trip alone and has agreed to see you safely to New Orleans," put in Marcel smoothly. It was best Honore know nothing of Gabby's plans to leave her husband.

Honore gave Gabby a quick hug. "Celeste will be pleased to have Gabby as a guest," she added. "I'm sure a change of scenery will do us both a world of good." Honore was thinking of Gabby's recent loss and her own loneliness following her sister's departure.

"Then it's all settled," announced Marcel. "Your ship leaves in two days."

"That doesn't give us much time," cried an excited Honore, jumping up to begin packing immediately. "Will you be able to join us?" Honore asked of Marcel before she left the room, suddenly mindful tht her brother would be left alone.

"I promise that I shall not be far behind you," he answered, looking directly at Gabby. Satisfied by his reply, Honore scampered up the stairs, leaving Marcel and Gabby alone.

"*Merci*, Marcel," Gabby said warmly. "Not only have you arranged for me to leave Martinique but you have provided me with an excuse to do so. And I shall have Honore's delightful company besides. But are you sure your sister will welcome another guest? Do you think she will allow me to become governess to her children?"

"Do not worry, *cherie*," chided Marcel gently. "A letter has already been dispatched on a swift packet informing Celeste that you are to be afforded every courtesy as her guest. When I arrive is time enough to discuss your future. Until then you are companion and chaperone to Honore."

By the time he arrived in New Orleans, Marcel expected Gabby to come willingly to him. He would set her up as his mistress and in a grand house. If all he hoped came to pass he would even consider selling all his holdings on Martinique and moving permanently to New Orleans. Or perhaps they could all settle in France. It would not be difficult to arrange a suitable marriage for Honore in France and they would be out of Philippe's reach. It bothered Marcel not at all that he was taking another man's wife. Gabby was too good for Philippe, he reasoned. Teasing flirts like Cecily or vicious witches like Amalie were more to his liking. Perhaps he could even arrange for a divorce and marry Gabby himself.

Chapter Fourteen

GABBY STOOD beside Honore at the rail of the *Southern Star* as they entered the mouth of the Mississippe River, a cool winter breeze whipping their skirts around their legs. Gabby glanced fondly at Honore as the younger girl's excitement began to spark her own. Their passage to New Orleans had been a pleasant interlude. Honore had seen to it that Gabby did not become bored and her constant chatter often saved Gabby from dwelling too much on the past.

Gabby pulled her warm cloak closer about her and thought fleetingly of the coming Christmas season. She had hoped to be with her own little family at Bellefontaine when Christmas arrived, but fate had willed otherwise. Her arms still ached to hold the babe Philippe had heartlessly accused her of murdering. Not even Honore's sunny disposition and welcome company could dispel her longing. Sadly she realized that as long as she remained estranged from her husband she would never hold a child of her own in her arms.

When Gabby first learned from Marcel that the *Southern Star* was a ship of Philippe's line she had nearly refused to board her until Marcel had sworn to her that there was no way possible for her husband to learn that she was a passenger. Marcel had even taken the precaution of listing her as Madame Marcel Duvall on the manifest. He had also carefully checked the passenger list and found that none of his close acquaintances traveled aboard the *Southern Star*. As far as Gabby could tell, her departure from Martinique went completely unheralded.

Soon the ramparts came into view and Gabby became as

animated as Honore to be once more in the first city she had set foot in when she arrived from France and which she still held in warm regard. She thought briefly of Jean Lafitte and of her friend Marie and wondered if those heroes of the battle of New Orleans still resided on Barataria.

The *Southern Star* eased into a berth along the long row of docks and Honore began anxiously scanning the wharf for her sister. Amid the bustle of busy sailors on the ship and the throng of people along the ramparts, Honore was unable to identify a familiar face. But to Gabby's horror the face of a man she had hoped never to see again emerged from amid the crowd to stand on the dock waiting for the gangplank to be lowered into place. Thunderstruck, Gabby could only watch in silence as Philippe boarded the ship, spoke briefly with the captain, then walked unerringly in her direction.

Honore spied Philippe as he advanced on them and gave a cry of surprise. "Gabby!" she gasped. "Your husband is in New Orleans and has come to meet you!" Completely unaware of Gabby's estrangement from Philippe, Honore continued enthusiastically, "I am so happy for you! How exciting to be reunited with your husband so unexpectedly!"

Gabby winced at Honore's words but had no time to think of an appropriate reply before Philippe was upon them.

"*Ma chere,*" he greeted with mock tenderness that rang falsely in Gabby's ears, "I am so happy you chose to join me for the holidays."

It was obvious to Gabby that Philippe's great show of affection was for the benefit of all within hearing as he took her into his arms and tenderly kissed her. If she didn't know better Gabby could almost believe that Philippe was glad to see her.

"How . . . how did you know I was aboard the *Southern Star?*" stammered Gabby when she finally found her voice.

"Later," he returned smoothly. His words conveyed little by way of an explanation but the twitch in the muscle along his jawline warned Gabby to silence. "First we must find Honore's sister and when we are alone I will tell you what you want to know. I will also demonstrate just how happy I am to see you," he added, an underlying thread of malice in his voice. Gabby stiffened but fought hard to keep the smile on her lips.

"But, Monsieur Philippe," protested Honor innocently, "Gabby was to be Celeste's guest. Does this mean her plans are altered? Marcel expects Gabby to be at our sister's home when he arrives. Did you know Gabby has been staying with us?" Gabby swallowed the lump of fear rising in her throat. Honore's innocent words sounded condemning even to her own ears. What would Philippe think? she wondered fearfully.

"I am sure your brother will be the first to agree that my wife and I have been parted long enough," he said lightly, but with steely undertones. "She will join me aboard the *Windward* where her company will be most welcome during the long weeks to come." Gabby blanced and would have protested had not Philippe's threatening look forewarned her. "Come, ladies," he announced curtly, "shall we disembark?"

It took no time at all once they were ashore to locate Celeste. She waited inside her carriage on the perimeter of the crowded dock and in spite of her own predicament, Gabby smiled at the tender greeting between sisters. After far too short a time she found herself taking leave of them with tears glistening in her violet eyes, Philippe's grip upon her arms tightening painfully as she watched them depart.

"We shall meet again on Martinique," Honore promised, giving Gabby a final squeeze before climbing into the carriage. "Is there a message you wish me to convey to my brother?" she asked, unaware of Philippe's icy eyes at the mention of Marcel's name.

"*Oui,*" murmured Gabby with a wary glance at Philippe,

"tell him . . ."

"Thank him for seeing that my wife reached me safely," Philippe interjected, dropping his arm to encompass Gabby's tiny waist. Then they were alone.

"Shall we leave, *ma chere?*" Philippe asked. The timbre of his voice sounded low and strained to Gabby and her knees began to tremble. What would Philippe do to her? There could be no doubt in his mind that she was leaving him and Honore had inadvertently let slip that she had been staying in Marcel's townhouse. Naturally he'll assume the worst, Gabby thought ruefully.

Quaking inwardly, she allowed herself to be guided along the docks until they reached the *Windward's* berth. She resisted only momentarily before giving in to Philippe's none too gentle prodding up the gangplank. They were met by a stern-looking, gray-haired man whom Philippe introduced as Captain Bouvier, the replacement for Captain Giscard. He seemed to have been expecting her and after a formal word of welcome went about his business.

Then Gabby was rapidly propelled toward the cabin she had previously shared with Philippe on her crossing from France. Shoved rudely inside the room, she stumbled, clutching at a chair for support, but unable to stop herself sprawled at Philippe's feet. She had all she could do to keep from crying out as Philippe stood menacingly over her, feet wide apart, hands on hips, his darkening features more frightening than she remembered.

"Up to your old tricks again, *ma cherie?*" he said scathingly. "I can tell by your face that you hoped never to see me again. I am sorry to disappoint you." His steely gaze held her captive to the deck.

"How did you know I was aboard the *Southern Star?*" Gabby demanded with more bravery than she felt at that moment.

"Your lover Marcel sent a message to his sister on one of

my packets," Philippe explained in a brittle voice. "I happened to be in New Orleans when it arrived and the message was put into my hands by the captain. I recognized the name of Marcel's sister and read the letter out of curiosity before sending it on to its destination. To say I was shocked would be an understatement." He paused to glare accusingly down on Gabby. "To learn that one's own wife had become whore to a man he despised is hardly what I would call welcome news. How long has Marcel been your lover? How long have you been living with him? I imagine you have set St. Pierre agog with your shameless behavior. What's even more despicable is that you used poor, innocent Honore to cover your affair."

Gabby made to rise but Philippe held her firmly to the deck with his booted foot. "It's not what you think, Philippe!" denied Gabby hotly. "Marcel is my friend, nothing more! If you knew why . . ."

"I don't want to hear it!" bellowed Philippe, removing his foot from her stomach. "Do you think I have forgotten or forgiven you for your indiscretion with Captain Stone? It appears that the innocent girl who wished to become a nun has turned whore as well as murderess!" Wincing, Gabby closed her ears against his cruel, hurtful tirade.

How dare he act so self-righteous, Gabby fumed. How dare he condemn her after she found him in the arms of his mistress. Aloud she said, "I am sorry for you, Philippe. You accuse me unjustly. Will you not hear me out before you judge me? I am not the only one who has sinned."

Her words must have hit a raw nerve for his dark face grew fierce. "Enough!" he ordered harshly. "Your idle prattle bores me." He looked down upon her with disgust. "Get up!"

When Gabby made no move to obey, Philippe grasped her hands and pulled her roughly to her feet. His gray eyes narrowed in guarded scrutiny, moving from her face insinuatingly down her curvacious body. "You appear quite recovered," he said. "Apparently Marcel has been most careful with your health."

Forcefully he pulled her into his arms, his fingers sinking into the soft hair at the back of her head, tightening, holding her motionless for the cruel descent of his hard lips. She could not move, could hardly breathe under the controlled savagery of his passion. Gabby could feel the steady beat of his heart, feel the hardness of his body against hers, stiff and unyielding like the man himself. His other hand ravaged the soft curves of her body. She remained rigid and unmoving beneath his violent onslaught until he flung her from him in disgust, the feel of her tense, defiant body sending him into a rage.

"Do you prefer the gentle touch of your lover to mine?" Philippe asked icily.

Anger prompted Gabby to retaliate. "Perhaps I do." She was immediately sorry she had provoked him as she found herself lifted bodily and flung to the bed, pinned beneath Philippe's punishing strength. With deft hands he undressed her, her feeble struggles serving only to enflame him. When she was divested of every stitch of clothing and lay naked and exposed, Philippe silently and grimly removed his own clothes. With bleak eyes Gabby saw the state of his arousal and turned her head from the strangely disquieting sight of his strong, masculine body. He laughed sardonically when he saw the direction of her gaze.

"How do I compare to your other lovers?" he taunted cruelly. "Surely you haven't forgotten so soon the extent of my passion?"

Enraged by his words, Gabby tried to strike out at him but found her wrists captured and pinned above her head. Philippe lay full length atop her, her breasts pressed into his massive chest. Freeing one hand, Gabby clawed instinctively for Philippe's eyes. His head snapped back as her fingers raked the side of his neck, immediately drawing blood.

Gray eyes blazed with anger as well as passion. "Don't fight me, you little hellcat," he warned ominously. "I own you. You are mine. I can take you at will. This is the law." Then he wrenched her free arm up to join the other over her head. Her hands grew numb, her shoulders straining in their sockets. She watched with perverse fascination as the blood from the grooves in his neck dripped upon her breast. Almost cruelly Philippe lowered his mouth to her trembling lips as his free hand plundered her body. Tears of frustration welled in Gabby's eyes but did little to stop Philippe's onslaught. Then, without warning, she sensed a change in him as his body relaxed and almost tenderly he explored the moist corners of her eyelids, the smooth curve of her cheek, the hollow at the base of her neck. His quickening breath seared her flesh, setting off in her an uncontrollable shudder as his lips trailed fiery kisses to the taut peaks of her breasts.

Involuntarily, a low moan issued forth from Gabby's throat and Philippe's flinty eyes glinted in savage satisfaction when he heard it. It had been so long since Gabby had been loved that once Philippe had awakened her sleeping passion she could scarcely control her rising emotions. Her body remembered the tenderness he was capable of and yearned to experience it once again. Then all pretense of tenderness fled as Philippe continued his ruthless plunder.

Gabby lunged under him, every muscle straining to throw him from her, but the effort served only to instill him with a need to hurt her. The rigid muscles of his thighs pressed into her soft body and his hands ravaged her flesh with a directness she could not thwart. When he tore into her she cried out in agony but as he moved within her she experienced a growing weakness, a primitive urge toward surrender that had nothing to do with her will to resist.

With a will of its own Gabby's body began moving in rhythm to meet Philippe's thrusts. Sensing her surrender, Philippe released her hands and they immediately wound themselves about his neck, forcing him even deeper within her. There was no way Gabby could fight him now, no way she could deny him, or herself. A wild sob was torn from her throat and suddenly they found themselves adrift in a sea of ecstasy.

When Philippe finally eased his body away from Gabby, she turned on her side so he could not see her tears. She thought bitterly of Philippe's betrayal with Amalie, of his harsh accusations, and hated her body for responding to him almost as much as she hated the man himself. Alerted by her soft sobs, Philippe raised up on one elbow, his face momentarily losing its stony facade while he studied her in silent appraisal. A flicker of emotion coursed through him before his eyes once more became shuttered, his face a mask of icy reserve. He turned Gabby to face him.

"Why do you cry?" he asked with mock concern. "Don't you enjoy playing whore for your own husband?" His sardonic smile cut into her like a saber, his words twisting the blade more effectively than his hands ever could. "I ask no more of you than what your lovers would expect."

"Philippe, listen to me, please," Gabby cried angrily, determined to make him understand. "Marcel and I . . ."

"Enough!" Philippe ordered, immediately stilling her protests. "From this day on the name of no other man shall pass your lovely lips. You will be available to no one but me. You will be at my service and at my mercy."

"What happens when we return to Martinique?" Gabby asked, swallowing the nausea rising in her throat.

"Nothing will have changed," assured Philippe smoothly.

"And Amalie? Will she share your favors?"

Philippe's face darkened; Gabby quailed inwardly, only too aware of his foul temper. "What I do with Amalie is no concern of yours," he thundered.

"Then I wish you joy of her," Gabby ground out bitterly. "She might give you a bastard but only I can give you an

238

heir." For a brief moment she considered telling Philippe about the night Amalie had her taken from her bed to the altar of Damballa, but quickly discarded the idea, realizing that given his frame of mind Philippe would not believe her. Sighing wretchedly she turned away from him.

But Philippe was not ready to allow her respite. Gathering her against his hard chest and thighs he began to explore her body with a cold, methodical passion that left her chilled to the bone. Steeling herself against the sensations that his icy fingers evoked, Gabby was able to remain aloof while he took brutal pleasure from her ravaged flesh. Later, she was to wonder at the tenderness in his voice when he called out her name at the moment ecstasy washed over him.

Once he was sated, Philippe startled Gabby by abruptly rising and dressing swiftly, as if he could hardly wait to be rid of her. She had no way of knowing that he was shocked and dismayed by his inability to hold his emotions in check. He was moved more than he cared to admit by her facade of fragile vulnerability. Steeling himself against the conflicting turmoil raging within him, he stomped from the cabin, gathering up all of Gabby's clothes along the way and taking them with him. The click of the lock grated loudly in Gabby's ears.

Gabby seethed with rage. She had been debased and degraded. It galled her to think that she would be used as nothing more than a sexual convenience! During the next days Philippe returned periodically to bring her meals and use her whenever the urge was upon him, informing her that she was being held captive because he could not trust her. Once at sea she would be allowed free use of the deck and be given her clothes back . . . but only if she behaved and promised not to entertain the crew with outbursts of hysterics. During Philippe's so-called amorous attacks Gabby remained beyond arousal, but her continued resistance only made her all the more desirable in his eyes. Her bitter words and cold body tended to make him use her more savagely than he intended and often he left her angrier at himself than at her.

Gabby watched morosely from the porthole as the *Windward* entered the Gulf of Mexico, shivering despite the blanket wrapped around her bruised body. Philippe still had not given her her clothes back and the cold air bit deeply into her bones. She wondered why he didn't just give up on her and let her go. Surely, somewhere in this world, there was a woman more to his liking, one submissive enough to please him.

With grim determination Philippe set out to break Gabby's will, but for some unknown reason he could not bring himself to cast her aside. Whenever he gazed into her defiant violet eyes he was torn apart. At times he desired nothing more than to take her into his arms and smother her with tenderness and love. And then there were times when her unresponsive, cold body and sassy words sent him into a rage. But willing or not, he was determined to have her. At this point, responsive or passive made little different to him. Never again would he allow himself to think of her as anything but a vessel for his lust. Never again would he lay bare his soul before a woman or give his heart in trust.

Because Gabby exhibited no signs of becoming submissive, Philippe continued to withhold her clothing as punishment. He hoped the humiliation and degradation he had subjected her to would soon have her begging, but he was mistaken. Gabby grew sullen and withdrawn. As much as Philippe hated to admit it, he sorely missed Gabby's passion, her sweet response to his lovemaking. His forceful ways left her bruised but otherwise undaunted, causing Philippe to rethink his tactics. Perhaps there was an easier way to tame her; a way that would be more to her liking but still not cost him his mastery over her.

Just before the *Windward* put into Charleston Gabby was

given her clothing back and told she could go wherever she pleased on deck. She eyed Philippe warily but wasted no time in dressing, regaining once more some shred of dignity. Although Philippe preferred her nude, he gallantly placed her cloak about her small shoulders before opening the door so she could proceed him out into the brisk air.

It seemed like ages since Gabby had walked about freely and she breathed deeply of the salt-laden air, feeling like one just let out of prison. Philippe could not help but smile at her obvious delight at being free again. For a brief moment the breath caught in his throat at the enchanting picture she made with the wind ruffling her silvery hair and whipping her skirts about her slim legs. At that moment Philippe wanted her more than he ever had before!

Without preliminary, Philippe grasped Gabby's elbow and forced her toward their cabin. Though clearly disappointed with her brief sojourn on deck, Gabby did not protest. Once inside, Philippe was startled by the first genuine warmth she had afforded him since he had forced her to accompany him aboard the *Windward*.

"*Merci*, Philippe," she smiled shyly. "I hope the next time I might remain on deck longer."

Hardening his heart against her feminine wiles, he ordered brusquely, "Take off your clothes!"

"What!"

"You heard me!"

"But why? You have just given them back to me," Gabby wailed in protest. "What have I done?"

"You have done nothing and you shall have your clothes back soon," Philippe promised, his eyes suddenly smoky with desire. There was no way Gabby could misconstrue his intention. His avid expression and hardening body told her he would have his way with or without her cooperation. And she did want her clothes back. With a wistful sigh, she removed her clothes, folded them neatly and placed them on a chair. By the time she finished, Philippe was disrobed, and she found herself gathered up in strong arms and deposited on the bed. She stiffened in resistance, but remembering how good it felt to be decently dressed and have a measure of freedom, relaxed within the circle of his arms, allowing his slow arousal of her body to take her back to the time when his lips and hands had been guided by love. Even now he had the ability to drive her wild with passion, and this time, in spite of his own rising ardor he took special care to satisfy her before succumbing to his own ecstasy. His entry was so gentle that Gabby, despite herself, gasped in delight, drawing him deep within her.

"*Mon dieu*, you are a witch!" he groaned, lost in a sea of desire.

For a brief eternity nothing else mattered to Gabby but the man transporting her to the brink of bliss. There was no Amalie, no Marcel, nothing but an exploding world where only Philippe had the power to take her. As the last burst of pleasure convulsed her she smiled up at Philippe only to have the smile freeze on her face when she saw his sardonic grin and self-satisfied curl to his lips.

"That was more like it, *ma chere*," he grinned, his hands lightly caressing her stomach. "I knew you could not resist forever. I am well aware of what that enticing body is capable of, for I taught you well. I hope that others after me appreciated my efforts," he taunted cruelly.

Gabby gasped, white dots of rage exploding behind her eyes, and before he could stop her Philippe felt the full imprint of her hand upon his face. Reflexively, he struck back, his own huge hand inflicting more damage than Gabby's smaller one.

Gabby's head reeled and blood filled her mouth as her stricken eyes sought Philippe's in numb disbelief. She willed back the tears but could not keep the pain from her face. Shocked by what he had done, Philippe jumped from the bed, moistened a towel in the water pitcher and gently wiped the blood from her mouth, his anger melted in remorseful apology, even though he could not voice it verbally. Then he cradled her in his arms, crooning softly until she fell asleep, sobbing softly into his chest.

Not only did Gabby have her clothes back but she was given the run of the ship. Since Philippe had struck her he had not attempted to take her again, except during the long hours of night when they shared the bed. Then, under the cover of darkness, he took his fill of her, sometimes with great tenderness, sometimes savagely, but always in silence. Gabby's body automatically responded even though her mind rebelled at the way he used her.

To Gabby's great surprise Philippe took her ashore at Charleston and showed her the sights in a rented gig. Although the day was cool, the wintry sun shone brightly and she enjoyed the outing immensely. The shops were filled with merchandise in anticipation of Christmas, which was a week away, and Gabby was saddened to think of the bleak holiday that awaited her aboard the *Windward*.

After Gabby had provoked Philippe into striking her he had tried to restrain his passion for her but whenever he pictured in his mind her lush body and huge violet eyes bright with desire he was driven by a power greater than his own weak will. For some unexplained reason she was as necessary to him as food and drink, more like a sickness in his blood. It would seem that after the pain she had caused him he would want nothing more to do with her, yet he clung to her, unwilling to relinquish her to another. Gabby was his; never again would another man put his brand upon her. He was determined to use her, debase her, even, until she no longer had a will of her own. Only then would he take her back to Bellefontaine.

Christmas came and went without fanfare. Philippe had turned a deaf ear to Gabby's pleas to be taken ashore again. She

243

wanted to buy a small creche, something to remind her of the meaning of Christmas no matter how empty the day would be. A light snow had fallen the night before and Gabby longed to trod upon the fresh, white ground. But Philippe went ashore alone after taking away Gabby's clothes once again. He expected to be gone the entire day making arrangements for a cargo of cotton and tobacco and did not trust her in his absence . . . not even under lock and key. He had thoughtfully provided a small stove for warmth and enough blankets to wrap herself in.

"Why do you continue to humiliate me, Philippe?" she had asked before he left. "If you hate me so why do you keep me with you?"

"I will never let you go, Gabby," he said with controlled emotion. "You are mine. No other man shall have you again." Then he was out the door before he could see tears of bewilderment and anguish gather in her eyes.

As the day lengthened, Gabby's stomach rumbled as delicious odors of food from the galley wafted into the cabin. With each passing hour it became increasingly evident that Philippe had forgotten to order food for her and she railed at his neglect, especially on Christmas Day. Darkness fell, and even the meager supply of wood for the stove ran out. Gabby crawled into bed in an effort to keep from freezing. She fell asleep, but not before vowing anew the promise she made to herself to leave Philippe at the first opportunity.

It was nearly dawn when Philippe returned but Gabby was sleeping so deeply she did not hear him moving somewhat unsteadily about the cabin, cursing softly when he stumbled into the furniture. It was some time before he slid into bed, soaking up her warmth as he pulled her roughly against him. The sudden contact of her warmth against his chilled body brought her startlingly awake. The strong smell of whiskey assaulted her senses, and then she caught a whiff of musky

244

perfume. She struggled against him but was no match for his superior strength.

"Want you," he muttered unevenly as his hands fumbled at her breasts.

"You're drunk!" she accused. "And . . . and you've been with another woman!"

"Need you," Philippe insisted drunkenly.

"Go back to where you came from!" Gabby spat venomously.

"Want only you," he muttered, easing his muscular frame atop her smaller one. "Love me, Gabby. Show me what makes men so eager for you."

"You disgust me, Philippe!"

"Ah, but I can't seem to get enough of you." As if to prove his words he entered her roughly, causing Gabby to utter a cry of pain before going limp, holding herself aloof from his drunken onslaught. Finally, he was finished, and Gabby breathed deeply when his weight shifted from her. Almost immediately he was asleep. Not so Gabby who lay awake a long time, her body curled up in a tight ball.

Even though Philippe had little sleep the night before he was the first to awaken. Gabby was turned toward him, her soft breath fanning his cheek. His heart skipped a beat and he wondered at his ability to treat her as he did. He studied her face intently. It was an extraordinary face, both arresting and provocative, with a sweetness and purity that belied her true nature. Cursing, he left the warm bed, quickly dressed and let himself out of the cabin after a fleeting glance around the room to check on his preparations of the night before.

Gabby awoke slowly, stretching her arms and legs lazily. Instinctively she reached for Philippe and opened her eyes when her hands failed to meet with warm flesh. She sat up and her violet eyes grew round and big when she saw the creche neatly arranged atop Philippe's sea chest. Beside it sat a small box gaudily wrapped in bright paper and tied with a huge bow. Gabby slid from bed and moved to the creche, picking up each tiny, hand-carved figure, marveling at the intricate work. Only after she had thoroughly examined the creche did she allow herself to focus upon the box, touching it gingerly before taking it up, her hands shaking as she removed the wrappings. She treated it as if she expected something to jump out at her, but finally the cover fell away and Gabby gasped in stunned shock at the contents. Nestled in a cocoon of soft cotton lay a pair of amethyst earrings the exact shade of her eyes. How could Philippe use her so foully and still care enough to buy her such an expensive gift? Never would she understand the strange man she had married. Conflicting emotions warred within her. Everything about Philippe was a contradiction. He had only to touch her to send her to soaring ecstasy . . . or to the depths of Hell.

An insistant knocking on the door interrupted her reverie. Absently she called. "Who is it?"

"Seaman Laville, Madame St. Cyr," announced the man standing at the other side of the door. "May I come in? Your husband ordered your trunk of clothing brought to the cabin."

"Come in," called Gabby, surprised when the door opened without benefit of key. Had Philippe forgotten to lock her in? she wondered uneasily. What kind of game was he playing now?

If Seaman Laville thought it odd that Gabby stood clothed in nothing but a rough blanket he gave no hint of it. Neither did the two sailors who carried her trunk. Placing the trunk at the end of the bed and wishing her a Merry Christmas, they left, carefully closing the door behind them. Though Gabby strained her ears she heard no telltale click suggesting she had been locked in again.

With a cry of joy Gabby fell upon the trunk and found that all the clothing she had brought from Martinique was still inside. Discarding some of the lightweight dresses inappropriate to nothern climes, she chose a medium weight wool in a becoming shade of mauve. Selecting lacetrimmed undergarments and mauve slippers to match the dress, she set them aside while she washed in the icy water from the pitcher on the wash stand. After dressing quickly in the chill air, she took up her silver brush and began to work out the tangles in her pale hair until it was smooth and shiny. As a final touch she fastened the amethyst earrings in her ears. She had finished none too soon for Philippe entered at that moment bearing a large tray. The delicious odors wafting from beneath the linen cloth covering the tray set her mouth to watering.

"Very becoming," Philippe murmured, his brittle gaze sweeping over her lush curves, "but I like you just as well without clothing." Then his eyes caught the glitter at her earlobes.

Seeing the direction of his stare, Gabby's hands automatically flew to her ears. "*Merci*, Philippe, they are exquisite." His face softened for a brief moment before his usual mask of indifference hooded his features. "And the creche, I love it. But I have nothing to give you in return."

"Christmas should be a time of joy no matter what one has done," he muttered with obvious embarrassment. Then taking her hand he led her to the table where he carefully laid out the festive breakfast, urging her to eat while it was still hot.

Gabby attacked the food almost greedily and Philippe had time to ponder the reasoning behind his generosity as he watched her eat, his eyes never wavering from her face. He very nearly hadn't returned to the ship at all last night. With business at an end he had tried to take his leave of Gordon Blake, the man he had been dealing with for tobacco. But Blake had insisted on bringing Philippe to his home for Christmas dinner. There was no way Philippe could gracefully

247

refuse so he had reluctantly agreed to join Blake and his family in their sumptuous home for a late supper. In addition to Blake and his wife were the couple's two sons and their wives, and their lovely, black-eyed daughter named Lee Ann whose thinly veiled, flirtatious glances were directed at Philippe all evening. Later he had allowed himself to be persuaded to spend the night with the Blakes, the gleam in Lee Ann's eyes promising more than a good night's rest.

Once in his room, Philippe had undressed, climbed between the sheets and immediately fallen into a drunken sleep, the amount of brandy he had consumed during the course of the evening having made him more than a little tipsy. He had awakened confused and befuddled, disturbed by the rustle of clothing. He struggled to rise from his stupor but his spinning head made him drop back heavily against the pillow. A smooth, silken body came into his arms and involuntarily his hands reached out to draw Lee Ann's supple, willing flesh urgently against his hardening body.

She moaned, and he sought her lips, all vestige of drunkenness vanished as they parted beneath the pressure, becoming pliant, then demanding. Her hands found and grasped his member, leaving no mistake about her intent. She became like a wildcat, scratching, biting, devouring him with her lips and her body. But even as his flesh responded to her his thoughts strayed to Gabby, held captive in a tiny room by now grown cold and bleak, her loneliness and despair the result of his senseless abuse.

There was no way Lee Ann would allow Philippe's thoughts to linger on another woman as she eagerly drew him into her scalding flesh with a cry of pleasure, welcoming his hard, cruel thrust gleefully, urging him on with soft words of encouragement. For some yet obscure reason Philippe wanted to punish Lee Ann for not being the woman he really wanted in his bed, but the harder he tried to hurt her, the louder her cries of encouragement. For Lee Ann it was over too soon as

248

Philippe flung himself off her with a disgusted grunt that she mistook for satisfaction. Almost immediately her soft, even breathing told Philippe she was asleep.

Still dazed from too much alcohol, Philippe wanted nothing more than to return to the *Windward* and Gabby. In fact, something compelled him to rise from the bed and dress. Without a backward glance at the sleeping Lee Ann curled up contentedly in his bed, he noiselessly let himself out of the house and, despite the later hour, made directly for the nearest jewelry shop where he pounded loudly on the door until a sleepy-eyed, disgruntled proprietor let him in. But once the man realized that Philippe wished to purchase one of his most expensive pieces of jewelry his anger immediately cooled.

Now, as he watched in silence as Gabby devoured her breakfast, his eyes softened, remembering the first time he had aroused her passion. She had resisted mightily his frequent assaults upon her body until the raging storm as well as his own ardor finally sparked a response in her, unleashing the passion he knew her capable of. With a start he realized that he preferred her willing and eager for him and thought wistfully on the loving woman she had once been.

Gabby sat back in her chair, pushed her empty plate away and sighed contentedly. "I can't remember when anything tasted so good," she said, smiling like a cat who had just lapped up a saucer of cream.

"I can't remember when I've seen you eat so much, *ma petite*," Philippe replied, a crooked grin easing his stony face, "except when . . ." Suddenly he broke off and stared narrowly at her, his eyes searching her features before sliding over her reed-slim body. Abruptly he arose and left the cabin, carefully closing but not locking the door behind him.

Later that day Gabby bravely opened the door to her cabin and strode defiantly on deck, the stubborn tilt to her chin daring anyone to stop her. She was surprised to find the ship nearly deserted until she remembered that they had probably gone ashore to celebrate Christmas. Though the wind was chilly the sun shone brightly and Gabby turned her face toward the welcome warmth. Without warning Philippe appeared at her elbow. "Be careful you don't become chilled in this cool breeze and catch a cold, *ma chere*," he cautioned, thoroughly confusing Gabby to his changing moods.

"Would you care, Philippe?" she asked, turning to face him, violet eyes wide and questioning.

"Mais oui, ma petite," he answered archly. "Ill you would be of no use to me. A weak body holds little appeal for me."

Gabby blanched and had to hold on to the railing for support. Would she ever become immune to Philippe's cruelty? she thought resentfully, swallowing hard on the constriction in her throat. Turning on her heel, she deliberately walked away from him, but he followed close behind, until they were both inside their cabin.

"We leave Charleston tomorrow," he said with studied indifference.

"To return to Martinique?" asked Gabby hopefully.

"No, our next port of call is Norfolk."

"That means we will be at sea many more weeks," replied Gabby dismally.

"Oui," Philippe responded coolly. "Perhaps in the coming weeks you will learn the meaning of faithfulness."

"Just as you shall," replied Gabby softly, a slow smile curving her lips at Philippe's startled look.

Chapter Fifteen

COLD, SLEET-DRIVEN winds added considerably to the length of time it took to reach Norfolk. Day after day Philippe continued to demand his marital rights, sometimes with little consideration for Gabby's feelings and at other times with such tenderness that she was at odds with her own emotions. If at any time during their curious relationship Gabby experienced the least bit of softening in Philippe's attitude, he immediately negated it with cruel taunts and callous disregard.

On the day Norfolk came into view Gabby was standing at the railing buffeted by strong winds. The rough seas made it nearly impossible to keep her balance. Suddenly, nausea rose in her throat like gorge and try as she might she could not keep from spewing the breakfast she had just eaten into the sea. Waves of dizziness sent her reeling and just when she feared she would fall overboard, a pair of strong arms tightened around her waist and she felt herself being lifted from her feet.

Gabby slowly opened her eyes and when her vision cleared saw that she was lying on the bed and that Philippe was tenderly sponging her face with a wet cloth. "Do you feel better, *ma petite?*" he asked, concern evident in his voice if not in his eyes.

"*Oui*, Philippe," Gabby answered, trying to rise.

"No, do not get up yet. I have no wish to see you lying at my feet."

Obediently Gabby lay back against the pillows. She needed no one to tell her what had caused her nausea or made her swoon. She knew without a doubt that she was pregnant again! Would Philippe be pleased, she wondered, eying him warily. She certainly was not!

Her uneasy thoughts were rudely interrupted when Philippe placed a hand on her flat stomach and asked, "Whose child is it, Gabby?" His blunt accusation shocked her.

"*Mon dieu*, Phillipe, how can you ask such a thing? No one but you could have fathered this child!"

"How can you be so sure?" he said icily. "I took you not two weeks after you left Duvall. There is no way you can be certain who fathered your child."

"Philippe! Please believe me! There has been no one but you!"

"Save your breath, *ma chere*. I know Duvall as well as I know your own passionate nature." Then he removed his hand from her stomach and began to pace the small cabin. "The fault lies with me," he went on bitterly, "for taking you without thinking, for allowing lust to cloud my judgment. I swore I would never again find myself doubting the paternity of a child conceived by my wife. *Mon dieu*, Gabby, what have you done to me!"

Gabby could almost feel sorry for him. "I have done nothing to you, Philippe," she retaliated. "But I can see that in your mind I am guilty of adultery. If you don't believe me, let me go. I will make my own way and somehow provide for my child without you. Divorce me! It's not impossible these days. Just don't treat me like your whore!"

"I can't let you go!" Philippe cried in anguish. "Don't you understand that? No, of course you don't," he said, answering his own question. "How could you when I don't understand myself. You are in my blood, my brain. The scent and feel and taste of you are with me always. You are mine and I will never let you go. No other man will have you again.

I can hate you, despise what you did to me, yet I cannot let you go. You nourish my body and feed my soul!''

His tortured words shocked and bewildered Gabby who listened, mouth agape, violet eyes unbelieving. How could he need her but not love her? She could not help but ask the question burning on the tip of her tongue. ''What of the babe? What are your feelings toward the child I carry?'' she asked hesitantly, knowing that his response could change the course of her life.

Philippe was quiet for so long that Gabby thought he hadn't heard her. When he finally spoke, an all-encompassing emptiness invaded her soul. ''In all honesty I do not believe that I have sired this child,'' he confessed. ''I will do my best to be a good father because there is a remote possibility that the child is mine. I can promise you nothing more.''

Philippe's words sent a cold chill down Gabby's spine. She could not bear to think of Philippe's firstborn being treated any differently from any subsequent children they might have. In her heart she knew she had no choice but to leave Philippe and raise her child with all the love and affection it deserved.

''And once the child is born,'' Philippe continued blithely, ''I shall not let you out of my sight until you conceive again, for only then can I be certain that my own flesh and blood and not some bastard will inherit Bellefontaine.''

''You monster; despicable cad!'' Gabby sobbed, jumping up from the bed to pound her small fists ineffectually against Philippe's chest. Bewilderment, despair, defeat engulfed her. ''I shall love this child above any others you might force upon me!''

Philippe's eyes grew black with rage as he flung her from him. In his own mind her words reinforced his belief that

Gabby carried Duvall's child. He grew even angrier when he realized that he still wanted her knowing the extent of her treachery. He stomped from the cabin, fully intending to have nothing more to do with her. Once his business in Norfolk was concluded he would order the *Windward* back to Martinique where he would seclude Gabby at Bellefontaine and have her closely watched, for he could not allow her to destroy another child no matter who had fathered it. The nagging feeling that he had sired the child was never far from his thoughts. His doubts would plague him the rest of his life.

Philippe did not return to the cabin that night and Gabby was relieved. She supposed he had slept in one of the empty passenger cabins but in truth cared little what he did as long as he stayed away from her with his teasing lips and hands. It was nearly impossible to remain passionless under his expert probings. She hated herself anew each time she responded to him. And until now he had been unrelenting in demanding his due from her body.

The next morning after having disgorged the breakfast Seaman Laville brought to her, Gabby stood at the railing and watched Philippe walk down the gangplank and disappear into the winding streets along the waterfront. Even though it was snowing and bitterly cold Gabby wished she could have gone ashore herself. She still harbored notions of fleeing and only awaited the opportunity. As if reading her mind, Laville appeared and requested she return to her cabin.

"It is must too inclement to remain on desk, Madame St. Cyr," he suggested, grasping her elbow and leading her gently but firmly toward the cabin. "Are you ill?" he asked solicitously when he saw her pale face. "Perhaps some hot tea would help revive you."

"*Merci*, no," answered Gabby, silently cursing Philippe for appointing Laville her watchdog.

From that moment on wherever Gabby went Laville

hovered nearby. She found herself spending long hours in her cabin huddled around a small stove just to escape his constant company. Philippe had not returned to the ship and Gabby supposed he was sampling the charms of Virginia women! She certainly would put nothing past him.

Later, picking at the supper Laville had brought her, Gabby wondered why Philippe had not yet returned. Suddenly there was much shouting and running back and forth on deck and she flung open the cabin door to inquire about the commotion. She watched a few minutes until she recognized Laville hurrying by with a bucket in each hand and stopped him.

"What is happening?" she asked, wondering at the excitement all around her.

"An accident," Laville answered hurriedly. "A fire below deck. Some of the men lit a stove to keep themselves warm and a spark ignited some clothing nearby. All hands are engaged in dousing it so you'd best stay in your cabin." Then he was gone.

Gabby had no intention of remaining inside her cabin. This was just the opportunity she had prayed for. With all hands engaged in putting out the fire and Philippe gone ashore, she knew the time had come to make good her escape. Quickly, she donned her warmest dress and sturdiest shoes. From the depths of her trunk she took a reticule that she had filled with coins before leaving Martinique and fastened it to her waist. Then she pulled on a hooded pelisse and quietly slipped from the ship.

Gabby had no idea where she was going but wanted to get as far away from the harbor as possible before her absence was discovered. She hoped to find a decent inn or boarding house far removed from the dock area. She had enough money to last until she found employment if she was frugal. Her pregnancy did not show and it would be several months yet before she had to worry about that problem. In the meantime she would work and save enough money to buy passage to New Orleans where she hoped Marcel's sister would help her.

Gabby's pelisse was covered with a light dusting of wet snow and her shoes were soaked through. Shivering, she pulled the cloak even closer about her slim form. In her aimless wandering she soon found herself in a shabby, rundown section of town. Several times she was accosted by rough-looking men as she hurried along the dark streets. She could see inviting lights of an inn ahead and thought longingly of a blazing fire and warm bed.

Approaching the inn cautiously, Gabby paused briefly in the warm glow flooding through an open window. Raucous laughter and loud, boisterous voices, both male and female, greeted her ears and instinctively she knew it would be no place for a lady alone to stay. With a pang of disappointment she moved on determined to find a more appropriate lodging before she froze to death. Suddenly, a hard hand grasped her shoulder, holding her like a band of steel. Gabby felt a constriction in her chest and nearly choked with fright. How had Philippe found her so soon? she thought irrationally.

Gathering her strength she turned to face a complete stranger dressed in rough seaman's garb and reeling slightly from side to side as if far gone from drink.

"Ah," the man sighed when he saw her small, upturned face. "I knew this'd be my lucky day but I just didn't know how lucky." He draped a large arm possessively around Gabby's waist and pulled her close.

"Please, Monsieur," Gabby gasped, panicstricken, "I am not . . . !" But she got no further.

"A Frenchy!" the big man exclaimed at Gabby's first words. "Damned if Big Jake ain't got hisself a Frenchy! How much, mamselle? How much for a good tumble?" he repeated, pulling impatiently at her clothes.

"I'm not what you think!" Gabby cried frantically, fear gnawing at her insides. "Let me go!"

"Aw, don't play coy with me, Frenchy," Big Jake said, shoving his face so close to hers that she gagged at the foulness of his rum-laden breath. "No lady would be out alone at this time of night. Do you have a room?"

Gabby could only stare.

"Never mind, the inn will do right well," he said dragging her toward the doorway. Finally realizing that her words of protest were having little if any effect upon the big brute, Gabby began to struggle, desperately trying to break his hold upon her. In her efforts to escape, her reticule became dislodged and it hit the frozen ground, spilling out coins all around her feet.

"Whew!" whistled Big Jake. "You sure been a busy gal tonight, Frenchy." With one hand tight about Gabby's wrist Big Jake bent to retrieve her coins and push them back into the reticule. He raised a shaggy eyebrow when she reached for it and stuffed it in his pocket, laughing off Gabby's feeble attempts to take it from him. "After you show me a few of those tricks you French gals are famous for I'll consider giving it back to you. But only if you please me."

Gabby found herself being forced roughly through the door and into the inn by Big Jake while her impassioned pleas went unnoticed amid the throng of men and women intent on their own pleasure.

"A room!" demanded Big Jake gruffly, slamming a coin down in front of the innkeeper.

"Up the stairs and first door on the right," responded the innkeeper with a knowing leer on his coarse features.

"Help, Monsieur, please help!" pleaded Gabby, near hysteria.

The innkeeper laughed crudely, answering, "Don't look to me like Big Jake needs any help, little lady, but if he don't satisfy you I'll be glad to oblige. Always did fancy a Frenchy!"

"You're right," guffawed Big Jake, "don't need no help.

All I need right now is this here little French whore and a big bed.'' Without further ado, he hoisted Gabby over one huge shoulder and took the steps two at a time followed by loud cat calls and vulgar laughter from the crowded common room.

Nearly faint from fear, Gabby's small fists beat ineffectually against Big Jake's broad back. "Please, Monsieur, please let me go,'' she begged. "I am not a . . . not a . . . not what you think!''

Suddenly a door along the long corridor opened and a tall, well-dressed man stepped out. "What is going on?'' he demanded when he saw Gabby struggling with Big Jake and heard her entreaties.

"Help me, Monsieur, please help me!'' Gabby cried, holding her hands out to the man.

"Stay out of this, mister,'' growled Big Jake. "I just got me a Frenchy for the night and she's the type what likes it rough. She'll tame down once Big Jake puts it to her.''

"No! No!'' denied Gabby. "I am not what he thinks. I am a respectable woman!''

"Unhand the lady, Jake!'' ordered the man who Gabby had begun to look upon as a savior.

"Like hell!'' sputtered an enraged Jake. "She's mine. Go find your own whore!''

Suddenly Gabby found herself lying on the floor. The stranger had let loose a blow to Big Jake's chin that sent him reeling across the hall causing him to release his hold on Gabby. Immediately Jake was on his feet facing the man who threatened to rob him of his pleasure, his eyes glazed with pain and hatred. But in his drunken state he was no match for the cool, calculated blows of the other man. Big Jake found himself more on his back than on his feet.

"Had enough?'' the stranger asked, panting from his efforts.

Apparently Big Jake had for he rose somewhat unsteadily

to his feet and slunk off, but not before muttering darkly, "You and that whore ain't heard the last of Big Jake, yet."

Ignoring Big Jake's threats the man turned his attentions toward Gabby. "Are you hurt, my dear?" he asked solicitously as he helped her to her feet.

"I am unharmed, Monsieur, thanks to you," murmured Gabby gratefully as she swayed unsteadily against her rescuer. The ordeal with Big Jake had effected her more than she cared to admit and all of a sudden everything started receding into the distance until she was aware of nothing but blackness.

Gabby struggled into consciousness, disoriented and bewildered. Glancing around she saw that the room she was in, though small and sparsely furnished, was warm and cozy and she snuggled more deeply beneath the comforter covering her. A male voice startled her and she looked around for the owner of the low, pleasant tones.

"I see you are awake, my dear," Gabby gazed into a pair of deepset, brown eyes in a long, rather ascetic face. Then it all came rushing back to her. The man smiling down on her was the same man who had rescued her from the clutches of Big Jake. Beneath the covers Gabby shuddered.

"Are you cold, my dear?" asked the man kindly.

"No," answered Gabby hesitantly. "I was just thinking about what had nearly happened to me." Then she focused her huge, violet eyes full on the man, studying him with intent interest. For some unknown reason he shrank back from her guileless stare. "*Merci*, Monsieur, I don't know how to thank you, but I will trouble you no longer." She made to get out of bed but started violently when she discovered she was nude beneath the covers. "Monsieur!" Gabby gasped in outrage, quickly pulling the quilt to her chin. "What is the meaning of this?"

"Now, honey," the man soothed in a placating tone,

"don't get your feathers ruffled. Your clothes were wet and I figured you would catch your death if I didn't get them off you. I assure you I did not molest you in any way," he added quickly at her wary look. His assurances did nothing to relieve Gabby's embarrassment or still her fears.

"If you will be good enough to return my clothing and leave the room I will dress and be on my way."

"Where will you go? I found no money on your person."

"*Mon dieu!*" cried Gabby in genuine distress, "my reticule, my money! Big Jake stole my money!" She began to cry, huge sobs racking her small body. What would she do? Where could she go without money?

"Do you have any relatives in Norfolk?"

Gabby shook her head.

"What about friends?"

Again the negative shake.

"You obviously are not an American. Where did you come from? I think you owe me an explanation seeing as how I saved you from rape, or worse."

Of course he was right but Gabby had no intention of telling him the truth. She knew nothing about the man and though he seemed kind and had done her a great service she had no idea what his intentions toward her were.

"Let's start with your name," the man suggested gently.

"My name? It's . . . Lisa," lied Gabby. "Lisa La Farge."

"That's a good start, Lisa. Where are you from. Your accent is obviously French."

"*Oui*, I am French," admitted Gabby. "I arrived in Norfolk from . . . France only today."

"If you have no friends or relatives in Norfolk how do you intend to live? Why did you, a woman alone, choose to leave France in the beginning? And how did you come to meet a man like Big Jake?" His questions seemed endless.

"I was on my way to find lodgings for the night when I was accosted by that . . . that . . . Big Jake." She shuddered when

260

she spoke his name. "He mistook me for a . . . a . . ."

"Lady of the night?" interjected the stranger whose name she had yet to learn.

"*Oui,*" whispered Gabby in a low voice, a becoming tinge staining her pale cheeks. "As for earning a living," she continued quickly to cover her embarrassment, "I had hoped to find employment as a governess or perhaps a dressmaker's assistant. I am not without education, Monsieur."

"I can see you have breeding, my dear, which makes your situation all the more desperate. You don't seem the type to be on your own." Suddenly he became aware of Gabby's pale face and the lavender shadows marring the delicate skin beneath her eyes. "But you are exhausted!" he exclaimed with obvious concern. "And here I am questioning you when what you need is a good night's sleep. This has all been too much for you. You must spend the night here."

"No, I cannot!" Gabby cried with growing pain. "Why, I don't even know your name, or anything about you, Monsieur . . . Monsieur . . ."

"Mike, my dear. Mike Renfro. And now that the introductions are over I insist you get some rest."

"I cannot stay here, Monsieur Ren . . ."

"Mike," he insisted.

"*Oui*, Mike. It would not be right for me to stay here. This is your room."

"Would it be right for you to return to the streets and be mistaken again for a whore?" His blunt language shocked Gabby but also made her aware of her plight. Wavering, she thought on the alternative to spending the night in Mike's room. Lack of funds would force her to return to the *Windward* and Philippe. Did she want that?

"I promise I will remain a perfect gentleman and in the morning I personally will help you find suitable employment."

Gabby had to admit the offer was enticing. She was exhausted beyond endurance and Mike did seem trustworthy. He treated her far more gently than Philippe would if she returned to the ship. "Where will you sleep?" she asked, turning her violet gaze on him.

"Right here on a pallet, my dear," Mike replied without hesitation, "in case Big Jake takes it into his head to return. You heard his threat." Almost absently he crossed over to the bureau and removed a bottle from a cubbyhole. "Now, my dear Lisa, I think a small brandy is in order, to relax you and help you sleep."

"No, Monsieur Mike," protested Gabby, "I don't think . . ."

"You are too beautiful to think," replied Mike smoothly, pouring a small amount of the amber liquid into a glass. Turning his back on Gabby he was occupied a few moments over the glass before handing it to her. "Drink up," he ordered, sounding like a stern father.

Dutifully Gabby lifted the glass to her lips and drained it, coughing at the unaccustomed burning in her throat. Almost immediately she was suffused with a warmth that started at her toes and continued to the roots of her silvery hair. She blinked as Mike's thin frame began to recede from view, and her feathery lashes sank lower and lower until they rested on her pale cheeks.

"Tired," she muttered drowsily, "so tired."

"Sleep, my lovely Lisa, sleep," crooned Mike softly.

Nearly an hour passed while Mike kept guard over Gabby, his eyes glued to the steady rise and fall of her full breasts beneath the quilt. He felt remorse for what he was about to do to her but there was no help for it. She wasn't the first innocent to be taken advantage of nor likely to be the last. He nearly jumped out of his chair when a soft rapping noise interrupted his thoughts.

Moving quietly, he opened the door to admit a woman whose flamboyant beauty and dazzling figure demanded immediate respect. Flaming red hair surrounded a face with small, finely defined features and bright eyes whose strange color reminded one of pieces of amber. Of medium height, her figure was voluptuous. Though past the first blush of youth her full blown beauty was totally arresting.

"Glad you could come so quickly, Daisy," said Mike by way of greeting.

"Where is this paragon of beauty?" Daisy asked, casting a delicate, raised eyebrow around the darkened room.

"Drugged," grunted Mike pointing to the bed.

"Well, let's see the merchandise," replied Daisy crudely as she moved to the bed. With one graceful motion she flung aside the quilt covering Gabby's nude form. The soft lamp glow clothed her perfect figure in a golden shroud, revealing it in all its glory.

Daisy drew in her breath sharply, then let it out slowly. "My God!" she exclaimed, "you've really outdone yourself this time, Mike. That body," she whistled appreciatively, "small, but all woman." Then she weighed several strands of pale hair in her well-shaped hands. "Breathtaking! You've earned yourself a bonus for this one, Mike. Enough to feed your habit for a good long time."

"I don't know," shrugged Mike skeptically. "You won't find this one so willing. An innocent! Truly an innocent!"

"Are you turning soft?" quipped Daisy, her voice calculating.

"Nothing like that. It's just that she isn't like the others."

"Don't worry about her. I'll take good care of her. French, did you say?"

"Yes, French."

"Good! Good!" Daisy's luminous eyes glittered like jewels as she rubbed her hands together, hardly able to believe her good fortune. She'd never employed a French woman before, but if she knew anything about men, and her knowledge was considerable, they would go crazy over her.

"Wrap her in a quilt and carry her down the back stairs," ordered Daisy, becoming brisk and businesslike. "My carriage is waiting at the rear entrance." Within a short time Gabby's fate was settled without her knowledge by two perfect strangers.

Slowly Gabby untangled herself from the web of sleep, surprised to see bright sunlight streaming through the window. Her last conscious thought was of drinking the brandy Mike had given her. She must have fallen asleep almost immediately, she reasoned, for her sleep was complete and undisturbed. With catlike grace she stretched luxuriously under the satin sheets. Satin! When had the sheets been changed from the coarse linen that adorned Mike's bed? Panic-stricken, Gabby studied her surroundings. The room was large and gaudy with imported French furniture. The walls were painted a vivid pink and hung with pictures depicting young, nude women in sexual poses, most of them embarrassingly explicit. Gabby made a rise but gave up when pains in her head caused her to fall back against the soft pillow. That's when she discovered she was still naked and glanced around furtively in search of her clothes which seemed to be missing. Confusion reigned and her head seemed to explode in a million tiny fragments.

At that moment the door opened and a flame-haired woman entered carrying a tray. To Gabby the lady appeared very beautiful and sophisticated, being tastefully dressed in the latest fashion.

"Good morning, honey," she said in a broad American twang, unlike the soft southern drawl of New Orleans. "I am Daisy Wilson and you are a guest in my home."

"How did I get here?" questioned Gabby uneasily.

"Mike brought you, honey."

"Mike? Where is he?"

"Gone about his business, I suppose," replied Daisy blandly.

Gabby closed her eyes, massaging her aching temples with her fingertips. It was all so perplexing.

"You seem confused, honey," smiled Daisy. "Maybe I'd better explain. Here," she said, placing the tray across Gabby's lap, "drink your coffee while I tell you how you came to be in my home."

When Gabby sat up, the sheet covering her fell away baring her breasts. Daisy's eyes glittered at the sight of the perfect creamy globes tilting deliciously upward, already calculating the money Gabby would earn for her. Flustered, Gabby pulled the sheet up to her neck and began sipping the coffee to cover her embarrassment.

Tearing her eyes away from Gabby's enticing body, Daisy began her explanation. "Mike is a friend and . . . uh . . . business associate. After you fell asleep last night he sent a message to me asking if I would give shelter to a young woman in distress. Of course I could not refuse."

"Why can't I remember leaving the inn?" Gabby asked, her eyes troubled.

"You were exhausted, honey. And it's no wonder. Mike told me about your . . . uh . . . ordeal with Big Jake. He's a bad one all right. Mike thought you would be safer in my home as well as more comfortable. He just picked you up, quilt and all, and brought you here in a carriage."

"*Merci*, Daisy," said Gabby gratefully. "I owe you a great deal and I don't know how I shall ever repay you."

"Perhaps we'll find a way," murmured Daisy, arching a curved eyebrow. At Gabby's questioning stare, she continued. "What do you intend to do, honey? Mike tells me you have no relatives or friends in Norfolk. A girl like you can't go roaming the streets alone."

"I intend to seek employment," announced Gabby firmly as she made to rise from the bed. With a cry of dismay she fell back against the pillow, clutching her temples with shaking hands as a sharp pain pierced her brain.

"Here now, honey," clucked Daisy, all worry and concern, "there's no need to rush off. It's obvious you aren't well. Just you lay back and rest."

"But I cannot pay you for my room and board," persisted Gabby, tears glistening in her eyes.

"Did I ask for payment?" asked Daisy huffily. "Don't fret, we'll figure something out. Right now I think it's time we had a woman to woman talk. What Mike told me about you was sketchy at best. You might as well tell me the truth, honey. Who are you running from and why?" Daisy's brittle gaze seemed to penetrate her very soul. "You can begin by telling me your real name."

"My real name is Lisa La Farge," lied Gabby, lowering her eyes. There was no reason for Daisy Wilson to know her real name.

"All right, honey, I'll accept that because it makes no real difference anyway. And you obviously are French so that part of your story is believable. Who are you running from? The law? Your parents? Your husband?"

Gabby had no recourse but to tell Daisy the truth. Part of the truth, that is. "To understand my situation I must begin at the beginning," Gabby replied in a soft voice, reliving that day in her mind when she first saw Philippe.

"I'm all ears, honey."

"I was placed in a convent by my parents at the age of eight and remained with the nuns until I was eighteen."

"My God!" interrupted Daisy. "With that face and body! A nun! My God!" Then she looked sheepishly at Gabby. "All right, all right, I promise to keep quiet until you are finished."

"A week before I was to take my vows my parents appeared with a man they said I was to marry in three days time. You can imagine how I felt! To be torn from the only home I had ever known, from people who loved me to become the wife of a man who frightened me was like a death sentence. But in

266

the end there was no way to avoid it. I became the bride of Philippe St. . . . La Farge," she amended.

So, she wasn't a virgin, Daisy thought. No matter, being French made up for her lack of virginity.

"I remained with my husband nearly two years but in the end I could no longer bear his unbending nature or his cruelty so I left him and took the first ship bound for America. He has no idea where I am and I shall never return to him."

"I cannot believe your husband, or any man for that matter, could be indifferent to your charms let alone treat you in the manner you have just described. Is that the whole of it?" asked Daisy suspiciously. "Or do you have a lover waiting someplace for you?"

"I have no lover!" denied Gabby with such conviction that Daisy was inclined to believe her.

After her long recitation Gabby was perspiring profusely and her face grew pale. The drug she had been given the night before still plagued her although she thought her weakness was due to her pregnancy and her ordeal with Big Jake.

Gabby's state of near collapse did not go unnoticed by Daisy. "I can see that you are not yourself yet and here I am pestering you with all kinds of questions. Tell you what," she said, flashing Gabby a huge smile, "I'll have breakfast sent to your room and then I'll see that no one disturbs you so you can have a nice long rest. How's that sound, honey? We can talk further when you feel better."

"You are very kind, Daisy. *Merci.* Somehow I will find a way to repay you."

"I'm sure you will, honey. I'm sure you will."

Gabby only picked at the tempting array of food one of the servants carried in to her a little while later. Her eyes grew heavy as she nibbled at a roll and drank coffee. Finally, unable to keep her eyes open a moment longer, she set the tray aside, snuggled down into the satin sheets and was soon asleep.

When Gabby awoke purple shadows flitted about the room but the warm glow from the fireplace dispelled the gloom as well as the cold. Her head no longer throbbed and she felt almost normal again. She was also ravenously hungry. Spying a wrapper lying at the foot of the bed, Gabby arose, put it on and tied the belt securely around her waist. Then she walked somewhat unsteadily to the window and stared in awe at the breathtaking sight that met her eyes. The world before her lay covered with a mantle of purest white, nearly unblemished by human trespassers. Paying more attention now to her surroundings, Gabby saw that the room she occupied was on the second floor and that the street below appeared to be quiet and well kept. She became so engrossed in studying the scene outside that she failed to hear the door to her room open and close. It was the mouthwatering aroma of food that finally alerted her to the fact that she was no longer alone. She turned just in time to see a small, pretty black woman in a maid's crisp uniform set a heavily laden tray on the table by the fireplace.

"Miz Wilson sent this," the girl announced, running dark eyes over Gabby in swift appraisal. "She said for you to eat and she'll be in to see you later."

Gabby needed no further urging. She took her place at the table while the maid silently ladled a rich, savory soup into a bowl. She gobbled it down embarrassingly fast but the maid seemed not to notice as she whisked away the empty bowl and replaced it with a meat pie filled with succulent chunks of beef and several kinds of root vegetables, which she washed down with hot tea. The maid departed while Gabby ate greedily, only to return a short time later with an apple cobbler rich with the smell of cinnamon and topped with generous spoonfuls of clotted cream. The maid watched wide eyed while Gabby made short work of it. Then she gathered up the dirty dishes and quietly left shaking her head in awe, unable to believe the French woman's voracious appetite.

Pleasantly stuffed, Gabby took her place before the window again, a puzzled frown creasing her smooth brow when she saw three men approach the front door followed a few minutes later by two more men. Vague stirrings of misgiving gathered in her breast like a hard knot, the reason for which Gabby did not know. A soft rap on the door to her bedroom brought her musings to an end and she turned just as Daisy entered.

Gabby's mouth fell open in admiration when she beheld the older woman. Never had she seen anyone more startlingly dressed. The cobalt blue of her lowcut, satin gown contrasted vividly with her amber eyes. At intervals the full skirt was drawn up with black lace bows revealing a scarlet underskirt. The bodice was sleeveless and drawn tight to push the tops of her white breasts upward, nearly baring them to their pink nipples. She carried a black lace fan and had pearls woven skillfully into her flaming locks.

"You look much better, honey," Daisy said in her throaty voice. "I knew all you needed was a rest and a belly full of good food."

"I was ravenous and I'm afraid I made a pig of myself," Gabby admitted shyly. "But I do feel much better."

Daisy laughed. "Millie told me she never saw a lady eat like you." Gabby hung her head in embarrassment but said nothing.

Daisy moved nervously about the room snapping her fan open and shut with loud popping noises. Suddenly she turned and faced Gabby. "I'm going to come right to the point, honey," Daisy began, eyeing Gabby speculatively. "What kind of employment do you hope to gain?"

"I have been well educated," Gabby replied. "I feel more than qualified to become a governess."

"That's all well and good but Norfolk is a seaport and its inhabitants rough seamen and their families. Hardly the sort to employ a governess.''

"I am very good with a needle,'' added Gabby hopefully.

"Ha,'' laughed Daisy caustically, "hardly a profitable way to make a living.''

"I will do what I must to survive.'' Gabby's chin rose several inches and her violet eyes darkened with determination.

"Perhaps you should return to your husband.''

"Never!'' cried Gabby vehemently.

That's just what Daisy wanted to hear. "Then sit down and listen to what I have to say. I may be able to solve all your problems.''

Skeptical, but nevertheless interested, Gabby perched at the edge of the bed prepared to hear Daisy out.

"I am prepared to offer you employment. The pay is excellent, you can live here in my house, eat good food and wear beautiful clothes.'' Daisy paused to observe Gabby's reaction to her words.

"What would I have to do?'' asked Gabby warily.

"My God! Mike was right, you are an innocent!'' exclaimed Daisy incredulously. "Haven't you guessed by now where you are or for that matter what I am?'' Although things were beginning to take shape in her mind, Gabby shook her head. "You are in the best house of prostitution in Norfolk, possibly in all of Virginia,'' bragged Daisy proudly. "I am the owner.''

All the color drained from Gabby's face and for a moment she thought she might lose her excellent supper. "And . . . and you want me to work for you?'' she asked in disbelief. "But Mike knew I was not that kind of woman. Why did he bring me here?''

Daisy's coarse laughter rang out. "Mike and I have a business arrangement; he keeps an eye out for girls like you who might otherwise end up on the streets and I provide the wherewithal to feed a very expensive habit of his. Most of the young women he brings to me are decent, but destitute, like yourself, but nearly always they decide to remain with me. Mike has proved invaluable to me during our long association.''

"You mean you pay him for supplying you with unsuspecting women?" Gabby asked, stunned. "But he seemed such a gentleman, and so kind and helpful."

"Of course," agreed Daisy. "Unfortunately Mike has a very expensive habit that I won't go into at this time, but his superb judgment and excellent eye for women have proved profitable for both of us. That is one of the reasons my house is the best and most popular one around. No ordinary street walker for Daisy Wilson's establishment!"

"I'm afraid Mike's trouble will earn him naught this time," asserted Gabby indignantly. "I would never consent to prostitute myself!"

"Isn't that what you did when you were forced into marriage?" asked Daisy slyly.

Daisy's words stunned Gabby into silence. Acting as Philippe's whore was exactly the role she played of late. Though at one time they had loved one another until Amalie had destroyed whatever had been between them.

"Well, honey, what do you say?"

"If you will return my dress I will leave," insisted Gabby, wanting nothing more to do with Daisy or her profession.

"No so fast, Lisa," said Daisy smugly, putting a restraining hand on Gabby's arm as she prepared to leave. "Where will you go? It is already dark outside. Have you forgotten Big Jake so soon?"

Gabby hesitated. She could always return to the ship. Facing Philippe and his anger was better than what Daisy offered.

Sensing Gabby's indecision Daisy pressed on. "Maybe you'd like to think about it while you rest here a day or two," she suggested helpfully.

"There is nothing to think about. I must leave now."

"Hold on, honey," soothed Daisy. "Do you think me so heartless that I would turn you out on a snowy night with no place to go? Even if you refuse my offer I couldn't do that to you." Gabby lowered her lashes so Daisy could not read the relief in expressive eyes.

"Besides, Lisa, you are obviously in no shape to leave here for at least several days. You are deathly pale and weak. What you need is a few days of rest and quiet. You'll find no one is eager to hire a sickly woman."

Gabby realized the wisdom of Daisy's words but she was not beguiled by them. She was unwilling to pay for her room and board in the manner in which Daisy suggested and wondered if the madam would try to hold her against her will. Aloud she said, "The only way I can remain under your roof is if I am allowed to do some small service to pay for my keep. In a day or two I will leave and seek employment."

"That sounds fair enough," agreed Daisy readily, almost too readily, Gabby thought. "You said you were good with a needle. My girls rarely have time to mend or repair their own clothing. While you are regaining your strength you can mend their dresses and do me and my girls a great service."

"And I wouldn't have to leave this room?" asked Gabby suspiciously. "Or . . . or be forced to do anything I didn't want to do?"

"Lisa, I promise you no one will force you into anything against your will," replied Daisy archly.

"In that case, I accept your generous offer and if you will send some of the garments in need of repair to me I shall start on them immediately."

"No hurry, honey. Tomorrow is soon enough. Right now I think a hot bath is in order. Would you like that?"

"Very much," smiled Gabby gratefully. "I was unable to take a fresh water bath aboard ship. In fact, I have not been in a real bathtub since I left . . . France."

"Well, then," grinned Daisy, "I'll send one up to your room."

As if on cue, the same maid who had waited on Gabby before entered the room bearing a tray with a wine bottle and two glasses. She set them on the table, then turned to Daisy. "You want that bath set up now, Miz Wilson?"

"As soon as Lisa joins me in a glass of wine, Millie," Daisy told her as she carefully poured out two glasses of clear, ruby liquid. After casting a curiously pitying look in Gabby's direction, Millie quietly left the room.

"I don't think . . ." began Gabby gazing doubtfully at the wine.

"No protests," admonished Daisy as she handed the glass to Gabby. "One small glass of wine never hurt anyone. Might even do you some good."

After Daisy's generosity it would be churlish for Gabby to refuse to share a glass of wine with her. The woman had taken her in and had not insisted she turn prostitute even though she had obviously paid Mike a great deal of money for her. With a smile of gratitude Gabby raised the glass to her lips and sipped appreciatively. It tasted surprisingly good, cool and crisp, and before Gabby knew it her glass was empty even though Daisy's remained untouched.

"I have to leave now, honey. Business, you know. Millie will be in soon with your bath." Running a practiced eye over Gabby's small form, she continued. "I'll send up something suitable for you to wear to bed and some perfume for your bathwater. You just sit back and relax, Millie will take care of you." Then she picked up the half empty wine bottle and carried it with her from the room, leaving behind her own untouched glass.

Heaving a pleased sigh Gabby sat back and closed her eyes. She felt surprisingly good, her whole body vibrated with a feeling of well-being. Matters had taken a decided turn for the better for her and perhaps she could get on with her own life now. She thought of Philippe's child nestled under her breast and absentmindedly rubbed her palms against her nipples, shocked to find them fully erect, as if stimulated by a lover's caress. She moaned and was surprised by the sound coming from her own throat. If she could have but seen herself, Gabby would have been horrified. Her violet eyes were darkened by a look that often preceded lovemaking; her lips were open and softly inviting, moistened continually by the tip of her red tongue. Under her own fingertips her body quivered, eager with anticipation. In a trancelike state, she picked up Daisy's untouched wine glass and thirstily gulped down the contents.

Chapter Sixteen

LOST IN his own melancholy, Philippe sprawled carelessly in a chair, his long legs spread before him, a glass of brandy in his hand, his feelings masked by the bored look marring his handsome face. He surveyed the scene around him with cool disdain. It was the same scene he had been a party to for the past two evenings. Unwilling to return to the ship, knowing full well that he couldn't stay away from Gabby, he had instead sought the gay, uncomplicated company of Daisy Wilson's whores. But even during his most intimate moments with one of Daisy's beautiful and talented girls, thoughts of violet eyes and long, pale hair intruded upon his pleasure.

Gabby's pregnancy had unwittingly presented him with a monumental dilemma. She knew how badly he wanted an heir, just like she knew there was no way possible to tell who had sired the child she carried. In his heart he realized that he could be the father as well as Duvall. Irrationally, Philippe discounted entirely the possibility that Gabby and Marcel had not been lovers as she had insisted. But he was no fool. He still could count. Only if the babe was born a full nine months after he had made love to her in New Orleans would he accept responsibility. Philippe cursed under his breath, drawing the unwanted attention of some of the girls milling about the room in various states of undress. He had thought to forget Gabby for a while by spending some time in the arms of another woman but here he was mooning over a woman who was as much a whore as any one of Daisy's girls! No! thought Philippe, modifying his opinion. Gabby could never be like one of Daisy's whores. Though she might give herself in love she would never sell herself!

Philippe's flinty gaze swept the room falling on the elegantly garbed, flame-haired woman who had just entered. He hadn't had Daisy yet, but knew tht she would be more than willing if he wanted her . . . perhaps tonight . . . He heard she only took men occasionally, but her brittle eyes had told him that she would be available to him if he wished. He noticed that Daisy was making some kind of announcement and tried hard to concentrate his rather besotted brain on her words.

"Gentlemen," Daisy said loudly, quickly gathering the attention of every man assembled in her tastefully furnished drawingroom. "Tonight everyone is in for a treat." She paused dramatically, smiling slyly when she saw that she had the undivided attention of all her customers.

"For the first time this house has in its employ a genuine Frenchwoman of astounding beauty." The room grew deathly still. "She is young and perfect in every respect and thus demands a greater . . . uh . . . fee." From the moment Philippe heard "Frenchwoman" his attention did not waver from Daisy's words.

"Where is this Frenchy?" asked one of the men.

"Yah, Daisy," joined in another, "let's see the merchandise. I want to see what we are paying for?"

"Patience! Patience!" laughed Daisy, pleased by the way things were going. "Every man present will get a look. But only through a peephole."

"What's the matter, Daisy?" asked a distinguished-looking older man. "Does this Frenchy think she's too good to mingle with your other whores?"

Thinking quickly, Daisy answered, "This girl is from the most expensive, highest class house in Paris, and has knowledge of many ways to delight a man that not even my girls are aware of. Eventually she will accommodate every one of you but tonight will be special for only one of you. She has entertained royalty and is in a class all by herself," Daisy announced expansively, making up lies as she went along.

Clearly the clientele were intrigued. A Frenchy straight from a Paris bordello! A mystery woman too high class to associate with Daisy's other girls!

At that point Philippe lost interrest. A Frenchwoman held no mysticism for him. He had one of the most beautiful, enticing Frenchwomen alive aboard the *Windward* whom he was having great difficulty purging from his mind. He wanted nothing more to do with Frenchwomen.

"Follow me, boys, if you want a glimpse of my little Frenchy taking a bath," Daisy said mysteriously, leading the way up the long staircase. "But don't be shocked or surprised at anything you see!" Except for Philippe every man present trooped en masse behind a strutting Daisy, chattering excitedly among themelves.

Gabby stood up and stretched luxuriously. The steaming tub looked inviting and smelled deliciously of jasmine. She yanked impatiently at the belt of her wrapper, anxious to ease her aching body into the warm water. Relaxing in water up to her waist, Gabby found it difficult to concentrate. It was an effort to remember where she was and why she was here in the first place. Her brain seemed frozen, unable to sort through emotions and feelings. For some unexplained reason her body trembled with a need she found hard to describe.

Placing her hands over her full breasts and arching her back, Gabby felt her nipples press against her palms, hard, pulsating, demanding attention. Moving downward over the still taunt stomach, the gently swelling hips, her restless fingers sought and found the core of her womanhood.

Gabby started in embarrassment, looking sheepish when the door silently opened and Millie glided through with a tiny bit of froth in her hands, which she placed at the foot of the bed. Millie's eyes slid almost guiltily from Gabby's nude body before she departed, leaving Gabby to complete her bath in private.

As if in a dream Gabby picked up the fragrant soap and began to lather her body. Suddenly, an uncontrollable urge caused her to drop the soap and run her hand sensuously over her slippery body, stroking, caressing, in wild abandon, panting and gasping with a need her drugged mind could not control. Desperate to be loved, to experience the thrill of a man's hands upon her hot flesh, to feel him deep within her body. Eyes wide open, moist lips parted, her hands worked feverishly, probing, massaging, assuaging her burning need.

That scintillating scene greeted pair after pair of glazed eyes peering through the peephole into Gabby's room. One by one Daisy's customers filed past the opening gazing lustfully at the unsuspecting enchantress whose sensuous body was writhing and twitching beneath her own fingertips.

"My God!" exclaimed a man clutching the bulge in his crotch as he came away from the peephole. "I never seen anything like it!"

"Hot little bitch!" cried another with gleaming eyes.

"Jesus!" mouthed a youth no older than a boy, "think what she could do to a man in bed." His eyes glazed over with a kind of reverence.

After each man had a turn at the peephole, Daisy led them back downstairs. Philippe watched with amusement as Daisy's customers returned to the parlor, the manifestations of their lust clearly visible to his eyes. Whatever they had seen had evidently affected them deeply. Daisy allowed them a few moments to pull themselves together, moving to stand beside Philippe while they spoke quietly, speculatively with one another.

"What about you, Mr. St. Cyr?" Daisy asked, cocking an eyebrow provocatively. "Are you so immune to beauty that you have no desire to look upon it?"

"Your French whore holds no interest for me," said Philippe coolly. "One of your other girls will do just as well. Or," he paused dramatically, "perhaps you are free."

Daisy eyed Philippe appreciatively before breaking out in raucous laughter. She had to admit she had been attracted to him since he had first come into her house two nights ago. His lean, hard body and cool composure intrigued her from the beginning. She seldom serviced any of the customers herself but somehow she sensed that taking Philippe into her bed would be a pleasurable experience for both of them.

Philippe's face darkened menacingly at Daisy's laughter, mistaking it for mockery. Abruptly, he lunged to his feet in an affort to leave when he felt a hand on his arm and looked down to see Daisy's eyes burning into his with a searing yellowish flame.

"Wait, honey, don't leave," she pleaded, her throaty voice promising delights yet to come. "I wasn't laughing at you, only at myself. I never thought I'd jump at the chance to bed one of my customers, but somehow, I can hardly wait. When I finish with the business at hand I'll make you glad you waited for me." The pressure of her soft body against his left Philippe little doubt of her desire for him.

Philippe watched lazily as Daisy's compact body moved gracefully across the room to the knot of men she had led down the stairs just minutes before. He saw, rather than heard, the brisk negotiations going on between the madam and the group of hot, eager men. Daisy's brilliant smile told Philippe that a highly satisfactory agreement had been reached. After a nod toward a husky, crude-looking man, obviously a wealthy merchant, Daisy returned to Philippe who watched with detached interest as the merchant bounded up the stairs two at a time to the cheers and catcalls of the other men.

"Don't let her wear you out, Rafe," someone shouted.

"Bet that little Frenchy knows how to use her mouth," laughed another, making an obscene gesture with his hand.

Philippe closed his mind to their jeers, turning his attention instead to Daisy, hoping her ample charms and wide experience in bed could occupy his mind and body long enough to shut out disturbing thoughts of a deceitful, silver-maned minx whose diminutive body nearly drove him wild with desire.

"A very profitable evening," murmured Daisy, clutching Philippe's arm close to her body, her eyes dark with desire. A self-satisfied smile curving her red lips, she wasted no time in leading Philippe up the stairs to her room. She was pleased in more ways than one. She had just obtained the highest price ever for the French girl, Lisa, and the drugged wine had worked far better than she could have wished. Most of the men were paring off with one girl or another, and best of all, she anticipated a long night of passion in the arms of the handsome man beside her.

Only when the water had grown cold did Gabby become aware of the need to get out of the tub and dry herself before the warm fire to stop her shivering. Stepping gingerly from the tub and using the soft towel Millie had provided Gabby began to rub her trembling body, a dreamy, far-off look glazing her face. The fire from the grate illuminated her pale, alabaster skin. Dropping the towel she moved languorously toward the bed and donned the bit of frothy lace she supposed was a nightgown. The garment Daisy had provided for Gabby was completely transparent with thins straps holding up a low-cut bodice that tied beneath the breasts with a satin ribbon and fell in sheer, graceful folds about her slim legs. Throughout it all, Gabby could concentrate on nothing but her throbbing, tingling body. Panting from the intensity of her emotions, she could barely keep her hands from straying to her tormented flesh.

As she stood beside the bed, confused, uncertain what to do next, the door opened to admit a stockily built man whose heavy, crude features seemed in distinct contract to his expensive clothing.

"My God!" he breathed reverently, "you're even lovelier close up. And worth every penny I paid!"

"Monsieur?" asked Gabby with a puzzled frown. Why was she in a bedroom with a strange man inappropriately dressed in almost nothing? she wondered vaguely.

"An honest to God Frenchy," breathed Rafe in lewd fascination. "Name's Rafe, Mademoiselle," he informed her as he eagerly advanced upon the cowering girl. "You and me are going to get along just fine."

The look in Rafe's beady eyes was unmistakable and even as Gabby was repulsed by the man himself, her flesh strained toward him. All conscious thought fled as her body took on a will of its own. She was aware of nothing; at that moment nothing mattered except assuaging the terrible throbbing tormenting her feverish flesh.

In a flash Rafe tore the revealing nightgown from Gabby's body and fell upon her with an insatiable lust, plying his hands and lips to her straining flesh, her cries and moans of encouragement driving him to a frenzy. She pulled at Rafe's clothes like a mad woman until he finally managed to cast them off. Then he picked her up and threw her on the bed, his hard, stocky bulk falling heavily upon her.

Gabby's tortured body was aflame as it never had been before. While Rafe plied his hands and mouth to every crevice, every opening on her smooth, perfumed flesh, she writhed and moaned, cresting peak after peak, yet strangely unsatisfied. Several times in her delirium, she called out Philippe's name but if Rafe noticed he said nothing. When finally he plunged his engorged member into her velvet wetness she screamed with pain at his brutal entrance, yet clawed his body closer, pulling his mouth to her pulsating nipples. With a blaze that threatened to consume her she climaxed just as Rafe's pounding ceased and he collapsed atop her panting and gasping for breath.

"So you like old Rafe, huh, Frenchy?" he laughed crudely when he finally found his breath. "Well, I got plenty more where that come from."

Gabby was far from sated. "More! More! Please more!" she begged an astonished but pleased Rafe.

"Sure, honey. Right after you show me a few of those tricks Daisy said you were famous for."

Gabby stared at him uncomprehendingly as he knelt above her, twisting his hands hurtfully into her hair to pull her face into position. Hungrily, she accepted him without protest, the yearning within her driving her to the brink of insanity.

"Jesus!" Rafe cried, his body convulsing with intense pleasure. "Jesus! Jesus! Jesus!"

In the room next to Gabby's, Philippe and Daisy lay entwined in each other's arms, their bodies wet with perspiration. Philippe had found Daisy quick to passion and his deft caresses had aroused her to a feverish pitch. Her own strokings and petting, meant to enflame, somehow fell far short of their goal. Philippe could not help but compare Daisy's flabby flesh to Gabby's taut, smooth body. But if Philippe's passion was not sufficiently aroused, Daisy did not notice. She was too caught up in her own pleasure to pay attention to Philippe's lack of response. Besides, he was careful to bring Daisy to a thundering climax even if his own was dismally lacking. Soon after their first encounter, Daisy was eager for him again and once more Philippe found himself plunging into her, outwardly exhibiting a passion equal to her own yet somehow remaining unscathed.

Daisy lay replete and spent while Philippe dozed beside her. She smiled fondly at him while he muttered in French, only one word coming out clearly. Gabby! Who or what a

Gabby was, Daisy neither knew or cared. She was only sorry that Philippe had told her the was leaving for Martinique the next day. She sighed and thought to waken him again for another round of lovemaking when she suddenly remembered the girl, Lisa, in the next room and wondered how Rafe was progressing with her. She eased from the bed and moved to the peephole.

Somehow, through the fog of sleep, Daisy's laughter and mutterings came through to Philippe and he reluctantly opened his eyes to find the cause of Daisy's mirth. He saw her looking through a small aperture in the wall.

"What is it, Daisy?" he asked sleepily. "What are you looking at?"

"The little Frenchy is nearly devouring Rafe and that clumsy oaf is pounding the tiny thing senseless. But what's more amazing is that she is begging for more. I've never seen anything like it," Daisy repeated with awe. "I've never seen it work so well."

"What work so well?" asked Philippe, curiosity getting the better of him.

"Er . . . nothing, honey, just talking to myself."

"Come back to bed," Philippe urged, watching her nude body through slumberous eyes.

Daisy would have liked nothing better than to snuggle next to Philippe's hard, virile body but she was held spellbound by the passionate couple in the next room. "He sure is getting his money's worth. I hope he don't pull any of that silvery hair from her head. God, it's beautiful! Almost like pale silk."

Somewhere in Philippe's befogged brain a little bell rang and he began paying closer attention to Daisy's words. "What did you say her name was?" he asked, suddenly alert.

"She says it's Lisa, but who knows? Lisa La Farge. Sounds French enough," replied Daisy, shrugging daintily. "Jesus! Look what she's doing to old Rafe now!" Her well-manicured hands began to work over her own body while Philippe jumped from the bed with a curse, shock and disbelief marching across his face.

"Impossible!" he cried out when Daisy divulged the girl's last name. It was the same as Gabby's maiden name! "I left her well protected aboard the *Windward*. How would she get here?" Rudely he shoved Daisy from the peephole and fit his own eye to it. What he saw froze the blood in his veins. A red rage exploded behind his brain and Daisy stepped back in alarm.

"What's the matter, honey?" she asked, suddenly frightened by the madman she had taken to her bed. "What are you talking about? You had your chance to look at the French girl before and you turned it down." She sidled next to Philippe, prodding him with her bare breasts in an attempt to divert him. After watching the spectacle in the next room she was more than ready for him again. "Come back to bed," she urged in her throaty voice.

But Philippe neither heard nor felt Daisy. What he had just witnessed had left him shocked and speechless. Against all odds, the Frenchwoman in bed with the man Daisy called Rafe was Gabby! Her naked, sweat-drenched body was being pounded into the mattress by Rafe, his heavy frame nearly smothering the smaller form beneath him. But it was Gabby's face that held Philippe in thrall. Her eyes were narrowed slits of lust, her smile wanton, her moist lips open and greedy. He could almost hear her moans and words of encouragement as her small hands worked over Rafe's husky body. She must have almost worn the man out because his face was red and he was perspiring profusely all the while his buttocks rose and fell in quick jerking motions, the lust-crazed woman beneath him consuming every ounce of his flagging energy.

Finally, the horror of what he was witnessing hit Philippe with the full force of a sledgehammer blow to his stomach and he had all he could do to keep the vomit from spewing from his throat. "*Mon dieu!*" he cursed violently. "What have you done to her?"

Daisy was stunned by Philippe's reaction. What could he care about a little French whore? she wondered. For that's what she was. Daisy didn't for one minute swallow that sob story about the convent and a cruel husband. Her prowess in the bedroom disproved the convent upbringing if nothing else did.

"What's it to you, honey?" Daisy purred in her sexiest voice, hoping to lure Philippe back to bed.

"Damn you to hell, Daisy!" exploded Philippe, his rage turning against the woman standing beside him. "That's my wife in there with that maniac!" Pulling on his clothes with one hand and holding on to Daisy's wrist with the other, Philippe ran from the room, a nude Daisy in tow.

"Your wife!" gasped Daisy, wincing when Philippe tightening his grip on her wrist. "No! It can't be. She's nothing but a French whore!"

Ignoring Daisy, Philippe burst into the next room dragging the madam with him. Hearing Gabby's tormented cries nearly tore him apart. But when she called his name out in agony his tortured face bore all the signs of madness.

The man atop Gabby was so engrossed in the writhing body beneath him he did not hear Philippe enter. "Name's Rafe, you little bitch," grunted Rafe, "and I'm every bit as good as your Philippe, whoever the hell he is, but damn if you ain't wore me out."

Suddenly his sweating body left the bed and sailed across the room, landing heavily at Daisy's bare feet. He was too near exhaustion to do more than gasp in surprise.

"Get out, you scum!" ordered Philippe, outrage burning in him like a hot brand. "Get out before I kill you!"

Despite his exhaustion, Rafe stumbled unsteadily to his feet, grabbed his clothes and announced with more bravery than he felt, "Sure, sure, can't satisfy that little whore anyhow. But I got to hand it to you, Daisy, you got a gold mine in that Frenchy. Takes to it like there's no tomorrow." Then, seeing the murderous look on Philippe's face, he scudded out the door, frantically pulling on his clothes.

Daisy made to follow but Philippe caught her wrist again and pulled her close to the bed. "What have you given her?" he demanded angrily, pointing to Gabby.

"Nothing! Nothing!" she insisted, becoming more frightened by the minute. "Are you sure she's your wife?"

"She is my wife," Philippe stated grimly, "and I know she has been drugged or she wouldn't be here. I have no aversion to killing a woman, Daisy, so tell me the truth." His hand tightened, raising her arm behind her back until she screamed out in agony.

"All right! All right! I'll tell you, only don't break my arm, for God's sake!"

"For your sake it had better be the truth!" It was all Philippe could do to tear his eyes from Gabby and the agony she was experiencing.

"I only gave her a stimulant to make her more . . . er . . . willing."

Philippe cursed loudly. "How much, damn you, how much did you give her?"

"Only a few drops in a glass of wine. Not enough to harm her. I've used it many times before with no ill effects . . . only . . ."

"Only what?" demanded Philippe, increasing the pressure on Daisy's arm.

"I've . . . I've never seen it work so . . . so . . . thoroughly," Daisy stammered, wincing in pain.

"Did you leave the bottle in the room when you left her?"

"No! No! I carried it out with me." Then light dawned on Daisy's terrified face. "My glass," she gasped. "I left my untouched glass of wine in the room and . . ." She broke off and glanced toward the table at two empty glasses. Philippe followed the direction of her gaze and needed no further explanation to realize that Gabby had downed the contents of both glasses of drugged wine!

"If your damned stimulant harms her or her child I will come back and kill you with my own hands," promised Philippe through clenched teeth.

"Your wife is . . . pregnant?" gasped Daisy, certain that she was facing sure death. "How could I know? She mentioned no child to me."

"How did she come to be in your house?" Philippe asked, exerting more pressure to Daisy's arm. Knowing Gabby he realized she would never have come willingly to a house of prostitution.

"A friend of mine saved Lisa . . . er . . . whatever her name is, from being raped by a sailor named Big Jake, and he brought her here to me."

"She came willingly?" asked Philippe, disbelief evident on his face. He knew Gabby well enough to know her convent uprbringing would not countenance selling herself no matter how desperate she was. "The truth!" he demanded when Daisy hesitated. "If I find out you've lied to me I'll tell the police you kidnapped my wife."

Daisy had no choice but to tell Philippe everything she knew about Gabby and how she came to be in a house of prostitution. When she finished, she cocked an eyebrow at Philippe and asked with no small amount of curiosity, "Are you the cruel husband she was running away from? That's a story I'd like to hear, honey!"

A small muscle twitched in Philippe's chin and he balled his fists to keep from striking the madam. "She was drugged twice!" he cried out in alarm. "Your friend Mike drugged her in order to transport her here!"

Daisy shrank from the menace evident in his voice. "She was given only a sleeping draught the first night," she countered. "Do you think I would allow her to be harmed? She represented a sizable investment on my part."

"But what about the child she carries? Will the sleeping draught or the stimulant harm the babe?" Philippe demanded, nearly demented with anxiety.

"I don't know," admitted Daisy hesitantly. "But I'm sure she will be fine once the effects of the drug wears off. It's never harmed anyone before."

"By all that's holy you'd better be right," warned Philippe ominously, causing Daisy to shiver with apprehension.

All of a sudden the anger drained from Philippe's body. His main concern now was getting Gabby out of the whorehouse and safely aboard the *Windward* where he could look after her properly. Releasing Daisy's bruised arm, he gathered up Gabby, satin sheet and all, in his brawny arms, cradling her as one would a small child. She seemed to weigh nothing at all as he carried her from the room.

As if aware of Philippe's arms around her, Gabby moaned and pressed even closer to him. "It's all right, *ma chere*," he whispered tenderly. "Nothing or no one will harm you again. I shall look after you always." Turning to Daisy once more, he ordered brusquely, "Have your carriage brought around back." When she was slow to move, he gave her a vicious shove. "Move, damn your whoring hide, move!"

Gabbing up Gabby's discarded wrapper, Daisy drew it about her and hurried down the back stairs to do his bidding. By the time Philippe reached the rear door with his slight burden a carriage and driver were waiting. Soon they were speeding toward the *Windward*.

After ordering the captain to set a course immediately for Martinique, Philippe carried Gabby to their cabin and placed her gently on the bed. Then he asked a concerned Seaman Laville who was hovering anxiously nearby to bring hot water, disinfectant, and towels. Only when Laville had provided these items and gone about his duties did Philippe uncover Gabby and minutely inspect the numerous bites and scratches scattered over her nude body.

Loudly cursing Big Jake, Mike, Daisy, and Rafe, Philippe gently cleansed and applied disinfectant to each bruise and hurt. Then he washed every inch of her, wincing in pain and disgust as he wiped all traces of Rafe's ravishment from between her thighs.

All the while Philippe worked gently over Gabby the drug continued to ravage her body and mind as she twitched and strained toward his tender touch, her flesh still yearning, needing. Finally satisfied that he had attended to even the smallest bruise he drew the cover over her and pulled a chair close by to begin the vigil of waiting out the after-effects of the drugs she had been given, praying that she would not abort.

Philippe must have dozed because he awoke with a start to find Gabby awake and sitting in bed, wild-eyed and distressed. She appeared not to know him although she called his name over and over.

"What it is, *ma chere?*" he asked, his face taut with worry. "How can I help you?"

"Take me! Please take me! I'm afire!" she gasped, clutching out at him. "Why are you making me suffer this way? Make love to me!" Her lower lip tembled and Philippe felt a great compassion as well as pity for her. She had no idea what she was doing and Philippe fervently hoped that she would remember nothing of what took place in Daisy's establishment, for she would never hear it from his lips.

His heart was nearly wrenched from his chest as Gabby continued her pleading. No longer able to bear her misery, he moved from the chair to the bed and took her in his arms in order to stop her violent trembling. After that it seemed only natural to cover her mouth with his to still her sobs and small cries of abandonment. What followed was inevitable.

"Hurry! Hurry!" Gabby urged as she tore at Philippe's clothing. Even though he knew she was still reacting to the aphrodisiac in her system there was no way that Philippe could resist. Besides, he reasoned, his own passion taking wing, she was obviously in an agony of need and who better to assuage that need than her own husband? At least he would take her with gentleness and care, unlike that animal, Rafe, who pounded at her with unbridled lust.

Philippe made tender love to Gabby and she appeared to recognize him as the lust-crazed glaze began to fade from her violet eyes, replaced by a soft, luminous glow. Even her trembling subsided as Philippe moved slowly within her. Her cries of completion, when they came, were no longer those of a frenzied animal, but like a woman in love being made love to by a man who loved her.

Immediately afterward Gabby curled contentedly in Philippe's arms and fell into a deep, natural sleep. Philippe watched her carefully for a long time before he, too, drifted into an uneasy sleep.

Philippe awoke first and watched Gabby's face, serene in sleep, loath to move and disturb her peaceful slumber. He thought back over his life and to the terrible injustices he had forced upon both Gabby and Cecily. Everything that had happened had been his fault; his pride, his stubbornness, his jealousy had nearly lost him everything he held dear. He knew in his heart that after Gabby's latest attempt to leave him that he could no longer force her to remain with him against her will lest she destroy herself in another such escapade. He would never divorce her, but neither would he insist that she live with him.

His total disregard for her feelings while he held her in virtual captivity aboard the *Windward* had been responsible for her ordeal at Daisy's unscrupulous hands. He could never forgive himself for that! Even now he erupted in a cold sweat when he thought about Rafe's desecration of her frail body and fervently prayed that she would remember none of it. Never would he reveal to her the manner in which she had been shamed and abused, not even if his heart broke from the pain of concealing the truth. Had he not shamed and abused her himself?" he thought guiltily.

"*Mon dieu!* How have you endured?" Philippe cried remorsefully, hugging Gabby's body close.

With deep longing piercing his soul he recalled the time when they were happy and in love, a time when they joyfully awaited the birth of their child. His feelings for her still were intense, moving, but they now included distrust. Was it possible to regain what they once felt for one another?

Gabby stirred in Philippe's arms and slowly opened her eyes, her face blank with bewilderment, a small frown marring the smooth skin of her forehead. "*Mon dieu!*" she cried, clutching at her temples. "Why does my head hurt so?"

She looked at Philippe, as if seeing him for the first time, and memories came flooding back like rushing water. She recalled her recent escape from the *Windward* and waking up in Daisy Wilson's establishment, but further than that her mind refused to cooperate. She was whirling around in a dark void where only fleeting glimpses of vague, shadowy memories, some too horrendous to contemplate, confused her thoughts and clouded her brain.

"How did you find me?" she finally asked, feeling Philippe's intense, gray eyes upon her. "Did Daisy . . . ?"

Philippe watched Gabby warily, and when it became certain that she recalled nothing of the night before, he said, "One of the sailors aboard the *Windward* recognized you when you were carried into Daisy's house and notified me. When I arrived and identified myself as your husband Daisy had no choice but to release you to me."

"I . . . I can't remember," Gabby agonized, squeezing her

temples in frustration. "Are you certain that is how it happened?" Gingerly she flexed her limps and wondered at the soreness she felt over most of her body. "My baby!" It was more a cry of distress than a question as her hands clutched at her taut stomach.

"All is well, *ma petite,*" Philippe soothed. "The child still lies safely within you. And the reason you can remember nothing is because Daisy gave you a sleeping potion."

Gabby sighed hugely, and all did seem well until she happened to glance down at herself and was horrified to discover her flawless skin marred with a multitude of bruises, scratches, and teeth marks. Even her scalp felt as if her hair had been torn from her head.

"What have you done to me, Philippe?" she cried accusingly. "Why have you abused me when I was unconscious and could not defend myself? If your brutality costs me my child I shall never forgive you!"

Philippe blanched, his face deathly white beneath his tan. Until this moment he hadn't thought what he would tell Gabby when she discovered the bruises inflicted by Rafe. Unless he wanted her to learn the truth, which he swore never to divulge, he had no choice but to accept the blame.

"Your child is safe, *ma chere,*" assured Philippe. "As for hurting you, I . . . I . . ." What could he say?

"Don't make excuses, Philippe!" rage Gabby, in a flash of anger. "You have only to look at my body to see that I have been foully used!" Only then did she become aware that she still lay within the circle of her husband's arms, and she pulled away, glaring at him with such a look of loathing that Philippe was too shocked for speech. To cover his rampant emotions he arose from bed and began dressing.

Gabby, too, made to get out of bed but immediately fell back grasping her head and moaning. Philippe was instantly at her side.

"Lie back, *ma petite,*" he urged gently. "Rest until you feel well enough to get up. I'll not bother you again," he promised, settling her tenderly against the pillow as if he cared deeply for her. Gabby watched, warily, fearfully. Only when he left the room did she relax and give in to the sickness that pillaged her bruised and battered body.

Gabby was still abed when Philippe returned later with breakfast, her violet eyes luminous in her pale face, her body trembling, ill and wretched. Philippe realized that it was too soon to be entirely certain whether or not she would lose the child. And if that should happen he was powerless to prevent it. There was nothing for it but to insist she remain in bed and watch her carefully.

"I brought your breakfast, *ma chere,*" he said cheerfully, placing the tray on the bed beside her.

"I . . . I cannot eat," Gabby murmured, sickened by the sight of food.

"You must," urged Philippe gently. "If not for yourself, then for your child."

His kind words did little to ease Gabby's troubled mind. Why was he being so solicitous, so tender? she wondered wistfully. Had he devised some new method of punishment? She watched him through cautious eyes as he picked up a spoon and proceeded to feed her as one would a child. Gabby was so surprised by his unaccustomed kindness that she automatically opened her mouth. When nearly all the food from the tray had been consumed and Gabby protested that she could not force down another mouthful, Philippe set the tray aside and studied her intently for several minutes without speaking. Gabby had the distinct feeling that he was trying to memorize her features. The silence between them grew almost painful. At last Philippe spoke.

"Gabby, if you haven't noticed, the *Windward* is on open sea. We left Norfolk last night." Gabby remained silent. "Our destination is Martinique. I . . . I think you need to consult with a doctor concerning your pregnancy. Martinique is the best place for you to be at this time."

"Why should you care, Philippe? This child means nothing to you."

"You are still my wife," came Philippe's feeble reply. His next words rendered her speechless, his voice low, tortured. "When we reach Martinique you are free to do as you please. I . . . I will not force you to return to Bellefontaine with me, or resume relations. Whether or not you choose to function as my wife will be your choice alone."

"Do you mean to divorce me, Philippe?" Gabby asked, mouth agape, stunned by her husband's complete about-face.

"No!" protested Philippe loudly. Then more quietly, "I will never consent to a divorce."

"Then what do you mean? I don't understand, Philippe. What new type of cruelty are you inflicting on me?"

"I have done much thinking since I found you at Daisy Wilson's and I have come to the inevitable conclusion that you and I would be constantly warring with one another if I forced you to return to Bellefontaine and resume our marriage. For one thing, this child would always come between us. I am as certain of this as I am that I could not live with you in the same house and not make love to you. You are far too desirable to keep my hands off you." He paused, clearing his throat, as if speaking was causing him pain.

Gabby listened closely but found Philippe's words impossible to believe, not trusting herself to ask how he meant to free her. All the while he spoke his face remained inscrutable, his eyes hooded, only a muscle twitching along his jawline betrayed what he might be feeling.

"When we reach Martinique," Philippe continued, as if reading her mind, "you are free to choose where and how you want to live your life. You can return with me to Belle-fontaine, become wife to me in every way, remain at my townhouse in St. Pierre, or . . . or . . . go to Duvall, if that is what you really want. I won't stand in your way."

Gabby was stunned as well as perplexed. Did he actually mean what he said? she wondered. Would he really allow her to live openly with Marcel without benefit of a divorce? For obvious reasons she could not reside with Philippe at Belle-fontaine. Nor did she choose to occupy the townhouse where both Philippe and Amalie could easily approach her. She had to think of Philippe's child, protect it from Amalie, even from Philippe himself. She knew instinctively that Marcel would welcome her into his home, would make no demands upon her, would even care for her child. But did she want that? Eventually he would expect more from her than mere friendship, and under the circumstances his expectations would not be unreasonable. She knew Marcel loved her. How long could a man in love be satisfied with chaste kisses and passionless embraces? Once her baby was born he would want to become her lover, and out of gratitude she would not, could not, refuse him. Perhaps, she mused, perhaps . . . she could come to love him as she had once loved Philippe.

Philippe watched through a smoldering, gray mist while Gabby mulled over and decided her own future. He was care-ful to keep the anxiety from his face but in his heart he already knew her decision as ominous shadows from the past suddenly appeared to plague him.

At last Gabby's violet eyes impaled Philippe as they probbed into the depths of his soul. Before her final decision was made she felt obligated to speak once more of their child. She owed it to that innocent being to try for a reconciliation, to convince him that she had not betrayed him with Marcel. Drawing a deep, agonizing breath, she asked, "If I return to Bellefontaine, become your wife in every sense of the word, won't you find it in your heart to accept and love this child as your own?" Long, feathery lashes lowered to disguise her emotions, Gabby waited with bated breath for Philippe's answer; a few simple words that could change the course of her life.

"May *le bon dieu* forgive me but I cannot!" cried Philippe, nearly choking on his own words, cursing the pride that refused to give her the benefit of the doubt; a doubt that would follow him to his grave.

"I carry your child, Philippe," Gabby insisted softly, sorrowfully. "It could not be otherwise. You are the father of this child just as you sired the son I lost. As long as you believe me an adulteress, I cannot return with you to Bellefontaine nor live as your wife."

Bowing to the inevitable, eyes sad, yet resigned, Philippe said, "You will go to Duvall." It was a statement of fact rather than a question.

Until that moment Gabby had not been certain she would go to Marcel. But Philippe's unplacating tone and grim expression made her mind up for her. "If Marcel will have me I will go to him," she said, her eyes sliding from his stricken face.

"Of course he will have you," retorted Philippe cuttingly, "a child needs his father, does he not, *ma petite?*"

Gabby could only stare at him. Could this be the same man who had vowed never to let her go? His biting words bolstered her determination to accept whatever freedom he offered and make a life for her and her child without him. "So be it," Gabby whispered, her voice barely audible.

"Before I allow you to go your own way," Philippe continued, his face stony, "I would ask but two things of you." Still mistrustful, Gabby did not respond, eyeing him sullenly. "First, the moment we reach Martinique I insist you be examined by Dr. Renaud." He went on when Gabby voiced no objection. "Second, as long as we remain man and wife I shall continue to support you. I will arrange with my

296

bank for you to draw funds whenever you need them. I refuse to allow Duvall to support my wife."

Gabby digested all this slowly. She had no objection to consulting Dr. Renaud, and as for supporting her, it was no more than right. She would be less dependent upon Marcel if she had her own monies and Philippe's child would be denied nothing.

"I agree, Philippe," she said tiredly, surprised at the ease with which her freedom had been accomplished.

"Then we have nothing more to discuss, *cherie*. I probably won't see much of you during the remainder of the voyage. Seaman Laville will see to your needs from now on until we reach Martinique. My only wish for you now is to rest, recover your strength and . . . and . . ." He could not continue, his emotions were too near to the surface, too raw. Turning abruptly, he left the cabin. Gabby glared at his retreating back, hurt, bewildered, confused . . . and strangely bereft.

True to his word, Philippe made no attempt to see Gabby during the following weeks. She had no idea where he slept and cared less. At least he wasn't torturing her body with his constant lovemaking, demanding from her more than she was willing to give. She had followed his suggestion though and spent long hours in bed regaining her health throughout the tedious voyage, stuffing herself with enough food to please even Seaman Laville who hovered over her like a mother hen.

The farther south they traveled the milder the weather became and Gabby took to the deck for exercise as well as from bordeom. Ofttimes she sensed someone watching as she strolled and would turn abruptly to find Philippe's hooded, smoky gaze upon her, intense yet unreadable. Whenever that happened he would nod curtly before turning away.

Thus the days passed. Although Gabby rested, ate, and exercised regularly, she remained desperately thin; her huge, violet eyes seemed to swallow up her pale face. She was not actually ill, but she sensed something strange—like a poison sapping away her meager strength. Not only was she plagued by the feeling that all was not well with her and her child, she experienced a deep sense of loss, as if a light had gone out of her life.

On her last night aboard the *Windward* Gabby decided to retire immediately after supper. She wanted to be up early to catch her first glimpse of Mt. Pelee and the white sand beaches surrounding Martinique. She now considered Martinique her home and was pleased to be returning.

Almost absently she began her preparations for bed. Sighing, she lifted her chemise over her head and studied her slightly rounded stomach in the mirror over the nightstand, thinking of how she would look in a few more months.

Suddenly the door opened and Philippe entered, looking just as startled as Gabby to have intruded upon such an intimate scene. The sight of her flawless white body poised on the edge of confusion held him in thrall. "Very fetching, *ma chere*," he drawled lazily, twin flames of desire darkening his smoky gaze.

"Philippe! What are you doing here!" gasped Gabby, frantically searching the small room for her wrapper.

"I came to pack my belongings," he said, his voice hoarse with desire, "but seeing you like this . . . *mon dieu*, I am only human!" Gabby backed away from his burning eyes, scorched by the raw passion radiating from his hardening body. Unconsciously she covered her protruding abdomen with her hands as if to protect her child from his lust. Instantly he was beside her, drawing her tembling blody into his arms.

"Gabby, *ma chere*, I want you! Let me love you one last time!"

To Gabby's ears it sounded almost as if he were a drowning man begging to be saved. This was not the same man who had taken her brutally time after time, debasing, abusing her. This strange man acted as if he truly needed her. What deception was he playing at? she wondered even as her flesh strained toward his burning touch.

When she made no protest, Philippe wasted no time, carrying Gabby to the bed and hastily shedding his clothes. It seemed like only moments before his lips were claiming hers, savagely, yet not without a hint of tenderness. He outlined the tender shape of her mouth with his tongue, memorizing, before plunging into the sweetness within. She felt his hunger, was overpowered by it, and then she felt her own hunger answering. She stiffened, feeling his mouth move downward to pull at an erect nipple, pausing at the slight bulge of her stomach, hands caressing lovingly, almost reverently. Still he continued his downward journey. Gabby could feel him large and tumescent against her and she moaned in spite of herself as a warm, pleasurable lassitude swept her along on a tide of passion.

"Soon, *ma chere*, soon," crooned Philippe, whispering words of love. "I want to worship every inch of you one more time."

And he proceeded to do just that. Not an inch of her body was inviolate. Though she was ready for him he would not be hurried. Even her small cries and gasps of pleasure when he found a particular spot vulnerable to his lips and hands could not persuade him from his quest. Then his mouth found the place he sought and Gabby arched her back to him, pulling him even closer, encircling him with her legs as he tasted, taunted, teased, his tongue hungry for her honeyed warmth.

"Now, Philippe!" Gabby cried, writhing, moaning, ecstasy driving her out of her mind.

Spurred by her words, Philippe plunged into her velvet wetness, afraid he would hurt her, yet powerless to contain his need. To his surprise, Gabby ground her pelvis into his, stunning him by the passion he had unleashed in her as well as by the intensity of her response.

Gabby wanted all of him, and as if to prove it, she flung her arms and legs around his driving body, locking him securely. Lost in the soft recesses of her body, Philippe slowed his pace, savoring, enjoying fully her welcoming flesh. Gabby's blood boiled, great rivers of molten lava flowed through her veins and she grasped and clutched Philippe even closer. Sensing her urgency, Philippe quickened his movements, plunging down, down, down, into the velvet honey of her. At the onset of her long, wailing cry, he covered her lips with his, taking, muffling the sounds with his own mouth until they mingled and became like thunder in his ears.

Lying side by side, panting loudly, bodies touching, they descended slowly from the towering passion they had just shared. When Philippe could finally speak his voice was tinged with sadness. "A fitting adieu, *ma chere*. One that will remain with me forever."

Gabby could not trust herself to speak. She wanted their final parting to be as friendly as possible given their circumstances and anything she could say would cause more dissension. She could not face another altercation, knowing in her heart that though Philippe desired her body he could never bring himself to believe her, or trust her. Sighing wretchedly, Gabby sensed that they had just said their last farewell in such a way as to prove that her love for him was not entirely dead . . . but it was too late . . . too late.

Hearing her sigh, Philippe was assailed by feelings of guilt and remorse, thinking that he had taken advantage of her again, used her to satisfy his need for her, a need that would torment him for the rest of his life. So before he did or said something to anger her he rose from the bed, careful not to touch her, fearing he might take her again, and began to dress.

"I shall be on hand to escort you ashore, Gabby," Philippe

said as he fumbled with the buttons on his soft, linen shirt, his eyes carefully averted from her enticing body, utterly desirable despite her pregnancy.

"Whatever for? Everyone will soon be aware that we have separated."

"Perhaps not," Philippe said mysteriously.

Fully dressed Philippe finally found the courage to face Gabby. He ached to make love to her again, to purge her mind and body of Duvall by sheer force of strength. Then his eyes fell upon the curve of her stomach and his mouth hardened. By all that was right and holy the child she carried should be his, not Duvall's! With a will of its own his hand crept out to caress the smooth roundness. Gabby flinched but made no move to stop him, waiting for him to say something, anything. With a curse, Philippe flung himself away and out the door into the dark, lonely night.

Philippe was waiting for Gabby the next morning when she emerged from her cabin, mauve shadows marring the pale skin beneath her eyes. With cool detachment that belied his true feelings he offered her his arm and together they descended the gangplank.

Gabby was immediately caught up with the sights and sounds of the island. Her eyes and ears were so filled with the teeming life and colorful people happily going about their business that she was unaware Philippe had hired a carriage until she found herself being handed inside.

"Where are we going, Philippe?" she questioned. "I thought you said . . ."

"Relax, Gabby, you will see your precious Marcel soon enough. But first we are going to visit Dr. Renaud. I can only remain in St. Pierre a few days before I must see my plantation."

Dr. Renaud finished his examination and sat down to talk with Philippe while Gabby dressed.

"How is my wife, doctor?" asked Philippe with grave concern. "To my eyes she appears frail in comparison with her previous pregnancy."

"I cannot understand it, Monsieur St. Cyr," began the doctor, shaking his shaggy head of graying hair. "I can find nothing physically wrong with your wife, yet . . . you are correct in your thinking. There seems to be something intangible undermining her health. We must watch her closely if she is to be delivered safely."

"It's just as I feared," muttered Philippe darkly. "Doctor, there are complications to my wife's pregnancy that you are unaware of." He paused, considering how much of the truth he should reveal to the good doctor. "What I am about to tell you must be held in the strictest confidence."

"I am not in the habit of discussing my patients with anyone," bristled Dr. Renaud huffily.

"I do not mean to question your integrity," assured Philippe hastily. "Let me explain. While the *Windward* was docked in Norfolk, my wife took it upon herself to go ashore alone after I forbade her to do so. She became lost and was accosted by a common seaman and nearly raped. To further complicate matters she was rescued by a procurer for a house of prostitution and given a sleeping potion to render her senseless and then a double dose of a powerful stimulant in an effort to force her to their will."

"*Sacre dieu!*" cursed the doctor, his eyes saucers of anger and disgust.

"Luckily," lied Philippe smoothly, "I found her before any harm was done to her and brought her back to the ship."

"The poor child! What a shock to her system, especially in her delicate condition," agonized the good doctor, immediately searching his mind for the names of aphrodisiacs she could have been given.

"Doctor," said Philippe, lowering his voice, "my wife does not remember any of her ordeal and I would prefer to keep it that way. If she had blocked the episode from her mind I see no reason to enlighten her."

"Wise, very wise," agreed Dr. Renaud, nodding his head sagely. Privately, he felt much was left unsaid, that something horrible had happened to Madame St. Cyr in Norfolk.

"My main concern is Gabby's health and the welfare of the child. Is it possible the babe could have been harmed by the drugs my wife was forced to ingest?"

"*Mon ami,*" stated the doctor. "I do not know what drugs your wife was given; there are dozens capable of producing the results you described. We all know of their initial effect but what damage, if any, they have on an unborn fetus is anybody's guess. We can only wait, watch, and pray. Of course, in light of what you have just disclosed, I shall insist that your wife remain in St. Pierre under my care. Bellefontaine is too remote."

"My thinking exactly, doctor," agreed Philippe with alacrity. "But unfortunately I cannot remain in St. Pierre. It's imperative I return to my responsibilities at Bellefontaine."

"Under the circumstances I do not think it advisable for Madame St. Cyr to remain at your townhouse alone except for servants."

"I assumed as much, Doctor," nodded Philippe. "With this in mind I have arranged for my . . . friend . . . Marcel Duvall, to look after Gabby. He lives in St. Pierre most of the time, leaving the running of Le Chateau to his excellent overseer. She will reside in his townhouse, under his care, until the child is born." Philippe could not help but notice the doctor's startled look.

"Er . . . rather unusual, isn't it, Monsieur St. Cyr? There is bound to be much gossip about such an . . . er . . . arrangement."

"But I am certain you will not allow such talk to take root, Doctor," Philippe continued, his eyes narrow shards of ice. "My wife remains in St. Pierre at your insistence and her

303

living arrangements meet with my complete approval. Armed with this knowledge you should have little difficulty quelling malicious gossipers bent on destroying her reputation.''

"You can rest assured, *mon ami*," asserted the doctor, stiffening his bent shoulders, "that not one damaging word shall be spoken against your lovely wife in my presence. She has been through too much to be hurt by idle talk. And I am sure that Duvall will not be remiss in his duty toward the wife of a friend such as yourself.''

Philippe breathed a sigh of relief. He had eased the compromising situation Gabby was about to enter upon in the only way he knew how. He felt he owed her that much. Dr. Renaud would see to her health as well as guard her reputation, at least until the child was born. Suddenly, a thought entered his mind. He had failed to ask the most important question of all.

"When will the child be born, Doctor?"

"These things are hard to predict exactly, but according to my calculations you should be a father by the end of August or first part of September.''

Swiftly counting in his head Philippe reckoned that the child could be his only if born after the first of September. Any date before that would definitely prove that Marcel had sired the babe just as he suspected.

Just then Gabby entered the room. "Well, Doctor," she asked, her smooth face showing signs of strain and fatigue, "am I healthy enough to please you?"

"I can find nothing wrong with you, Madame St. Cyr, that plenty of nourishing food and the mild climate of Martinique won't cure," answered the doctor with bluff hardiness.

"I somehow sense, Doctor," Gabby admitted softly, her eyes carefully averted from Philippe, "that this pregnancy isn't going as it should.'' Philippe could not help but wince at the accusing tone of her voice.

"Nonsense, *ma chere*. It is true that you are far too thin but the baby appears to be prospering. But for safety's sake I think it best that you remain in St. Pierre where I can keep close watch over you, and your husband has agreed."

Gabby slanted Philippe a blank look and opened her mouth to speak but Philippe allowed her no time to form her question. Immediately he rose, thanked the doctor, grasped Gabby's arm possessively, and led her from the doctor's office.

"Did you tell the doctor?" Gabby asked the moment they were outside.

"Tell him what, *ma chere?*"

"About our separation! He's bound to learn sooner or later."

"Not exactly," admitted Philippe somewhat guiltily. "What I told him was that I was unable to remain in St. Pierre with you because of pressing duties at Bellefontaine, and that my good friend Marcel Duvall would take you into his home and look after you until the child is born."

Gabby was utterly flabbergasted by Philippe's words. "Why? Why would you do that?"

"To protect you from slander," he said coldly. "I care what others say about you even if you do not!"

Gabby searched his face, but his features were carved from marble, his eyes unfathomable. Finally, his meaning became clear. "You mean only to protect yourself! It is your name you don't want maligned!"

"If that is what you believe . . ." he intoned dryly as he handed her into their rented carriage.

After seeing that Gabby was settled inside, Philippe shut the door and put his head inside the window. "I will not go with you to Duvall's house so we will make our adieus now. If you have need of me I will be at my townhouse for two more days. I've arranged for your trunks to be delivered to you. If there is anything you need from the plantation I will see that it reaches you. Perhaps you would like the baby clothes you made for *our* child?"

Gabby blanched, her pale face turning dead white. "I will let you know," she stammered, confused by Philippe's apparent lack of concern. "*Adieu*, Philippe," she whispered sadly, wistfully. "May *le bon dieu* deep you safe."

At her parting words Phillippe's face softened, gray eyes misty. Against his will his long arms reached for her inside the carriage, drawing her forward until he could reach her lips, covering them, gently, longingly, lovingly. His tongue tasting, savoring, as the kiss deepened, held, then released.

"*Au revoir, ma chere.*" Then he was gone, leaving Gabby stunned by the raw emotion evident in his parting kiss.

"*Adieu*, Philippe," she whispered into the emptiness of the coach, her heart strangely heavy with a grief she wished she did not feel.

Chapter Seventeen

GABBY HESITATED before Marcel's front door, her hand poised on the knocker, her mind in a turmoil. She realized that once she entered Marcel's house all hope of reconciling with Philippe was lost forever. But then, hadn't he already refused to claim his own babe? No, thought Gabby, resolutely firming her chin, Philippe did not deserve the son or daughter she would bear him. Her decision made, she grasped the knocker firmly, preparing to make her presence known. But before she could raise the heavy, brass object, a voice from behind startled her.

"Gabby, *cherie!* Is it really you? I have been out of my mind with worry since St. Cyr spirited you out of New Orleans!"

Gabby turned just as Marcel bounded through the front gate, a look of pure joy lighting his handsome features.

"Marcel!" sobbed Gabby, suddenly aware of how glad she was to see him.

"Where have you been, *cherie?*" Marcel asked, searching her pale face. What he saw made him gasp in shock and outrage as he drew Gabby into the protective circle of his arms. "What has he done to you, Gabby? *Mon dieu*, look at you, you are ill! If he has harmed you in any way I shall kill him!" Marcel announced with cold fury. The dark smudges beneath Gabby's eyes accentuated their violet hue and brought into focus her pale features. Her skin had the transparency of fine porcelain. All this Marcel noted with growing alarm.

Suddenly it all became too much for Gabby as Marcel's

face faded into the distance and she felt herself begin a slow descent to the ground. Then she knew no more.

Marcel, his face a mask of concern and love, had his arms around Gabby even as she began to crumple and lifted her weightless form, making his way into the house where he placed her gently on the sofa at the same time calling to his housekeeper to bring cool water and clean clothes. Then he began to unbutton Gabby's tight dress, starting at the high neckline and continuing to her waist where his fingers paused, noticing for the first time her thickened waistline and gently swelling stomach. He grit his teeth in barely suppressed anger but continued with his ministrations when his housekeeper, Tildy, arrived with the water and cloths.

Dismissing Tildy, Marcel tenderly bathed Gabby's flushed face and neck until her eyes began to flutter. "Gabby, *cherie,*" he crooned softly, "what has he done to you?"

Gabby's eyes blinked upon and she was momentarily stunned to find Marcel bending over her. She tried to answer but Marcel put a finger to her lips.

"Don't speak until your strength returns, *ma chere.* I shall send immediately for the doctor."

"No, Marcel!" Gabby replied, straining to rise. "I have just come from Dr. Renaud's office!"

"You have already seen a doctor?"

"*Oui,* Phillipe insisted on accompanying me there the moment we docked. Because . . . because of my . . . condition," Gabby stammered shyly. The pink staining her cheeks was the first sign of any color Marcel had seen on her pale face since he had found her standing on his doorstep.

"Philippe knows you are to bear his child?" Marcel was astounded. Why was Gabby here? Surely St. Cyr would not let her out of his sight now that she was carrying his heir, he reasoned.

"Philippe is well aware that I am pregnant," Gabby whispered in a voice so low Marcel had to bend to hear. "Only . . .

only . . . Oh, Marcel,'' Gabby sobbed, clutching at his shirt and hiding her head against his shoulder. "He refuses to believe the child is his!"

"*Mon dieu*, what a jackass! Who does he suppose the father to be?"

Gabby lifted her misty eyes and Marcel was shocked and angered at the pain and suffering mirrored in those violet depths. Even without being told he knew the answer. Gabby's words only confirmed it.

"He believes that we were lovers and that you sired the child before I left Martinique aboard the *Southern Star.*"

"If that were true I would be the happiest man alive, *cherie,*" Marcel said tenderly. And he was never more serious in his life. He would cherish a child by Gabby conceived from his own loins. Suddenly his jaw hardened, his fists clenched and his eyes became cold green emeralds.

"What did that fool do to you after he decided that child you carry was not his? Did he beat you? Starve you? From the looks of you it is obvious that you have been abused. Did he force you? Tell me, Gabby, tell me everything," insisted Marcel through clenched teeth. "The sooner I know the truth the sooner I can call him out and kill him. Once I make you a widow we will be wed."

"Marcel, please listen," begged Gabby. For some unexplained reason she did not want Philippe dead. "As soon as I learned I was with child I told Philippe, thinking he would be pleased. His reaction stunned me. He refused to believe I had remained faithful to him."

"The damn fool!" cursed Marcel bitterly. "Is that when he began abusing you?"

Gabby thought back to Norfolk and shuddered. "Just the opposite," she admitted slowly, still puzzling over Philippe's strange behavior after he found her at Daisy Wilson's. "Before that I was little more than his prisoner aboard the *Windward*. Philippe took away my clothes and forced me to submit to him. I think he was determined to either bend me to his will, or . . . or kill me.''

"Now I know I cannot allow him to live!" snarled Marcel. "What suffering you must have endured! But you said he changed after Norfolk. In what way?"

"*Oui*, he did change. But not before I tried once again to run away. There was no way I could remain with him and allow his own child to be treated as a bastard. So I left the ship while Philippe was ashore. Only . . . only . . ."

"What is it, *cherie?*" Then seeing Gabby's distressed face, Marcel was prompted to add, "Tell me only if you wish."

"Everything that happened in Norfolk is still fuzzy, distorted in my mind. I would rather not speak of it now."

"Of course, *cherie*, I will not press you."

Reassured by Marcel's gentle understanding, Gabby continued. "Needless to say Philippe found me and brought me back to the ship. For some unexplained reason I was ill and have not fully recovered."

"Are you certain St. Cyr did nothing to harm you? He did not neglect you while you lay ill?" asked Marcel sharply, the picture of Gabby sick and helpless before Philippe's anger vivid in his mind.

"No!" denied Gabby, recalling the bruises inflicted upon her defenseless body while she lay unconscious, but loath to reveal to Marcel the full extent of Philippe's cruelty. "Philippe was gentle and caring during my illness."

"Ha! I find that hard to believe!" sneered Marcel.

"It's true, Marcel, although I found it difficult to believe myself at that time. That's when he told me he would not stand in my way if I still wished to leave him."

"Philippe said that?" Marcel's face was a mask of disbelief. "Did he indicate that he might divorce you?"

"No! He made it clear that he would never consent to a divorce, that if I chose to . . . to live with you, it would be without benefit of divorce."

"And you still chose me under those circumstances, *ma chere?*" cried Marcel, tears springing to his eyes as he gathered her in his arms. "You shall never regret your decision, I promise. I shall always love and protect you."

"Wait, Marcel!" exclaimed Gabby, slipping from his embrace. "There is something you must understand. I cannot think beyond the birth of my child, I make no promises as to our future together."

"Your child is now my child by right of abandonment," stated Marcel firmly. "And once our child is born I shall take you to France and personally petition the courts for a divorce."

"You would do that for me?"

"For us, *cherie*, for us. Don't you know? Can't you guess? *Je t'aime, je t'aime.* I have loved you since the day I first saw you aboard the *Windward*, a young bride, unhappy in her marriage. Even then I hoped to have you one day for my own. Soon, it will become a reality."

Then, overcome by culmination of his wildest dreams, and by the hot flush of desire, Marcel buried his head between Gabby's breasts, planting moist kisses on her smooth flesh. His hand slipped to her stomach where he lovingly caressed the growing child he would love and cherish as his own.

"I believe you really mean it, Marcel," said Gabby wonderingly. "I believe you would love Philippe's child as your own."

"Our child, *cherie*," he corrected. "For I already accept responsibility. I would not hesitate to protect you both with my dying breath!"

"I believe you, Marcel," Gabby said wearily. "But I am in no way able to consider the future at this time. I am confused, hurt, and exhausted. Right now I need your friendship."

"My home is yours, *cherie*. I ask nothing of you, expect no payment but to be able to enjoy your company and share your

311

child. Now," he said brusquely, concerned by the lines of weariness marring her features, "up to bed with you." He lifted her easily in his brawny arms and carried her to the guest room, depositing her gently on the bed. "I will send Tildy up to help you."

Not until that moment did Gabby realize that she was bared to the waist. But now, as she followed Marcel's hot gaze, her face turned scarlet at his wistful look and her hands flew to pull the material of her bodice together.

"Forgive me, *cherie*," Marcel apologized sheepishly, "but I had to loosen your dress when you fainted."

"I understand, Marcel," murmured Gabby, blushing furiously, "there is no need to apologize. I . . . I am grateful to you."

"I want you to know that I will never take advantage of you or do anything to destroy whatever feelings you have for me. No matter how badly I want you I would never force myself on you as Philippe has done in the past."

Gabby relaxed visibly at his words and sighed wearily. "*Merci*, Marcel. You are so good to me. I only wish I . . . I could love you as you love me."

"It will come, *cherie*, it will come," he smiled confidently.

After Marcel left Gabby in Tildy's capable hands he let himself out of the house and strode with grim determination the short distance to the docks and entered a large building sporting a sign proclaiming it to be the offices of St. Cyr Enterprises. He looked neither right nor left but walked directly to a door emblazoned with the name of Philippe St. Cyr. Noting the intense look on Marcel's face, the clerk sitting at the desk in the outer office did nothing to stop him as he burst into Philippe's private office, slamming the door behind him.

Startled, Philippe looked up, but his hooded eyes effectively concealed his feelings when he saw Marcel, anger darkening his countenance.

"I thought I'd find you here, St. Cyr," Marcel said with deady calm.

Philippe's first thought was of Gabby. "What is it, Duvall? Has something happened to my wife?" Marcel could not help but note the way Philippe stressed the word "wife."

"My question exactly, St. Cyr. What has happened to her? Any fool can see she is unwell. If you won't tell me what is wrong with her I shall be forced to go to Dr. Renaud for an answer. If I find that you have harmed either Gabby or her child I shall kill you," Marcel said with cold fury, surprised at the depth of his own emotion.

A tremendously long silence loomed up while Philippe searched Marcel's face. Then, as if satisfied by what he saw, he said, "I don't blame you for being concerned about the welfare of your child, Duvall." Here he paused dramatically and when Marcel made no move to deny his words, Philippe's face hardened. "But that doesn't lessen my hatred for you. Twice in the past Gabrielle has left me, but this time I let her go because she carried your child. And after her terrifying experience in Norfolk I lacked the will to force her to return to Bellefontaine with me."

"Just what did happen in Norfolk?" Marcel insisted. "Gabby could not tell me about it without becoming distressed. I believe something so horrible happened to her there that her mind refuses to accept it. And I hold you responsible!"

Marcel was puzzled by the fleeting look of pain that crossed Philippe's face. "Because it concerns the welfare of your unborn child I will tell you exactly what took place in Norfolk when Gabby left the *Windward* on her own," sighed Philippe, his voice tinged with sadness. "I cannot tell you I am blameless because when I learned Gabby had been living as your mistress after I left Martinique I was livid with rage and determined to make her suffer for the indignity she heaped upon me. I admit freely that I dealt harshly with her

313

but I would not have done her bodily harm. I meant only to break her spirit until she became a loving, amenable wife to me. Then came the worst indignity of all . . . she discovered she was pregnant with your child. Oh, *oui*, she tried to convince me that the child was mine," laughed Philippe bitterly. "When I refused to believe her lies she left the ship at Norfolk deliberately thrusting herself into a situation that nearly cost her her own life as well as the life of her child."

Marcel's slitted eyes blazed hated at Philippe. Shock glazed his face as the sordid details of Gabby's ordeal in Daisy Wilson's house of prostitution came to light. At one point in the telling, Marcel sank into a chair and buried his head in his hands.

"*Mon dieu*, the memories of such foul treatment at unscrupulous hands must be eating away at her soul like some dread sickness! The depravities she engaged in while under the drug! I cannot bear the thought of that poor child's suffering!"

"Gabby does not remember what took place at Daisy Wilson's and if she means anything at all to you you must never reveal to her what I have told you this day."

"I love Gabby!" Marcel insisted vehemently. "I would never hurt her as you have done!"

"*Oui*," said Philippe wearily, readily accepting the blame heaped upon him by Marcel. "I believe you do love her."

"Then divorce her!"

"Never!"

"I fail to understand you, Philippe. You accuse your wife of adultery, even allow her to leave you for another man, yet refuse to divorce her. What manner of man are you?"

"My reasons are my own," muttered Philippe darkly. "What matters now is Gabby's health. She is in need of constant care. Her condition, according to Dr. Renaud, is delicate. He cannot even vouchsafe that the child has not been endangered by the drugs she has been given."

"Your concern is misplaced in view of your conduct toward her these past months. You realize that she will be devastated if she loses this baby. She desperately wants this child."

Philippe flinched, remembering all too well his own agony when Gabby lost their child in the banana groves. "Tell me, Duvall," he asked perversely, "were you surprised to learn you were to become a father?" The intensity of his gaze disconcerted Marcel. If ever there was a time to deny any past intimacies with Gabby, it was now. But if he did, Philippe would no doubt reclaim his wife. Therefore, his answer evoked no guilt in him.

"I was overjoyed to learn of Gabby's pregnancy," he said carefully. "This child will be most welcome. It just surprises me that you would consent to let her go."

Marcel's words sent Philippe's hopes plummeting. Though they were not what he wanted to hear they served to strengthen his belief that Marcel had sired Gabby's child. But then, he was not entirely stupid, he could count to nine as well as the next person. Time alone would be the determining factor. Suddenly he became aware of Marcel's expectant look, waiting for him to divulge his reasons for releasing Gabby.

Shifting uneasily, he said, "I realized that it would be a mistake to force Gabby to remain with me against her will. The deaths of two women are already on my conscience and I feared for her life. Better she live with you than die trying to escape from a marriage she obviously detested. I gave her a choice; the decision she made was hers alone."

With mixed feelings, Marcel accepted the finality of Philippe's words, though he distrusted Philippe's motives for letting Gabby go; for throughout his long dissertations his love for his wife was clearly visible. But he had obviously meant what he said. He would gladly put his wife into another man's keeping rather than cause her harm. That alone was proof of his love. Marcel had no doubt in his mind that Philippe would take his wife back even though he was convinced that she carried another man's child. Therefore, he reasoned, Philippe must never know that he and Gabby were not now and had never been lovers.

"For once in your life you used good judgment," agreed Marcel blandly.

Philippe glared balefully at Marcel. "Remember, Duvall, Gabby is still my wife. I shall never divorce her. And if you are thinking of making her a widow, forget it. I have escaped your snare once and can do so again."

Marcel blanched. Was St. Cyr aware of his futile attempts upon his life? he wondered. Aloud he said, "Your suspicions will gain you naught for nothing can be proved. In any case, it matters little to me whether you divorce Gabby. Once the child is born we will leave Martinique." Not waiting for a reply he turned to leave.

"Wait!" Philippe ordered, halting Marcel in his tracks. "I told you I would not interfere as long as you take good care of Gabby and I meant it. In return I request that you keep me apprised of her health during the coming months. Considering what you are gaining that is little enough to ask."

"If that is what it takes to keep you from annoying Gabby then I agree." Without further comment Marcel left Philippe's office as abruptly as he had entered.

Philippe sat brooding a long time after Marcel's departure. Why had Gabby lied about her relationship to Marcel? he wondered uneasily. Why had she insisted the child only be his. Confronted with the truth Marcel had denied nothing. Was there more here than met the eye? Angered, disillusioned, hurt, and confused, Philippe raised his huge fist and struck the desk with the full force of his awesome strength. The resounding crack that split the top of his desk and the pain in his hand combined effectively in clearing his mind of distressing images of Marcel and Gabby pleasurably engaged in the act of love.

The next day Philippe returned to Bellefontaine. Upon his arrival Amalie was on hand to help him dispel all thoughts of Gabby from his mind and body in the ways in which she excelled. But even her passionate welcome could not dim entirely the vision of a flaxen-haired beauty whose violet eyes, turned to him in love, had the ability to melt his heart.

True to his word, Marcel reported regularly to Philippe as Gabby's pregnancy progressed. These reports must have coincided with Dr. Renaud's for he appeared satisfied, choosing to remain at Bellefontaine rather than insinuate himself into Gabby's life at a time when serenity was important to her welfare. Part of the reason for the good report was Gabby's realization that she had nothing to fear from Philippe as he continued to absent herself from St. Pierre. Just knowing that she was loved and protected by Marcel also served to improve her mental state. That, in addition to plenty of rest and nourishing food, soon put roses back in her cheeks.

Marcel was more than pleased with Gabby's state of health since she had come to him. More and more he had come to think of the child she cared as his very own. He spent a good share of each day in Gabby's company and was amazed at the day to day changes in her face and figure. As her waist thickened and the baby grew, her features softened and she appeared lovelier than ever in his eyes. Once the child was born he was positive she would come to love him and he would have his heart's desire. They had grown quite comfortable with each other, more like married couples than friends. Even now Gabby allowed him certain liberties that normally would be granted only to a husband. She did not protest when he kissed her, nor pull away from him when he caressed her intimately. He especially loved to place his hand upon her stomach and feel the baby's movements. In Marcel's eyes, Gabby was never ungainly or awkward; she moved with the grace and beauty of a gazelle. But no matter how much he

317

wanted to make love to her, he curbed his desire. He vowed she would never suffer because of him and after Philippe had told him what had transpired in Norfolk he would never force himself on her. For the first time in his life he loved unselfishly. In his own mind, his love for Gabby was far stronger than Philippe's, who, according to rumor, had taken up again with his mistress.

Outwardly, Gabby appeared content. Marcel cared for her, and her health, while not robust, pleased the doctor. Inwardly, she was not as happy as she would have been had Philippe accepted his child and taken her to Bellefontaine with him. Because she realized the unlikelihood of such a thing happening she looked to Marcel more and more as her time grew near. He had been so good, so kind, that she had not the heart to deny him the kisses and caresses he seemed to crave. It warmed her heart to see the pleasure he derived from feeling the babe move in her stomach. At times Gabby could almost believe he was the father of her child!

At Bellefontaine Philippe busied himself with the cane harvest, driving himself relentlessly until he fell in bed each night too exhausted to even think. But that was the way he wanted it. His thoughts these days seemed only to lead in one direction . . . St. Pierre and Gabby. Even Amalie's golden body failed to push Gabby entirely from his mind. Once he had sated himself upon Amalie and the few moments of bliss were spent, he ordered her from his bed in self-loathing.

Nother Amalie could do seemed to inspire Philippe to the passion she knew him capable of; the spark, the fire of their lovemaking was sadly lacking. No matter how she teased and tantalized, his responses were always the same, automatic, remote, passionless. Sometimes, though, he became brutal and took her fiercely, his lust punishing. No matter what she did to please him, it produced the same results; after it was over he dismissed her from his bed as if she meant nothing to him but a vessel for his lust.

One night, in early August, after Philippe had received a note from Marcel concerning Gabby's state of health, he sat in his dimly lit room drinking until long past midnight, staring into space, his lean, dark face reflective. Had he not been miles away in his thoughts he would have heard soft footsteps padding across the room. Only when Amalie spoke softly in his ear was he aware of his presence.

"What do you want, Amalie?" he slurred thickly. "I have no need of your body this night."

Amalie flinched at his jeering words but did not let them deter her from her course, which was to replace Gabby in in Philippe's heart. "Let me love you tonight, Monsieur Philippe," she whispered silkily, winding her golden arms around his neck.

"Go away!" Philippe mumbled, shoving her rudely. Suddenly his hand closed on a firm, bare breast and Amalie moaned as Philippe unconsciously squeezed the warm flesh, feeling the nipple tugid against his palm. She swayed toward him and he pulled her onto his lap, burying his head in the soft curve of her neck.

"You need me," murmured Amalie huskily. "Only me. Forget her, she doesn't deserve you. Think of all the times she has betrayed you. Think only of your Amalie, Monsieur Philippe. Only Amalie loves you, *mon amour. Je t'adore!*"

"*Oui,*" agreed Philippe, fully aroused by her warm, sensuous flesh beneath his questing hands, shivering, straining toward his touch. Lifting Amalie from his lap, he rose unsteadily and stumbled with her to his bed. "Your soft, sweet flesh belongs to me. You alone have remained faithful to me."

His words were slurred but his hands were deft and sure as they traveled the length of her smooth body. His lips, sucking, seeking, drove her senseless with passion as they found the core of her desire. Philippe's own ardor was mounting steadily. He had not been so consumed with fire since the last time he had taken Gabby on the night before they docked.

"Come into me, *mon amour*, come into me," urged Amalie, arching to his hard, throbbing body, opening her legs to him.

Unable to hold back another moment Philippe lifted up and drove into her with the force of a sledgehammer. But instead of whimpering at the pain of his forceful entry, Amalie cried out in ecstasy, accepting every merciless stroke, urging him on with her hands and mouth as her legs grasped his body, pulling him closer, devouring him. She possessed such consummate feminine skills that her turning, writhing, moist body soon had him whirling in a vortex of passion where conscious thought dare not intrude. Philippe was unaware of his words at the moment of climax but Amalie heard them clearly.

"Gabby, *ma chere, je t'aime, je t'aime!*"

And then she was oblivious to all but her own thundering peak.

Later, while Philippe dozed, Amalie thought bitterly of his frenzied words and what they meant to her. Somehow she must prove to Philippe that she was the only one who could make him happy, that he did not need his faithless wife. Finally she felt him stir, his hands groping for her again. Immediately she was in his arms.

"You want Amalie again, Monsieur Philippe?" she asked seductively, her small hands already taunting his flesh. "Take me, I am yours. Even that pale wife you brought back from France realized it the moment she saw us together."

Philippe's body tensed, then froze, her words hitting him with the force of a physical blow. He grasped Amalie's shoulders in a bruising grip causing her to cry out.

"What did you mean by that remark, Amalie? When did Gabby see us together?" Her eyes were wide and horror-struck and she was momentarily struck dumb. "Answer me or I'll have your hide!"

Amalie was well aware of Philippe's vile temper when aroused and his dark moods and deemed him capable of doing her bodily harm. She had no choice but to answer his question. "Madame Gabby saw us making love the day that . . . that . . ."

"What day?" demanded Philippe ominously, his grip punishing.

"The day that she rode to Monsieur Marcel, the day she murdered your child!" she cried with growing alarm.

"*Mon dieu!*" cursed Philippe, looking at Amalie with loathing. "The shock of seeing us together must have driven her beyond sanity. No wonder she holds me responsible." In an agony of remorse he put his head in his hands and moaned. "I wish her nothing but happiness with Marcel. I owe her that much at least for my own betrayal."

"You are not angry with your Amalie?" asked the amazed Amalie, barely able to believe her good fortune. "If I realized you no longer cared for your wife I would not have offered her to Damballa. But then," she mused thoughtfully, "she might still be here if I had not . . ." Her sentence ended in a gurgle as Philippe's hands found her throat.

"Damballa? What has your infernal Obeah got to do with Gabby?" he asked with cold fury as he rose from the bed and lit a lamp, all signs of overindulgence vanished.

Amalie was truly terrified. She had not meant to divulge so much. If only Philippe hadn't found his runaway wife in New Orleans, she thought ruefully. She quaked inwardly at the look of pure malice in her lover's flinty eyes and instinctively knew the time had come to pay her dues.

"Tell me what happened, Amalie," commanded Philippe, his face a dark and deadly mask. "What did you do to Gabby after I left to cause her to leave Bellefontaine and go to Duvall? *Mon dieu!* She had barely recovered from a miscarriage and you dared to put her life in jeopardy again with your Obeah mumbo jumbo?"

"She was not harmed!" insisted Amalie, cringing beneath his venomous gaze.

But Philippe was driven beyond control. Twin flames of fury burned in his eyes. Before him was someone who had not only caused Gabby great suffering but had been the force behind their ultimate parting. With typical male conceit he had discounted entirely his own callous treatment during their first months of marriage and his past cruelties. In his mind, Amalie was the only one responsible for the loss of his child and ultimately his wife.

Without hesitation, Philippe lashed out cruelly, delivering a crushing blow to Amalie's face with his open palm. Reeling under the blow, she cringed when she saw him preparing to inflict yet another.

"Please, Monsieur Philippe, have pity!" she begged, one side of her face already beginning to swell. But Philippe was beyond pity. He was like a man possessed, unyielding, unfeeling, determined.

"The truth, you little bitch! What did you do to Gabby?"

"I'll tell you, only don't hit me again!" She watched through fearful cat's eyes as the huge, hurtful hand lowered before she spoke. "One night I . . . I had Madame Gabby taken from her bed and placed upon the altar of Damballa."

"Sacre bleu!" Philippe cursed. "You meant to sacrifice her to that . . . that snake?" He was incredulous to think that Amalie would go to such lengths to rid herself of a rival.

"No! No!" denied Amalie, fighting now for her life. "I would never have hurt her. I meant only to scare her into leaving you. I wanted you to love only me. We belong together, Monsieur Philippe. Didn't our coming together a short while ago prove that? Can you truly say that your wife pleases you as well as I? Surely her passion pales in compari-

322

son to the fire in my blood." Amalie's small hand inched confidently along Philippe's body until she grasped his manhood.

She was unprepared for Philippe's blow and her head veered sharply sideways. "What happened to Gabby on that altar?" he demanded, unappeased by her impassioned plea or her wild gropings.

Amalie realized there was no placating him; he would make her suffer until he learned everything there was to know. Head reeling from Philippe's telling blow, eyes nearly swollen shut, cheeks afire, she revealed all that had taken place upon the altar of Damballa, leaving out nothing except her frenzied coupling with the huge, black slave on the ground before the altar.

"I cannot believe that you could be so cruel," said Philippe, shaking his head in disbelief at the end of the telling. "If Gerard hadn't come upon the scene when he did who knows what might have happened. I've seen your Obeah rites. I know the kind of frenzy your people work yourselves into over that damned snake. No wonder Gabby left Belle-fontaine, she must have been driven mad with fright. Why that snake could have . . ."

That's as far as he got. While Philippe, eyes wide and horror-struck, tried to visualize Gabby's pale body on that cold, stone altar, Amalie saw her chance for escape and leaped from the bed like a sleek panther. Philippe, ever alert, grabbed her ankle before she cleared the bed, sending her crashing to the floor. Then he was stradding her inert form. When she made no move to rise, Philippe strode to the door, calling for Gerard in a voice loud enough to awaken all the house servants sleeping on the third floor.

Within minutes Gerard appeared at the door, lamp in hand, a bewildered look on his face. Tante Louise, a wrapper thrown over her nightgown, was not far behind.

"What is it, Monsieur Philippe?" Gerard asked sleepily.

The loud shriek coming from Tante Louise told Philippe that she had spied Amalie's bruised, nude body sprawled at his feet.

"What have you done to my *petite fille?*" she cried, moving swiftly to kneel beside her daughter. When she saw Amalie's swollen and battered face she began to wail pitifully. "What have you done to her? What have you done to her?"

"No more than she deserves," answered Philippe coldly. "I should take the whip to her. And you two are no better. How dare you conceal her dastardly tricks from me! Surely you couldn't have condoned what she did? *Mon dieu!* Gabby might have been bitten by that fer-de-lance, or raped by a sex-crazed slave!"

"No! No!" denied Gerard. "I reached her before any harm had been done. Amalie was jealous of Madame Gabby but she would never have hurt her!"

"I should whip her, or better yet, sell her!"

Tante Louise sucked in her breath sharply and rolled her eyes until only the whites showed.

Amalie, who by now had risen to a sitting position with her mother's help, threw herself at Philippe's feet, pleading, crying out, "Forgive me, Monsieur Philippe! Do not sell your Amalie! Whip me, but do not sell me, I beg you!"

Philippe gazed down dispassionately at the golden body that had once given him so much pleasure and he knew he could not bring himself to mar her beautiful flesh. There was but one alternative.

"Take her out of my sight and lock her in the servants' quarters," Philippe ordered, ignoring Gerard's stricken look.

"What are you going to do with my child, Monsieur Philippe?" asked Tante Louise, for the first time in her life finding herself hating her master. "She was born on Bellefontaine. This is her home. You took her when she was no more than a child. If you bear any love for me do not sell her!''

''I never want to set eyes on her again. After the cane is harvested I intend to sell her in St. Pierre.''

''But I belong to you!'' wailed Amalie. ''I want no other master! *Je t'aime! Je t'aime!*''

''You love only yourself,'' Philippe spat, unmoved by her pleas. ''There are many fine bordellos in St. Pierre and I will see that you are placed only in the best.''

Amalie's horror-stricken face followed Philippe as he turned away from her in disgust.

Chapter Eighteen

THE NEXT day Mt. Pelee began rumbling and belching thick wads of smoke and ash. Throughout the ages Pelee's occasional flare-ups had become commonplace among the islanders. After a few days the rumbling would cease and the spewing of fire and ash would slow to a halt. Everyone expected it to be the same this time and even the inhabitants of St. Pierre, the city most likely to be annihilated if a major eruption took place, went about their business as if there were no Mt. Pelee and the sooty ash that covered everything but a minor disturbance in their everyday lives. Most of the experts considered Mt. Pelee dormant for there had been no eruptions of major proportions for many, many years.

For the next two weeks the volcano continued with its fireworks and Philippe began to experience vague feelings of unease. Even the slaves sensed a force in the atmosphere that left them restless and discontented. They walked around with an air of expectancy, their eyes ever on the volcano towering above them.

But even if Mt. Pelee were to erupt, Philippe knew that Bellefontaine would be safe. The flow would take a path directly for St. Pierre and the sea, destroying everything that lay in its way.

Between the sultry August heat, the acrid ash residue clogging his throat, and his haste to complete the harvest so he could take Amalie to St. Pierre, Philippe was worn and exhausted. Only when the last of the cane was cut did he allow himself to relax and think of Gabby. He knew from both Marcel's and Dr. Renaud's reports that she was well and happy. The doctor still appeared vague on the exact date of the expected birth but Philippe surmised that the baby would be born within weeks. Perhaps he should call on her when he was in St Pierre, just to see if she needed anything . . . But even as he thought it, he knew he would not. Gabby did not love him; Marcel was the man she cared for. The best thing he could do for her was to stay out of her life.

The next day the sun was nearly obscured by thick clouds of gray ash. What rays found their way through to the ground were dim and diffused. In a carriage driven by Gerard, Philippe and Amalie set out at daybreak for St. Pierre. Amalie had long since given up pleading with Philippe. Her two weeks of enforced confinement had left her withdrawn and sullen. If she thought Philippe had relented in his attitude toward her, she was mistaken; his face, grim and determined, held no traces of remorse. Evidently he no longer felt a need for her body and he was bent on selling her to a bordello!

Amalie settled into a corner of the carriage, her yellow eyes narrowing as she thought of various methods of revenge, discarding one after another until her lips curved in a feline smile, sly, smug.

It was nearly dark when Philippe's carriage drew in before a large, brightly lit building in a section of the city that could not be called well-to-do but neither could it be considered a slum. There were many fine houses lining both sides of the street, all ablaze with lights. Philippe descended the carriage with Amalie in tow. To his surprise she did not resist but followed, chin thrust forward, shoulders squared, as he led the way to the front door, swinging her hips suggestively and tugging at the front of her peasant blouse until her dimpled shoulders gleamed like dull gold in the light of the rising moon.

At Philippe's knock, the door to the house opened; Amalie stopped abruptly in the portal, turning to Philippe, cat's eyes blazing, defiant, small white teeth bared. "You will pay for this, Monsieur Philippe!" she hissed. "One way or another you will be made to suffer!"

Then the door slammed, leaving Gerard staring after them, his features lined with sadness, his eyes bleak. Yet, he could not entirely hate his master. Hadn't he seen with his own eyes the fer-de-lance ready to strike at Madame Gabby's defenseless body with its deadly fangs? When Philippe emerged from the house, his expression grim as he entered the carriage, neither speaking nor looking at his driver, silently Gerard picked up the reins and turned the horses in the direction of Philippe's townhouse, casting one last, soulful glance over his shoulder.

In another part of the city, Gabby and Marcel, finished with their dinner, sat in the salle drinking coffee. Gabby, preoccupied with thoughts of her own, was quite unaware of Marcel's rapt eyes upon her, longing clearly visible in their brittle, emerald depths. His expression was dreamy, soft, and Marcel wondered if Gabby's thoughts were on the child she would soon bear. To him, Gabby was the essence of maternal beauty. Her face, gently rounded, and her figure, blossoming forth in the last stages of pregnancy, appeared lovelier than ever. She had been progressing normally in her pregnancy and Dr. Renaud expected no complications at delivery, which he now proclaimed would take place around mid-September, a short month away. Gabby's heavy sigh interrupted the poignant silence.

"What is it, *cherie?*" Marcel asked, his face filled with concern. "Is it the child?"

"No, Marcel," assured Gabby, directing a fond smile toward him. She was so grateful to him. How could she have managed without him? she wondered. "For some reason I am restless tonight. The babe moves constantly within me and it is increasingly difficult to assume a comfortable position."

"It can't be much longer, *cherie*. Soon the babe will be in your arms."

He placed a gentle hand on the great rise of her stomach and was rewarded with a steady thump, thump against his palm. Almost reverently he lowered his lips to the spot and moved his hand upward to cup an engorged breast. A tremor went through his body and when he raised his head, his eyes were shot with green fire. Ignoring Gabby's meak protest, Marcel sought her lips, the force of his kiss startling her by its intensity.

When he released her, Gabby felt drained of all strength. She had tried not to encourage Marcel's intimacies but was powerless to prevent his kisses and fondling. She almost dreaded the day her child would be born because it meant she would be forced into a decision she knew she must make: share a bed with Marcel or leave and make a life for herself and her child. Either choice would be a difficult one.

Now, as Marcel unbuttoned the top buttons of her dress and pressed hot kisses on her breasts, she pushed ineffectually at him and tried to rise. For some reason he seemed more abandoned tonight than he ever had before, almost as if the thought of the imminent birth of her child had released the passion he had held in check for so long.

"Do not pull away, *cherie*," Marcel begged. "I will do nothing to hurt you, you know that. I want only to touch you, to kiss you, to feel your flesh beneath my fingertips."

"I don't see how you can want to touch me like that, Marcel," Gabby complained. "I am gross and ungainly and surely unlovely to look upon."

"You have never been more beautiful in my eyes," said Marcel reverently, placing a chaste kiss on the top of her shining head. "Soon, *cherie*, soon," he promised, his eyes dark and sultry, "you will be mine."

Gabby breathed a sigh of relief when Tildy, Marcel's

housekeeper, chose that moment to interrupt. Her discreet knock was answered with some annoyance by Marcel who directed her to enter after allowing Gabby time to put herself in order. She came into the room followed by the groom from Le Chateau.

"Lionel!" Marcel exclaimed, jumping up from the couch. "What are you doing here? Has something happened at the plantation?"

"Bad trouble, Monsieur Marcel," moaned Lionel, shaking his shaggy head and rolling his black eyes skyward.

"Out with it, man!" shouted Marcel, losing patience with the slave's melodramatics. "Is it an uprising?"

"No! No! Nothing like that," replied Lionel hastily.

"Then what? Speak, man!"

"Fire, Monsieur Marcel, fire!" blurted Lionel breathlessly. "Everyone work hard to get cane harvested . . . fire start in the warehouse. Last night sparks from Pelee set off fire, destroy everything!"

"All the cane?" questioned Marcel bleakly.

"Everything," lamented Lionel.

"Damn, damn, damn!" cursed Marcel. "And the house, too?"

"House fine, Monsieur Marcel," smiled Lionel. "Overseer save house but he burned bad. He send me to fetch you. Say come quick!"

"Go with Tildy and get something to eat, then get some rest. We'll leave at dawn." Lionel turned and followed Tildy from the room leaving Marcel to pace back and forth nervously.

"I'm sorry, Marcel," began Gabby, feeling deeply Marcel's loss. "So great a loss must come as a shock to you. And your overseer, poor man."

"I can bear the loss of one year's crop, *cherie*," said Marcel turning toward Gabby with a gentle smile. "What really

330

bothers me is leaving you when you are so near your time."

"I have a whole month yet before the baby is due. By then you will have had time to see to your overseer and set your plantation to rights. Besides, isn't Honore due to arrive next week from New Orleans? You remember she wanted to be here in time for the birth. Once she arrives I will not be alone."

"I must return no matter how badly I wish to remain with you," sighed Marcel wretchedly. "And as you say, Honore will be here to look after you in my absence." He drew Gabby carefully into his arms. "I will be gone before you arise in the morning. Are you sure you shall be all right?" he asked, studying her intently. "The eruptions won't distress you? Your restlessness of late worries me and I don't want anything disturbing you at this point in your pregnancy."

Marcel's tender concern touched Gabby deeply. "I shall be fine," she assured him with more conviction than she felt at the moment. "Dr. Renaud is never far away and Tildy is quite capable of seeing to my needs. I don't want you worrying unnecessarily about me. Your overseer and your plantation are more important than I am right now."

"Nothing is more important than you, *cherie*. And one day I'll prove my love to you." Then he kissed her tenderly and led her up the stairs to her bedroom where he said goodbye after bestowing upon her such an intense look of love and longing that it left Gabby guilt-ridden to think that she could not return his feelings.

All that night Mt. Pelee boomed displeasure with the world and deposited a new layer of ash on everything beneath its gaze. Gabby was forced sometime during the night to close her windows and suffer in the stifling, airless room. She tossed and turned fitfully, finally falling asleep near dawn, her dreams filled strangely with Amalie and Damballa; dreams so real that she could almost feel that deadly serpent

331

creeping over her distended belly.

Awakening with a start, bathed in sweat, Gabby arched against the dull ache beginning in the small of her back, radiating to her stomach. Dismissing the twinges of pain, she heaved herself from the bed, her body heavy, her spirits fraught with vague feelings of foreboding. When the pain in her abdomen disappeared into a dull throbbing, she breathed in relief and began her day, unaware of the dark forces working against her.

Having spent the early cool of the day sewing on the baby's layette, by midafternoon Gabby was more than ready for a nap, exhausted from her insomnia of the night before. A knock on the door halted her slow progress up the stairs. Knowing Tildy was in the back kitchen probably asleep Gabby wearily retraced her steps to answer the insistent rapping. Her shock at finding Amalie standing before her was heightened by the fact that she had just last night experienced a disturbing dream involving Philippe's beautiful mistress.

"What do you want?" Gabby asked, trying to conceal the tremor in her voice. "You have Philippe to yourself now, why don't you leave me in peace?"

Amalie's strange cat's eyes narrowed on Gabby's protruding stomach. From the looks of her she was about ready to deliver, surmised Amalie, baring her teeth in a mirthless smile as she prepared to exact her due from the one person who stood between her and Philippe in a way guaranteed to hurt him most.

"Please let me in," begged Amalie when she realized that she was about to have the door slammed in her face. "Something terrible has happened to your husband."

Gabby froze, her hand on the door, giving Amalie the advantage she sought as her supple body snaked around Gabby's bulk into the foyer.

Her heart in her mouth, Gabby closed the door and turned awkwardly to face a gloating Amalie. "What has happened to Philippe?" she asked in a strangled voice, her face a tortured mask.

"He's dead!" revealed Amalie, reveling in her lie. "He was bitten by a fer-de-lance yesterday in the banana groves!"

Gabby's stomach heaved convulsively and she clutched at her throat, agony, disbelief, remorse marching across her face. "Philippe dead? No! No! It is not possible! I would have felt something if he were dead!"

Only then did she remember her strange lassitude and restlessness of the day before and the dark foreboding she experienced upon arising this morning. All the signs pointed to the one truth she was forced to acknowledge. Philippe was dead just as Amalie said!

Amalie slanted Gabby a sly look, afraid to show openly her delight at Gabby's obvious distress. "Do not fret, Madame Gabby," Amalie purred cruelly, "I was at Monsieur Philippe's side to give him comfort in his final hour. He clung to me and with his dying breath spoke of his love for me." She paused dramatically, noting with barely suppressed glee Gabby's stricken look before inflicting her killing blow. "When Monsieur returned to Bellefontaine without you I made him happier than he had ever been before. I shared his bed, his passion strong and fierce. Not once did he mention you or the bastard in your belly. He made love to me with wild abandon, crying out in . . ."

"Enough!" cried Gabby clapping her hands over her ears in an effort to blot out Amalie's hurtful words. "Why must you torment me? How can you speak so when Philippe lies dead?"

"Madame Gabby," said Amalie, squeezing out a few tears, "I have his last words to comfort me, memories of our shared passions to dispel my grief. And perhaps," she hinted in her throat voice, "perhaps I have more than that." Her hands moved suggestively to her stomach, accentuating the noticeable bulge beneath her colorful skirt.

Philippe's child? Did Amalie carry Philippe's child? No longer could Gabby bear the humiliation heaped upon her by Amalie and her spiteful taunts as she cluthed painfully at her middle, the babe lurching in her womb. Everything paled but the need to get away from Amalie, to give in to the grief racking her body in the privacy of her own room. With tremendous effort she moved heavily to the stairway and began the slow, painful ascent to the top, struggling to control her rampaging emotions in Amalie's disturbing presence.

Narrow eyes, Amalie watched Gabby's retreating back, waiting like a poised jaguar, fleet foot and treacherous, for the right moment to strike. And when it came her feet took wing as she darted lightly past Gabby's bulky form, until she stood directly above her blocking her path.

Gabby stared uncomprehendingly, her mind in a turmoil of confusion, her body contorted by pain, the menace in Amalie's feline features obvious. Struck dumb with horror, she watched as Amalie reached one slim arm beneath the waistband of her skirt and uncoiled an object that set her heart beating wildly in her chest. Amalie lovingly caressed the head of the fer-de-lance she held in her hands, murmuring softly to it before thrusting it within inches of Gabby's terror-stricken face. Just as its forked tongue flicked at Gabby's pale cheek, she stepped backward, emiting an earth-shattering scream as she lost her footing and tumbled head over heals to the bottom of the stairs where she lay arms and legs akimbo like a broken doll.

Scrambling down the stairs after Gabby, Amalie stared dispassionately for a moment at her bloodless face. When a nudge of her toe failed to evoke a response, she smiled grimly and quietly let herself out of the house, no one the wiser for her stealthy visit. Revenge was sweet! gloated Amalie. Perhaps now Monsieur Philippe would stop mooning over the wife he was too proud to admit he loved and buy back his faithful Amalie.

Gabby's scream had brought Tildy running from the kitchen but not in time to see Amalie leave the house. From the looks of Gabby's inert form Tildy was certain the poor girl was dead and began to wail and moan, imagining all sorts of punishment Monsieur Marcel would inflict upon her for allowing this catastrophe to befall his *petite amour*. Wringing her hands, she knelt beside Gabby's still form, praying for a miracle to happen.

The slight flutter of eyelashes against deathly white cheeks was the first sign of life in Gabby, but it was enough to galvanize Tildy into action. Within minutes, she had dispatched the gardener, Herman, for Dr. Renaud, making it clear to the youth that to return without the man would be tantamount to signing his own death warrant. For what was perhaps the first time in his life, Herman's feet miraculously sprouted wings and he sprinted off as if the devil himself was after him.

Tildy returned to her place beside Gabby, watching with grave concern as her swollen body jerked and convulsed at regular intervals. Just when Tildy thought she could no longer bear to listen to Gabby's screams of agony, Dr. Renaud rushed through the door, pushing Tildy aside roughly as he bent to examine his suffering patient.

"What happened?" he asked while he made a cursory examination to determine if any bones had been broken.

"I . . . I don't know, Monsieur Doctor," stammered Tildy shrugging her shoulders and spreading her hands out before her. "I was in the kitchen when I heard Madame Gabby cry out and arrived to find her so."

"There are no broken bones, thanks to *le bon dieu*," sighed the doctor sitting back on his haunches, "but she is definitely in labor. Where is Monsieur Duvall?"

"At Le Chateau," wailed Tildy, greatly distraught by the tragedy. "There was a fire and Lionel came for him. The overseer was badly burned."

"And Madame Gabby was left alone? At this stage of her pregnancy?"

"He left only this morning, and Mademoiselle Honore was to return to St. Pierre next week."

"Standing here talking isn't going to help Madame Gabby," Dr. Renaud exclaimed impatiently as another contraction ripped through Gabby's body. "You! Gardener!" he called, motioning to Herman who had been hovering in the background. "The two of us should be able to lift her and carry her upstairs. Gently, gently," he cautioned as they bent in unison to lift Gabby's convulsing body.

"Philippe!" moaned Gabby, softly at first, then ending in a crescendo of sound.

"She calls for her husband," said the doctor. "Is he here in St. Pierre?"

"I . . . if he is he has not been here," sniffed Tildy disdainfully, unable to keep the note of censure from her voice. Far be it from her to tell the doctor that Monsieur St. Cyr has not visited his wife once since she came to live in Monsieur Marcel's home. Surely his plantation did not keep him that busy! But she was too loyal to her master to start idle gossip.

"Go to St. Cyr's townhouse immediately," he ordered Herman once they had Gabby safely in bed. "If he is there tell he what happened. If he is not there send a messanger to Bellefontaine. Hurry, man!"

In surprising short older, Tildy had Gabby undressed and into a voluminous, white nightgown while the doctor fiddled with his instruments. Deeming that there was nothing constructive he could do at the moment, Dr. Renaud pulled a

336

chair close to the bed, placed a hand on Gabby's heaving stomach and brought out his watch to time the contractions. After several minutes had elapsed, he grunted, put the watch back in his pocket and bent closer to examine the purpling bruises on Gabby's face. Tildy hovered anxiously at his elbow until he sent her to the kitchen to boil water and fetch soft, clean cloths.

"Philippe!" Gabby croaked weakly, running the moist tip of her tongue across her dry lips. "Philippe! Dead! No! No!"

Her ramblings made no sense to the doctor. He thought she called for her husband and at the same time thought about the child she had lost.

"Your husband will be here in no time," promised Dr. Renaud, hoping against all odds that Philippe was in St. Pierre. Otherwise, it would be at least forty-eight hours before his arrival at his wife's bedside.

Gabby's eyes flew open, feverish, glazed with pain. "No! Philippe is dead!" Then she was engulfed in a paroxysm of agony and could speak no more.

"Poor child," muttered the doctor, stroking her arm in commiseration. Privately, he thought her chances of delivering a live, healthy child virtually nonexistent. At this moment even her life appeared in jeopardy. If only he could do something besides watch . . . and wait . . .

Unaware of the drama unfolding a few short blocks away, Philippe paced his room, his mind a turmoil of indecision. He had planned on returning to Bellefontaine the next day and he fought the urge to see Gabby before he left, fearing that his visit would unduly upset her at this late stage of her pregnancy. He was oblivious to all but his warring emotions until Gerard's voice startled him. But before he could grasp the meaning of the man's garbled words, a slim, black youth burst through the doorway delivering a message that left Philippe cold as death. He felt as if the earth had opened

337

beneath him, plunging him into a deep void. He barely had time to compose himeslf when Herman's next sentence sent a knife plunging into his bowels.

"Madame Gabby is calling for you. Dr. Renaud says if you don't hurry she will . . . she might not . . . !"

"Might not what? *Dieu! Dieu!* What are you trying to tell me? Is my wife dead?"

"No! She was alive when I left almost moments ago. Only . . . only . . . hurry before . . ."

Philippe was gone before the boy could finish.

Within minutes he was dismounting before Duvall's townhouse where a red-eyed Tildy met him at the door.

"My wife!" gasped Philippe between breaths. "What happened to her? Is she . . . is she . . . ?"

"She lives, Monsieur Philippe," added Tildy quickly when she saw Philippe's stricken look and white face. "She fell. Down the stairs. The doctor is with her now."

"Where is Marcel?" Philippe demanded angrily, glancing toward the room. "How could he allow such a thing to happen?" He was shaking with rage, his icy eyes blazing with anger.

"Monsieur Marcel was called to his plantation only this morning. A bad fire. His overseer was burned," Tildly explained fearfully, backing away from Philippe's cold fury.

At that moment a blood-curdling scream rent the air momentarily immobilizing Philippe. Somehow, he could not reconcile that inhuman sound to Gabby's voice. Dr. Renaud appeared at the top of the stairs, a harried frown creasing his weathered features. His expression lightened somewhat when he spied Philippe.

"Ah, St. Cyr," he called in a rush of relief. "*Le bon dieu* heard my prayers. Come up, man, come up. Your wife has been calling for you."

Philippe needed no further urging as he bounded up the stairs two at a time and entered Gabby's room behind the doctor. What he saw sent his senses reeling and cast him into a state of shock. Gabby, her face a mass of purpling bruises, lay twisting and writhing in the center of the bed, the mound of her stomach convulsed by wave after wave of contraction, her cries of pain enough to break his heart in two.

"Can't you help her, Doctor?" cried Philippe, rendered helpless by her suffering.

"We must wait on nature for these things," sighed the doctor wearily.

"Do you know how this happened? The accident, I mean?"

"I know no more than you. Tildy found your wife unconscious at the foot of the stairs. By the time I arrived her labor had already commenced."

"Do you think the sudden onset of labor pains could have precipitated the fall?" asked Philippe carefully. He could not help but take into account the date. Mid-August! Much too early for the child to be his!

"I am certain your wife would have gone full term had she not fallen down the stairs. One more month would have seen her safely delivered. I would have staked my life on it," he muttered shaking his shaggy head.

"That is something we shall never know for certain," said Philippe cryptically.

Suddenly Gabby roused, aware of a voice she had thought never to hear again. Had Philippe's spirit come back to haunt her? Or was the pain ripping her apart causing her to hallucinate?

"Philippe?" His name was a question on her lips.

"She calls for you," Dr. Renaud said turning to Philippe. "I will give you a few moments alone while I go downstairs for a cup of coffee. From the look of things it will be a long night."

Philippe took the chair beside the bed and grasped Gabby's trembling hands.

Gabby's eyes fluttered open and Philippe quailed at the look of fear mirrored in their violet depths. *Mon dieu*, he thought remorsefully, does she hate me so much?

Shaking her head from side to side, she cried out weakly, "Dead! Dead!"

Philippe thought she spoke of her babe and answered accordingly. "Your child lives, *ma chere*. See how he moves," he said, placing a hand on her quivering belly.

But even his words of encouragement did not seem to satisfy her. "Dead! Amalie! Dead!"

Amalie? What was Gabby saying? Was she reliving old memories in her delirum? Her next words sent Philippe's mind reeling.

"You're dead! Bitten by a snake! What is it you want from me, Philippe?" Her words were abruptly halted when another pain knifed through her and she clutched Philippe's hands in a bone-crushing grip. "Help me, Philippe! Help me!"

Philippe was truly puzzled. Why did Gabby think him dead. Had Marcel told her some preposterous life? What could he do or say to prove he was very much alive.

"Listen carefully, *ma chere*. I am not dead. I am flesh and blood. Here," he said, placing her hand against his cheek, "feel. I have come to help you." Very gently he pressed his lips against hers, feeling her soft breath mingling with his.

"But I was told . . ." Gabby was unable to continue as she was gripped in another paroxysm of pain, contorting her lovely features.

"Whoever told you I was dead was lying, *ma chere*." When she tried to speak he put a finger to her lips. "Shh! Don't try to talk. Save your strength. Let me hold you; let me absorb your pain." Privately, Philippe thought Gabby had dreamed up his death as a way of putting him out of her life forever. Pain does funny things to a person and Gabby was having more than her share of it at the moment.

Gabby seemed to relax as Philippe sat beside her on the bed and took her into his arms, cushioning her against the next onslaught of contractions convulsing her frail body. As she gritted her teeth and cried out, Philippe pressed his lips to her damp brow and whispered, *"Je t'aime, je t'aime."*

Soon Dr. Renaud returned to the room and examined Gabby, noting her weakening condition with growing alarm.

"Is there nothing you can do, Doctor?" Philippe pleaded as Gabby's unrelenting torture went on and on.

"I hesitate to introduce another drug into her system," remonstrated the doctor sternly. "If you are fainthearted then I strongly advise you to leave, for the worst is yet to come."

Philippe's jaw hardened. He would not, could not leave Gabby when she clung to him with such desperation. "I will remain," he replied with grim determination.

"Bon! I have a suspicion you will be needed."

Darkness had fallen and the room danced with shadows as Tildy, silent as a wraith, moved about lighting lamps. Dr. Renaud dozed lightly in a chair. Philippe flexed his muscles to ease the strain of supporting Gabby's writhing body, her contractions growing stronger and closer together while her cries grew more feeble.

Dr. Renaud yawned, stretched, and bent to examine Gabby once more, the grave look on his face sending Philippe's heart bounding from his chest.

"What is it, Doctor?" he asked fearfully.

"She grows weaker. Soon she will lack the strength to push the baby through the birth canal. I believe there to be a serious injury to her pelvic area, probably due to the fall. She is fully dilated but the baby remains firmly entrenched. If I am to save both mother and child your wife must find the will to assist."

"How can I help?" Philippe asked anxiously, willing to do anything to alleviate Gabby's suffering.

"I am going to try to get her to bear down. You can help by bracing her back and shoulders while she strains. Give her something to push against, so to speak." With a silent prayer he focused all his attentions on Gabby.

"Listen to me, Madame St. Cyr! You must help or your child will die! Do you hear me?"

"*Oui,*" came her weak replay. "Do not let my baby die!" Though her exhaustion was complete her fierce determination to bear Philippe a healthy child broke through her weariness and pain. Her own life was of minor importance.

"Bear down when I tell you, my child. The baby is too weak to do it on his own." Dr. Renaud placed a gentle hand on Gabby's abdomen and when he felt the next contraction, cried, "Push!"

Gabby strained with all her might but to no avail. For all her effort she had bitten through her lower lip and Philippe tenderly wiped the blood from her chin.

Once again the doctor commanded, "Push!" And once again Gabby's face purpled from her heroic attempts to follow the doctor's orders. This continued for what seemed like hours until the doctor cried exultantly, "I see the head!" Carefully, he inserted a set of forceps into the birth canal and eased the baby into the light of day.

The room was deathly still. Dr. Renaud worked over the infant an interminable length of time, then handed it to Tildy who was waiting nearby. Wrapping the baby in a soft cloth, she shuffled from the room, weeping silently.

"A girl," said Dr. Renaud, his face sad when he finally found the courage to face Philippe. "I'm sorry. The labor was too long. I could not save her. She was extraordinarily small and her lungs undeveloped." His voice was filled with compassion. Saving lives was one thing, but delivering stillborn babies was a chore he could easily forgo.

Philippe fought back a sob and buried his face in Gabby's

sweat-drenched hair. She appeared to be dozing and did not hear the doctor's words. "What now?" he asked, dazed.

"We wait for the afterbirth and hope there are no complications," pronounced the doctor hopefully. Then he put both hands on Gabby's still swollen stomach and kneaded gently. After a few moments, Gabby's limp body tensed, and she cried out.

"*Mon dieu!*" exclaimed the doctor, astonishment lighting his drawn features. "It can't be . . . it's not possible . . . yet . . ."

"What is it, Doctor?" cried Philippe, expecting to hear the worst as his arms tightened convulsively around Gabby.

"I had no idea your wife was carrying twins! Another child is about to make an appearance!"

"Twins!" Philippe barely had time to digest the doctor's incredible disclosure when Gabby convulsed and slammed her body down hard against him.

Almost immediately Dr. Renaud's jubilant voice rang out. "I have it! A boy! He lives, Philippe, he lives!" A lusty wail followed. Philippe listened in awe, tears streaming unashamedly down his cheeks.

From that moment on events moved swiftly. Tildy bore the baby away to clean him. He looked incredibly small and vulnerable in Philippe's eyes, and, for some reason, equally precious. How could he walk out of Gabby's life now after he had participated fully in bringing that tiny being into the world? Then all thoughts of the child fled as he looked down into Gabby's white face.

"My wife," he croaked, his mouth suddenly gone dry. "Will she . . . is she . . . ?"

"She is holding her own. Barring hemorrhaging or fever she should recover. I can truthfully say that had the birth been delayed another moment you would have neither wife nor child. But she is young, and given time, should recover completely."

"And the babe?"

"You heard him, *mon ami*," smiled the doctor, slapping Philippe on the back. "He is unusually robust for being a twin and premature at that. It is quite normal for twins to come into the world earlier than expected. It appears that this little fellow received more than his share of nourishment, leaving his sister too frail and weak to survive. But then, we cannot be certain that your wife's untimely fall was not the cause of the girl's death."

Tildy returned carrying a tiny bundle which she placed in the crook of Philippe's arm. Startled, he stared at the perfectly formed scrap of humanity amazed at his fight for survival. With his thumb he ruffed the soft blond fluff on the top of his son's head. The baby opened midnight blue eyes and gazed with grave concentration at his parent. Instinctively Philippe's grip tightened on the infant. He could not help but notice that the child had not one, single feature he could attribute to either himself or Marcel. Was the child his? Did the doctor speak the truth when he said twins were usually born early? Or was this helpless being the son of the man he hated? Unable to bear his tortured thoughts a moment longer, Philippe handed the baby to Gabby who had by then recovered somewhat and asked to see her son.

"Come with me, Philippe," urged the doctor, pulling Philippe from the room with him. "You look as if you could use a brandy and I'm sure Duvall has some of the best. Tildy will clean up your wife and you can see her again before I give her something to make her sleep. Time and rest are the best healers known to mankind."

Together they descended the stairs and helped themselves liberally to Marcel's excellent brandy. Both men were exhausted and they spoke sparingly, sipping their drinks in contemplative silence. After what seemed like an eternity Tildy entered the room to inform Philippe that Gabby was ready for visitors.

Philippe labored to his feet and tiredly climbed the stairs, struggling to compose his rampaging thoughts. What could he say to Gabby after his harsh treatment and hasty words of the past? His emotions ran rampant. But one truth stood out clearly in his mind; his love for Gabby was a patent, tangible force! The tiny infant he had cuddled in his arms was his no matter who the sire!

The sight that greeted him upon entering the bedroom was like a drug to his senses. Gabby, a beautiful smile curving her lips, was pressing a swollen breast to her son's budlike mouth, his lips hardly large enough to take in the engorged nipple. She gazed lovingly at the babe nuzzling at her breast before she turned to Philippe. He saw that her face was fuzzy from exhaustion and etched with lines of suffering and his heart went out to her.

"You're not dead," Gabby exclaimed wonderingly, violet eyes luminous in her pale face. "I thought . . . I thought I only imagined you were with me. Through all the pain your voice gave me courage. I could not have done it without you, Philippe. I . . . I . . . *merci.*" Gabby's eyes began to droop.

"Your son is beautiful, *ma chere*, just like his mother." His voice implied he meant every word. There was so much he wanted to say to her, so much to make up for. "I am grateful to *le bon dieu* for placing me in St. Pierre at the time of your need." No matter whose child he helped to birth, it was a rewarding experience, one he was not likely to forget. But why had Gabby thought him dead? Aloud, he asked, "Who told you I was dead? Was it Marcel?"

At the mention of Marcel's name Gabby roused from her stupor and smiled a secret smile. He had awaited the child's birth as anxiously as she. He could not have been more caring had he been the real father. How pleased he would be to learn of her son's birth.

"What is it, *cherie?*" asked Philippe, intrigued by the look on her face. "Why do you smile so sweetly?"

Gabby's exhaustion was such that she could barely concentrate on Philippe or his questions. Mustering what remained of her flagging strength, she murmured silently, "Marcel will be so pleased with our son." Those were her last words before she dozed off.

Philippe's gray eyes went murky, her words like a shaft of steel piercing his heart, leaving no doubt in his mind that he had just assisted with birthing Marcel's bastard! Yet, gazing down at the tiny, helpless being, he could not bring himself to despise him, not could he hate Gabby, for he alone had driven her into Marcel's bed as surely as he had lost what love she once held for him.

Bending to place a gentle kiss on her still lips, he murmured, "*Je t'aime, je t'aime, ma chere, adieu.*" Then he was gone, determined to divorce himself from the lives of Gabby, Marcel, and their son, though he could not bring himself to do it legally.

Chapter Nineteen

DURING THE month it took Gabby to recover from childbirth and the bruising fall down the stairs, Mt. Pelee settled down to an occasional rumble, much to the relief of the inhabitants of St. Pierre. Business continued as usual with hardly a second thought being given to that errant volcano.

Upon receiving Tildy's message announcing the birth of Gabby's son, Marcel had hastened back to St. Pierre to be with the woman he loved. The doctor had informed him about the multiple births and subsequent death of the tiny girl, stressing the importance of Philippe's presence during the long, difficult delivery. Marcel was on pins and needles until he learned that Philippe had returned to Bellefontaine almost immediately afterward, fearing Gabby's husband would demand her return. But since his hasty departure Marcel could only assume that Philippe still persisted with the fallacy that he was not the child's father and meant to claim neither his wife nor newborn son.

Marcel became immediately enamored of the baby boy. Already he had grown to love the sturdy little fellow whom Gabby had named Jean after Jean Lafitte whose courage and strength in face of adversity she greatly admired. And the name seemed apropos for the boy had survived against all odds.

If Gabby was hurt or disappointed at Philippe's desertion she chose not to mention it. In fact, she appeared outwardly to accept her husband's rejection of her and the baby, believing him happily ensconced at Bellefontaine with Amalie. Gabby had confided in Marcel, relating the facts concerning

Amalie's secretive visit and the cause of her fall. He was consumed with rage over the incident. He wanted to go immediately to Bellefontaine and confront Philippe with Amalie's violet act that nearly cost Gabby her life, but Gabby would not allow it, preferring no further contact with her husband or his mistress. In the holocaust of her mind everything that had happened to her was the result of those two lovers working hand in hand. How or why he had showed up unexpectedly on the day of Jean's birth remained somewhat of a mystery but Philippe's disappearance almost immediately afterward proved he cared little for her. But had she, she wondered, confused, in her delirium of pain and suffering, only dreamed his tender words of love?

As the days progressed nothing could take from Gabby the joy of holding her infant son in her arms. Sometimes she grieved for the tiny girl who was too frail to survive, but mostly she rejoiced in the son *le bon dieu* allowed to live and fill her life with a content and happiness she hadn't known for a long time.

Marcel was inordinately fond of little Jean. He usually could be found standing beside the baby's crib seemingly entranced by his tiny flutterings and mewings. One of his special pleasures was being present when the babe suckled at Gabby's full breast, imagining his own lips against the smooth mounds that Jean's rosebud mouth closed so greedily upon.

Marcel grew excited at the thought that Gabby would soon come to his bed and wondered at his patience until he realized that he loved her far too much to force her against her will, preferring to wait until she came to him willingly. Now that her recuperation was nearly complete he could barely conceal his anticipation. It was not difficult for Gabby to guess at his euphoria. She knew she would soon become the prize he had long awaited with such enduring patience.

She could think of no plausible reason to deny the man who loved her with gentle devotion and became the kind of father little Jean deserved and needed.

Mt. Pelee began erupting with renewed vigor on the day Jean reached the venerable age of one month. The fireworks spewing unceasingly from the crater's mouth were spectacular. Even the citizenry of St. Pierre, usually blasé about such happenings, sat up and took notice. Thin streams of red-hot lava flowed toward St. Pierre but so far had posed no danger. The eruptions continued unabated night and day for five days. Even the Obeah worshipers offered more than their usual number of sacrifices to Damballa in hopes to appease the God of the mountain. Then the eruption and spewing of lava ceased as suddenly as they began.

At Bellefontaine Philippe drove himself ruthlessly. Up at down, in bed at dusk, hard work his only defense against loneliness and his deep longing for Gabby. After long days and nights of soul-searching he convinced himself to swallow his pride and jealousy; his need and love for Gabby were too necessary to his life for him to relinquish her. And the ominous warnings coming from Mt. Pelee had him worried. He had never known Mt. Pelee to remain active for so long a period. Under normal circumstances, nary a puff of smoke could be seen coming from the dormant crater. Shuddering from a nagging fear he could not define, Philippe made up his mind to go to St. Pierre and beg Gabby to return with him to Bellefontaine with her son.

Philippe found himself on the road to St. Pierre on the day the eruptions from Mt. Pelee came to an abrupt halt. It was an arduous journey made even more so by the fingers of lava, now cooled, that had turned the Trace into a treacherous, rock-strewn obstacle course. It was long past dusk when he arrived in St. Pierre, going directly to his townhouse to spend the night nervously pacing the floor of his bedroom composing speeches. Philippe had no idea how he would react if Gabby refused to accompany him back to Bellefontaine. He refused to allow such thinking to cloud his mind. Somehow he had to persuade her that he loved her, needed her. Sleep became as elusive as Gabby during their turbulent years of marriage. Finally, near dawn, Philippe stretched out on the bed and drifted into a fitful sleep fraught with visions of eruptions, death, and destruction of monumental dimensions.

Gabby awoke instantly alert for sounds that might indicate further activity from Mr. Pelee, and hearing nothing but hungry wails coming from Jean in the next room, sighed deeply and relaxed. Soon, even Jean's cries ceased as his wet nurse put him to breast. At first Gabby had protested violently to the wet nurse, wishing to suckle the baby herself. But in the end she had reluctantly given in to Marcel's and Dr. Renaud's protestations that Jean needed more than she was able to provide. Because he was so small, he demanded frequent feedings, which Gabby, being in such fragile health, had been unable to meet. So to satisfy her maternal instincts and at the same time make good use of the milk flowing from her breasts she was allowed to suckle Jean three times a day with the wet nurse providing his feedings in between. A knock on the door ruptured her pleasant thoughts.

"Come in," Gabby called, thinking it to be Luella, the nurse, with Jean for his morning visit. She made it a habit of holding and cuddling her son each morning upon awakening. She was therefore surprised to see Marcel; even more surprised to see him close the door firmly before striding to her bedside.

"Is something wrong, Marcel?" Gabby asked nervously.

"Everything is perfect, *cherie*," smiled Marcel. "Just perfect." His emerald gaze never left her face as he casually sat down beside her. Only then did she notice the letter in his hand. Answering her silent question, Marcel held the letter aloft. "From Honore. I thought you might enjoy sharing her news with me."

Gabby clapped her hands delightedly. "How is the little scamp? Did she mention her new husband? Is she happy?"

Honore had not returned to St. Pierre as expected. A letter had arrived a day after Jean's birth informing them that she had fallen in love and would not be returning to St. Pierre. Celeste had approved of the match and the wedding would take place within the month. A letter from Celeste had followed enumerating the many qualities and eligibility of Honore's intended.

The arrangements had been heartily approved by Marcel and the wedding had taken place in New Orleans. Gabby's eyes misted as Marcel read Honore's letter aloud. The girl's happiness, her pleasure with her marriage, and their love for one another came through clearly in every word. When Marcel put the letter aside Gabby was weeping openly.

"What is it, *cherie?*" Marcel asked, concern apparent in his voice. "Are you ill?" Immediately he took her in his arms, intensely aware of every curve of her supple body through the flimsy material of her nightgown.

"Nothing is wrong, Marcel," Gabby sobbed in his shirt. "It's just that I am so happy for Honore. Her life, her marriage will be so different from my own. I hope she never loses the love and trust of the man she loves."

"*Ma chere*, happiness shall not elude you. I intend to make you as happy, if not happier, than Honore. I have some wonderful news for you. The *Reliance* sails for France in three weeks and I have booked passage for the three of us. I have already dispatched a letter to Linette requesting that her husband, Pierre, petition the courts in your behalf. By the time we arrive, obtaining your divorce should be merely a formality. Pierre Bonnard wields much influence, his legal prestige being considerable. We will be married the moment you are free to do so. Those cruel years as Philiippe's wife will soon become a thing of the past."

"So soon?" Gabby asked. "Must we leave Martinique so soon? I am not sure Dr. Renaud will allow me to leave. I am still under his care." She was dismayed by the suddenness of Marcel's announcement. Was she making excuses, she wondered, exasperated by her line of thinking. Philippe obviously did not want her so why should she delay her departure?

"The sea air will do you a world of good," Marcel stressed. "I'm sure the doctor will concur. He said your quick recovery was near miraculous. Is there some other reason behind your desire to linger in St. Pierre?" he asked, eyes narrowing speculatively.

"I . . . of course not," Gabby insisted a bit too heartily to Marcel's liking. "Jean and I will be ready to leave in three weeks."

"And was the doctor correct in telling me that your recovery is complete?"

"*Oui*, he was." Her voice came out a whisper but her answer was enough to set Marcel afire.

His hands could not be stilled as they caressed her scantily clad body. His lips reverently touched her eyes, slid along a smooth cheek, nuzzled her neck. Pushing her gown from her shoulders, baring her heavy breasts, his mouth sought a milk engorged nipple. Gabby gave a gasp of protest and shoved ineffectually at his hard chest, but her feeble struggles only served to further enflame him. Suddenly, starved so long of male affection, she found herself responding wildly to his lips and hands.

"You want me, *ma amour,* I know you do," murmured Marcel, his voice thick with desire. "Let me love you."

Taking Gabby's silence for acquiescence, Marcel stood up and began to shed his clothing, hands shaking, body trembling with long repressed desire. He had succeeded in

352

removing his jacket and cravat when the nursemaid burst into the room with little Jean in her arms.

Recoiling from the intimate scene, Luelle cried out, "Oh, Madame Gabby, forgive me! I thought you were alone!" Thoroughly flustered, the girl lowered her head to cover her confusion.

Hastily Gabby pulled the sheet up to cover her nakedness while the nursemaid focused her eyes everywhere but at Marcel and Gabby, aware of their obvious intent, though uncertain of the relationship between her master and the woman who was another man's wife. In an agony of embarrassment, she timidly approached the bed, thrust her small charge at Gabby and fled in a rush of embarrassment.

Marcel cursed under his breath, watching hungrily as Gabby put the gurgling child to her breast, which had begun to drip milk after Marcel's eager manipulations just moments before. Though bitterly disappointed, he could not help but smile as Jean's pink mouth pulled greedily at Gabby's nipple, his tiny fists kneading the flesh he longed to possess.

"Lucky tyke," he said softly, ruffling the baby's blond fuzz gently with a thumb. Then his hand slid upward to caress the tempting, white flesh visible above Jean's tiny face. "Tonight, *ma chere*," he murmured, green eyes intense with desire, "tonight you shall be mine." His meaning was quite clear, and against her will Gabby found herself anticipating the night ahead with a mixture of desire and dread.

Later that morning while Marcel was at his office, Tildy off to the market and Luella on an outing with Jean, Gabby sat in the salle trying to concentrate on a novel but having little luck. Her mind kept straying to the scene in her bedroom and how easy it was to respond to Marcel's ardor. For a long time she knew their coming together was inevitable. What did it matter if she gave in to Marcel before they were married? Who had a better right to her love? Certainly not Philippe, who by his absence made it perfectly clear that she was free to do as she pleased. At least Marcel's love did not hurt, was unwavering, and filled her with gentle contentment. She could do worse than become his wife. Why, then, did the feeling persist that she was betraying Philippe? Wasn't he, even now, betraying her with Amalie?

A loud knock at the door shattered the silence and with a frown of annoyance Gabby realized she was the only one in the house and, sighing deeply, moved to answer the summons. Shock followed astonishment when she found Philippe standing before her, a crooked grin flashing big and white in his tanned face.

"Philippe!" A pulse beat madly in her throat and she licked lips gone suddenly dry with the tip of her tongue.

"May I come in?"

Gabby was struck speechless as well as motionless. Finally, taking matters in his own hands, Philippe pushed open the door and entered before Gabby could object.

"I need to talk to you, Gabby," he pleaded, flashing her a look of entreaty. "Are you alone?"

Somehow finding her voice, Gabby croaked, "*Oui*, quite alone. Even Jean is out with his nurse." Dropping her eyes beneath Philippe's strange, smoky gaze, Gabby fought hard to control her raging emotions.

"Is there some place where we won't be disturbed?" Philippe asked, his eyes shifting toward the room he knew to be Marcel's study.

Wordlessly Gabby led the way to the small, intimate room instead of to the less private salle.

Philippe closed the door behind him, quietly turning the key in the lock, a soft, tender look glazing his features. "Jean," he said, tasting the name on his tongue. "So you named your son Jean. Does Marcel approve?"

"Marcel approves of everything I do," Gabby snapped waspishly, his question turning her resentful. Philippe

354

winced at the barely concealed insult but said nothing. "What do you want with me, Philippe?" she asked bitingly. "If you had cared at all about me or Jean you wouldn't have left St. Pierre without so much as a goodbye."

Philippe's eyes became inscrutable and he chose to ignore her question for the moment, deliberately changing the subject instead. "You are looking exceptionally well, *ma chere.*" His hot eyes devoured her figure from her trim waist to her full breasts, causing her to flush prettily under the intensity of his gaze. Without volition his hand reached out and caressed a silken cheek. When last he saw her, purple bruises marred her perfect skin. His fingers followed the curve of her jaw before falling away.

"Motherhood agrees with you, *ma petite.* You have never looked more beautiful . . . or desirable."

Completely unnerved, Gabby recoiled from his gentle touch. "What do you want, Philippe? Why have you come to taunt me?"

"Contrary to your belief I did not come here to torment you."

"Then why have you come?" she demanded, unmoved by his words.

"Can't you guess, Gabby?" He placed his hands on her shoulders and drew her forward until their bodies touched. Gabby found herself lost in depths as soft and hazy as a misty sea.

"Tell me, Philippe," Gabby urged softly, hope leaping in her breast. "Tell me why you are here." She suddenly recalled his words of love and encouragement throughout the long ordeal of Jean's birth.

"I want you, Gabby. I want you and Jean to return with me to Bellefontaine. I need you, your love, your gentleness, your passion. I need my wife. Ah Gabby, *ma chere, je t'aime, je t'aime!* I think I have loved you from the moment you

355

stood before me, your violet eyes blazing with rebellion, bravely defying your parents."

Gabby's heart quickened with gladness. Philippe loved her! Wanted her and his son! Then, in a motion so sudden it took them both by surprise, she found herself in his arms, bodies pressed close. All past hurts faded as he reacted instantly to her nearness.

His lips brushed her neck, her cheek, found her mouth, lovingly, longingly. Hungrily, Gabby returned his kisses, her hands winding around his neck, twining themselves in the dark hair curling at the nape of his neck. With eyes inches apart, each saw and recognized the other's need, urgent, vibrant, desperate. With mute agreement, Philippe began undressing Gabby while her fingers worked dexterously at the buttons on his shirt, his passion swelling with each passing moment. When she stood wrapped in the mantle of her own nudity and Philippe's proud body stood revealed in its own masculinity, they sank to the thickly carpeted floor, their mutual consent unspoken.

Perched on his elbow, Philippe watched the play of emotion upon Gabby's lovely features, reveling in the look of desire glazing her violet eyes. From the corner of his eye he noticed a drop of milk appear at the tip of an engorged nipple and run down the side of her breast. With a groan akin to pain he lapped up the droplet with the tip of his tongue. Gabby moaned and trembled as if from ague while Philippe gently caressed first one rosy breast and then the other with his tongue, the sensations driving her nearly out of her mind. When he lifted his head his mouth was white-rimmed and Gabby couldn't help but smile for he reminded her of Jean after he had just finished feeding.

"Do I please you, *ma chere?*" Philippe asked huskily when he saw her smile.

"Very much, *mon amour,*" she sighed contentedly.

"Say it again! Call me your lover!"

"*Mon amour,*" Gabby repeated sensuously. "Love me, *mon amour!* It has been so long!"

Philippe needed no further urging as he worshipped every inch of her body with his hands and lips. Her body arched and yielded, every pore, every nerve ending coming alive to his touch. He entered her gently, lovingly, and her body sang out as she opened herself to him as a flower opens to bright sunlight. His mouth closed down upon hers, hungrily, possessively, to still her small cries and moans. The sweet essence of her special fragrance swept over him with alluring promises of past pleasures reborn as his proud, unflagging manhood prodded her ecstatically higher and higher. Soon they were in a world where desire and gratification obscured all else. Philippe tensed, and, holding back his own climax, started anew until he felt Gabby begin her shattering ascent toward repletion. Only then did he allow his own journey to commence as together they whirled into the vortex of a volcano more powerful than Pelee.

Slowly Gabby returned from the heights of bliss to find Philippe smiling down on her. His smile was like nothing she had ever seen before.

"Do I amuse you, Philippe?" she asked lightly.

"I can't get over the miracle of you," he answered drowsily. "The taste, the smell, the feel of you is etched in my brain forever."

"Do you really mean what you said earlier? That you want me and Jean with you at Bellefontaine?"

"I have never been more serious in my life!"

"What about Amalie?" asked Gabby uneasily.

"Amalie is no longer at Bellefontaine." His tone was rich and caressing.

"You have given up Amalie for good?" she asked incredulously. "Where is she?"

"Amalie is . . . is with someone else." His voice held a caustic edge that Gabby could not define.

"But . . . but I thought you owned her!"

"No longer, *ma petite.*"

"You sold her?" Gabby found it hard to assimilate Philippe's bald announcement.

"I had no choice after I learned what she did to you. *Mon dieu*, Gabby, why didn't you tell me? I would have sent her away long ago had I been aware of her perfidy. Obeah rites are nothing to be taken lightly."

"My telling you would have made little difference. You were too angry with me at the time and convinced that I had become Marcel's mistress."

"But I also discovered why you risked your life and lost our child in the banana groves on your way to Marcel."

"You know?"

"*Oui*, Amalie confessed that she had seen you in the doorway watching that day I . . . I made love to her. I'm sorry, Gabby. The act was unintentional, completely unplanned, the first time anything like that had happened since I brought you to Bellefontaine. I never meant to take Amalie that afternoon. You will have to forgive me just as I forgive you for becoming Marcel's mistress after I left aboard the *Windward*. We can start over, you and I, begin our own family. But you need have no worry concerning Jean. I feel very close to the little fellow."

His words, meant to be healing, couldn't have hurt her more if he had hit her. "But I have never . . . I am not . . ." Her mouth was dry, her breath a hard knot in her throat.

"Shh, *ma chere*. No more lies between us. Marcel's son will become as my own. Have I not proved that by assisting at his delivery?"

"Jean is your son, Philippe," whispered Gabby, her voice choked. "Jean is your son!"

A tremendously long silence loomed up and Gabby grew

358

restive in Philippe's arms, shifting her weight away from him. He stared at her fixedly, beyond speech. Finally he said, "Believe me, Gabby, Jean will become like a son to me. Haven't I just promised you that?"

"*Become* like a son!" Gabby gasped with dismay.

"How can I convince you that I will love your son and treat him fairly?"

"Love him, treat him well, but not acknowledge him, isn't that what you really mean? Be honest with me, Philippe!"

"You want the truth? Then you shall have it. I cannot find it in my heart to claim your son, *ma chere*. There is still too much doubt in my mind."

"He shall never inherit your beloved Bellefontaine, isn't that what you are trying to say?"

"Isn't it enough that I will be raising another man's son? Do not ask me to leave Bellefontaine to a child whose paternity is in doubt. Our firstborn son shall inherit."

Philippe didn't wait for Gabby's response as his lips smashed down onto hers, hungry, wanting, needing, while the past rose up to haunt them like a spectre not yet laid to rest.

Gabby was beyond response. Her dreams of happiness as Philippe's wife lay shattered by mistrust and their past mistakes. Sensing her lack of passion, Philippe broke off the kiss, watching her face anxiously.

"I ask you one more time, Philippe, not to do this to yourself. Not to abandon me or your son," Gabby beseeched. "Jean could belong to no one but you for there has been no other man but you."

Philippe searched her face for a hint of the truth. "But the date," he insisted levelly. "Do you take me for a fool? I can count to nine!"

Gabby immediately saw the futility of her words. Though Philippe might love her, and in time come to love Jean, his pride would not allow him to relent. Something had convinced him that Marcel had sired little Jean. Tears blurring her eyes, Gabby struggled to rise.

"Hurry and dress, *ma chere*," Philippe ordered brusquely. "The moment the nurse returns with Jean we will leave for Bellefontaine. You can send for your clothes later." Despite their angry words only moments before, Philippe did not doubt for a minute that Gabby would leave with him.

"I am not going," Gabby said sadly as she began pulling on her clothes.

In the midst of his own dressing, Philippe stopped abruptly when he grasped the meaning of her words. "You refuse?" he asked, astounded. "How can you doubt my love after what we just experienced together? If you choose to remain with Duvall it will be the end for us, Gabby. I will not be so foolish to make the same mistake twice," he warned ominously.

Gabby's next words sent Philippe reeling with shock. "There is a good possibility I might never conceive again, and if I do, may not carry the child to term. Dr. Renaud said it has something to do with the injury to my pelvis caused by the fall down the stairs. It's a small miracle that Jean lived. So if you deny Jean now you may never have an heir as long as you remain married to me!"

Philippe fought to control the turmoil of emotion raging through his body. What choice did he have? Claim a child that could very well be a bastard or divorce his wife! "Twice you have destroyed me," he said wearily. "And both times by a fall. What caused your fall this time, Gabby? Certainly you can't blame me, or Amalie." Suddenly, in a flash of re-membrance, Philippe recalled Gabby's wild ravings during her difficult labor. "Who told you I was dead, Gabby?" he asked, eyes narrowed suspiciously.

"Amalie told me."

"Amalie! I find that hard to believe. I had just taken her to . . . to her new owner the night before."

"It's the truth," said Gabby bitterly. "She arrived at midafternoon and forced her way into the house by telling me you were dead from a snake bite. She . . . she even hinted that she carried your child."

"What happened?" questioned Philippe gently.

"Word of your . . . your sudden death upset me greatly. I started up the stairs with no other thought than to be alone with my grief. To my dismay Amalie darted up the stairs ahead of me, extracted a fer-de-lance from beneath her skirt and thrust it in my face." Philippe sucked in his breath in a gasp of pure rage. Gabby continued, the memory bringing tears to her eyes. "I felt that deadly tongue touch my cheek and recoiled in terror. I must have either fainted or tripped for I knew nothing more until I woke up with you beside me."

"Amalie again! Must I forever be plagued by wanton destruction of everything I hold dear?" Philippe anguished, burying his head in his hands. "If she had not caused your fall . . ."

"Would it have made a difference?"

"As things stand now . . ."

"As things stand now," Gabby continued when Philippe faltered, "we are no better off than we were when you left me here with Marcel. Nothing I say could change your mind about me."

Philippe did not dispute her words.

"*Adieu*, Philippe. May you find happiness and the heir you desire with another woman. Your pretence of love was short lived. For all intents and purposes, Jean belongs to Marcel. And after tonight, he can also claim me."

The meaning of Gabby's words were clear, leaving Philippe cold and empty. If she wasn't already Marcel's mistress, she was now ready and willing to share his bed. His avowal of love, his need for her, meant nothing, he thought resentfully, his face a dark, brooding mask as he dressed in

361

silence. He had begun the day in happy anticipation, their joyful coming together a portent of the future, but their final parting was the bitter ending. At issue was a tiny bundle of humanity whom Philippe realized he could easily learn to love. Perhaps already did. But it was too late for recriminations. Gabby could not, would not accept what he offered. She wanted more than he was willing to give.

Philippe strode stiffly from the room and angrily flung open the door leading to the outside nearly upsetting a startled Luella who was returning from her outing with Jean. Stunned by her collision with Philippe's imposing bulk, Luella would have fallen and dropped her ward had not Philippe snatched the blanketed bundle from her arms with one hand and steadied her with the other. While Luella regained her composure Philippe cradled Jean in the crook of his arm, startled by the intensity of the tot's eyes. Since he had last seen the child they had changed from midnight blue to a hazy blue-gray. His skin looked so petal soft that before Philippe knew what he was doing he brushed a finger gently against the smooth curve of the baby's cheek.

From behind Philippe, Gabby watched in contemplative silence while he caressed his son's face, a bemused smile softening his hard features. When he became aware of Gabby's gaze, he turned, thrust the baby into her arms and fled.

The moment Philippe disappeared from view a great lassitude overwhelmed Gabby, and if Luella had not taken Jean from her arms she would have dropped him. Concerned by Gabby's sudden pallor and violent trembling, Luella uttered a cry of distress, bringing Tildy from the kitchen.

"Take the baby to his room," Tildy ordered briskly, taking in the situation at a glance. "Hurry, Madame Gabby is ill, we must get her to bed."

Within minutes Luella had deposited Jean in his crib and returned to held Tildy put Gabby to bed. "I will summon the doctor," Tildy said, smoothing the covers over Gabby's slight form.

"No!" protested Gabby weakly. "I'm sure there is nothing wrong with me that a few hours rest won't cure. You'll see, tomorrow I will be back to normal."

Tildy looked skeptical but had no choice but to obey Gabby's wishes. She knew Monsieur Marcel would be home at suppertime and would know what to do. She had long ago surmised the situation between Gabby and Philippe and was well aware that Marcel harbored strong feelings for his *petit amour*.

The long afternoon passed into evening without showing any marked improvement in Gabby. During those interminable hours she had drifted in and out of sleep, at times wild imaginings filled her feverish brain. But through it all came the realization that one part of her life was over and done with. She had only Jean to think of now, and Marcel. No longer was there a reason to withhold herself from him.

Shreds of fog had begun to creep into the streets, half masking the dusk when Marcel returned home, quietly entering Gabby's room. Tildy had met him at the door with her distressing news and he had sent for the doctor immediately. He lit a lamp and gazed with consternation at Gabby's sweat-drenched face.

"*Mon dieu!*" he cried in alarm. "Why wasn't I informed earlier? You are ill, *cherie*, very ill."

Gabby moistened cracked lips with the tip of her tongue and tried to speak. Sensing her need, Marcel poured water from a pitcher at her bedside into a glass and held it to her lips. She drank greedily.

"I'll be fine tomorrow," Gabby promised with more conviction than she felt at that moment.

"The doctor will be here soon," soothed Marcel, brushing wispy strands of pale hair away from her forehead.

Within the hour Tildy ushered in Dr. Renaud who immediately sent everyone from the room before turning grave eyes on his patient. Marcel paced restlessly back and forth outside Gabby's door until he thought he would go mad with waiting.

Finally, Dr. Renaud came from the room, a thoughtful frown creasing his care-lined face. He closed the door behind him before speaking. "I must have the truth from you, Duvall, if I am expected to cure Madame St. Cyr's ailment." His fatigue-rimmed eyes bored into Marcel, his mind a hotbed of speculation. "I would know the nature of the relationship between you and Madame St. Cyr. She and the babe should be happily reunited with her husband at Bellefontaine by now. I was led to believe they would be."

"There is . . . they are separated," admitted Marcel grudgingly.

"I suspected as much from the first, but after St. Cyr assisted with the birth of his son I had thought . . ."

"Nothing has changed. When Gabby is well I intend to take her and the child to France and obtain a bill of divorcement. We will be married as soon as that's accomplished." Marcel offered no excuses, stating the facts as he saw them.

Dr. Renaud searched Marcel's face intently before posing his next question. A question he perhaps had no business asking. "Have you been . . . er . . . intimate with Madame St. Cyr?" During the doctor's thorough examination of Gabby he discovered that she had had sexual intercourse within the past twenty-four hours.

"Certainly not, Doctor!" denied Marcel indignantly. "It's true I love Gabby, but what do you take me for? I did not touch her before the child was born and since have not wished to hurt her in any way until she was completely healed from her difficult delivery."

"Hmm," mused the doctor rubbing his chin reflectively. He believed Duvall but it did not explain the indisputable evidence that she had been intimate with a man just hours ago. A sudden thought came to him. "Has Monsieur St. Cyr been to see his wife today?"

Marcel's eyes narrowed, then widened. What was the doctor getting at? he wondered, perplexed by the line of questioning. Of what possible use could this insane query be in diagnosing Gabby's illness? Aloud, he replied, "I doubt it, Doctor, but I can find out if it is important."

"I believe it to be," nodded the doctor sagely.

Without another word Marcel went in search of Tildy and Luella. What he learned troubled him greatly. Had Philippe's visit upset Gabby to the degree that it brought about illness? How had the doctor known? Suspicion of something he didn't care to name ate at his vitals. When he apprised Dr. Renaud of Philippe's visit earlier in the day, the doctor merely wagged his head in affirmation, carefully averting his eyes from Marcel.

"Do you think St. Cyr's visit is in some way responsible for Gabby's ailments?" asked Marcel, clearly upset.

"Actually, Duvall, the malady has me puzzled."

"Then why the questions concerning our . . . relationship?"

After careful consideration Dr. Renaud decided to keep his own counsel. Obviously St. Cyr and his wife had been intimate only hours before. And if that had occurred, the dissolution of their marriage was not the forgone conclusion Duvall thought it to be. Especially since Duvall himself had admitted he had never been intimate with the woman. But try as he might, the good doctor could discern no connection with St. Cyr's visit and his wife's illness. According to Duvall's information, St. Cyr's departure was hasty. Perhaps he and his wife had quarreled, the doctor surmised, and their parting had been less than amicable. The shock alone of first being intimate and then parting with bitter words could have been enough to bring on her illness. His mind finally made up, he answered Marcel's question. "It was essential for me to learn if something out of the ordinary occurred that could have caused a shock to her system and precipitated this illness. She still has not fully recovered from the birthing process."

"And what have you concluded?"

Dr. Renaud sighed hugely. "If I knew what took place between husband and wife this afternoon I would be more qualified to answer. Undoubtedly Madame St. Cyr is gravely ill. I assume St. Cyr told you about her terrible experience in Norfolk?" At Marcel's nod, he continued. "This fever may be just a latent manifestation of the drugs still warring in her weakened body."

"What can be done to help her?"

"Not much, I'm sorry to say. Make her as comfortable as possible, plenty of liquids and cool sponge baths. I'll leave some medicine to control the fever and return tomorrow unless summoned sooner."

He handed Marcel a small vial of dark liquid, then started down the stairs. "Oh, another thing," he reminded Marcel. "I prefer she doesn't nurse the baby until she is fever-free and has regained a measure of strength. If there is some infection raging in her blood we can't risk the baby's health. There is a chance he might pick it up through her milk. If her breasts become too painful," he added obliquely, "Luella will know what to do."

Marcel saw the doctor to the door and returned immediately to Gabby's beside where he remained during the entire night, bathing her feverish body with cool water and forcing liquids down her parched throat. He strained to make something out of her feverish gibberish but the only word that had come through clearly was, "Philippe," which she mumbled over and over until Marcel grew to hate the sound.

Sometime during the night Gabby awoke completely

lucid. She reached out tentively to touch Marcel's hand, causing him to start violently from his light doze.

"What is it, *cherie?*" he asked, seeing her violet gaze resting on him.

"I'm sorry, Marcel."

"About what, *mon amour?*"

"This night was to be special. I know you hoped . . . that is . . . you wanted . . ."

"Shhh," he soothed, placing a finger across her lips. "There will be other nights. We will have the rest of our lives to love one another."

"The rest of our lives," repeated Gabby bleakly before lapsing back into semiconsciousness.

The next day Dr. Renaud found his patient somewhat improved but still subject to bouts of fever and delirium. His original diagnosis and treatment still held so he left after warning Marcel to keep Gabby in bed until three days after her fever was gone. Unless her condition deteriorated, he advised Marcel, he would not return. After the doctor's departure Marcel reluctantly agreed to leave Gabby in Tildy's charge while he bathed and took a much deserved rest.

Several hours later Marcel's sleep was abruptly interrupted by Tildy who was shaking his shoulder vigorously to awaken him. He was immediately alert. "What is wrong? Has something happened to Gabby?"

"Madame Gabby is in pain," Tildy announced somewhat obliquely. "I . . . I . . . don't know what to do."

"What kind of pain?" Sensing Tildly's difficulty in expressing herself Marcel guessed immediately the nature of Gabby's distress. "Where is Luella?"

"Nursing the baby, Monsieur Marcel. Do you wish me to summon her?"

"No, leave her to her task. I will see to Madame Gabby myself. Go back to the kitchen."

Skeptical of Marcel's ability to alleviate Gabby's pain, Tildy nevertheless did as she was told. Within minutes Marcel had pulled on a robe and was beside Gabby, his sweeping glance immediately pinpointing the trouble.

"Jean! Bring Jean to me," Gabby pleaded. "I must feed him."

"The doctor has issued strict orders that only Luella be allowed to feed him during your illness." At Gabby's stricken look he continued soothingly, "You must think of your son. There is a good chance you might infect him through your milk."

"I . . . I had not thought of that," admitted Gabby weakly. "But what am I to do?" Although she had pulled the sheet up to her neck the telltale stain had seeped through her nightgown onto its snowy surface.

"Let me help you, *cherie*," said Marcel softly as he folded the sheet back and unbuttoned her nightgown to the waist, baring her milk-swollen breasts. Marcel was intrigued by the creamy fluid flowing from her engorged nipples that ran in rivulets down the sides of her breasts. Tentatively he reached out and lightly touched one and then the other pale globe. They felt hot and swollen to his touch and Gabby cried out in pain though his touch was infinitely gentle.

Without further hesitation Marcel lay down beside her and, ignoring her meek protests, took an engorged nipple in his mouth and suckled gently until the milk flowed freely, filling his mouth with the thick, sweet liquid. Loving her he did not moralize his action; he only meant to relieve the suffering of the woman he loved. Almost immediately the pain subsided in that breast, then disappeared altogether. Gabby sighed as Marcel moved to the other breast and began anew his ministrations. Pain free, Gabby grew drowsy. Feeling the tension leave her body, Marcel reluctantly raised his head from his pleasurable chore and tiptoed from the room after he placed a soft kiss on her lips, rebuttoned her nightgown and pulled the sheet up to her chin.

The following day, though Gabby appeared much improved, Marcel thought it best not to add to her distress by informing her that Philippe's lawyer had appeared at the door at an early hour with a document outlining Philippe's intent to seek a bill of divorcement through the French courts. The ground were adultery! Marcel's reasons for keeping it to himself for the time being were twofold. He feared she would refuse to continue with their voyage to France, and he believed that once they were away from Philippe she would grow to love him as much as he loved her. He had had many long agonizing hours to consider the reason behind Philippe's untimely visit on the day Gabby fell ill. He wondered what had taken place between husband and wife to change Philippe's mind about obtaining a divorce. Up until that day she had been adamant in his refusal to consider a divorce. But unless Gabby chose to tell him, Marcel's thoughts and suppositions were nothing but conjecture.

That night the city of St. Pierre was jolted from complacency by an eruption of violent proportions, the most forceful by far since Mt. Pelee had started on its road toward destruction. The next morning everything was covered with throat-clogging, gray ash, and hardened fingers of lava reached nearly to the city's edge. Not only that, but the eruptions did not cease. Pandemonium reigned as residents deserted the city in droves. Even the ships in the harbor prepared to sail out into open water, each taking on as many passengers as they were safely able to.

Three days later Gabby's strange malady had disappeared as swiftly as it had begun, leaving her weak but feverless. She was now up and about for longer periods of time each day. From a chair pulled to the closed window she watched in awe while the population of St. Pierre seemed to have gone mad.

Casting a wary eye on the continual flow of ash from the volcano, Gabby wondered uneasily if perhaps they shouldn't be making plans to leave the city. She had no wish to jeopardize Jean's life by remaining a moment longer than necessary in the city. Le Chateau, on the opposite side of the volcano, seemed the obvious choice. She said as much to Marcel when she dressed and joined him for supper that night.

"I was thinking the same thing, *cherie,*" Marcel admitted worriedly. "I had thought to wait and leave on the *Reliance* but I can no longer be certain if that is the wisest choice. I must do what I think best for you and Jean. And right now leaving St. Pierre seems the best thing to do. I suggest you pack tomorrow and the day after we will leave for Le Chateau. Don't take more than necessary," he cautioned. "We will make better time if we travel light."

The next day the sun did not once break through the thick clouds of ash hovering above the city. It was like perpetual night and Gabby could hardly wait to leave. That evening while Jean suckled ravenously at Gabby's breast—she had once again resumed his feedings—Marcel sat nearby, watching, a bemused smile curving his sensuous lips.

"Our son grows before my eyes, *cherie,*" he said, savoring his role as father to the infant. "I too would grow content were I in his place." His eyes sparkled mischievously but his gaze was intent upon Jean suckling contentedly at the tender white flesh.

Gabby flushed becomingly as she remembered the time Marcel had taken Jean's place at her breast. And yet, she felt that without him she could not exist. He had been her comfort and her solace since long before Jean was born.

"You are lovely tonight, *cherie,*" Marcel continued easily. "In fact, I have not seen you look so well since before Jean's birth." Naked desire was evident on his darkening visage.

Gabby had donned a lightweight silk dressing gown of a

370

soft mauve color accenting the deeper violet of her eyes. It clung softly to her slim body, falling away at the neckline while Jean nursed, exposing both creamy globes. Marcel's hot gaze feasted longingly on her loveliness.

"You have taken good care of me, Marcel," Gabby said shyly. "I owe you so much."

Marcel searched her face and drew in his breath sharply, her meaning becoming all too clear. Her eyes had become luminous, almost dreamy, her smile inviting.

Moving as if in a dream, Marcel approached Gabby slowly, hesitantly, carefully removing the sleeping Jean from her arms and left the room. When he returned moments later Gabby was still sitting where he had left her. She had not bothered to refasten the gaping edges of her dressing gown.

With infinite tenderness, handling her much as he would a fragile doll, Marcel lifted Gabby to her feet and slowly pushed the robe past her shoulders and over her slim hips until it lay in a shimmering pool at her ankles. She was naked beneath the robe and Marcel drew in his breath sharply as he gazed at her clothed in the mantle of her nudity, proud, regal. He had waited an eternity for this moment and his body reacted violently, hardening instantly. Sensing his emotion Gabby stepped forward until the tips of her breasts touched Marcel's chest. With an impassioned groan he lifted her into his arms and carried her to the bed. Never taking his eyes from her, he disrobed swiftly, and within minutes his maleness was pressing down upon her.

"Are you sure, *cherie?*" he asked, still unable to believe that she would finally be his. "Are you strong enough?" Vaguely he wondered what he would do if she were to say no.

Gabby's answer was more than he could hope for. "I want you to love me, Marcel. I need to belong to someone. You have proven your love for me and Jean many times over. Make me yours now, please!"

"*Coeur de mon coeur! Je t'aime, je t'aime,*" crooned

Marcel, his blood singing in his ears. His green eyes raked her, swept the length of her nakedness before he captured her lips with his in a kiss both tender and savage. He found it difficult to control the great surge of desire coursing through his body but was determined that Gabby should enjoy their first experience together as much as he knew he would. Deliberately, almost painfully, he slowed his breathing until his heart began beating normally once again. Assured now of his self-control, with one hand he stroked the silken flesh, throat, breasts, curve of her slender waist, hips, tasting, taking, savoring the sweet flesh he had dreamed about, longed for.

The moonlight had turned her cheeks to living ivory and he traced a finger gently along her jawline. Her hair, spread about her like a cloak appeared as molten silver, her eyes deepening to fathomless pools of velvet. His lips, seeking, questing, burning, touched gently to every sensitive area of her body, the hollow of her neck, her breasts, her navel, the tiny bud of her womanhood. His hands, so gentle, so sure, neglected no part of her body while his turgid manhood pressed urgently against her thigh.

When penetration finally came it was with a sharp, clean thrust that made Gabby gasp as she rose to his hard body with throbbing joy. If she had any doubt as to the quality of her response, she need not have worried. No woman alive could have withstood for long Marcel's expert caresses and words of love. And Gabby was no exception. Before long she was quivering and trembling with a passion equal to Marcel's, her small cries of delight setting his blood afire as no other woman had before nore was likely to again.

"How I've longed and dreamed for this moment," cried Marcel ecstatically, as spasms of erotic shivers splintered through him signaling the beginning of his journey to a world where nothing existed but bliss. "Now you are mine! Truly mine!"

Gabby barely heard his words, she was so caught up in the moment, the act, this man who truly loved her, who moved so forcefully within her, prodding her ever higher until she joined him in his journey toward ecstasy. Marcel covered her mouth with his until her cries were stilled. Only when she had quieted did he allow his own climax to rip through his body in tearing spasms. But even at the peak of his ecstasy Marcel was made aware of a name he had come to hate, a name Gabby had cried out before he had smothered her cries. "Philippe!" *Mon dieu*, how he hated that accursed name!

Gabby slowly opened her eyes feeling as if she had just come down from a high mountain, surprised to see Marcel leaning above her on one elbow, his features soft and dreamy.

"You are not sorry, are you, *cherie?*" he asked, searching her face for traces of regret.

Sorry? She was sorry perhaps that Philippe could not find it in his heart to love her as much as Marcel did; sorry to see her son lose his birthright; but no, she was not sorry that she had given herself to Marcel, that she had shown her gratitude in the only way she knew how. Just as she had shown Rob so long ago. Marcel had made her his and she had no regrets.

Gabby's answer was so long in coming that Marcel experienced a twinge of pain. When her answer finally came it made all the waiting worthwhile.

"I feel no remorse, Marcel. You have been patient and loving and I am glad you have finally made me yours."

"It was well worth the wait, *cherie,*" he whispered tenderly, more than pleased with her answer. "Did . . . did I please you?"

"Did you doubt it?" Gabby asked shyly.

Marcel smiled. There was no doubt in his mind that Gabby had enjoyed their passionate encounter. Her cries of delight and ardent response to his caresses told him that much. What he did still doubt were her feelings for him. A woman in love did not have the name of another man on her lips at the peak of her joy. It was obvious to Marcel that Gabby still held strong feelings for her husband, no matter how cruelly he had treated her in the past.

"You were so gentle, so tender," Gabby continued, fearing that she had somehow hurt his feelings when he remained silent for so long, staring pensively into space. "Nothing like . . . like . . ."

"Don't mention that name to me, *cherie*." His voice was soft, but Gabby could detect an underlying hint of steel. "You and I and our child will go to France as planned and you will soon forget you ever belonged to another. The past died tonight with our coming together. Our loving made you mine for all time."

Gabby sighed, a nagging guilt tugging at her heart. Could she ever return Marcel's love wholeheartedly without recriminations? she wondered wretchedly. She drifted off to sleep listening to his heart beats keeping time to the ominous rumbling coming from somewhere deep within Mt. Pelee.

When Gabby woke next it was still dark and at first she thought Luella had put Jean to her breast. But when she opened her eyes she saw Marcel's tousled head bending over her, lips tugging gently at an erect nipple. She touched his hair. Startled, he raised up, a sheepish expression on his face when he realized he had awakened her. He could not help but want her again and when his passion would not be quelled began his tender ministration.

"I'm sorry, *cherie*," he apologized guiltily. "My need for you is so great that I could not help but feast at so bountiful a table. I think I could easily become addicted. Soon I shall become as fat as Jean."

Gabby smiled at his boyish delight in her. "Do not apologize, *mon coeur*," she chided gently. "Although you may have to fight Jean for the right, you are free to feast to your heart's content." Before long time for words was past as Marcel once more lost himself in sweet, willing flesh.

The next day the lovers awoke to a day as bleak and dreary as the previous one. Only now the situation became more desperate; a dull, red glow was clearly visible at the neck of Pelee. Shortly after dawn Marcel readied the carriage that would carry them from St. Pierre while Gabby prepared Jean for the journey. Soon they joined the maelstrom of traffic leaving the city. It seemed to take forever before they had gained the serpentine graveled road winding up St. Pierre's amphitheater of hills. But before they were able to enter the Trace itself, they were met by a pair of soldiers from the government troops sent over in a vanguard from Fort-de-France to protect the beleaguered city from looters. Both soldiers stood in the middle of the roadway, pistols drawn.

"What is it, Sergeant?" asked Marcel after he reluctantly halted the carriage at the barricade. "It's imperative that I reach my plantation by nightfall."

"Not if you intend traveling along the Trace, Monsieur!" replied the soldier. "In places the road no longer exists. We are here to prevent anyone from entering."

"Are you sure?" gasped Marcel, quailing inwardly. With the Trace gone so was their last link to safety.

"It would be suicide to attempt that road. Think of your wife and child. Go back to St. Pierre. You would be safer there than on the Trace."

It was obvious to Gabby that Marcel was shaken but trying hard not to show it as ashen-faced he turned the rig and headed resolutely back to the city, masking his rising fears behind stony features. There was no longer any doubt in either of their minds that Pelee was about to erupt. If not today, then the day after that or the day after that. The big mystery was what trajectory it would take. Judging from the ash and lava flow during the past month, St. Pierre had no hope of escaping unscathed.

Marcel handed Gabby out of the carriage. "Don't unpack, *cherie*. If there is some way to escape the city I'll find it," he promised, kissing her gently on the lips and ruffling Jean's fuzzy head before hurrying away.

During the hours that Marcel was gone Gabby paced nervously, ever mindful of Pelee's dramatic performance. She was nearly wild with anxiety when he finally returned, a wide grin splayed across his handsome features.

"Hurry, Gabby," he urged when she met him at the door. "Get Jean. We're leaving!"

"How? The soldiers said the Trace was impassable."

"We're not going to Le Chateau. I don't have time to explain. Just hurry or we'll be too late!"

"Too late for what? Please, Marcel!"

Seeing that she would not move until she learned their destination, he hurried explained. "The *Windward* is in the harbor but sails within the hour. Her captain deemed the situation in St. Pierre critical and is loading as many women and children aboard as he can safely handle. As the owner's wife you are automatically guaranteed passage as long as you arrive before she sails."

"What about you?" Gabby protested. "Is there no place for you?"

"Please hurry, *cherie*," Marcel urged desperately. "We will talk later."

A loud rumbling and new spewing of ash and rock from Pelee hastened Gabby's steps. Within ten minutes they were in the carriage once more and inching their way to the docks through throngs of people wandering aimlessly about. Before they had traveled very far Marcel realized that there was no way they could reach the *Windward* before she sailed unless they abandoned the carriage and set out on foot. Cradling Jean in his arms he took Gabby by the hand and led her through the crowded streets.

As they neared the docks the crowds became so dense that Marcel had to hand Jean to Gabby and literally fight every inch of the way, pulling them through the passage he opened. Marcel cursed when he realized the cause of the mass of humanity swelling the docks.

The *Windward* loomed before them. On the gangplank stood a flank of sailors holding back a crowd of fear-crazed people with long, sharp pikes. Already the ship was spilling with human cargo. It was obvious to everyone but the people on the docks trying to board her that she was already over-loaded.

"They are waiting for you, *cherie*," Marcel called to Gabby as he clawed his way forward in hand to hand combat. They gained the foot of the gangplank not a moment too soon. To their dismay, the seamen were retreating to the deck preparing to run in the gangplank and cast off the lines holding the ship to the dock.

"Wait!" cried Marcel frantically above the roar of the crowd. "Madame St. Cyr and her child have arrived! Let them board!"

Suddenly the captain's worried face appeared at the railing and, recognizing Gabby, he sent two sailors to escort her aboard. When Gabby realized that Marcel was not coming with her she clung to his hand, panic-stricken to think that she might never see him again. "Marcel!" she cried as he gently loosened her hold upon his fingers.

"Go aboard, Gabby," Marcel commanded, tears misting his eyes. "Take care of our son." Then he lifted her hand to his lips and tenderly kissed her fingertips before he was jostled back amidst the throngs, his parting words echoing in her ears. "*Je t'aime, je t'aime!*"

"Marcel! Marcel!" Gabby cried, trying in vain to find his face amid the sea of people. "Please take care of yourself!" If only she could return his words of love!

Just then the captain appeared above her, peering over the rail. "Hurry, Madame St. Cyr! We can delay no longer."

Squaring her slight shoulders, Gabby turned and resolutely followed the sailors on board the ship, clutching Jean to her breast. Almost immediately the gangplank was run in and the moorings cast. A puff of wind filled the sails and the *Windward* nosed out of the harbor. A strange lump gathered in her throat when she turned to view the thousands of desperate people left behind in the doomed city. Was Marcel one of those doomed, she wondered, choking back a sob.

Gabby had no more time to dwell on Marcel's fate for Captain Bovier, whom she remembered from her previous journey, appeared at her side. "Look to Pelee, Madame St. Cyr," he said, pointing to where the glow at its neck had grown brighter with each passing hour. "I would have been safely out to sea by now had I not waited for your arrival. Had you delayed one moment longer I would have been forced to leave without you. It's strange that Monsieur St. Cyr would leave his wife and child in the city at a time like this."

Gabby flushed. "My . . . husband wanted me to return to Bellefontaine with him but I had not recovered sufficiently from childbirth to hazard the journey," lied Gabby, unwilling to divulge at this time the true status of her marriage.

Seeming to lose interest in the subject, the captain grunted out a reply that he had duties to perform and left her standing at the railing watching the shoreline recede from view. Finally, when there was nothing left to see, Gabby made her way through the people milling aimlessly on deck to the cabin she had shared with Philippe through both happy and sad times.

Chapter Twenty

EACH PASSING day found Philippe viewing Mt. Pelée with growing alarm. Since the day he had left Gabby and little Jean in St. Pierre he had been plagued with conflicting emotions. He was angry. He was sad. He was bereft. He was hurt by Gabby's rejection, discounting his own rejection of her and his son. Afterward, he had been so distraught that he made straight for his lawyer's office before allowing second thoughts to muddy his thinking. Then he left immediately for Bellefontaine where he plunged wholeheartedly into the arduous task of processing his newly cut cane into sugar and rum. The heat was oppressive; the air too humid, too still. A deep sense of foreboding prevailed. Even the natives went about their work as if doom's day were near, sensing as only the supersititious can the presence of an awesome, all-powerful force.

No matter how hard Philippe tried to banish thoughts of Gabby from his mind, he found himself dreaming of her as she had been at the final parting. Her outpouring of love, her need for him had been amply demonstrated by her passionate response to their tumultuous joining. Even her words had proclaimed her love for him. Why then, when he confessed his own love, had she thrown it back at him by insisting Jean was his son?

Weren't their love and need for one another enough? he reasoned irrationally. Perhaps, given time, he would feel differently, especially in view of the fact that Gabby might never bear another child. But it was a decision he would have had to come to himself.

Philippe wondered if the divorce papers he had signed had made Gabby happy. Certainly Marcel must have been overjoyed to learn that soon he would be able to legalize their relationship as well as openly claim his son. Philippe cursed bitterly. By all that's right and holy Jean should be his son!

"Damn! Damn! Damn!" he exploded, causing the slaves working nearby to shake their heads sadly, knowing full well the reason for his discontent. Why did he allow anger and pride to rule his life? he wondered, casting a guilty eye around him when he realized his embittered outburst had been observed.

In a fit of despondency, Philippe had even taken a pretty mulatto to his bed. Suzette had been born on the plantation but was too young and too afraid of Amalie to flaunt herself before Philippe. But with Amalie out of the way and Philippe's wife nowhere in sight, Suzette grew bold and displayed her ripe sixteen-year-old body before her master, promising delights he could not resist. Her skin, the color of *café au lait*, still held the dewy bloom of youth and her rich, black hair hung in rippling waves to the middle of her back. The night Philippe finally took her to his bed, she had teased and taunted him mercilessly, appearing from nowhere to entice him with her flashing, black velvet eyes, pushing out her breasts until they strained against her flimsy blouse. Without a word, his face set in grim lines, he had grasped Suzette by the wrist, pulling her along after him into the house, past a wide-eyed Tante Louise and into his bedroom.

Allowing neither of them time to disrobe, Philippe flung her on her back on the bed and mounted her with a violence that surprised even him. It was as if he wanted to punish her for the sins of every woman on earth. Philippe was dismayed as well as shocked to find Suzette a virgin. Immediately he became more gentle, but quickly learned Suzette wanted no gentleness. Once the initial pain of entry was past, she was like a young tigress, urging him on until he had broken through her maidenhead. Without missing a beat, Suzette gave herself up body and soul to the act she had long anticipated, saving herself for this very moment with this very man.

Philippe had to admit, although grudgingly, that Suzette had entered his life at a time when he feared for his sanity. To lose himself in her sweet, young flesh had been like a balm . . . for a while. After the first week or two, even venting his lust upon voracious little Suzette was not enough to coax him from his doldrums. She had been no more than a pleasurable diversion, unable to completely fill the void left by Gabby. There were times he even longed for Jean's soft downy head nestled in the crook of his arm.

On the morning Gabby and Jean boarded the *Windward*, Philippe stood in the fields of cut cane beyond the house, eyes focused on Pelee, his heart in his mouth. The dull glow at the neck of the crater grew redder by the minute, the spewing of ash and rock a continuing process now; a sooty mist blocked out the sun casting the world below into dim shadows. He could plainly see white-hot fingers of lava splaying downward from the cone.

The awesome sight inspired fear in Philippe's breast. With sinking hear the realized that Gabby and Jean lay in the direct path of Pelee's lava flow! Suddenly he was possessed by a conviction that in only a matter of hours the mountain would blow apart. St. Pierre, the only town in its path of destruction, would disappear in a sea of molten lava! Never once did he consider that the flow could take a different direction, that it could destroy Bellefontaine. Irrationally, it was at that moment when the possibility existed that neither Gabby nor her son would survive Mt. Pelee that Philippe came to a momentous decision.

Mounting his horse, he rode at breakneck speed through the stubble of cane back toward the house. Once in his room he threw together a change of clothes and shaving gear and, calling to Gerard, left instructions for his overseer.

Philippe was barely beyond the banana groves when it happened. It struck with hurricane force, a searing wind that swept down from the mountain. His horse reared in terror and Philippe fought desperately to control him and keep his seat. The banana trees around him bent nearly to the ground and he could feel the heat generated by the wind burning his body. As quickly as it came it was gone. With a wary eye on the mountain Philippe coaxed his mount on with gentle words.

Suddenly the glow at the neck of Pelee was spreading above him as a blinding, red ball blossomed out of the side of the crater. The volcano exploded, and exploded, and exploded, and the ground beneath him rocked with each new shock. Black smoke spewed up from the throat of the volcano and the entire side of the mountain flew away. A white cloud shot with flame burst out of the gaping hole in the volcano's side and hurled downward toward the sea.

Philippe stood frozen in his tracks, immobilized by terror, staring slack-jawed as the steaming flow of lava sweeping down the bed of the Roxelaine River raced directly for St. Pierre. Even as Philippe urged his courageous horse forward he knew that nothing or no one could survive once that tremendous flow of lava reached the city. But still he could not turn back. He plunged headlong into the gloom, seeing neither the gravel roadbed of the Trace nor the fallen away sides of ravines, for the darkness had obliterated the sun with the first eruption. He traveled in absolute silence, an unnatural silence for not even the normal sounds of birds or animals could be heard.

Suddenly, his horse lunged, and he felt himself lurch wildly into space. He was falling over the edge of a ravine, drifting, turning, nearly dreamlike, hurtling slowly downward. Philippe heard his horse scream in fright. He felt like screaming himself. Then he hit the water.

When he tried to move, there was a sharp throbbing in his head. The heat was unbearable and he wanted a drink of water. Hearing the rush of water, he reached out, felt rough, jagged rocks. Memory came rushing back with startling clarity. Rising on an elbow he saw that somehow he had reached the rocks after his fall into the river. Looking up he realized that he had fallen over twenty-five feet and he was amazed at the miracle of his survival. Another miracle made itself known when, looking around to get his bearings, he spied his horse on the opposite side of the river calmly grazing at a clump of grass.

Waiting a few moments until his head stopped spinning, Philippe stood up, stepped to the edge of the water and threw himself in. The only way he knew of reaching St. Pierre in time to save Gabby and his son was on horseback. He began to swim against the current with long, hard strokes. Though not wide, the river had been swollen by recent storms and Philippe struggled hard against the undertow. But he was a strong swimmer and, given his superior strength and determination, he finally reached the other side only a little downstream from his horse. Choking for breath a minute or two, he pulled himself up onto the bank where he lay gulping huge lungsful of air before starting off toward his mount.

Making his way back to the road, Philippe found it strewn with ashes so hot he could feel the heat of them through the soles of his boots. The trees around him were no longer green and the breadfruit limbs lay on the ground broken by mud and ash, their leaves stripped bare. With each turn Philippe strained for a glimpse of St. Pierre, but could see nothing of th e city. And when he came to the tiny, picturesque village upriver of St. Pierre his heart sank with dread. What had been a beautiful little village where a small mountain stream met the Roxelaine River now lay stripped of all but four or five houses. The rest was a chaos of broken tiles, twisted iron and scorched remains of furniture. Trees had been up-rooted, even stone and cement houses had been demolished.

At this point Philippe began to meet vacant-eyed refugees, their hair and faces begrimed with a thick coating of ash. Their clothing was no better. Philippe searched each face carefully before turning away in bitter disappointment. When he tried to question them, they only stumbled past, not answering. Finally, one bleak face turned back when Philippe cried out, "What happened in St. Pierre? Did the lava reach the city?"

"No, not lava," the man answered, his eyes bleak and lined with ash.

Philippe felt a great weight lift from his shoulders. "Thank *le bon dieu* the lava didn't reach the city," he breathed in an outpouring of relief.

"A cloud of steam, Monsieur," the man clarified. "There is nothing left of St. Pierre."

Philippe fought for control. "What about survivors other than yourselves? A woman, young, beautiful, with a child."

"I saw many such as you describe, Monsieur. All dead."

Philippe did not stop him when he turned and continued up the trail after his companions, his hollow eyes filled with horrors enough to last a lifetime.

Suddenly the man stopped, looking back over his shoulder at Philippe. "Turn back! You won't be able to get near the city. Whoever you have there is sure to be gone!"

But Philippe would not be deterred. Face grim, body taut, he forced his horse onward. Gabby and his son had to be alive! When at last he came to the city, he knew why the man on the road tried to dissuade him. The destruction was almost beyond belief.

Plantations and cane fields were sheets of flames around the city, and every ship that had the misfortune of still being in the harbor was aflame. After a cursory inventory Philippe saw that none of the burning ships belonged to him. The shore was a tangle of wreckage and carnage, afloat with dead bodies. St. Pierre was a wasteland of devastation. The city still blazed, the stench of burning wood and flesh overpowering.

The first corpses to meet Philippe's eyes, their bodies bloated, skin blistered and blackened, caused him to retch. But he pushed onward until his horse would go no farther. Abandoning his mount, Philippe continued on foot. It wasn't long before he realized the city would have to cool down before he could begin his search for Gabby. Retreating to the outskirts of the city Philippe began his seemingly interminable wait.

It was two days before the smoldering ruins of St. Pierre had cooled enough for him to enter. Making his way through the all but obliterated streets, he went first to the place where Marcel lived. Nothing remained to show where the townhouse once had been. Tier after tier of broken walls lay all around him. The roads were blocked by corpses of people who had fled into the streets to die in agony. Philippe poked around in a disheartened manner among the bodies but after a while gave up in despair. His only hope now was that somehow Marcel had gotten Gabby and Jean out of the city in time.

Though his eyes stung from the acrid smoke and intense heat he went on scanning the destruction for familiar landmarks. Gone were the twin towers of the cathedral, vanished was the military hospital but for one wall. Most incredible of all was that not even the walls of the fortress were standing.

Philippe wandered over the city, finally finding himself at the harbor. He was surprised to see a ship anchored off shore and a long boat pulling away loaded with marines. He waited until they reached shore. Then he learned that the *Windward*, his own ship, reached Fort-de-France with news of the destruction and a ship had been dispatched along with a column of marines to search for survivors. Philippe joined the search.

The rest of that day and the next the rescuers fanned the city for survivors. They had set up a hospital of sorts against the lone wall of the military hospital and by the second day a disappointing number of people were lined up beneath it, most of them dying. On the second day, Philippe was surprised to see the sun appear through the haze of the smoking mountain. The top of Pelee's crater had been blown away and the denuded slope below gave mute evidence of the mountain's destructive power. The lush jungle had become a gray, furrowed desert of ash and mud. And the Roxelaine valley a corridor along which death and destruction had flowed into the city of St. Pierre. Although nothing but ash, stone, scalding steam had reached the town, the devastation had been complete and unbelievable.

On that same day Philippe found himself before the ruins of a house whose remaining front entrance he barely recognized. After staring intently at it several minutes, he turned away to continue his search. A moan, soft as a whisper caught his attention. He retraced his steps, listened again, and again the sound, raspy, yet recognizable as human. Galvanized into action, Philippe moved toward the sound, sought and found what he was looking for beneath a broken section of wall. A woman, hardly recognizable as such, alive, barely. Her body was blackened, her face a twisted mass of pain. The fact that she was alive and conscious at all was a miracle. Philippe bent over the woman's battered body and she opened her eyes. Her voice, when she spoke, was thick and choked, but Philippe had no doubt that the agonizing mewing sound coming from the dying woman belonged to Amalie.

"Monsieur Philippe," croaked Amalie, clawing at him with blackened hands. "You have come for your Amalie! Ah, but it is too late, too late!"

"Not too late, Amalie," lied Philippe, feeling nothing but

pity and compassion for the pitiful hulk that was once his beautiful mistress.

"Too late, too late," moaned Amalie again. "Forgive me, *mon amour*. Forgive me before I die!"

"Later, Amalie, don't try to talk now," soothed Philippe.

"There will be no later for me. I cannot face *le bon dieu* without your forgiveness."

Philippe nodded his head wearily. He had no choice but to listen to Amalie's dying words.

"I wanted your wife dead. It was my intense jealousy that killed her and the child she carried when she fell down the stairs. I thought that with her dead you would come back for me." She paused, swallowed with difficulty, then went on doggedly. "But you did not come, Monsieur Philippe. I waited but you did not come. Did you find another to take my place?"

"Listen, Amalie," Philippe murmured, placing his mouth close to her ear. "The fall did not kill Gabby. It hastened her labor, but she lived. As did one of the twins she bore. A boy. Only the tiny girl did not live to see the light of day."

"And . . . they . . . have . . . survived . . . Pelee?"

"I . . . don't know," Philippe admitted, his voice broken with anguish. "I . . . have not found their bodies."

With a strength sometimes afforded the dying, Amalie pulled Philippe closer until his face was inches from her own tortured features. "I forgave you long ago for selling me. Now it is your turn to forgive me."

If forgiving Amalie brought her peace of mind Philippe saw no reason to withhold it from her. Feeling nothing but sadness, he said, "I forgive you, Amalie. The rest is up to *le bon dieu*."

Immediately she loosened her hold on him and fell back. Her yellow cat's eyes glamed with a strange light. "Now kill me, Monsieur Philippe. Kill me . . . ! For . . . what . . . we

387

. . . once . . . meant . . . to . . . each . . . other . . . kill . . . me."

Philippe sat back on his haunches staring at the black and blistered face and broken body that once had given him so much pleasure. He never doubted for a moment that she loved him as thoroughly as she was capable. A great and over-whelming sadness came over him. Her suffering was awesome to watch, her death imminent. But yet, how could he . . . !

"Kill . . . me . . . ! I . . . beg . . . you!" Amalie implored, her impassioned plea cutting into Philippe like a sword.

Rising, Philippe pulled out the pistol one of the marines had given him to ward off looters, and took deliberate aim at Amalie's heart.

"*Je t'aime,*" she mouthed moments before he pulled the trigger.

Philippe doggedly made his way back to the hastily erected hospital. He sank to the ground, resting his back against a large chunk of cement. Someone handed him a cup of coffee and plate of food. Automatically he ate and drank, his emotions masked by extreme weariness. He had found no trace of Gabby or Jean, or even of Marcel. In all likelihood, he surmised, sighing wretchedly, they lay dead beneath the steaming rubble of the city. To add further to his distress, he had just shot his former mistress! Philippe set his plate and cup down and buried his head in his hands, too numb to cry, too dazed to think, too sick at heart to live. Without Gabby life had no meaning. Even his beloved Bellefontaine paled in comparison.

The drone of voices nearby disturbed Philippe's melancholy. He could not help but overheard the conversation. Raising his head, he saw the doctor sent over with the marines bending over a charred body. Two assistants hovered close by.

"Poor fellow," said the doctor, shaking his head in commiseration. "I cannot imagine how he survived this long."

"We found him down by the harbor lying half in, half out of the water," replied one of the men. "That's probably why he's still alive. The water must have protected him from suffering burns serious enough to kill him outright."

"Will he live?" ask the second man.

"Not a chance," answered the doctor matter-of-factly, shrugging his shoulders. "Not one survivor among the thousands of people in St. Pierre when Pelee erupted."

"Listen!" said the first man. "What is he saying?"

"Sounds like he is calling for someone. His wife, probably, and more than likely dead. There! He is calling out again!" said the doctor, cocking his ear closer to the dying man. "Gabby. Yes, that is the name. I'll give him something to ease his passing."

Philippe was on his feet instantly, all signs of exhaustion gone from his body. "Wait!" he commanded, startling the doctor by his outburst. "I think I know that man. May I speak with him?"

The doctor shrugged his shoulders and wordlessly moved off to another blackened hulk just brought in to the make-shift hospital.

The moment Philippe looked into Marcel's blistered face and pain-crazed eyes he knew time was fast running out. Bending close to Marcel's ear he called out his name. It took a few minutes for the dying man to focus his eyes and when he did recognition was instantaneous.

"Philippe!" he croaked through lips parched and nearly skinless.

"Gabby!" Philippe cried out, his eyes crazed with fear. "Where is Gabby? And . . . and my son?"

An eternity passed before Marcel answered. And in that eternity Philippe died a thousand deaths.

"Alive! And Jean also. I put them aboard the *Windward* only moments before she sailed from the harbor."

"*Merci! Merci*, Marcel!" breathed Philippe, suddenly

drained of all emotion. Several minutes passed before he gained some semblance of control. Then he said, "No matter what happened in the past you negated it in an instant by that unselfish act. Henceforth I shall always remember you as the man who saved my wife and son."

"Your son, Philippe?" Marcel was growing weak, yet his tone was rebuking.

"*Oui,* my son," repeated Philippe firmly. "Gabby is still legally my wife and that makes Jean my son no matter who sired him." Never had Philippe sounded more decisive.

"How could you ever doubt it? I never would have thought you such a fool. Gabby has always been yours. Never mine . . . never. Jean is your son."

"Don't try to talk," cautioned Philippe as Marcel's voice seemed to fade away. "I'll call the doctor."

"No!" forbade Marcel. "Time is running out for me. Let me talk. But first, water, please!"

Looking around, Philippe spied a crock of water nearby and, using a broken dipper, trickled some into the raw slash that had been Marcel's mouth. After a few minutes he began speaking again.

"Take care of her, *mon ami.* I loved her more than I thought possible to love another human. I loved your son, too. I would have been proud to claim him. It's . . . it's better this way. She was . . . never . . . mine. Never . . . loved . . . me. Yours, Philippe, always . . . yours."

Marcel's eyes were wild now, his pain naked, palpable. Philippe turned to call the doctor.

"No!" rallied Marcel, sensing Philippe's purpose. "Not through. Hear . . . me . . . out."

Philippe had always heard confession was good for the soul and this day had proved the theory. First Amalie had begged to be heard and now Marcel seemed in need of similar service as he rambled on through cracked lips.

"Go to Gabby, Philippe. She and Jean need you. I loved her. *Mon dieu*, how I loved her!" he mumbled almost incoherently. "My love for her was pure, unsullied. I . . . I never touched her, though *le bon dieu* knows I wanted her. Believe me, *mon ami*, I am a dying man. I would not lie to you."

Philippe was prepared to go to Gabby whether she had been Marcel's mistress or not. It just didn't matter anymore. But Marcel's dying words filled his heart with joy.

"I . . . I find it hard to believe that in all those months you lived in the same house you and Gabby . . ."

"Never!" lied Marcel vehemently, knowing in his heart that *le bon dieu* would forgive him for his falsehood. He discounted that one time Gabby had allowed him to make love to her. In his heart he knew she came to him only out of gratitude. Philippe's name on her lips at the most intimate of moments proved as much.

"Two weeks ago those words would have been the most welcome words in the world. Today they mean nothing. I love Gabby no matter what has transpired in the past. I only hope my foolish pride hasn't destroyed whatever feelings she once held for me," confessed Philippe fervently.

A grimace creased Marcel's face. "Come closer, *mon ami*," he whispered, his voice failing noticeably now. "I beg you not to divulge to Gabby what I am about to reveal to you. After I am gone I want her to know only good of me." Philippe waited patiently, well aware of what was to come. "I'm glad I didn't kill you. All those times, in France, aboard the *Windward*, in New Orleans. I deeply regret Captain Stone's death. I killed him, too. Found out from Gabby he was on an important mission to obtain war supplies. Had to stop him. Orders."

"And Captain Giscard's accident aboard the *Windward*?" urged Philippe gently. He might as well hear everything.

"Him, too. Sorry. Had to stop documents from reaching General Jackson. Failed. Failed miserably."

"Why, Marcel? For the love of *le bon dieu*, why? You with your French heritage. Did you love the English so much?"

"Money, *mon ami*, money. My father left Le Chateau debt-ridden. Both my sisters needed a dowry to attract husbands worthy of their station. The English money saw both Linette and Honore well and happily wed. Without it they would have had to settle for much less. In the final analysis try not to judge me too harshly."

Privately Philippe thought he would have found another way out of financial difficulty. But a dying man deserved some shred of dignity no matter what his sins. Aloud he said, "What you did, Marcel, is now between you and *le bon dieu*.

"Then . . . you . . . won't . . . tell . . . Gabby?"

"No, Marcel, the past is buried."

"*Merci* . . . *mon ami*. Tell . . . her . . . tell . . .her . . . I love . . ." His voice faltered in mid-sentence. And stopped.

"I believe you did, *mon ami*," replied Philippe softly, knowing Marcel was beyond hearing. "I believe you did."

Philippe started violently when the doctor touched his shoulder. "Your friend?" he asked compassionately, closing the dead man's eyes.

Philippe hesitated a full minute before answering. "A friend? Yes, Doctor, you might call him that."

"Sorry, *mon ami*," replied the doctor. "Be glad he wasn't a loved one." More prophetic words were never spoken.

Five days later the marines left the wasteland of St. Pierre. Not one person discovered alive in the rubble had remained that way for long. When the disheartened men climbed aboard their ship for the trip back to Fort-de-France, Philippe was among them, tired, dirty, but happy beyond belief.

Aboard the *Windward*, Gabby cradled Jean, let him search for and find her breast, and then let herself relax and enjoy the sensation of watching and feeling him suckle. Jean was all she had left. After word had reached Fort-de-France of the complete devastation wrought by Pelee on St. Pierre, Gabby knew in her heart that Marcel was dead. If he were alive he would have found some way to reach her, or barring that, to send word. A tear slid down her cheek as she silently mourned the only true friend she had ever had. He had loved her more than Philippe had, proving it over and over by word and deed.

Though she was reasonably certain Marcel was dead, Gabby had no way of knowing whether Philippe lived. If he were at Bellefontaine at the time of the eruption he would not have been harmed. But if he happened to be in St. Pierre . . . Gabby shuddered. Somehow the thought of Philippe's death affected her in a way Marcel's demise never could. But whether Philippe was dead or alive made little difference at this point in her life. For all practical purposes she and Jean were alone in the world. She was now forced to make her own way, to forge a life for herself and Jean. No longer did she have Marcel to shelter and protect them. Even his last thoughts had been of her and Jean. Before he had turned back from the *Windward* he had pressed a sheaf of bills into her hand. At least now she and Jean would not go wanting.

Now she was faced with a dilemma. Captain Bovier had informed her that he planned on sailing back to St. Pierre the next day to see if Philippe had left orders for him. With St. Pierre no longer in existence it seemed likely that a new home port would be established for Philippe's shipping line. In his own mind the captain had no doubt as to Philippe's well-being, for if he were in St. Pierre at the time of the eruption he would have met the *Windward* when she docked.

At least Gabby had the means to purchase passage to New Orleans, or even France, if she wished. Both Honore and Linette would welcome her and Jean and give them shelter until she found a way to support the two of them. Why did it have to end like this? Gabby wondered sadly. She was so caught up in her own thoughts that she failed to realize that Jean had eaten his fill and slept contentedly, her nipple lax in his pink, rosebud mouth, a dribble of milk running down his tiny chin. Still undecided what course to follow once she left Martinique, Gabby sighed hugely, closed her eyes and wearily rested her head against the back of the chair.

The moon sent shafts of molten silver through the porthole but still Gabby did not awaken. Though her arms had relaxed, she did not loosen her hold on little Jean who also slept soundly. When Philippe quietly entered the cabin, his breath caught painfully in his throat; his hard-sinewed frame went slack with tenderness. Gabby's madonnalike features were limned by pale moonbeams caressing her body. There was a porcelain loveliness about her from her silvery tresses shimmering against translucent skin to the faint violet smudges beneath her eyes. Jean slept peacefully in her arms, his small face damp against her breast. The memory of his own face pressed against those creamy globes was etched upon the tissues of his brain. At that moment it seemed to Philippe that everything he ever wanted or dreamed of was embodied in those two sleeping figures.

Careful, so as not to awaken her, Philippe lifted Jean from the crook of Gabby's arm. His eyes were diamond bright with unshed tears as he held his son whom he had so carelessly abandoned. With one finger he tenderly traced the curve of Jean's downy cheek, and smiled when he opened his tiny mouth searching for a plump nipple. Reluctantly Philippe put his son down in the makeshift crib Seaman Laville had fashioned when Gabby first came aboard. Only when he was certain the baby still slept soundly did Philippe turn back to his wife, scooping her up in his arms as if she were thistle-down and placing her in the center of the bed that held for him memories too complicated to sort out at that moment. He could feel the soft, stirring rustle of her breath against his cheek.

Gabby awoke abruptly, immediately sensing something was amiss. Arms held her down like two steel hands. In panic, she became irrational, crying, and hammering her small fists against a rock hard chest. "Jean!" she cried, "What have you done with my baby?" Then she recognized Philippe, eyes wide in disbelief and shock.

"Our son is in his bed, *ma chere*," soothed Philippe softly, "sleeping. He is beautiful, nearly as beautiful as his mother."

"Your son!" bridled Gabby, wide awake now. "Why should you want him now when you could have claimed him months ago? Nothing has changed!"

"You have every right to be angry, Gabby," admitted Philippe, guilt riding him heavily. "Only my stubborn pride prevented me from claiming my son. I knew in my heart that I had sired Jean. Even if . . . even if Jean were not mine I would still claim him."

"I can't believe what I am hearing, Philippe," exclaimed Gabby, completely and totally bewildered.

"It's true, *ma chere*," Philippe stated emphatically. "Jean is my son and heir! I loved him from the moment he emerged into the world."

Gabby held her breath, unwilling to shatter the fragile beginning they had just established as she searched his face for some hint of mockery.

Philippe grew alarmed at the continued silence. "I . . . am I . . . is it too late?" His look was so woebegone and sad that Gabby had to smile. He mistook the meaning behind her smile as he grasped her shoulders, pulling her close as if afraid she would get away. "Tell me it is not too late," he begged. "Have I completely destroyed the love you once held for me?"

Because of their past, their mistakes, their trials, and their bitter words, Gabby was afraid to commit herself. She needed time to sort out her emotions, to learn the cause of his change of heart. "How did you find me?" he asked, deciding that talking about anything at all was preferable to answering Philippe's plea for reconciliation.

"Marcel told me he had put you and Jean aboard the *Windward.*"

"Then he is alive!" cried Gabby, jubilant. Her relief and joy caused a twinge of pain to crease Philippe's face. Had she come to love Marcel so much? he agonized.

"No, *ma chere,*" Philippe said gently. "Marcel died shortly after he was found amid the ruins of St. Pierre. He lived long enough to tell me about you and Jean. I will be grateful to him for the rest of my life. The gift of life he gave to you and Jean more than compensates for his past offenses against me."

"He was so good to me . . . and Jean," sobbed Gabby, her heart wrenching painfully in her breast. "He loved us, Philippe, truly, and without reservations. Can you understand that?"

"I know, and I understand," admitted Philippe, amazed that he really did understand. "I believe he loved you as much as I do. His last words were of you."

Gabby was sobbing softly now, and Philippe wanted only to comfort her as he caressed and soothed her, pressing his lips against her bright head.

"Mourn if you must, *mon amour,* I really do understand your feelings. Only know that I will never do anything to cause you to seek comfort and protection from another man. No one will ever hurt you, including myself!"

"You've said that before, Philippe," chided Gabby, wanting desperately to believe but afraid of being hurt yet another time, if not now, then later.

"I know that in the past I have been an arrogant bastard. I

deliberately hardened my heart against you, admitting to no one, least of all myself, how much I loved you, needed you, how empty my life has been without you. My greatest fear was that my love should destroy you as it did all the women I loved."

"You cannot blame yourself entirely for Cecily's death. I thought we had settled that before."

"No matter. The blame is mine," theorized Philippe, shrugging his wide shoulders. "If I had let her go, had not forced her to conceive a child she did not want, had not loved her so desperately, she might still be alive."

"Philippe . . . I . . ."

"Wait!" Philippe intervened, holding a hand out. "Let me continue. Cecily's death is only a part of the tragedy plaguing me. There is yet another death attributed to me. The death of one I held more dear than Cecily even."

Gabby's mind was restless with speculation. Had there been another woman in his life? she wondered, her eyes turning dark, nearly jet in the shadows as she waited for Philippe to continue.

"I loved my mother as I never loved another human being. Until you came along." He paused, his face registering pain at the dredged-up memories.

"Your mother? But . . . ."

"She died when I was ten years old," interrupted Philippe. "I . . . she died because of me."

"But . . . how . . .?"

"She and I were on our way to St. Pierre one day when a wheel came off our carriage. We were thrown into a ravine and fell into the rain-swollen river. I was knocked unconscious and my mother held my head above water until Gerard reached us. She insisted that he take me ashore first. When he returned for her it was too late. Keeping me from drowning had so weakened her that she could not stay afloat until Gerard returned for her."

397

"It's insane to blame yourself for her death," cried Gabby, torn apart by his guilt as if it were her own.

"After my mother's death my father could not stand the sight of me. I know he blamed me for surviving when she did not. Soon afterward he shipped me off to France to be educated. I returned to become master of Bellefontaine after his death eleven years later."

"I'm sorry, Philippe. It was cruel of your father to hold you responsible for your mother's death." Her heart ached for the rejected child he must have been, banished from his beloved Bellefontaine, forgotten by his father, much as she had been by her thoughtless parents.

"Then I found Cecily and dared love again," continued Philippe. "Only . . . she didn't return that love, and in the name of love I was responsible for her death, also. Don't you see?" he anguished. "How could I love again, fearing that my love would claim another life? Then, against my will I fell deeply in love with you, a mere girl who dared defy me."

"You had a strange way of showing your love," reminded Gabby gently. "Strange, yet, at times tender. But always with a fury that left me breathless."

"I felt I could protect you only by holding myself aloof and rendering you submissive to my will. I was determined to break your will, to make you into something you could never be. At first I didn't want your love, only your obedience."

"But I loved you, *mon coeur,*" Gabby murmured against his chest, delighting in the feel of soft hairs tickling her cheeks. "If only you weren't bent on destroying that love."

"*Mon dieu,* Gabby!" cried Philippe in alarm. "Have my insane fears and foolish pride destroyed your love? Have I lost my son as well?"

"I . . . don't know, Philippe," admitted Gabby truthfully. "So much hate and animosity has passed between us. What if Marcel had been my lover? What about Rob?"

"All that doesn't matter. I told you before the past is

dead. My life is nothing without you and Jean."

As if to accentuate his words Philippe captured her lips, gently nudging them open with his tongue, seeking the sweet breath within. Slowly, Gabby began to respond; her pulse leaped, her limbs went liquid as she melted against his hard body. His hands played restlessly over her back, clutching her slim hips against him, cupping a soft breast.

Before Gabby realized what was happening, Philippe was undressing her with fingers suddenly gone numb. When she lay clothed only in shimmering moonbeans she tore off his own clothing and lay beside her, gathering her close. The sweet essence of her perfume swept over him with alluring promises of past pleasures reborn.

"I want you, *ma chere*," he whispered against her fragrant flesh. "I need you with every fiber of my being."

Gabby lay still, so still that Philippe thought she had fallen asleep. But her eyes were wide open and staring directly at him, her breathing shallow, labored.

"Do not be afraid of me, *amour*. I will never hurt you again. If you don't want me, you have only to say the word and I will go away."

She said nothing.

With a contented sigh Philippe kissed Gabby deeply, offering her his tongue, which she accepted, hungrily. His mouth moved to her breast, adoring first one and then the other, tugging at the turgid nipple with his teeth until he felt her shudder. With his lips he burned a trail of fire across her stomach to the moistness between her thighs. She stiffened, but Philippe gently nudged her legs apart and raised her hips. She gave a startled cry when she felt his tongue, hot, questing, probing. She arched her back, muffling a moan with the back of her hand. Then she gyrated her hips wildly until sparks ignited inside her brain and she writhed in abandon, crying out again and again as a burst of white hot flame seared her flesh.

Only when she had quieted did Philippe raise up, entering her with a gentleness and reverence that surprised her.

"This is where I belong, *ma chere*," he whispered huskily as he moved deep within her.

How perfect, how complete! Gabby exulted. The pain of it swelled to agony, a sweet, blissful agony that filled her body until she felt she would explode of it. And then she did, at the same time Philippe began his own blazing eruption.

Later, lying with his head upon her breast, Philippe was nearly asleep when Gabby whispered his name.

"What is it, *ma petite?*" he answered lazily.

"Not long ago I hated you, but now . . ."

"Now you love me," he finished. "Is that what you are trying to say?"

"I think so. But how can that be?"

"What is hate but an extension of love? You and I, *ma chere*, have lived a lifetime of hate. From this day forward let us know only of love."

"I want to believe that, Philippe. Truly I do. Only . . ."

"We shall go on a long voyage," he continued blithely, despite her voiced misgiving. "The three of us. Anywhere you want, England, France, America." His eyes danced with happiness.

Gabby's eyes sparkled in response. Dare she hope that after knowing nothing but the dark side of love all these years she was finally to experience that which Philippe had long denied her? It was as if she had finally burst out of a long, dark tunnel into the light of day. And at the end was the beginning of forever.